John Ralston Saul wa[...]n Alberta, Manitoba, Onta[...] ill he earned a Ph.D. between King's College, London and the Ecole Libre des Sciences Politiques in Paris. The subject was Charles de Gaulle. He then ran an investment company in Paris before returning to Calgary to join Petro-Canada on its first day of operations. As Assistant to the Chairman, he was closely involved in the creation of the company and in its first three years of spectacular growth. He has since been involved in Asian trade and has travelled with guerilla groups behind the lines in the Sahara and in the jungles of South-East Asia.

By the same author

*Bird of Prey*
*Baraka*

JOHN RALSTON SAUL

# The Next Best Thing

**GRAFTON BOOKS**

A Division of the Collins Publishing Group

LONDON GLASGOW
TORONTO SYDNEY AUCKLAND

Grafton Books
A Division of the Collins Publishing Group
8 Grafton Street, London W1X 3LA

Special overseas edition 1986

First published in Great Britain by
Grafton Books 1986

ISBN 0-586-06871-6

Printed and bound in Great Britain by
Cox & Wyman Ltd, Reading

Set in Times

For

Seng Harn
killed in his house by a friend

Pichai Khunseng
former Shan commander

and Norman Bottorff

Once the heart is mastered, wisdom is born.

*Pali text*

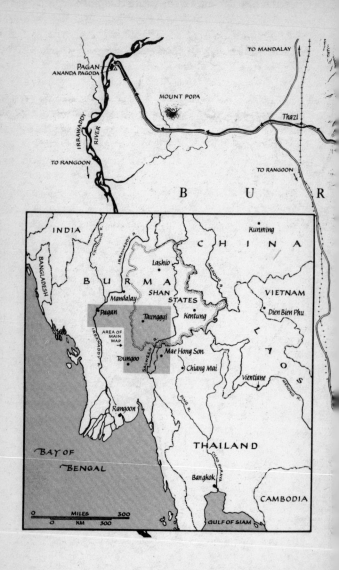

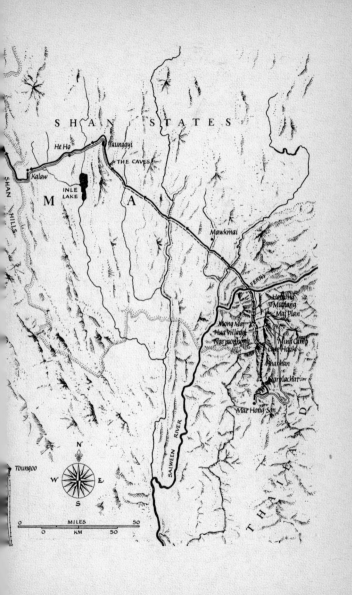

S H A N   S T A T E S

SHAN HILLS

He Ho
Taunggyi
Kalaw
THE CAVES
INLE LAKE

M                    A

Mawkmai

FERRY

Homong
Mutiang
Mai Pian

Mong Mai
Hua Village
Narmoohong

Mini Camp
Gawi Hpak

Bhakhan

Kunglachat

Mae Hong Son

SALWEEN RIVER

T H A I L A N D

Toungoo

N
W        E
S

MILES
0                    50
0        KM        50

# 1

The river ferry was a clumsy, wooden affair, low in the water. On the post against which the pilot supported himself an elaborately painted sign limited the passengers to fifteen. The paint was faded. More than thirty Thais huddled out of the sun, bracing themselves upright and back from the spray thrown by the fast water taxis, in whose wake the ferry wallowed across the brown water of the Chao Phraya, from Bangkok side to the slums of Thonburi, down towards the main port. Spenser was the only foreigner, his head a good twelve inches above the Thais and bent to avoid the beams of the roof; his eyes betraying a half-crazed look, a weakness for the wild card.

The pilot aimed his boat straight at the floating dock. An instant before collision, he threw the wheel around to port, at which the passengers crowded along the starboard rail, sinking the gunnel close to water level. The crash brought on a rush that carried Spenser stumbling up from the rocking boat onto the floating platform. This lurched as they pushed ahead onto a larger, swaying jetty, where a crowd waited in the shade of tin sheeting to take their place, and from there he was pushed on up a sagging gangway to shore.

In the narrow alley he managed to stand aside, balancing himself on the mud between two stagnant pools with his back against a wire fence. He was in the latter half of his thirties and wore a summer suit cut by a good, standard London tailor. His shirt was from a conservative shop half way down Jermyn Street – in the bleaching light of the Orient only a close look would have confirmed it to be striped and those stripes to be pink.

The smells of putrefaction rose up around him to meet the

weight of the sun's rays. Although it was four o'clock, there was not yet any shade and everything exposed had absorbed the day's heat, which now radiated back from all angles.

Out of his jacket, Spenser pulled a sheet of instructions written in Thai Sanskrit and began to push it mutely in front of the stragglers from the boat. He was not one of those Englishmen who believed that, by speaking his own language louder, foreigners could be made to understand.

His expression of self-effacement was surprising given the look in his eyes and the wide jaw bone that suggested force. Thick brown hair was combed straight back from a strong forehead and worn slightly too long. He was flushed from the heat; a function of racial colour not of physical condition, because his body betrayed only the slightest hints of urban male decline. In any case, this was something of which Spenser was unaware. He didn't notice his own physical existence on a daily basis. He was too intent on the things that interested him. It was that which gave substance to his unrestrained look, even in the heat of a slum alley.

A boy, who had been hanging around the dock, came up and tried to take the paper from his hand. Spenser showed it to him. The last few passengers pushed by while the child puzzled over the writing until it was clear that he could not read and that no one else remained in the alley. The boy started ahead and beckoned him to follow towards a maze of openings. Spenser picked his way slowly among the stretches of mud and the piles of rotting food, so that by the time he reached a first group of two-storey buildings – some of rough cement, others of wood – the boy was shouting into a doorway. An old man came out and read the instructions. He explained the route at length in Thai, while Spenser leaned against the wall of the house, managing to shade the back of his head from at least the direct heat of the sun, while his attention retreated into misty imprecision. Waiting, immobile, he could not escape sensing where each piece of his clothes clung to his skin. He wiped the sweat from his face yet again.

They wound their way on through a network of alleys in which the confusion of stalls and of noise and of smells soon made the passages appear indistinguishable one from the other. It was the boy who did the searching, while Spenser concentrated on not losing sight of his darting form and on avoiding the motor bikes and *tuc-tucs* which surged out of nowhere with a guttural explosion of gears, like an uncontrolled percussion bass in the orchestra that had swallowed him. Every few minutes they stopped for the note to be reinterpreted by someone fresh – a fruit seller followed by a man seated on the ground repairing shoes, then an old woman crouched in her doorway – each time setting off again on what seemed to be a repetition of their wandering. In a short street very much like the others a voice called out from above,

'Hey *farang*! You're James Spenser, eh?' It was a thick voice tinged with mockery.

Spenser twisted his head back to find the view blocked by a wood balcony one high floor above him. The building rose no further. A white man was leaning over, his features blurred by the sun's glare.

The man gestured, 'The knob's in front of you.'

Spenser gave the boy ten *baht* and pushed the door open. Inside the heat was worse. There was a clammy, over-used feel to the air. A disjointed chorus of girls' voices paused in the half-light, then began again.

He was in a surprisingly large workshop with a rough floor of loose boards between which the smell of the mud rose up. Four neon bars on the walls threw a weak yellow light that outlined jumbled piles of bamboo and rattan. These were stacked to the ceiling and in their shadows the girls worked. He guessed there were two dozen of them; the nearest in her early teens, if that. They were weaving rattan furniture and the only other sound was of the strips snapping into place.

A rough staircase led up to a single office that ran the length of the building's façade. It was furnished with two paper-littered desks and four cane chairs. The only decorations were a photograph of the King hung beside that of the Queen. The opposite wall was broken by three open doors cut into the front of the building. He walked through onto the balcony, which creaked beneath his step and stretched a good yard out over the street, itself little more than four yards wide.

The white man sat in a rattan armchair beneath the shade cast by the eaves, a large glass of beer in his hand. He was blond, almost pretty in a muscular way, but this was marred by a brutal edge, immediately felt yet not tied to anything concrete. He looked up with a stare somehow off-centre. Spenser put it down to drink. Beyond him was a table laden with bottles of Kloster beer and beyond that, at the far end of the balcony, a second armchair. The man wore cream cotton trousers and a blue sports shirt, both neatly pressed. He was in his early forties.

'So you found your way.' His disappointment was clear. He pointed across the table at the empty chair. His hand curved back to grasp his beer and he lowered his eyes to take a long, concentrated drink that emptied a third of the glass, before staring back up at Spenser. 'What do you want?' He held the stare for a few seconds. 'You must want something.'

Spenser squeezed by to drop into the empty chair. 'What I want right now is a beer.'

The other man gave a short laugh and leaned sideways to push a bottle part-way across the table. 'No more glasses.' He paused. 'Sorry.' It wasn't an apology.

Spenser drank from the bottle before saying as pleasantly as he could manage, 'I assume you're John Field.' This was met by silence. He took another drink. 'Is this your factory?'

Field cut in sharply, '*Farangs* can't own property. You know, foreigners.'

4

'You have a Thai front man, I suppose?'

'There are no Thais in business. He's Chinese-Thai. You want him? He's downstairs with the rattan.' It was clear he was tired of correcting people's inexplicable ignorance. 'And no, he is not my partner. This is his sweat-shop. One hundred per cent his. I just pimp for him … clients! I find him clients.'

Spenser nodded patiently. 'As I told you on the phone, your name was given to …'

'Don't give me that English crap. Someone must have given it or you wouldn't be here. So now you're here, eh. What are you up to? Selling stolen goods or buying them?' Field said the words with wry detachment. 'What's my percentage for helping?' His voice was raised above the noise from the street without appearing strained.

This time Spenser laughed. 'Actually I'm interested in some religious figures.'

'Interested?' The word rolled over his tongue. 'So what else is new? This is the pillage capital of the east. What religious figures?' It was as if he were hearing about religion for the first time.

'In Burma.'

'That's no big deal. They've cornered the market on corruption and inefficiency.' The phrase seemed to please him. 'I doubt if I can help you.'

'Actually, I wasn't really after your help. I have an introduction to a dealer here. A Ying Chai.'

'Ha. Well if there's something to steal, he'll certainly know how to do it, if he hasn't taken it already. Don't tell him too much or he'll do it without you. So, what do you want from me?'

Spenser allowed uncertainty to the surface. 'Nothing really. It's just that I was told I should meet you. That you've been here long enough to know every …'

'Crook in town, governmental or otherwise,'

Spenser nodded with a smile. 'That if I got into trouble you might help get me out of it.'

5

'That's the straightest thing I've heard this week.' Field peered at him. 'So I'm the man to know? Great. Eighteen years ago, when I got here from Montreal, you could make a decent buck writing stories out of Bangkok. Then the wars ended and the countries fell, so all these displaced journalists horned in. I mean, this is the only place left unless you write tourism garbage out of Peking.' He paused to think about that. 'Who's interested anyway, eh? I hardly write now. Instead I make use of my contacts,' he looked away to empty his glass and refill it, 'selling garden furniture.' Field examined Spenser carefully. 'You don't look like a crook.'

'I'm not.'

The answer was dismissed by Field with a laugh as he leaned over the balcony edge to point down the alley. 'Here's Blake.'

The man indicated was still fifty yards away. Spenser realized that his own arrival must have been noticed at the same distance; Field watching him search from house to house, and waiting till the last moment to call out. The man he called Blake walked close to the opposite side of the alley. In comparison to the Thais around him, he was heavy-set. A discreet version of a Hawaiian shirt hung outside his trousers. His hair was black and thinning, brushed over from below the natural part. He might have been an American tourist, perhaps lost, had it not been for the way he slid unobtrusively through the alley, avoiding the mud and the refuse without seeming effort. By some form of osmosis he appeared aware of everything about him. This could be sensed even from the balcony. Blake's eyes had not risen and yet Spenser felt his own presence already noted and taken into account. Periodically the man looked around, but this was done with perfectly normal curiosity.

'You'll see.' Field betrayed enthusiasm. 'Out of the crowds of second-rate escapees we get, he's one of the few remarkable *farang*.' The comment invited no reply.

Only then did Spenser notice a woman walking just ahead of Blake, picking her way down the middle of the alley. She was taller than the crowd, through which she moved with elegance, her face hidden by a black straw hat. The red chiffon blouse, the pleated black skirt, the lizard sandals melted away before the impression which she herself made. It was of delicacy and of common sense; of accepting her surroundings while holding herself apart from them.

Spenser turned to Field, 'Does she come with him?'

'Mai Lau?' He nodded. 'Look, they don't laugh at her. Not even envy. She makes them feel they could be like her. She has a corrupting character.'

'I don't think I'd mind.'

Field looked up in reply but didn't smile.

The building was of such minimal construction that they felt the balcony move as the door below opened and closed. A soft, restrained voice called out in Thai; a voice difficult to associate with the man just seen in the street, but which nevertheless penetrated up through the office and out onto the balcony.

'Up!' Field shouted over his shoulder.

Blake took in the balcony before he reached them. His face was devoid of lines, like a healthy child, so that he had no apparent age. He put out a large hand to grasp Field's. 'It's good to see you.' The voice was quieter than would have seemed possible. There was a deep, warm ring to it; American and well-meaning. Blake stood back, close against the wall, from where he smiled inquisitively at Spenser. It was the smile of a man in control.

'This is a friend, James Spenser.' Field paused before the word friend. It was used only to avoid wasting time over explanations.

Spenser felt his own hand being enveloped. He looked down. Blake's was square and immaculately clean. The arm was large and meaty; the skin disfigured by a number of swollen insect bites painted over with orange disinfectant. The man was shorter than he had expected and the ease of his movement made him seem slight, when in fact he was square and solid.

'I'm Blake.' He said it slowly lest something be missed. The expression on his face was as soft as the voice.

Behind him the woman arrived. Field kissed her and began in Thai before remembering a curt wave of introduction. 'This is Li Mai Lau. Mr Spenser.'

She nodded as she sank onto Field's rattan chair. Beneath the hat her skin had the pale flawlessness of the inside of eggshell. She fixed a non-commmittal smile and said nothing. Her eyes at first appeared enormous; but it was the size of the irises which created the impression – they were black and left little room for white around the edges. Blake placed his chair close to hers and pulled back partially through the open door into the office, where he could not be seen from the street. Tea was produced for both of them.

The conversation that followed was about Blake having come down to Bangkok to look at the furniture. He was certain that up north he could supply cheaper weavers. This he explained in his spare style, as if teaching children. After ten minutes Field took him downstairs to the workshop.

Spenser smiled at the woman, then drank from his bottle of beer, then looked at her again. He was reflecting on how large a bottle it was to be drinking from when she broke the silence.

'Apparently you were admiring me down in the mud.' She indicated the street below. There was the hint of an English public school in her voice, but it was much clearer than usually produced by that training and the cadence was clipped.

'I didn't realize you spoke English.'

'I'm from Hong Kong.'

'The way you were introduced didn't suggest that.' He had meant it as an apology, but it came out wrong and he trailed off.

8

She smiled with a row of perfect teeth. 'That's just John giving you a difficult time. My other name is Marea.'

He waved over the edge of the balcony. 'It was a remarkable sight – beauty and fashion advancing through the people. An allegory.'

She slapped the table with the tips of the fingers of her right hand; a short, controlled gesture in place of a laugh. 'I haven't been fashionable for a long time.' She had the hands of a classical Chinese painting – small, the fingers tapering gently without any hint of knuckles. 'I'm afraid you're showing ignorance. These are copies of old clothes. The woman who does it for me can't work from photographs or I could be updated.'

He shrugged good-naturedly, 'I was talking about the effect, not the details. "May God be praised for women."'

'"That give up all mind,"' she threw back. 'You should finish your sentences, Mr Spenser. Why do men have such a soft spot for Yeats? My mind is one of the few things I still own and don't intend giving up.'

'But you follow your husband into the slums to compare sweat-shop salaries?'

'Oh, this is a holiday for me. Besides I don't like to be left alone. And Matthew doesn't like to leave me alone.'

'I can understand that.'

'I don't think so,' she replied, and lost interest in the conversation. Her eyes wandered away.

As she chose to look down into the street, he was able to focus on her. The bones of her arms were so fine that he could imagine his fingers squeezing twice around the wrists. He digested this detail without it being what held his eye. She had the same effect on him as a wonderful sculpture; details of perfection could be catalogued, but the beauty was within, around, behind. He concentrated on her hands and felt them moving out, floating to an embrace. And then her body rising from its place to touch his. The illusion had surrounded him before he heard the others coming back up the stairs. Then he saw her again, quite still, staring down into the street. When Field appeared, she asked,

'Do our girls underbid yours?'

He ignored the irony. 'There is more than price, Li Mai Lau. We have to look at the workmanship.'

She began mocking him, 'You mean it's still not cheap enough?'

Field laughed.

'Do you see that man at the noodle stall?' Blake interrupted.

They looked down and across the street. Ten yards from the house was a wooden cart, on one end of which sat a wire cage that kept flies off the uncooked noodles – they had the colour and consistency of raw tripe. The other end was metal-lined, with a pot of water hung over a charcoal fire. One of four bamboo stools was occupied, the client leaning back against a house wall as he sucked at his bowl of noodles with the help of a spoon. Nothing appeared to differentiate him from the others in the street. Blake instructed Field in the form of a request,

'Will you please tell him to go away. Now. Before I leave here.' His Sunday-school diction married well with a melodramatic phrase.

Field laughed, 'Why should he?' Then added with annoyance, 'For that matter, why should I?'

Blake seemed not to have noticed Field's questions. 'If not I will kill him. Perhaps not in this street, but today.'

Marea put her hand onto Blake's arm. 'You know he won't leave, Matthew.' But she withdrew it without further sign.

Something in Blake's manner made Field saunter from the balcony and go down the stairs. Blake had again seated himself half inside and went on talking business as if Spenser were involved.

'My people could finish the tables by September. Maybe the large chairs will take a little longer. The girls up north are not so fast at complicated work.'

His gaze was fixed kindly on Spenser, who registered little of what was said, his own attention being on the street, where Field appeared – his whiteness exaggerated by the view from above – and without great conviction walked over to the man, thereby blocking him from sight. Nothing could be made of their conversation. By the time it ended the client had finished his noodles and sat idly against the wall watching the white man recross the alley. No questions were asked after Field's reappearance on the balcony. He volunteered nothing. They went on to settle delivery dates and to discuss the contract, over which Blake gave the impression of an honest, caring man. Within ten minutes the details were agreed and he got up to leave. Marea rose at the same time.

Once they were out of hearing, Field asked, 'What did you think of him?' He had forgotten his annoyance on Spenser's arrival.

Marea appeared below and began along the centre of the alley, with Blake directly behind.

'Profoundly boring,' Spenser replied before he could catch himself, 'apart from his weakness for dramatics. And apart from his wife.'

Field didn't seem to mind. 'Who said she was his wife?'

They watched Blake draw even with the noodle stall. He walked on without glancing to the side, then abruptly changed his mind and swung around, covering the distance without appearing to rush, but so quickly that the man had no time to rise. Blake stood close above him with one hand spread across his chest, pinning him to the stool. The American said something and they saw the man reply. Blake's other hand came up and pushed him hard against the wall. Then he stepped back and walked on down the alley. The man made no move to follow. The incident had been so rapid, so quiet, so intensely private that not even the Thai who was boiling his noodles a few feet away had paid attention.

11

'What you see withdrawing from this alley,' Field picked up, 'is the backside of a grandson of God. That makes him one-quarter divine in his own right.'

'I don't suppose it's a help in the furniture business?'

'You're fast to judge, Spenser.'

'And what does that mean?'

'Blake is a funny guy. Complicated. He has too many enemies and nothing to show for it, except Marea, and she's a liability. He's the closest thing I know to an untouchable.' As he said that, the couple disappeared from view. 'His grandfather came out to Burma as a missionary in the 1890s. Baptist, of course. The second largest Baptist community in the world is still locked up behind the borders of Burma. This first Blake didn't want to stick around on the plain with the other missionaries, so he pushed east into the mountains. That's the Shan States. The British had half-conquered, half-bribed the Shans the year before. He rode across half a dozen mountain ranges to Kentung, a market town in a valley. There were hardly any tracks then. In fact, there are hardly any now except for the opium trails.' He paused. 'I exaggerate for dramatic effect. The English eventually built a road to Kentung. Guerrillas mostly control it.

'Anyway, Blake's grandfather set up in the market place with the Bible and started preaching. No luck. The Shans had and have an unbeatable combination of Buddhism and animism, plus contempt for outsiders – so they ignored him. But the hill tribes came down regularly to buy and sell. One group, the Lahu, happened to have a prophesy on the books – something along these lines – We can't find God, no matter how we search. But when the time comes, he'll find us, don't you worry, eh. As luck would have it the prophet had gone into detail – a white man on a white horse and carrying the scriptures of God. Blake fitted the bill. He converted them all – 15,000 in five years. That is a physical miracle at least, because we're talking about hill tribes hidden away in what's

12

still the most obscure part not only of Burma, but of Asia. The ladies in Michigan tried to question the quality of his conversions. I believe they raised the spectre of a personality cult. But success was an unbeatable argument and the man-God just stayed where he was, doing good works.

'When the time came, he passed his divine qualities to his son and had the good grace to leave the country before dying. The son went right on preaching until the last war, when he also doubled as an agent behind Japanese lines for the American army. In fact he never bothered to leave. He kept his wife and child with him. The wife died but the child seemed to like the filth in the jungle. That was Matthew. You just met him. After the war the Burmese became independent and threw them out, so the Blakes retreated south across the mountains to a small town called Mae Hong Son, just on the Thai side of the border. Matthew's father used it as a base to carry on both functions – son of God and intelligence gathering. I'd say the intelligence business was starting to take up most of his time. The border there is mountain-jungle. Impossible to control. He used to go in and out of Burma whenever he wanted.

'He sent his son to the States long enough to get a degree, then brought him back and pressed him into both family businesses. During the Vietnam war Matthew Blake was the only American who could organize the hill tribes into fighting units without totally corrupting them and himself. I'd say he's still the best guerrilla leader in Asia. Then the other Americans went home. Of course Matthew stayed behind – a third-generation Lahu god who happens to hold an American passport. He's been trying to figure out what to do with himself ever since.'

'Don't the Americans still need his services?'

'I told you, he has too many enemies. The Thai government would expel him if they got hold of a decent excuse. Nobody's playing his game. He's a prehistoric leftover.' Field drained

13

his beer. 'So I can't help you? Pity. Listen, I've got to go. My daughter's waiting for me. Come to my house tomorrow night and we'll discuss it. I'll walk you to the ferry.'

As they climbed to their feet, they noticed that the man at the noodle stall was lying half on his back on the ground, with one leg hooked up and over the stool. They could see a narrow red line that began at his mouth and spread down across his cheek. There was also a small stain on the front of his shirt. The owner paid no attention. Nor did the passers-by.

Field was momentarily mesmerized, then pulled himself together. 'It's not important.' He drew Spenser inside. 'They'll pretend the guy's a drunk and dump the body tonight. Nobody wants to deal with the police. They're too expensive.' He led the way downstairs, where he stopped between the workshop, still filled with weavers, and the front door. 'It's a dirty business.' Field was talking about the girls. 'I guess it is better than working in a brothel. Of course, they could make more money with their bodies, at least for a while.' He looked them over in the dimming light. 'They haven't got the looks.'

He pulled open the door and led the way down the centre of the alley without looking to either side.

# 2

The death of the man at the noodle stall did not shock Spenser. Instead it revived the only other death he had witnessed - that of his father. He said nothing to Field and was careful to hide his emotion, yet the blood on the man's face stayed with him that night as he lay awake, isolated from Bangkok by the vacuum of his double-glazed, air-conditioned room.

He had been standing by his father in their Paulton Square

house in Chelsea. That house had been his father's only good business deal; he had bought it during the war, one week after a string of bombs fell on the square. 'The bottom,' went his standard joke, 'had fallen out of the market.' Spenser's childhood, indeed his whole youth, had been wrapped up in its four narrow floors. He could still recreate, as if standing before them, each of the drawings his father had discovered over the years – in poky shops or unidentified in auctions – and brought home in triumph thanks to the ignorance of the world in general. While the pictures on the walls grew into a valuable collection and the house was eventually worth a small fortune, his father was a buyer not a seller. Having bought the best of something, he could think of no reason to part with it. They therefore lived in relative poverty and were never able to repaper or repaint or recover – those were his mother's dreams, which always took second place to her husband's. His mother still lived there, alone, imprisoned by thirty years of her husband's obsessions, and no doubt she would continue that way until she died in another thirty years or so.

Spenser had been sixteen and home on a school holiday. The fourth floor was devoted to a study where his father worked. He was just fifty, but had been sick for the past two years and had gradually taken on a high pink colour with a swollen air that broke down and deformed any remaining hints of youth. They had been standing in the study before an unframed red chalk drawing of men on horseback, which Spenser had seen correctly was French and eighteenth-century, but his father egged him on to say more, so he guessed that it was Canova. This was greeted by a 'Ha!' of triumph, on the tail of which came a demonstration of all the obvious traits that made the choice ridiculous.

His father loved to exercise his skill and to become excited in the process – to celebrate his genius by transforming intellect into emotion; a kind of verbal orgasm – just as he

15

loved to discover that a museum department had made a mistake, because they would have to call him in and pay him something to set them right. For this reason he followed the auctions closely, waiting for inevitable errors – undetected fakes, bad acquisitions, mistaken attributions. The result was what he called his 'stupid money'. Their stupidity, his money. He also did it to reassert regularly his own reputation among the mafia of official experts.

For his son's benefit he went into a long dithyramb about the legs of a particular horse before going on to point out something self-evident that Spenser had missed about the grouping of the riders, when blood came spattering out of his mouth among the words. It flew in tiny drops onto the drawing. In his surprise, his father put out a hand to touch them and, as they smeared across the uneven surface of the paper and the lines of the horsemen, a flow of blood followed and he was suddenly bent double in agony, vomiting it and coughing as it filled his lungs.

At first Spenser stared in horror. Out of the contorted heaving, his father stretched a hand for help and Spenser took it and half-carried him to a sofa. Only then did he cry for help. The rest was blurred, except that his father went on vomiting in agony until he was dead; which took some five minutes. In the empty silence of the seconds that followed, Spenser noticed his own hands, stained with blood. He went to the bathroom and scrubbed them long after the flesh hurt. Then he locked himself in his bedroom where he began to cry. Later they told him that his father had drowned in his own blood, or words to that effect.

Lying in his Bangkok room, he waited through the night, unable to sleep; not because he had been horrified by the man's death in the alley. He had not. Death, as Spenser knew it, could only be a violent shock and something to which there was no reply. Being reminded of the inevitable violence kept him awake only because it led to a void without reply.

16

In the morning, before the heat built up, he was driven to Ying Chai's shop. He had sent a note the day before to introduce himself. It wasn't far; just around the corner from the Erawan Hotel, but he didn't want to walk back when the sun was high.

The shop took up the ground floor of a new office building. Its mirrored door swung open onto a monumental display of gold-lacquered buddhas – nineteenth-century Burmese and of no great interest. Behind these were glass cases laid out and lit as in a museum. The shop walls hung with heavy mauve brocade that framed the ceiling – a patchwork of elaborately carved panels, probably collected from old houses and monasteries. He waded forward through the carpeting with the caress of silent air-conditioning on his cheeks towards a young girl, who looked more like an object for sale than an assistant. She watched him approach without breaking her pose. He asked for Ying Chai and was told to wait. Spenser rapidly examined what was in the cases; it all appeared genuine, but none of it remarkable. Certainly not in comparison to the décor of the shop.

The sound of laboured breathing made him turn to find an old woman steering herself with a cane at a limping pace between the cases. On her head was a black wig, curled in the fluffed-out style of the fifties. This helmet balanced the weight of her body, which from the breasts on down was considerable and without form. She wore lime green tights to give her legs support; but the visual effect was to create bulges in every direction. Her make-up had been applied as a thick mask. That, combined with the slackening of the flesh, made it impossible to judge her race. Spenser paid little attention until he realized that he was her destination.

'Ying Chai is unwell,' she said in a surprisingly strong voice as she drew close. Her English was considered and old-fashioned, in the convent-school style. The cadence was further confused by her difficult breathing. 'I am his wife. A letter came from London from Percival Gordon to warn us that you would call. He is an old friend.' With her free hand she gave a sharp tug at her tights, pulling the top up higher. Stretched over this new layer of flesh, the elasticized cloth created fresh bulges for a few seconds before gravity caused the waistband to slide back down to its previous level. 'An old client. It seems you are the new genius of the Victoria and Albert.' The name Victoria came out in four clear syllables, suggesting that the women were related, or at least acquainted in some distant past.

Spenser offered a smile of self-effacement. 'Gordon is a friend of mine, so he exaggerates. I was in their Indian Department until last month.' At the word 'until', he saw a light dim in her eyes and then extinguish. 'I'm afraid I'm not buying for the museum. I'm here on my own.'

Using her cane as a rudder, she swung herself about and began walking away. Over her shoulder she managed to shout, 'No matter. We shall sit down.' Without slowing she took another pull at her tights.

He was led into a room whose main decoration was a disorder of ledgers littering shelves and stacked in corners. Half a dozen sculptures were scattered over a teak desk and two credenzas, upon which they acted as paperweights. He saw that three of the sculptures were exceptional and that this was where she did her real business. The magnificent shop was designed for the passing trade. On one end of the desk was a bas-relief of a disciple seated with his feet to one side. It was three inches by four and had been roughly broken out of a larger sculpture. Spenser had difficulty keeping his eyes away. Near it was a Khmer statue of Vishnu, standing more than two feet high. As Ying Chai's wife lowered herself onto her cushioned chair behind the desk, she saw Spenser eyeing the Khmer.

'Do you like it?' she suggested.

Spenser moved around the statue with sudden physical

agility and ran his hand over the surface. 'Of course it's a fake.'

She made a loud noise, which sounded like, 'Ah!' before adding in a neutral voice, 'Do you think so?'

'Certainly. The ear lobes are too long. And why is the hair so roughly cut at the back? Look, they've mixed two periods in the shoulder. You would only find muscles this size on an early piece.' Like his father, he became animated when examining an object; like a toy wound up and let loose. And when the object was false or badly done, a natural anger came out, as if this crime against excellence had been aimed directly at himself. He put his eye close to it. 'The surface roughness is supposed to be root marks, but there's no dirt in the holes. They must have dropped hot plastic on and ripped it off cold.'

These flaws, which sounded so obvious, were in fact minute and invisible to most eyes, even to those of most experts. But for Spenser they were childish details; mere specifics which could be explained. They had nothing to do with the central flaw that had first caught his eye – the absence of the essential. The magic of creation was missing; the irrational, the unexpected, the irregularity, the spirit which could make a sculpture more than an object. It was something he could never explain, but only feel. This spiritual eye was what set him apart from his peers.

Mrs Ying was nodding and had put on a pair of glasses. Spenser caught himself before he asked whether she had bought the sculpture without realizing or was responsible for its production. She pulled herself upright and examined the statue for a good two minutes. 'Well done, Mr Spenser! You sound like our friend Gordon. Now, he has very good eyes. Is he coming to visit us?'

'I think he's too old now.' Spenser tapped the fake as he sat down across from Mrs Ying. 'Perhaps that's why I'm here.'

Her eyes swung back to the Khmer, which seemed to need an explanation. 'Some fool brought that in yesterday. I had

19

not yet examined it. He must take the thing away. Ever since the wars began in Cambodia, we receive a steady supply. And now much of it is like this one.'

The girl from the shop brought pale green tea – in low, wide cups.

'Very pretty,' Spenser said, as he raised his.

'Not for sale,' she replied. 'What is it you are interested in? Perhaps I can have something brought up.' She put both hands to the waist of her tights and gave them a tug while trying to raise her bottom from the chair.

'Mr Gordon suggested I approach you with a proposition. I want to get some pieces out of Burma.'

She put up a hand to stop him. On three fingers there were rings of imperial jade. Behind, the flesh could be seen hanging down beneath her arm. 'What do you mean? Do you want to go and take them and bring them out yourself?'

'I realize I can't do it alone. But I know the market in Europe. The risk is worth taking.'

'Unlikely!' she erupted, with a suddenness that caused her mass to quiver, after which she settled motionless into her chair, staring down at the desk. She might have been dead. Spenser had begun to wonder if she were all right when her eyes came up and fixed on him. 'These things are too complicated now. Too many people watch us. The laws are too strict. What we sell is not permitted to leave the country because too many Americans turn buddhas into lamps. Imagine Jesus Christ on the cross with a light bulb in each hand? No, Mr Spenser. No.' A glimmer of her convent-school training seeped out in the tone lent to Christ's name. Again she fell motionless, this time staring at him.

It was a curious speech to have made since they both knew that every piece she sold went to a foreigner and left the country illegally. What was more, every piece in her shop had originally been stolen by someone. And every foreign museum and foreign collection was made up almost entirely

20

of objects which had originally been stolen. That was the function of a museum: to protect stolen goods. She patted her wig to confirm it was still in place.

'Now,' she sighed, 'I wait. Things come to me. Sometimes they are good. Rarely they are wonderful. But if they are too good we cannot sell them because they are too well known. People do not want objects they cannot show or resell.'

'What about that?' Spenser pointed at the small bas-relief on the desk. There was a covetous ring to his voice which she did not miss.

Her hand, warmed by the chunks of lime green jade, picked it up kindly. 'This is very good. Do you know where it is from?'

'Burmese. Pagan.'

By now she expected him to get it right, so no notice was taken of his quick reply. 'Two peasants living at Pagan knocked this off a sculpture in the Ananda Pagoda. So rough, so clumsy. They did not need to lose the legs. And they sold it to an Australian tourist for 100 US dollars. He carried it out in his suitcase and sold it to me for 500. If only it had not already appeared in a book, I might sell it for 50,000.'

'But as it is?'

'I might get fifteen.'

Spenser reached out to take the fragment from her. He caressed it with a warmth unexpected between a human and an object. This caress stretched on into a long silence during which he held the sculpture close, not to examine it, but simply to feel it in his hands. 'I'll give you ten. Cash.'

Momentary surprise was quickly disguised by an energetic tug at her waistband. 'This is the first Pagan piece to come out in years.' She no doubt regretted not having begun at a higher figure, then with a shrug decided not to barter. 'Done. Out of friendship for Percival Gordon; but you must show it to him. He must see that we still find the best things.'

'I want you to send it to Gordon.'

She nodded in understanding. 'You are buying for him.'

'No. It's a present. I told you. I'm on my own. Will you be able to send it?'

The question was dismissed as irrelevant. 'That is the easy part. The customs officers take standard bribes by weight. I shall make a present of that to you.'

'Marvellous,' Spenser laughed. He was delighted with himself. Giving the statue to Gordon was an unnecessary gesture. One he could only just afford. But why not? He knew the pleasure it would bring. In comparison to the freedom the old man had pushed him towards, this was a mere token offering. He held out the sculpture. 'I'll bring the money over tomorrow.'

She grasped it with a motherly smile, her thoughts scarcely disguised: $10,000 for a present! The young man was clearly capable of buying again. Perhaps he was more than a client. He was, after all, a friend's friend who deserved her help. 'I shall think of someone for you. Someone in the north. Someone honest who still goes into Burma. You must be careful.' She leaned forward with an urgency that pierced her make-up. 'Never deal with a Thai. They are short-sighted thieves. You give them $200 to send a piece out of the country; $100 for them, $100 for the customs man. They keep $150 for themselves and the customs man is unhappy. You must only deal with Chinese. You can go up and down Asia from Seoul to Jakarta, it is the Chinese who run things. They know about proper business. Ask Percival Gordon. Every piece we ever sent him got through. No, I shall find someone for you.'

'Marvellous,' Spenser said to liberate himself. 'I'll come in the afternoon.'

Through the clammy heat of sunset he arrived at John Field's house. It was hidden in a compound shared with five other houses, separated one from the other by canals and gardens, all of which were overgrown. The guardian made no attempt to help open the gate. He was content to lie in his string vest and shorts on the raised floor of his shelter, from where he watched the hotel driver struggle. When asked, he pointed towards a clump of trees within which Field's house was buried, then turned his radio up still higher lest anything else be demanded of him.

The door was opened by a girl of seven in bare feet who spoke no English, but acted as though he were expected. Spenser wondered if this were Field's daughter and left his shoes at the end of a row of sandals and loafers outside. He followed the girl across a half-furnished room enclosed on two sides by walls of wire screening that opened onto a canal. At one end of the room was a simple dining-table; at the other were four cane chairs padded with leather cushions. The two solid walls were hidden by shelves of unfinished wood, stacked rather than lined with books. There was an air of disordered neglect about the room that was softened by the rich sounds of birds swooping over the canal outside, their music flowing through the screens as if they were within.

The girl led the way up a staircase and along a short corridor at the end of which she pushed open a door. Spenser found himself in a bedroom where Field lay naked on his side, his back turned to a woman propped up by pillows and talking straight ahead of herself in anger. She was dark with a flat face and breasts that were full and uncovered, along with the rest. Propped forward as she was, the breasts arched out prow-like, the nipples spreading over a good part of the surface. Her voice charged around the full vocal register of Thai, moving suddenly from whispers to shouts to whining before beginning to whisper again. Her right hand was stretched towards Field, whom she periodically slapped on the shoulder or the backside, hard enough to emphasize her point in an unfriendly way. He was not bothering to defend himself. On his face was an expression of boredom.

23

Before Spenser could turn about to leave, she noticed him and immediately waved and shouted as if he were part of the problem.

Field sat up. 'You're here. Good.' He jumped out of the bed, wrapped a sarong around his waist and pushed ahead of Spenser back downstairs.

'I'm afraid your daughter led me up.'

'My daughter?' He stopped on the stairs to look up at Spenser. 'Christ, that's not my daughter. Forget it anyway, forget it. That's the way she is, growing up like her mother, eh. That bitch you just met. I couldn't get one without the other, so I took both.'

Downstairs he flipped on a ceiling fan. A bottle of Mekong, the Thai whisky, sat on a shelf surrounded by books. Field filled two glasses, then set off in search of ice and soda and slices of lemon. He came back and dropped them in.

'Drink this.' He threw himself on to a chair, pulling up another one for his feet. 'Sit down. Funny thing about women here. They come from the north, girls like her, without money or education or anything – I mean she comes straight out of a rice paddy, eh. Mind you, she picked up a few things before she got to my house. And there they are with nothing – Jesus, I mean nothing – in the new Sodom and Gomorrah. So they make their way with their bodies.' He saw that his glass was already empty, lurched to his feet to fill it and splashed some more into Spenser's without being asked. 'But they know what they want in return. It's a fair deal, eh. And they know others are waiting to take their place. Most of them play it pretty fair so long as it lasts. Not like your white equivalent.' He noticed that Spenser was only half-listening. 'She'll get us some dinner,' Field added, then looked up the stairs, 'eventually,' and took another long gulp that emptied half his glass. 'I'm starting to think she isn't like most of them.'

They lapsed into silence while Field mused over his fate. Then he stretched out his legs without turning to Spenser.

'It's not really her fault. Funny you should think her daughter was mine. She's all Thai, that one. Came out of the village with her mother. There's some idiot husband still back in the paddies. Now my daughter is a pretty thing. And smart, not like her mother. There's a bitch. A stupid bitch. She's what caused that little scene you just saved me from. The idiot came here this afternoon to wheedle more money. I wasn't around, only Miss Boobs upstairs was, so they shouted at each other for an hour. Current queen versus original queen. The battle for the crown, eh. Great public entertainment. Thank God I wasn't here! She wants the money for herself. Not for Songlin, that's my girl. I give them lots. I put her in a good school. Her mother wants the money so she can play Mah Jong all day. I should take Songlin away from her. That's what I should do.' This was said with a determination inspired by Mekong.

The ceiling fan was not enough to keep the room cool when the screens were closed, blocking any breeze. But with darkness the sound of birds had died away to be replaced by that of mosquitoes, so nothing could be opened. Already bugs had found their way in and Field's words were accompanied by the orchestration of his snatching mosquitoes out of the air with his left hand and squashing them in his fist. Spenser emptied his glass once and then a second time, just to keep cool and to occupy himself during the monologue. Having described his first love in Bangkok and his latest, Field went on, if only to prove that he was sometimes happy, at least in the early days of each affair. It began as an amusing patter that turned into a summing-up of his private life, perhaps in preparation for yet another change. By then Spenser had taken to refilling his own glass. When the woman came down the stairs and began making noise in the kitchen, just out of their sight, Field focused on his guest.

'Is Ying Chai interested?'

Spenser no longer felt up to talking. 'I saw his wife. He's dead, or almost, and she isn't far behind.'

'I figured that. Past glories. I thought maybe you knew something I didn't.'

Spenser shook his head. 'I can't see the Ying Chais, Mr and Mrs, on a jungle expedition. She said she would find someone in the north, near the border, who could get me through the Shan States to central Burma.'

'She's right. This place is full of specialists. The north has the smugglers,' he enumerated, 'drugs, jade, rubber sandals, antiques, motor cycles, birth control pills and on and on. Some things they run into Burma. Some things they run out. The smugglers are the poor hewers of wood. The stuff coming south they sell to middlemen who bring it on down to Bangkok. The élite here buys everything for a song and exports it at great profit. You might as well go straight to the people who are going to do the job. You'll find the middlemen seven hundred kilometres north in Chiang Mai. It's a schizophrenic little town. On your left are the tourists spending twenty-four hours with the suburban hill tribes and their picturesque poppy fields. On your right are the jade houses, fronting for the drug runners who control sixty per cent of the world's heroin. They also kill a lot of people. It's a romantic place, but the people you want are another 300 kilometres north, right on the border.' He examined Spenser with a not unfriendly stare. 'What I don't get is why you want to do whatever it is you want to do.'

At first Spenser seemed not to hear the question. He had gone to Field's house fully intending to tell him everything; and now, with five Mekongs inside him, the desire was gone. 'It's not very complicated really. I'm an expert in Burmese art and I've worked out that there are some pieces at Pagan which are scarcely guarded. All I have to do is get them away from there. They're rather large.'

'So your luggage won't do?'

'200-pound statues. Carved stone.'

'It's the jungle trails for you.'

'That's the only hard part. I've got the buyers. I even have the cash to finance everything.'

'I wouldn't tell too many people that.'

'No. You're the only one.'

Spenser's assurance was annoying Field. 'Great,' he said, 'but I still don't understand.'

'Oh,' Spenser shrugged, 'things got turned around somehow.' Field was staring at him intently and he felt obliged to go on. 'It's not just to make the money,' he laughed at himself, 'because I'll make a fortune out of it. A fucking fortune. It isn't that ... Look at you. You're not hanging around here for the list of bar girls I've just heard.'

Field shrugged. 'I'm transparent. A lot of us came out here to get away. That wasn't how we put it. We thought we'd come because of Vietnam, but that was just an excuse. It was an American war, eh. Only I'm Canadian. There were lots of Brits, Australians, French, everything. There hadn't been a good excuse to go east since the traders and missionaries were thrown out of most places. When the war ended some of us went home. Not many. Some had been killed. The rest are still here; a few up-country, but mostly in Bangkok. It was great till then. Lots of stories. When they ran out it got so I was editing my life, you know. So I gave it up. Now I don't worry. I live a rough first draft. Here,' he tapped the arm of the chair, 'I am away. Away from them.' His hand waved in a wide arc as if all of western society were crouching in the shadows beyond the screened windows. 'They can't touch me while I'm held in the soft embrace of the East.' He laughed to show he was joking, which made it less of a joke. 'The soft grip. But that has nothing to do with you.'

'Yes and no. I want to go back ... I had two obsessions when I left school. One was a love of beautiful things. The other was a day-dream about what I'd do with this love. I thought I'd go into a museum and surround myself with it all. I'm sure it sounds sterile to you, but to have them there to touch … and to try to make other people feel them the way I do. The propagation of excellence; that was how I saw it. Only everyone I worked with saw it differently. They had a career ahead of them. They didn't care about the beautiful objects except as the tools of their trade. And the museum was so poor I couldn't even bring pieces up from the basement. You know, who would retype the catalogue? Who would adjust the insurance? So I discovered it wasn't enough to be surrounded by what I loved. I had to own them. I had to be free to do what I wanted with them. All I needed was one good find to finance this trip. I made it. And when this is done, I'll be free to do whatever I want.'

'And that's it?'

'More or less.' Spenser felt he had said enough.

'No little troubles along the way?' Field's eyes were still fixed on him.

'Not really. The trouble is getting someone to help me now.'

'Like hell,' Field shouted at him. 'Your mouth muscles stopped working when you got to the good part.' He shouted again, this time to the kitchen, 'Hey, Bua, we need some food or Mr Spenser's teeth are going to fall out.'

The woman came around the corner and said in a tiny voice, all soft soprano, 'What you want, John?'

He told her something in Thai which made her laugh, then turned back to Spenser. 'You'll see. Bua is a crummy cook. One thing. You'll end up in a border town. I don't know which one. It'll depend on how many trails into the Shan States are open these days. I've given up following which little group is fighting which. There must be a dozen pseudo-nationalistic smugglers, each with a band of soldiers. Sometimes a couple of hundred. Sometimes a couple of thousand. Always fighting each other over control of the

28

trails. But if you happen to end up in Mae Hong Son, stay away from Blake.'

Spenser revived, 'Why?'

'You came for advice. I'm giving it.'

'I thought he was desperate for jobs.'

'Doesn't mean you've got to give him yours.' They looked at each other through an alcoholic haze. 'You were there yesterday. You saw what happened. Do you know anything about where you want to go, apart from your buddhas?' As this made no impression he added in an irritable way, 'The word anarchy. You know it? Generally defined as an abstract idea for nuts. Well the Shan States are practical anarchy put into physical effect. Nothing is fixed in place. Nobody calls the shots. There is no main line. Just a gigantic, rich vacuum inhabited by a lot of clever men, who fight with each other for little victories and money on ground they can't control for more than one hour over a hundred yards.'

'But you said he was the finest guerrilla leader this side of the moon.'

Field got to his feet and waved his hands under Spenser's eyes. 'All you want are some stupid little statues. What you've got to do is tiptoe over the border and up a trail, snatch them, and tiptoe back. No noise. No attention paid. What you need is a second-rate little smuggler, not some crazy General Patton who used to drink a bottle of scotch a day to give himself the nerve to lead armies of Neanderthal hill pygmies up cliffs under machine-gun fire.'

'At the moment he's all I've got.' Spenser led him on.

'Go on, asshole! Hire him! He'll take your money, eh, but you'll end up fighting his wars. Not snatching your babies and running away to happiness.'

'So you think I should take your advice.'

Field suddenly realized he was being teased. He leaned forward to give Spenser a light slap on the cheek. 'That's right.'

# 3

What Spenser told Field of himself was perfectly accurate thanks to sins of omission. The next morning he regretted his reticence. He was in need of a friend and knew that to win Field over he would have to enter into a confessional without walls; but there was nothing in his own background to prepare him for massive revelation.

It was true that he was driven by a love of beautiful things. Not of beauty; there was nothing abstract about him. It was the objects themselves that he loved. Not that he was driven by a craving to own them. Just to see them, to touch them, to hold them, as if he were their lover; something quite different from the creator who could never exist side by side with his creation. It was all, as Cocteau had said, a question of sex.

At the age of nine he had first been sent out alone by his father to haunt the museums. He was to report back on what he had seen, with detailed descriptions and judgements. His father was devoted to tests. At first Spenser had treated this as a game, and organized meetings with his friends in one museum or another, where they would rush about rooms of armour or of Egyptian tombs, playing.

One day his friends didn't appear and he found himself waiting at the British Museum in a room of Khmer statues. For a while he sat patiently, then fidgeted, then found himself staring at the statues because he had nothing else to do. Slowly, imperceptibly the figures came alive. At first he thought he had fallen asleep and was dreaming. But that thought alone was enough to make him realize he was awake and that the statues were moving with some power of their own. His father's long speeches on the divine state of genius caused him to think it was the spirit of their creators that made them vibrant. For Spenser, it was the conversion on the road to Damascus.

He spoke of this to no-one, out of fear that his friends would think him peculiar, if not crazy; not even to his father. After all, Spenser was deprived by his conversion of the normal tools of rebellion given to any youth. How could he hate the beauty his father loved when that beauty carried him into a world of hallucinations; him alone? He had a secret key to the universe of dreams. All he could do was hold back the knowledge of his fervour and then, without consciously intending to do so, concentrate on what his father knew nothing about – bronze and stone, given that his father's obsession was with drawings and paintings. As his first experience had been with Khmer sculpture, the boy became devoted to things oriental. There the older man was unable to follow.

Spenser's passion at that stage involved little more than his imagination. He came into a room. He sat. He waited. And the objects revealed themselves to him. The next station in his development came over a year later. He was sitting before a case of Indian figures in the Victoria and Albert when a friend of his father's crossed through the gallery on the way upstairs to his office. The curator recognized the child and broke into his reverie.

It was the first time Spenser had been caught in the act and, luckily, at least that was the child's reasoning, by someone who was not a threat. Before he could weigh the consequences, Spenser poured out all of his feelings with what must have appeared to be wild infantile enthusiasm. The museum official was delighted and offered to take him down to the stock-rooms, where the boy would be able to see the rest of the collection. In the shadows of the long tiled corridors through which he was led, remains of dead civilizations lined either side, looming over him in a jungle of twisting arches and undefinable ruins. Behind a locked door,

31

lights revealed a sea of statues which over the years had been jammed into this room devoted to India and south Asia. Some were in cases, others on the floor. The older man unlocked a case and handed a small buddha of Pagan to Spenser. He took it carefully in his hands and, without expecting or seeking anything, felt a vibration slip up through his fingers into his arms and chest. He let the statue drop, but recovered in time to catch it and forced his fingers tight about the stone while the sensation spread and grew in strength. He looked in confusion at the curator only to realize that his experience was within and invisible to others. As he digested this, its intensity swelled and swelled until he was overcome with a sense of communion that sated itself before retreating into mere vibrations. He handed the statue back and reassured himself that one object had brought on this reaction, which could not be repeated, and he avoided even looking at that object as it was replaced on its shelf.

The older man took out a figure carved from a piece of crystal. It was a disciple of the Buddha. 'This one's not bad. Not the same thing, of course.' He handed it to Spenser, who hesitated to take the buddha. Then he couldn't stop himself and the same sensation surged through his body.

That evening he mentioned to his father that he had met a Mr Ramsey at the museum. His father replied sardonically,

'The only thing that changes at the V and A is the religion. The place is either in the hands of Catholic sodomites or Protestant sodomites.' Spenser's face must have betrayed confusion because his father added, 'I say, he didn't take you into his office or anything, did he?'

What he meant by 'anything' wasn't clear to Spenser, who thought it best to reply in the negative.

Throughout his years at Winchester and later at university, he knew that he could find comfort by shutting himself up alone with the few objects he owned. From the beginning he had his father's talent for finding things, but added to it was

32

the ability to sell what he had bought in order to buy something better. In the beginning it was a matter of no more than a pound or two, but this desire to trade in order to increase his personal pleasure contradicted the training he received at school.

He often wondered why he was at a school famous for producing slaves to convention with perfect manners. Slaves of the highest quality, but so much the opposite of his father, who had been educated at home and hated organized society with all its limitations and obligations, and who himself had no manners. At first Spenser suspected he had been sent to Winchester as a test – to see whether he could break out of the mould and become one of the eccentric exceptions to the rule. Later he felt his father was trying to destroy any risk of competition from a son; or simply couldn't be bothered dealing with a child who was becoming as unpredictable and troublesome as himself.

His father's death dragged Spenser down into a confused depression, so that he suffered without awareness of pain, as if permanently stumbling through thick fog. The day after the funeral he escaped to the V and A, where he fixed himself before his favourite statues and stared with amorphous hostility. He didn't question this sudden hostility. Yet within seconds the sculptures began to move wildly in a way he had never before felt. They flowed out from their stands, reaching for him, encircling him, enrobing his senses, breaking away barriers, caressing his face until tears flowed effortlessly. Silent, easy tears, endlessly emptying him. He reached down for his handkerchief only to find his trousers strained by an erection. The undulations rolling through his chest and head with uncontrollable turbulence abruptly turned with tidal force to rise from his groin, pushing the tears away. He rushed along the galleries to closet himself in a men's cubicle, where his whole body was overcome with shuddering and the waves passed through him.

Then he sat on the seat in a trance. His grief was gone. Death had shrunk away to a distant bench. Walls separating him from the beauty of the statues had collapsed all around. The beauty had been released. And what had changed to bring on this freedom? There could only be his father's death.

Spenser went back along the corridors to the statues and sat before them. A deep calm settled upon him. Where the sight of these forms had once created a hypnotic sensation akin to fear, he now felt himself floating in pleasure. Yet even in this pleasure, something was being held back. Some secret. Some vision. Some truth. The figures had embraced him, but it was a wilful not an open embrace.

A few weeks later he returned to school, where the confused depression once again overtook him. He became obsessed by the need to see beautiful objects in order to find release. It was a good six months before his mind began to clear and he was able to talk to other students as if they existed. Even then his passionate link to beauty remained.

At least on the surface, Spenser began his career as a typical Wykehamist. His desire was to serve the state – which in his case meant going into a museum and working his way to the top. If he served well, his reward would be increased responsibility. His own skills, added to the memory of his father's reputation, meant that when the time came he was snapped up as an Assistant Keeper by the V and A.

At first he found no contradiction between service and collection. The museum paid him little, but he was used to being short of money. For a few years he got by as most of his friends did – he lived off the deb circuit and country weekends; and because he was normally agreeable, he was asked to dinners by eager girls preparing for the right marriage.

What cash he had was used to build up his small collection of statues in the two-room flat he rented in Kensington. This pattern evolved little with time, except that his friends gradually got married and he was gradually paid more, which still amounted to next to nothing.

He spent little time with those of his contemporaries who worked in the museums. Most of them were the paper scholars he detested, more interested in careers than in beautiful objects. Their success seemed to be in contradiction to his own, rather than a complement. He felt constantly out of step and therefore ignored them. The museum's poverty was more difficult to accept; though he refused to be upset when it could not finance the rotation of its own collection, let alone buy important pieces that came on the market. He simply got on with his work and was mildly surprised each time his skills were recognized. At thirty-two he was made a Deputy Keeper; one of the youngest ever, and therefore destined to be Keeper. More important than that, he was quite happy so long as he could continue buying and selling for himself, risking a few hundred pounds, sometimes even a thousand. A single unwritten rule limited him ˉ it was not done to buy in the same field as one's department. He didn't mind. His career was devoted to India and Burma; his private life to Thailand, Cambodia, China and Japan.

He spent a good deal of time in the sale rooms, keeping his eyes open for himself and for his department. It was there he first focused on the fact that some people grew rich by using their skills; not only rich, but in the process they kept the best for themselves. He became accustomed to watching the rings of dealers seal up the bidding despite the awareness of the auctioneers and the museums; and this before the sales began. Then he got to know the dealers himself because it was through their hands and through those of a few odd mavericks that the most beautiful pieces passed.

He was more shocked to discover that some auction houses thought nothing of undervaluing objects in order to buy them for their own stocks through blind bidders. These pieces would later reappear for sale elsewhere at their proper price, thanks to proper attribution.

All this time he rarely lasted with a girl for more than a few months. His elusiveness at first made them more eager to catch him. Then they became wary as his reputation spread. It seemed that if a woman didn't share his passion for things of beauty he was soon bored, and by its nature this passion could never be truly shared. He didn't ask himself why such a personal, even secret, obsession should control his emotions. He accepted as self-evident that all his loves should be inextricably linked. And since his passion was irrational, he had no control over its demands; yet they were gradually isolating him from the world to which he belonged – apparently the real world – without delivering the secret he was certain had been promised on his father's death.

Shortly after being named a Deputy Keeper, he went to a friend's house in Devon for the weekend and met Anne. She had the grace of a figure in a Japanese drawing – a fineness such that the mere thought of touching her gave him pleasure. And when, a few weeks later, he in fact touched her, it was with a sense of climbing ashore. She sought nothing from him; no moral protection or direction. If anything she protected him. And Spenser, whose family had always lived in chosen isolation and who himself had been slipping farther into marginal waters, reached out for her hand.

There was something more. Her own family had been amateur collectors for generations, which helped her to understand his obsession, and before long he was spending his weekends in Devon, where her parents' house was littered with the particular tastes of three centuries. Sometimes opportunity had played a role. The Second Opium War, for example, had placed a young officer before six undefended Chinese buddhas of the tenth-century. They now dominated the drawing-room.

Spenser felt at home in this large brick house and, more important, he felt for the first time in his life that he belonged

36

to the normal world. He was amazed by how much pleasure the sensation gave him.

Her parents and her brothers, who periodically came down for the weekend, knew about sculpture, even oriental sculpture. They all took a great delight in explaining the origins and the quality of the pieces in the house. But they also talked about family and farming and ordinary human events, which he listened to as if arriving from another planet.

The third station in his development came in December, a year and a half before his resignation. He had gone to Christie's for the exhibition of a major oriental sale and found nothing worth bidding on for his own department and nothing he could afford for himself. On his way out he was stopped at the bottom of the stairs by an assistant keeper from the Far East Department of the museum; someone Spenser generally avoided. There was a smell about him which suggested school lockers and his mind was lost permanently in bureaucratic forms. Hair lay heavy and dank upon the rim of his glasses. Spenser could visualize the wife who cut it with her sewing scissors.

'I don't suppose you'd do me a favour, Spenser.' He didn't wait for a reply. 'I've got to buy a drawing in this wretched sale tomorrow, but I can't come. Do it for me, won't you. I'd be awfully grateful. Number 72. Go have a look. I'll ring you about the price.'

Spenser wandered back up to the sale-rooms. There was nothing magical about number 72. It was just the sort of safe purchase that would look good on the man's record. The museum already had one almost the same.

Only then was Spenser's eye drawn to the picture hung beside it – a Hangchow scene. There was a lilt to it, a certain flow which he couldn't place. He checked 73 in the catalogue. It was unattributed. He turned to the price estimates. £200. Spenser stared at the drawing again and followed the familiar lines. Then it came to him. Had no one else seen it? A Daogi like that was worth £10,000. Was it really an error? He forced himself not to look again, lest he draw attention; in any case, every detail of it was imprinted on his mind. If he could get it, he knew exactly what he would do – resell it to buy a wonderful bronze he had been seduced by in a gallery the week before; unfairly seduced, as it was beyond his means.

The man from 'Far East' telephoned him late in the afternoon and asked Spenser not to pay more than £2,000 for his drawing.

'It was 72?' Spenser asked.

'Yes. Yes. The Tang Yin.'

'And there was nothing else you liked?'

'Terrible lot of trash!'

Spenser laughed dutifully. 'It was just that I thought 73 quite a nice drawing.'

'Really?' The man paused, indifferent. 'Didn't notice.'

The next day there was a snowstorm in London, which reduced the number of bidders. Spenser bought 72 for the museum and 73 for himself. It cost £120. His hand trembled as he wrote the cheque – not in the excitement of winning out, but with the passion of the true eye. Nothing had called it forth in the last easy months and suddenly it surged up from nowhere. He waded through the slush to a dealer on Bond Street, just to have confirmation of what he suspected. Only when he got there did he notice that his loafers were soaked through.

The dealer offered him £7,000 straight away. Spenser refused. He wanted to sell it for the maximum and explained that it was his lucky piece. Then he told him the story.

At eleven the following morning, the man from 'Far East' stormed into Spenser's office. Via the grapevine he had heard everything. With his back stiff and his buttocks stuck out, he placed himself before Spenser's desk and shouted. 'You tricked me!' His feet danced as he talked. His voice was high-pitched and slightly out of control. The effect was of an unplucked but castrated cock trying to pee. 'You knew of course. You knew you were making an ass of me.' An unnatural, meaningless smile filled with teeth broke the mask of the man's face.

'I guessed what it might be and took a chance – I didn't make a fool of you. You didn't want it.'

'You didn't tell me.'

'I told you I liked it. I asked you if you wanted it.' Spenser lost patience. 'Anyway it's not my department. I can buy what I want.'

'Well you must give it back to us!'

'Fuck off.'

The man was still for a moment, as if another cock had come into the yard, bigger and not castrated. 'We won't let it drop. People are laughing.' He added with an air of generosity, 'We shall give you what you paid.'

'Get out!' Spenser jumped to his feet and swung his fist at the man. He stopped himself at the last second and stared at the clenched hand. He could scarcely focus. The other man had gone white and was also staring at it. Spenser grabbed him by the shoulders and pushed him into the hallway, then slammed the door.

An hour later the Keeper of Far East called and began pressuring him. Then his own boss came in to make it clear that technically he could keep the picture, if he didn't mind damaging his career.

They were interrupted by a secretary. Melting snow was leaking through the glass roofs into the hall of wood carvings. This happened every time there was heavy rain, but they couldn't afford to have the roof repaired, so the Keeper broke off the meeting and led the way, running down the stairs and through galleries, gathering large plastic sheets from strategically placed cupboards as they went and dragging them on to cover the endangered pieces. In the midst of this, the Keeper found time to warn him that the question of the

Chinese drawing was not closed.

When he got home in the early darkness of winter, Spenser sat on a hard chair and looked around at the wooden Japanese figure lying on the sofa and the large crystal eighteenth-century buddha and his other loves and fell into a trance of depression. He was roused by the arrival of Anne to whom he told the whole story. She was on his side, as he knew she would be. He was morally in the right and the others were simply jealous. He went through it again and again with her and only towards the end did she point out the obvious – that he was obliged to give in. That or destroy his career. Spenser could but agree. And yet he went to the museum the next morning with a feeling of having betrayed himself; a feeling that he no longer belonged there.

It was two days later that he saw Percival Gordon walking up the stairs to the Christie's showrooms. Without thinking why, Spenser followed him into an exhibition of old master drawings. He had never met Gordon, but a myth surrounded him. He was one of the few men Spenser's father had constantly praised – a man who bought and sold only for his own pleasure and in a great variety of areas. Everyone considered him an expert without being able to say exactly how or why. This had been going on for a long time. He was in his seventies.

Spenser put himself near the door and watched Gordon glide through the room, limp and yet restrained. No concrete gesture or expression showed him to be conscious, except perhaps the restraint, which was romanticism disguised as disinterest. Gordon took the arm of a well-known dealer and said to him,

'I've just been quoting you. I'm doing a catalogue for Artemis. Do you remember what you said about Uccello?'

The other man murmured and they moved together around the wall examining the pictures. Gordon was tall and wafer-thin. He pulled the drawings towards himself roughly,

40

as if they were the kind of woman who could be bought or sold. There was the assurance of total knowledge, not love. Love was what he hoped to find among the tawdry display,

'Look at that blue. They've cleaned it. Very peculiar … Look at that line. Now isn't that a pretty thing?'

His profile was like a quarter moon, the tip of the nose rolling into the deep long valley of a sunken mouth before rising on out to the tip of his chin. His lips hung as low on his face as they would go, turned down not with displeasure, but with minimalization. Despite his appearance, it was easy to see in him the boy who had talked loud of shooting and art fifty years before, with his mouth enthusiastic upon his face and breaking into uncontrolled laughter. But that had been gradually flattened out. First by the imitation of sophistication – Adam's fear of nakedness. Then by the heavier, real thing when he was in his thirties and his mouth had taken on the brittleness of plaster, only to melt into the present marginal admittance of life, which passed for fatigue but was actually the romantic's controlled resentment before what the world expected of him.

There was no preening, no self-esteem. His languidness was asexual: a sense of himself – not of his role or his intellect or his pride – but a moral sense of whom he supposed himself to be. Nobody in particular. Just himself. And upon that ethereal confidence all the rest hung, like washing on a still day. As to anything private, that was hidden.

On his way out of the room, he pretended to notice for the first time that he was being watched.

'You're Spenser's boy.' It was a strange phrase to throw at someone thirty-five years old. He extended a long transparent hand and took the young man's arm. 'What are you doing for lunch?'

'Nothing.'

'Then lunch with me.'

In the street he held onto Spenser's arm, guiding him

without explanation. They turned towards St James's and when they were away from anyone who might overhear, he half-whispered, like a boy sharing a secret,

'I heard about your caper.' He flashed an innocent smile. 'They're a bunch of shits, you know. Not worth the paper they push.' He walked on again, in silence. Then stopped long enough to say, 'You shouldn't have given it back, you know.'

'I can't afford to resign.'

'Afford?' He stared at Spenser in disbelief. 'Afford? That drawing was worth two years of your salary.'

Spenser hadn't thought of it that way and said nothing. They turned up St James's and into Gordon's club. He led the way by the porter in his cage, through a first drawing-room into a second, both of which were almost empty because it was scarcely noon, and on past two Japanese screens into the bar at the back, where he leaned against a leather fire rail to warm himself. A sullen trio stood in another corner mumbling to each other. Gordon hadn't said a word since Spenser's reply in the street and still seemed shaken by it.

In an attempt to get himself back on track, he threw out, 'Would you like a glass of champagne?' only to look at Spenser doubtfully. 'Or do you drink gin?' He paused and looked over at the barman without listening to his guest's reply. 'No, I think champagne's the answer.'

When he had got himself and his guest upstairs and seated by a window under the barrelled ceiling of the dining-room, he told Spenser to order a game mousse and salmon, then slouched himself across the table into a position where he could talk only inches from Spenser's plate. Against the pale walls of the room his face almost disappeared.

'Look here. I don't know what you think you're doing working in that mausoleum. I know you. I know all about you. I've read your articles. What do you get paid for them? A pissing five pounds? I hear the gossip. You're good. You'll get one of the big houses before you're dead. But do you want it?

42

My guess is no. You've got the eye and you'd rather use your edge. Those people you work with, they don't love art. They don't even like it. It frightens them. They'd like to take a perfect photograph of every masterpiece, then destroy the masterpiece. They want to be in control. I've seen you in the sale-rooms. I've seen the way you pick things up.' He threw himself back in his chair with his arms out. 'They look at art through a prophylactic!'

Spenser was so surprised that he whispered, 'What do you expect me to do?'

'The next time you find something, don't give it back.'

He had known the answer before he asked the question. He had known already when he returned the Chinese drawing.

A month later Spenser was standing in a sale-room before a small dancing Shiva. According to the catalogue it was nothing, but he knew immediately what it was – one of a row of four from a temple in north India. Two were still there. One was in the Metropolitan and one was missing – probably in the cellars of a stockbroker whose grandfather had been in the Indian civil service. Wherever it had been, it was now a foot away and calling to him.

He felt someone take his arm and turn him around. It was a dealer whom few people liked, but who had a talent for turning up wonderful pieces with doubtful origins. He was called Berek, a Yugoslav by birth.

'Don't stare,' was all he said until they were in the corridor outside. He whispered, 'So you noticed. Come on. I saw your face.' He laughed. 'An expression of sheer amazement. I think we are the only two. Do you want it?'

'I'd love it, but I can't. It's my department.' The dealer showed relief. 'On the other hand, I think my department would like it. I'm obliged to tell them.' He said this apparently in earnest.

'Come on, Spenser. I'll outbid you, so why push the price up? I'll make you a deal. You let my buy it. I'll sell it to your

43

department and I'll give you half. What can they afford?' As Spenser said nothing, he talked on. 'You'll make a good £5,000 out of it. They owe you that much. Don't play the sucker twice.'

Spenser flushed with embarrassment. So everyone knew about the Chinese drawing. And they were all laughing at him. He had himself sat in on so many conversations when someone was mocked for his errors or naïvety. Was that all he had gained by his honesty? Ridicule. And hatred from his colleagues for trying something they would never dare try. And all of that without a single person showing greater interest in the beauty of the object than its correct attribution and its price. He didn't think about it. He stopped himself from thinking and said yes. Once it was said he felt himself coming alive in a way he hadn't since his childhood visits to the museums.

With the £6,000 Spenser eventually received, he bought a Japanese lacquer monk sitting on a low chair. It was four feet high and he placed it in his drawing-room as if it were part of the family. Only that evening did he tell Anne what he had done. The shock that came over her face couldn't have been missed. This time there was no question of him being morally in the right. He made no attempt to explain or to justify himself. There was nothing he could say. Her devotion to him quickly swept away the shock and transformed itself into protective love.

'I'm just trying to understand, James. Perhaps you don't want a career; perhaps you shouldn't have returned the Chinese drawing.' When he picked up on none of that, she added, 'Well, you've have your revenge now,' meaning life could go back to normal.

He wanted to explain himself. To make it easier for her to accept, but could think of no way to do it. At the time his dishonesty felt dishonest; an enormous act that would change his life. However, nothing changed. Instead he received more invitations to write and to lecture. The gods smiled.

Early in the spring he came across a reference in a nineteenth-century art magazine lying around the house in Devon. It interested him so much that he cancelled all but the essentials of his daily existence in order to find out more. The reference was to a family in Wales who owned fifty life-size buddhas. Apart from that one mention, he discovered nothing, so on weekends he began driving off from Anne's house to spend the day in Wales asking questions. At first she came with him, then after a time she lost interest and waited at home. He wondered periodically himself why he was doing it, but five months later his questions led him to an estate in north Wales.

A retired officer confirmed that his great grandfather had commanded a regiment in the 'Burmese conquest' and had brought home a shipload of junk plundered from a monastery. It was out on an estate farm where a cousin lived.

It was dusk when Spenser drove down a muddy track towards the farm. In the time it took to find the door of the stone house and to wait for it to be opened by a farmer – who had once been a gentleman farmer, but now did it himself between drinks – the night had come on. It took another hour of talking before they made their way across the mud of the farmyard to a large stone barn. There was no electricity inside. The farmer shoved open the doors and flashed his light. Dozens of eyes shone back. On five rows of platforms sat large bronze buddhas with quartz eyes. They were eighteenth-century and not of enormous value, but altogether Spenser guessed they could be sold for around £300,000. He offered the farmer £3,000 to empty his barn and drove back to Devon.

That night, lying beside Anne, he waited until they were in darkness before telling her what had happened. She absorbed his excitement and rolled over to kiss him.

'The people at the museum will look so silly. You've done it

45

without them. I feel a bit sorry for the farmer.'

'These aren't for the museum,' he said quickly. 'They're not good enough. The museum wouldn't want them.'

She was silent. 'What are they for then?'

'For me. To sell. I should clear well over £100,000.'

'And that's all right?'

'Of course it is, Anne.'

'Good.' She said this as if to block any doubt. '£100,000. How wonderful.'

It was a tentative acceptance. And of course she was right. He would never tell the museum. He felt anger rising against her. Why couldn't she just accept? 'The museum doesn't matter, Anne. Listen! This will change everything.' He pulled her back into his arms, crushing her gently to force away the shadow separating them. For the first time, he felt he must protect her; that she could not deal with all that he might do. What he was going to do. If she couldn't understand, he would have to present things in a way that she could accept. Suddenly, he was afraid that he might lose her. 'Anne,' he caressed the length of her back as he held her tight, 'we'll get married.' The drunk farmer and the quartz eyes faded away and he knew everything would be all right.

It was after three in the morning when he awoke, unable to sleep, and went down to the drawing-room. He switched on a single lamp, which cast shadows from the six Chinese buddhas. It was curious how still they were. He threw himself on to a sofa with his legs up. All six statues were beautiful, yet he had never been able to bring them alive. This thought gave him a start. He had never really tried, he reflected. But then trying had nothing to do with it. He looked around the room. It struck him for the first time that the house was filled with a beauty that sat heavy and still. How many times would he have to come there, how many hours, before he could bring these buddhas to life? They had been aggressively possessed at first by the passion of one family member, then literally forgotten by the generations that followed and were busy aggressively possessing other things. Had passion, in so quickly turning to indifference, left the genius within them to wither away over the centuries of meaningless ownership? In truth, they were like clutter. He thought of Anne. The line of her back turning into the curve of hips. Each weekend he came to this house with love. But love of what? Of dormant ownership? Looking around he was certain of his need for her. But desire was missing from that. Simple desire. Did he want her? Suddenly Spenser wondered whether they had been talking to each other over the last year or to themselves. It wasn't enough to need her. And what did she want? Spenser realized he had no idea and felt stupid ... self-centred. He looked around the room. If she loved this clutter or was even attached to it, she could never understand what drove him. The thought was no sooner out than he was ashamed of it. Was that why he had suggested marriage? To cover the void. He felt a terrible anger against himself and did not go back upstairs.

The next morning he left before breakfast saying that he must see his Yugoslav dealer as early as possible. Berek agreed to pick up the buddhas from the farmer, store them and sell them as best he could. Again they agreed to split the profit evenly.

Spenser walked out of the dealer's gallery into the warm street air and abruptly, now that all was in place, realized he had not questioned his own actions for months. Not since he had seen the reference in the magazine. He had been hypnotized and carried along an obsessive path. He was technically within his rights to do the deal. There could be no doubt of that. But he was in the wrong on every other count. And he had done it for what? Not for beauty or excellence. Just for money. But no, he reflected, it wasn't for the money. It was to escape the need for money. To escape every need. To scrape himself clean. And now that was done.

He felt free. He was free. It was a clear September afternoon. he walked a few blocks towards the bus with this sense of freedom swinging faster and faster until suddenly it wasn't possible to ride back on a forty pence ticket to a chair behind a desk. It wasn't enough. He looked up. Brown's Hotel was just ahead. He searched frantically through his pockets, then his diary and wallet, where he found Percival Gordon's card. Spenser ran inside to use their telephone.

Gordon lived in the Albany. At first glance there was little in his apartment and Gordon himself said, as he led the way, 'I have a very small collection, but each thing is the best. Why should I bother with more?'

In the fading sun by a drawing-room window were two Peking chairs so light and so designed that they appeared to fly. Between them was a scroll table and on it was a half empty bottle of champagne beside one flute. Gordon produced a second glass and filled it.

'By beginning at eleven each morning, I can sip my way through a bottle in time to have one glass left for bed. It's very good for the sinews.' He drew out the last word into something mysterious.

Spenser's eyes began to adjust and he saw that the impression of emptiness around him was in fact a symphony of perfection. Each piece of furniture, each picture, each object, wherever it came from or whatever its period, was married to the rest by virtue of its excellence. Gordon had surrounded himself with a seamless cloak of beauty. He waited in his Peking chair, as if it had been made for him, and said nothing until Spenser had finished looking.

'Have you come to weep or is there a tale to tell?'

Spenser sat down in the other chair to describe in detail what he had done. As he spoke he realized there had never been any real confusion in his mind.

Gordon's mouth hung impassive, hinting neither approval

nor disapproval. 'And what will you do when you have completed your transaction?'

'Get out of London,' Spenser threw back. 'Cut them all out.'

At that Gordon jumped to his feet with an energy totally out of character. 'Yes! Yes! Cut them out. This,' he swept his arms around the room, 'this is a preparation for death. Get away from those sordid sale-rooms filled with dirty old men trading old loves and new loves endlessly among themselves. Oh, the recycling of emotion.' He threw his hands up to clasp either side of his head. 'I cannot bear it! ... But I am too old to cut them out. Oh, I never did anything truly of my own. Little adventures, yes. I always had a little something tucked in my pocket when I crossed a border. They never miss it. But no ... in your place ... I would ...' He stopped himself and sat back down in his chair, where he closed his eyes to consider his words. 'At Pagan on the Irrawaddy there are 5,000 temples in ruin. A few of them are among the greatest creations of the world. From the eleventh century to the thirteenth the Kings of Burma ruled there, with four million people in the city alone. Now a few peasants live here and there beneath the ruins in bamboo huts. Nothing else.' He drew himself in and smiled apologetically, 'But that you know. I am treading on your subject.' He sighed audibly. 'The society of man is the most delicate of flowering plants. Mistreated, ignored, grown foolish or over ambitious or too weak or too strong it does not wither but explodes in a mere second and disappears so completely it might never have existed. Its survival depends not on the good reading of warnings but on the correct actions of the society itself. A seed of imbalance appears at first to be nothing. But then it swells and germinates and flourishes into blossom. And no matter how beautiful the flower, its seeds will destroy the garden. The creative genius that you and I worship is a minor by-product that dies with

49

the rest. Sometimes a few isolated objects escape. Little more. That is the lesson of history. Look at Angkor. We found it abandoned and saved the carcass for its beauty. Now the carcass has become a battleground and even the ruins are being destroyed. Pagan is waiting for the last vengeance of history. You could get there first.'

At the mention of Pagan, Spenser knew he had been right to come. Something was waiting for him and Gordon was the messenger. 'Have you seen it?' Spenser asked.

'I passed through. They fly a small plane in a few times a week. A handful of the curious can sleep in a guest-house. There is a little museum which is well locked up at night, but the best is still in the temples.' He crossed the room and came back with a book of photographs. 'You know this? Here's the best. In the Ananda Pagoda there are 1500 statues, but in the outer corridor there is a series of eighty depicting the life of the Buddha.' He began flicking through the pages. 'Even through these terrible photographs they come alive. You know, with the lacquer taken off no one could prove they were the same. Everyone would know, but no one could prove it.'

Spenser bent over the book. He knew of the statues. They were stone. Three feet high. The lacquer merely coarsened them. It had been added as a base for gold leaf and could easily be removed. The photos gave little but he could see beyond the images, so that his eyes were mesmerized. 'What would I do with them?'

'For a start you'd have to limit the stink or no one would buy them. I could help you. I know collectors who would take the risk. Each one of these is worth close to a million dollars. You might get $200,000 with a bit of luck. You could feed them out slowly. Eventually even the museums would want them. They would wait until the next disaster strikes Burma and then, in the disorder, who would think to blame them? They are hired to get the best. So you would have saved these wonderful things and made yourself a fortune.'

Spenser leaned across the book. 'And kept the best for myself ... and for you.'

Gordon smiled. 'You will see. It's not the possessing.'

'How beautiful.' Spenser turned the pages carefully, no longer listening.

It took Berek another five months to sell the bronze buddhas. When it was done he asked Spenser to celebrate over lunch at a restaurant off Piccadilly. It was a crowded, noisy place in the brasserie style, filled with people on the make wearing purchased signet rings and practised accents. They exuded a hungry vulgarity and begged to be loved, which they knew they would be if they could hold on to their money long enough.

Berek was not alone. He had with him the two American dealers who had bought the buddhas in a single lot. Their idea was to sell them in California where oriental religions were fashionable and could be played upon. As Spenser sat down, Berek threw a thick envelope on to the empty plate before him.

'What's this? Spenser picked it up.

'Take a look,' he replied loudly.

Spenser ripped it open. Inside was a wad of hundred pound notes. He quickly stuffed it in his jacket, furious. 'Why did you do that?' He stopped himself from looking around.

'Because that's your fee.'

'I don't understand.' He looked at the three smiling faces. A doubt came into his mind. 'How much is there?'

'£20,000.'

'What! You owe me ...'

'I've restructured the deal.' It's much harder to sell these things than to find them. What I really owe you is a finder's fee.' Berek laughed at Spenser's confusion. 'Is there someone you'd like to complain to?'

Spenser felt his heart pounding until it deafened him. He

51

pushed back his chair and managed to get to his feet. The other three watched him curiously. Then, without warning, he threw out his fist and caught Berek in the face, knocking him on to the floor with his chair. The restaurant turned in abrupt silence.

'I'll skip lunch,' Spenser said.

He walked across the park to the museum and on arrival sat down to write his letter of resignation. With £20,000 he would have enough.

# 4

Carlos Santana was awoken by an irritation, or was it a sensation, familiar and yet unwanted. On the assumption that it came from mosquitoes, he waved his hand over his face. The five nails were long and unclean. But it was still the summer dryness in Mae Hong Son. The few surviving mosquitoes usually ignored his dried body in preference for juicier flesh.

He ran his tongue around the seven remaining teeth. Their roots were so exposed, their colour so yellow shot through with black that they in turn would soon fall. He drew his top lip down over the teeth; a motion that also pulled the lids back from his eyes. After a time they focused, although their muddy quality remained. Between himself and the low wooden beams there were no insects. His eyes moved in an arc towards his toes until he saw his wife, crouched on her knees, caressing his genitals.

'No!' he shouted. 'No!' and pushed her away. He looked with dismay at the beginnings of an erection and shouted at her again in Hua, but she had understood. 'Not the day the monk dies.'

His rib cage pushed out aggressively against the slack, mottled skin. What was it that made her persist? He had not given into her for ten years, not since her fourth child. Yet still she slept on a mattress in the corner so that she might attack him when her Spirits told her the moment was ripe.

'Go make food for the monk! He will die today.' Santana moaned to himself, 'To have an erection the day he dies.'

His English came out with an uneven accent, sometimes slipping back into Spanish habits, sometimes confused with a word of Hua. English was the language in which he had chosen to finish his life because he spoke it badly and in any case it had had nothing to do with the important moments of his existence. The words did not touch him. Their sound evoked no memories, good or bad. That and abstinence from the flesh were two of his successes since becoming a Buddhist. Two concrete steps over twenty years. In truth he no longer spoke any language properly. He preferred silence.

His wife ignored the order and jumped to her feet to rush around the room spraying insect killer into the corners and under the furniture. He felt the morning heat already building. 'Stop it! The stink. You will kill me.' In the absence of sex she had become increasingly attached to killing insects. 'I will stink by the side of the dying monk.'

She stopped at the thought of the bad luck that might imply. There were moments when Santana thought her appreciation of the modern world was limited to a spray tin. But then he remembered the insects in her village and could hardly blame her.

'Manee, go downstairs. Food for the monk. Special today.'

This time she obeyed. He couldn't help but notice that, despite her negligence, she had held on to her looks. Plump, but all together. She said she was thirty-six. Well, he was sixty-one and had given her ten years of sex plus four children. That was enough. He had earned the last ten years of abstinence.

'Lik!' he shouted. 'Lik!'

His third child, a boy of fifteen, came running up the stairs.

They had been expecting a load during the night from across the border.

'The men, have they come?'

The boy shook his head. Santana had allowed his children to be brought up by his wife. That also was a way to cut any attachments to life. They belonged to her world. If necessary, one day, they could go back to her tribe.

'Your uncle, he has not come?'

The boy shook his head again.

Santana's last job had been for the Americans – training hill tribes to fight Communists on the Burmese border. He had been hired by Blake's father, the second Lahu god, in the fifties and had spent five years organizing a tribe called the Hua. In 1962 he got out, with a wife and a family connection that would keep his shop filled by whatever antiques were left to be smuggled across the Burmese border.

'The uncle never comes on time.' Santana's apparent anger hid a certain relief. He was glad not to buy stolen buddhas on the day the monk died.

That failing needed no amplification – dishonesty was dishonesty. Selling buddhas was worse than dishonest. He had been filled with scruples when he began in the business, limiting himself to artifacts and dancing nats. These had gradually become scarce and he increasingly poor. But his scruples had held. At the same time he had begun his flirtation with Buddhism and one day in a temple had admired an early statue of the Buddha. The monk had picked it up and given it to Santana. 'Could you keep it for a time? We have so little space here.' Santana had been about to point out that it already had a space. Instead he made a large donation to the temple. After a time he had realized that the statue need not be returned. He had in fact bought it. In horror he donated the figure to another temple, where the monks were known to be honest, but from then on he allowed

54

himself to buy buddhas, provided they had been stolen by others.

He reached for a pair of scissors by the bed and began clipping his toe-nails; he clipped his nails rather than clean them. Lik stood close by to gather up the black slivers as they sprang in different directions. He would bury them or burn them lest they be used against his father by an enemy. Santana got to his feet and pulled on some old trousers. He had given up underwear. The noise of the main door opening below drew him to the top of the stairs. An English voice asked,

'Is Carlos Santana here?'

His wife hesitated, 'He nooh here.'

'When will he be back?'

'Don't know.'

'Today?'

'Nooh.'

'When?'

'He nooh tell me.' She hesitated again. 'Next month.'

'Please give him this card. I'll come back.'

The door closed and Santana heard the card being ripped up. She must have thought the man looked unlucky. He laughed to himself. How could she understand his Buddhism when hers was racked with superstition and spirits and ritual. He was certain that when she bowed in front of a buddha, she was worshipping an idol. It might as well have been a spirit or a nat. Well, it was no worse than his mother had been with her saints and her Virgin Mary. In any case, it wasn't his affair. His own actions were quite enough to deal with.

He came down the stairs and ate some rice. His wife had laid a table of soup and noodles with meat, but he left them, as he always did. He took the containers of food for the monk and went out through the side-door on to a patch of dried earth and crab grass. There was a pervasive smell of burning

55

in the air. He looked up at the line of hills on either side, only to see that the sky was tinted brown with smoke. It was the same every year. From February on, the hills baked and were covered with sporadic fires which were left to burn themselves out. It would last another month, until the rains began in July. Through the dry season the valley collected heat; during the rains it was a swamp.

His house was on the main street – there was only one other road and they ran parallel the full length of the town along the bottom of the valley. They began at the airstrip and ended just before the small lake, where the monastery grounds blocked their path. The main road was paved, the one behind was gravel. Like all but three of the houses in Mae Hong Son, his was of wood, raised up off the ground, with carved roof panels and shutters in place of glass.

At the back of the house was a shed in which his sons created old furniture. At the side was an eucalyptus tree encased by a cage. This mass of wire was a lunatic thing rising from the ground into the branches, which it used as support. Inside were five monkeys. He had no idea why he kept them. Perhaps to remind himself that he was as ugly as they.

He noticed Spenser watching from the far side of the road and guessed that this was the early caller. The piercing stare would certainly have been considered dangerous by his wife. But Santana had other things on his mind. He threw some scraps to the monkeys which, given his stooped body, seemed to require great effort. Then he shouted to Lik to remove the shutters from the shop at the front of the house. Most of his clients were Bangkok merchants who flew in now and again. He was expecting no one that week, but perhaps the Englishman was a buyer. When his son had the shutters off, Santana walked out into the street and turned right, past the peeling cement façade of the Mitr Niton Hotel on the other side. He noticed Spenser follow at a distance.

The hotel's three storeys made it the tallest building in

town, along with the neatly painted Thai Military Bank next door. The cement trinity of Mae Hong Son was completed on Santana's side of the street by a large house, whose iron balconies were painted bright red. The house itself was set back behind a wall with broken glass embedded along the top. A sign on the wall in Thai, Chinese and English read 'Jine Senn Jade House'.

It was the monk's duty to come out with his bowl and give the people a chance to earn merit by filling it with food, but that was academic given his weakened state. The container Santana carried was filled with delicacies far finer than the scraps a monk was meant to eat indiscriminately, merely to keep alive. In any case, he would certainly eat none of it – and if he did, it would be a deathbed failing. The Spaniard wondered if his offering weren't really intended as a temptation. Why should the monk escape, perhaps really escape once and for all from this existence, and leave his friend still a prisoner of his illusions of reality?

Santana walked in a dissected manner, each joint its own master. It was the cumulative result of attacks by malaria and dysentery and hepatitis, among other afflictions which his body had survived. Fifty steps from the house he turned left down to the lake – it was more a pond – and to the right around the edge on a dirt lane until he reached the grounds of the monastery. The temple was at the centre. It was in the rural style; a wood pavilion raised high on stilts and covered with a tin roof. The solid brick tower of the stupa rose before it, fifty feet into the air. Its wide base was painted white. The elegant upper half was covered in gold leaf. From the top, two sets of bells hung motionless, in the absence of the slightest breeze. On either side of the temple, beneath the shade of trees, were the huts in which the monks lived.

He went first to the stupa and walked around it once, stopping beneath the niche where the statue of the Buddha sat. He genuflected and muttered, 'I take refuge in the

Buddha.' It was said without sentiment. He meant only that he did it in honour of one who had escaped. Then he went to the monk's hut.

They had carried him out beneath a tree, where he lay on his side, a blanket beneath him and cushions behind. His right arm was crooked to prop up his head. Around him eight other monks were seated. Santana put the food down at the old man's feet and placed himself close to his head. One of the monks had to move sideways, which he did with some grumbling.

The old man was transparent. He had stopped eating a week before, when he realized he was close to death. There had been a time when he had enjoyed talking English to the ruined Spaniard. It was a language he had learnt sixty years before from an English consul who had also liked to discuss religion. And Santana knew himself to be rare among westerners in that he was not attracted to the marginal fields of Buddhism, such as the Tibetan, where the teachings had been so buried in pagan superstition that their meaning was reversed. It was curious that Santana should seek the heart of the Buddha's ideas and that the monk should have been able to offer so little guidance. They had no common past to work with – Santana was bound by experiences both foreign and so terrifying that the monk could not find within himself the words to help. And now he could do nothing. Conversation was a strong cord, binding him to his body, when he sought only to cut himself free.

Santana leaned down and whispered, 'Bikku, I must talk to you a last time. I have no love for this world. I know there is no happiness here, but I am held by my misfortune . . .' He felt a fool and stopped of his own accord.

The monk drew breath to fill his lungs enough to speak. 'You are living in nirvana, but the veil of ego blinds you.'

'The veil of pain,' Santana said, more to himself than to the other.

58

The monk projected a hollow voice. 'If you complete the journey you will be sorrowless and rid of all bonds. There will be no burning of the passions. Because you are unaware of yourself, life is an illusive solid. When you become aware, it will be a realistic void.'

This effort left him gasping. The others watched in silence. His breathing became so slight that one of them leaned forward to see whether he was still alive. They remained there for an hour and well into a second hour.

Santana's eyes were drawn down to the scrub grass in front of the monk's blanket, where a caterpillar was edging its way between them. At first he thought it was a maggot and his eyes were fixed in horror that it would turn in his direction. He could feel a tide of nausea rising up within him. It was only when a small phalanx of ants appeared and began attacking the caterpillar that the other monks were distracted from their meditation. The ants ran as a single body and threw themselves at the caterpillar, rolling it over with each attack and stinging it. The viciousness of the scene far outweighed the size of those involved. Santana and the monks sat transfixed; he on the edge of nausea, they by the cruelty. The white softness of the caterpillar's skin had a tender quality and it was large enough for its agony to be recognizable. They watched in discomfort but did not move.

Suddenly the old monk reached out with his left hand and tattooed the ground to frighten off the ants. He snatched the caterpillar up, rolled it gently into his palm and drew it close to his eyes. It was already dead. He put it down on the blanket before him. 'Not today,' he said. 'Today I will live. Tomorrow.'

Santana pulled himself to his feet and walked away to a grove of trees where he vomited. The good things of life he had no trouble giving up. It was the wounds that held on. In Barcelona, as a teenager, he had been an anarchist and had escaped the final massacres only by fleeing to France. What

59

stayed with him from that violence was the smell of rotting meat. With many of the other escaped anarchists, he had gone into the Foreign Legion and had spent the war in Algeria. Afterwards they sent him to Indo-China and eventually, along with the rest of the Foreign Legion, to Dien Bien Phu.

His battalion had been allotted Isabella, where they lived in the mud with their own faeces. After three months he had been saved by a wound and put in the bomb-proof hospital – a complex of dark caverns dug out under the mud. As the number of wounded grew, these tunnels were extended until they stretched beneath the graveyard, also growing with freshly-killed soldiers. It was then that the maggots began oozing through the mud ceilings and dropping down to eat at the open wounds of the living. The doctors calmed the panic by explaining that this was good; maggots ate only dead flesh and therefore cleaned the wounds. It was an interesting argument, but Santana had had to be tied to his cot. When the surrender came, he had been in and beneath the mud for five months.

He had the misfortune to get better just in time to be marched by the Viet Minh to the prison camp – 300 miles with his hands tied behind his back. They were untied in the evening. Of 10,000 on the road, 7,000 died. A friend developed gangrene from the tight binding on his wrists. To save himself he used a jack-knife to cut off his own diseased arm. All of that Santana survived, and when he saw a maggot or smelt rotting flesh, the horror heaved up from within him. The old monk had never seen such things. He had an ego so much less tortured from which to escape.

Santana struggled back to his house and shouted as he came through the front door. 'Manee, I want to smoke. Get me a pipe ready.'

She slid her feet along the boards into the store, where she could see the tension on his face. 'Nooh now. Later.'

'I want it now!'

She pointed behind him. Santana turned around. The Englishman had paused in the doorway to listen, but he now came forward across the creaking floor and put out his hand.

'My name is Spenser. Ying Chai gave me your name. I asked for you this morning.'

'You want to buy something?' Santana tried to drive his pain back into the depths. He could feel a sweat coming on, though the low room was cool.

With the shutters off, a draught was drawn through the openings. Around the walls were polished shelves filled by lacquer betel boxes, wood carvings and buddhas. Most of them were fake.

'Perhaps,' Spenser replied. 'But I'm only interested in twelfth-century or earlier.'

'Have a look.' He turned away to mop his face with a cloth his wife used for polishing.

Spenser walked around the room with a serious, respectful air, after which he said politely, 'These are not as old as they might be.'

Santana tried to make sense of the expression on the man's face. Only with difficulty could he concentrate on its features. What did he mean? Impatiently the Spaniard moved back through an arch. 'I have better things in the next room.'

He turned on a light and pushed his wife, who shuffled ahead, spraying under tables with her tin of insecticide. In the second room the objects were real, without having any special quality. Again Spenser looked around carefully before asking,

'Do you have anything older?'

That was all Santana needed in his present state; someone with money and nothing to sell him. Normally he would have invited the buyer into his sitting-room and brought out his good pieces. At the moment he had none. That was what he hoped his brother-in-law might be carrying across the border.

He pulled himself together enough to say, 'I will have some things tonight. You will come tomorrow?'

'I'll come in the morning.' Spenser smiled politely and backed his way out.

When he was gone, Santana said to his wife, 'I want a pipe.' He climbed to his bedroom and lay down. A few moments later she followed with a wax lamp and set up her tools on the low table by the bed.

She warmed and kneaded the opium with what amounted to affection. It was the closest she could come to his sex. The smoking, she knew, would sap his desire. If Santana would not come to bed with her, nor would he go with anyone else. She heated the blackened putty a last time and put it to the side of the pipe, then asked,

'Monk die?'

'No.'

She handed the pipe to him. 'You still go to temple?'

'Tomorrow.'

He took a deep breath. Before he began to slip down into a boundless calm, he repeated to himself that this also was a failing, this blurring of the mind. Escape from the world had to be a conscious act, not a cowardly withdrawal into a dark cave. How often had he felt his cravings grow like a creeper to strangle his freedom and then go on growing like monsters in search of mythical combat? It was a great failing, far greater than the commerce of buddhas, because it came from a fear of himself.

From a distance and scarcely an hour earlier Spenser had seen the Spaniard stumble to his feet among the monks, disappear under the trees to vomit and stagger home. He had no idea what it meant and followed, only to discover in their short conversation that the man had been overcome by some sort of nervous attack. Spenser got out of the shop as quickly as he could and drifted back towards the monastery.

There were a few people on the street; mostly hillsmen carrying sacks towards a small market by the airstrip. Spenser passed his hotel and cut down towards the lake, lizards darting along the edge of the dry, weedy ditch beside his feet. The Spaniard's face stayed with him – the unfocused eyes as much as the handful of teeth over which the lips could not close. The long dirty fingers jerking in uncontrolled directions had been like an evocation from the side of the damned on judgement day.

Spenser found himself in the monastery grounds, standing aimlessly beneath the temple porch. As Santana had done, he followed the overgrown dirt path around the base of the stupa until he came to the niche that held the buddha. It was an ornate, even coarse, painted figure. He could not imagine for what reason Santana came there.

The monks still waited before the old man. Spenser slipped closer to them and sat under a shade tree. A dog infested by weeping sores sniffed up to him, but barked and shied away, no doubt frightened by the smell of butter that came off most Europeans like a rancid perfume. Around Spenser the patchy grass had been withered to a light brown, matching the earth, and the leaves on the trees were dusty with the stillness of the long, dry season.

He had arrived that morning in a twin-prop plane, which four days a week did a turnaround flight from Chiang Mai. The flight took fifty minutes, versus ten hours on the road that twisted up north and west through the hills towards the border town. Of the other twenty or so passengers, most were soldiers returning from leave or peasants. There were also four middle-aged men squeezed into tight shirts and bell-bottom trousers. Their feet were protected by transparent silk socks over which elaborate Italian sandals had been fitted. They carried pigskin purses and wore sun glasses. Had they not been Thai and had there not been jungle below covered by a smoke haze, they might have been mistaken for property developers in Marseilles or Miami.

The plane had dropped over a pcak into the Mae Hong Son valley and held to the centre of the strip. There was a mountain river on one side and the town was on the other. The four men pushed out of the plane first, to be greeted at the foot of the steps by a thin, young Thai in a red Lacoste T-shirt and French jeans. He fitted to the form of his clothes, not they to him, because he was soft without a line of his own. The backside of his jeans rounded into a flat, wide shape, like that of a plump woman. On each wrist there was a fine gold chain. His face escaped down towards his neck, interrupted only by a long hair which he affected on one cheek and periodically fiddled with. Spenser saw him lead the others through the one-room terminal, which was more like a shed, and out to a Mercedes sports car, into which they squeezed. The remaining passengers walked the three hundred yards into town or paid to ride in the back of a pick-up truck. Spenser chose to pay.

Sitting now in the monastery, his gaze was held by the transparency of the old monk. No. He was translucent. It reminded him of the quartz buddha in his London apartment – particularly as the sun struck it from behind in the afternoon. He watched the old man, expecting him to come to life, and was drawn into the wait for death until he lost track of the time. The colour around him softened once the shade was thrown no longer by the trees, but by the lowness of the rays. It was his thirst which recalled him to conscious thought.

He got up to leave the temple grounds, intending to go back to his hotel, across the road from Santana's house. The gate leading out to the dirt track was blocked by a Land Rover. As he turned to squeeze around it, the side-door opened.

'Spenser!'

He looked back and recognized Matthew Blake, leaning across the seat.

64

'I have been waiting some time. Jump in.' His voice was friendly. He was wearing another Hawaiian shirt.

Spenser rested his hand on the door-frame before looking up with irritation, 'What do you mean, waiting? How did you know I was in town?'

A single guffaw indicated the impossibility of not knowing. 'Get in.' Blake's voice became momentarily thin. 'This is an awkward place to be seen talking.'

He only annoyed Spenser further. Awkward? For whom? Field had done well to warn him. But Blake continued to hold the door open and Spenser's main concern was his own thirst. 'I need a drink,' he said, to escape.

'Yes, yes. Get in.' Blake started the motor of the Land Rover, which began moving away before Spenser had finished climbing up.

They drove around the opposite shore of the lake – where a cow was tethered on the low ground – and up the hill on the far side, following lanes past jungle gardens and balconied wooden houses raised on stilts. Blake drove with great care. His eyes were constantly watching in all directions. After a minute's silence, he asked,

'What were you doing with Santana?'

'I was ... Why are you following me around?'

Blake ignored Spenser's anger. 'Just as well I found you before anyone else did. Someone must have seen us together in Bangkok the other day and now you turn up here. You have made it awkward. Open to misinterpretation.' Blake's process of reasoning presented itself in such a simple manner that complication seemed to be the greatest of sins. He fell back on his Sunday school voice to which was added fatherly disapproval. 'What are you doing here?'

'Misinterpreting what?'

'Don't be childish.'

Spenser thought about the man lying dead at the noodle stall. 'I'm in the antique business.'

'That's an obvious answer.' Blake meant it was a lie. 'You

didn't come from London to see a man like Santana.' He glanced around at Spenser. His eyes were earnest and large. 'All I want to do is make sure neither of us gets the other into trouble.'

'I've done nothing. You're the one causing trouble.' Spenser could still feel the earnest enquiry beside him. 'I want to bring some buddhas out of Burma.'

'Buddhas?' Blake showed relief. 'That would be fine. Santana is good at that. Where does he pick them up?'

'Pagan.'

He considered this new fact. 'Well, that's no good.'

'What do you mean?'

Blake ignored the question. 'What does Santana say?'

'I haven't asked yet,' Spenser admitted.

'When you do, let me know. He may try to lead you on. You said "bring out". You mean take?'

'Yes.'

Blake shook his head. Now that he had the answers to his questions, he lost interest in the subject and went on to another, without noticing Spenser's agitation. 'We are going to visit a lady who is very close to General Krit, who commands this area. If there is any confusion about the two of us in people's minds, he will straighten it out. All you have to do is smile.'

He went back to his driving. They had left the town by way of the road past the army base and climbed a dirt track along a ridge of small hills covered in brown scrub. The airstrip was down below them to the left. To the right, settled in a clearing between two hills, was a round mirrored building which resembled a revolving restaurant that had been carried off the top of its skyscraper by a freak cyclone and plonked on the ground in the middle of another world. Spenser was so surprised to see this that he put Blake's comments aside. He would soon find out for himself what Santana had to offer and was leery enough of Blake to avoid involving him in any

66

way. They turned towards the unrevolving restaurant.

'As you can see, the friendship of General Krit is worth something. The electricity lines, for example, come from the army camp where there is a generator.'

Above a red awning, which ran out onto the dirt parking lot, a sign flashed: 'HONEY'S'. Blake led the way through a first pair of glass doors and, a few yards later, a second pair. They were met by a blast of air-conditioning and of badly played disco music which filled the darkened circular room lined with mirrors. Three rings of empty booths capable of seating a good 200 ran around in decreasing circles to embrace the dance floor, where a single table was occupied by young men. Before them on a raised platform at the core of the sphere, an all-girl band played. Their music was amplified from a multitude of speakers. Along the wall opposite the door there was a glassed-in cage, built like a miniature Roman theatre. Its curved tiers were carpeted and on them sat a half a dozen girls in evening dresses. They wore numbered badges.

Blake chose a booth in the outer ring, just beyond the cage, where he sat with his back to the wall. Of the girls behind glass, one could have been a grandmother. Above her, another wore heavy glasses and was cross-eyed. Two at the back were knitting. Most of their faces were flat and their noses wide, which meant they were from tribes.

Spenser leaned across the table. 'Big time in the jungle?'

Blake shrugged. 'I am not an expert. A lot of money comes through town. With Krit around, some of it must stop here.' He called a waitress. The one recognizable word in their conversation was, 'Honey.' When the waitress had gone, Blake decided to add, 'She used to have a little dump. In those days her friend Krit was on his first tour here, as a colonel. Now he's back as the general and she's richer.'

'What does he do for her?'

'Krit? Oh, he's involved in most things.'

A woman wove her way towards them through the rings of booths at a trot, propelled by the sharp angle of her high heels. She wore an electric blue silk dress that stood out against the dark skin. Her beauty was only slightly marred by a glossy sheen that spoke more of cash than of allure. Her hair, which was perfectly black, was pulled up into a luxuriant halo.

'Blake! Blake!' She shouted when she was still five yards away. It was an imperious voice, filled with metallic warmth. 'You come to see me at last.' She melded down beside him. Her skin had the flush of someone who defined success as having the right to eat and drink for one's pleasure. 'First time you come my new place, eh. Not since you got that girl.' She was oblivious to how this embarrassed him and turned to call the waitress back. 'Bring beer. Who's this?' She raised her chin in the direction of Spenser.

Blake went into an explanation in Thai, from which only the names of Spenser and Krit stood out. She nodded her head from time to time in a mechanical way and made sounds of understanding or agreement. They broke off when the young man in the Lacoste T-shirt from the airport came in leading his four friends. All five looked around before placing themselves with care at a booth near the door.

'Who is that?' Spenser interrupted.

'A Haw,' Blake replied. 'A Chinese. He trades in jade.'

'What's special about that?'

'He fronts for his uncle, Khun Minh.' Spenser continued to look blank. 'Who has a private army on the border.'

'Your friend pretty ignorant,' Honey laughed and they went back to their conversation in Thai.

Spenser lost interest. He drank his beer and, when he saw that Blake hadn't touched the other, drank that as well. His eyes wandered back to the glass cage. He was interrupted by the firm grasp of Honey's fingers on his arm.

'Hey, Blake. Your friend bored. Go take a girl,' she

encouraged Spenser. 'No! No, go on. I make you a present. Only quick 'cause we fill up soon. Hey!' She waved to the waitress and pointed at the cage, shouting instructions. The girl shouted back and Honey translated for Spenser. 'Take number 42. She's good for English taste.'

'That's all right,' Spenser insisted. 'Later.'

She looked at him in a matter of fact way. 'Later cost money.'

'That's all right,' Spenser repeated.

She shrugged and went on talking with Blake. An hour later they left and Blake offered to drop Spenser at his hotel. The American seemed satisfied. His only conversation as they drove, apart from a jocular, 'That will fix them,' when they pulled away from Honey's, was to explain that General Krit had been too ambitious. He had been promoted from colonel – thus losing his profitable northern regimental command – to general and a job in Bangkok. Two years later he had been involved in the peripheries of an unsuccessful coup and had been sent back up to Mae Hong Son. It was a punishment, but one with comfort. This time he was commander of the entire area and could therefore get a percentage from the full panoply of illegal border trade; to say nothing of illegal immigration, protection, licences, promotions and so on.

'He's an old pro,' Blake said. 'Back in the sixties he even resold rifles that the US supplied to the Thai army to fight Communists.'

'To whom?'

'Oh, not to the Communists,' Blake reassured him. 'To the opium armies and the other smugglers.'

# 5

Spenser went to bed that night with photographs of the eighty statues from the Ananda Pagoda. He intended to choose the twenty most beautiful and memorize their features. Everything would happen quickly when they got to Pagan and, no doubt, in darkness, so it would be up to him to ensure they took only the best. He spread the photographs out around himself on the three single mattresses laid side by side over a large platform in the corner of his room. The sheets were stained. The room was a cement shell with a five-speed ceiling fan, a bare light bulb over the bed and a single window covered by a damaged screen which, like a lobster trap, let the mosquitoes in and didn't let them out. The room rate was five dollars a night.

The more he stared at the photos, the more frustrated he became. He could see that the statues were wonderful; but the flat, black and white images hid not only the details of physical beauty but all the living genius which would be self-evident were they standing before him. It was possible to eliminate five or six, but no more.

He was still shuffling from picture to picture at three a.m. when he heard a delicate knocking. There had been no sound of footsteps. He waited in silence. The knocking began again, louder, and was followed by a voice,

'Please, Mr Spenser, please, open door.'

'Who is it?'

'For Mr Blake. Open please.'

Spenser pulled on his trousers and called out, 'What do you want?'

'Urgent. You must come.'

Spenser unlatched the door. It was immediately shoved in

against him. A man of no more than five feet, with skin much darker than the Thais, stood in the middle of the room, looking around.

'You must come quickly.' He snatched Spenser's shirt off a nail and flung it at him, then found shoes and socks which he placed at Spenser's feet.

'Tell me what's going on or I won't come.'

The small man grabbed Spenser's nearest arm and forcibly began to help him with his shirt. 'No time now.'

There wasn't time to be furious or frightened. He was bundled down the stairs to the street and into a Land Rover, where Marea, Blake's friend, sat waiting. She was in a shirt and trousers, her hair tied up behind. Before she could do more than nod, the small man had climbed behind the wheel.

'OK, we go,' he said, and threw the machine into gear.

'What's going ...' Spenser began.

Marea cut him off, 'They came after Matthew had fallen asleep. It was a truck filled with men. Policemen I think.' She sat close to Spenser with her head turned so that she could speak straight into his ear. It was a curious sensation. In the darkness he could feel the breath rushing in sharply with the sound of her voice. 'The boys wanted to fight but we could never have got away. Not all of us. Matthew wouldn't let them fight.' She had one hand out to brace herself against the dashboard as they swerved around corners heading towards the military camp. 'They took him in the truck. I've been telephoning everyone we know for the last two hours. No one would come to the phone. Thirty minutes ago a servant called me from General Krit's house.'

'Is that who took him?'

'Of course not. He was brought to Krit's house afterwards. I don't know what they've done to him. Where did you go with Matthew this afternoon?'

'To see a friend of Krit's.'

'Honey? Matthew is a fool. He doesn't understand these

71

people. He only understands them in the hills.'

She watched in silence as the headlights followed the road. Spenser had been expecting an explanation which still had not materialized. He said irritably, 'If you had come to the door instead of this ...' He indicated the driver.

'Jalaw,' Marea provided.

'I would not have had to be wrestled down the stairs.'

She looked at him in surprise. 'I couldn't be seen going to your room.'

Her delicacy struck Spenser as odd. 'What am I doing here?'

Again she seemed surprised at the question. 'They asked for you.'

'I don't know what's going on.'

'It doesn't matter, Mr Spenser. Matthew must need an alibi. Just get him out of there.'

The Land Rover pulled up in front of a walled compound. A soldier came out and Marea spoke to him, giving what sounded like orders, to which he replied every few seconds with a bobbing of his head, 'Kap.' And then again, 'Kap.' Eventually he opened the gate. They drove up to a house built in a series of interlocking triangles. Krit had brought in an architect. He had also used army trucks to carry in the material and had lent the architect and the trucks to his friend, Honey. Marea put her hand on Spenser's thigh and tightened her fingers.

'You do know how to lie?'

He took the gesture to be inadvertent, but felt the blood abruptly surge within him. 'I'll see what they say.'

'Krit's a bastard. He doesn't care so long as he looks good when it's over.'

'Aren't you coming in?'

'I can't. I'll wait here.' She reached over him and opened the door.

A platoon of soldiers was standing around on the porch.

Spenser made his way through them, crossed the flagstones and climbed some marble steps. The door was opened before he reached it by a young police officer whose manner showed that he had been educated and trained in the United States. He checked that Spenser was indeed whom they were waiting for and led him up a spiral staircase towards the sound of a maudlin American love song. At the top of the steps was a large room shaped like two interlocking triangles. The modern architecture bore no relationship to the decoration within, which was a mixture of Thai and Chinese, at its most gilded and baroque.

In the near end of the room's first triangle, Blake was stretched out on a sofa. There was a cut on his lip and another beside his left eye. His face was swollen. He wore a ripped T-shirt stained with blood that in turn had stained the peach-coloured silk on which he lay. Both eyes were puffed up and closed. The young officer saluted a middle-aged Thai in silk pyjamas and a paisley silk dressing-gown who was walking across the room holding a glass, from which he drank before recrossing the room. His winter weight outfit would have been impossibly hot had not the air-conditioning maintained a glacial temperature. The first thing Spenser noticed was the remarkable length of General Krit's ear lobes. He assumed the man was General Krit. In the far triangle of the room a man and a woman were crouched on the floor fiddling with a record player from which Neil Diamond sang. The woman wore a St Laurent dressing-gown in bright pink silk, down the back of which her hair hung long and black. Her face was made-up like that of a starlet.

Without looking at her, Krit said, 'I told you to turn it off.' She turned it down and went on flipping through the records. The General shouted at the man lounging beside her. 'Pong Hsi Kun! Make her turn it off.'

Pong smiled, revealing just how much his decayed teeth jutted out. Apart from thick glasses, he wore only a sarong, wrapped around his pale and fleshy body. He had the consistency of someone who did neither physical work nor exercise. 'Do as your husband says, my dear. Turn it off.'

She lowered it a little further. Pong reached over, covering her hand, and made it complete the operation.

'You're no fun, Pong.'

He smiled at her. 'I came all the way from Bangkok to visit and after two days I'm your marriage counsellor.' He looked up at Krit. 'I'm supposed to be your financial adviser. Remember?'

Krit threw up his free arm. 'If you were such an adviser, backer, smart man, I wouldn't be stuck a thousand kilometres north of Bangkok.'

Pong shrugged good-naturedly. Only then did Krit notice Spenser standing at the door and wave at him to come in. He ordered the young officer to stay where he was in the entrance. 'Is this Spenser?'

Blake managed to open one eye and nodded with difficulty.

The General raised his glass as if to say – let's get on with it – then announced to Blake, 'You would be dead had I not come to the rescue.' The voice was suddenly edged with stage formalism. 'Even so, I found out just in time. When a policeman is killed, do you not think the police will react?'

Blake pushed himself on to his side and forced out slurred words. 'It has nothing to do with me.'

'We'll see!' the General shouted. 'We will see!' He had perfectly smooth skin over which wrinkles had recently shot. They could be dated to his exile from Bangkok and were cut like knife marks across the rest, which remained smooth and child-like. At the same time he had lost the calm for which he had always been known. In the company of Pong and his other Chinese backers in Bangkok he had taken up their habit of drinking brandy, which he did throughout the day with a touch of soda. His eyes were agitated and burning. His friends called this charisma; his enemies said it was frustrated ambition mixed with alcohol. He turned to Spenser.

'You, what were you doing there?'

'Where?' Spenser was bewildered.

'With Blake in Bangkok, what ...' he turned to the young officer for guidance.

'Eight days ago, Sir.'

Krit turned back to Spenser. 'What were you doing there?'

'I saw Mr Blake once in Bangkok, at a rattan factory. I was on business.'

'Business? Business with Blake?'

'No. I met him by chance at the factory. My business was with a man called John Field.'

'Field!' Krit paused before turning to Blake. 'Was Field there?' When Blake nodded, Krit strode over to the young officer in the doorway to make his point. 'Not even an idiot like Blake would kill a man with a journalist as a witness.' The officer did not react, but Krit seemed much calmer. 'So Field was there. Always in an awkward place.' Suddenly he remembered Spenser. 'You still haven't answered my question. What business?'

Blake found enough strength to break in, 'Tell him. He thinks you are involved in something much more complicated. Your buddhas will not bother the General.' When Spenser said nothing, Blake added, 'My friend collects statues. Burmese buddhas.' The slur had gone from his voice.

'Shut up!' Krit shouted. 'Let him explain.'

Spenser saw he was trapped. At least, as he hadn't yet broken a law, there was nothing they could punish him for. Besides which, in a bizarre way he was enjoying himself. He had at first been concerned for Blake, but now he wondered if the American's injuries weren't being exaggerated by ham acting, because apart from a few cuts and a bit of swelling, he seemed perfectly all right. His hair, for example, was combed up over the thinning top; a difficult feat for someone who could neither open his eyes nor lift his arms. Spenser sketched out what he had come to do, while Krit listened with scant interest.

Eventually the General cut him off, 'That's your business. If you want to go into Burma I can't advise you.'

Blake moved his hand to get their attention. 'Spenser will give you a memento when he comes out.'

'Oh, that isn't necessary.' Krit feigned surprise and gratitude. 'Although I do have a personal interest in historical pieces. I suppose Blake gave you some advice in Bangkok?'

The General's wife put the record back on quietly. Her husband showed no signs of having noticed.

'That's right,' Spenser said. 'I understand he knows the Shan hills quite well.'

'And did you see this man who was killed?'

'I'm afraid I don't know what you're talking about.'

'No. I don't suppose you do. So Blake has two witnesses. You and Field, who is an old friend of mine from the press.' He turned purposefully to the young officer. 'It would appear that your people have questioned Mr Blake, but do they have witnesses?'

'Only indications, Sir.'

'They appear to have been wrong.' The officer reacted with mimed acceptance, but Krit had another question for him. 'You did not explain how this narcotics agent came to be killed.'

'I do not know, Sir.'

'I mean, what were the circumstances of the death?'

'He was following Mr Blake, Sir.'

Krit waited for more. When nothing came, he asked, 'Why?'

'Information gathering, Sir.'

'Ah.' Krit nodded. 'He doesn't seem to have collected much.'

'That we cannot know, Sir, as he is dead.'

'Then we must release Mr Blake. Please inform your

76

people.' He dismissed the officer, who saluted. Behind his back, Krit gave a boyish laugh. 'So, I have done my Pontius Pilate number, Blake. What's more, you see, I am better than a Roman. I deliver up you gods only to your friends. Not to the crucifying mob. You see.' He glanced over his shoulder and was surprised to find the officer still waiting. 'Thank you, Major.'

'Border Police!' The words were called out in a lazy voice from the far end of the room. Spenser had forgotten about Pong Hsi Kun, lounging like a silent jellyfish on the floor. Everyone stared at him in surprise. 'I said Border Police. The murdered man was not from the narcotics division, as your officer has implied. He was from the Border Police. From Mae Hong Son as a matter of fact.'

Krit shouted at the major, 'Come here! Is this true?'

'I believe so, Sir.'

'From my command?'

'Yes, Sir.'

'What was he doing in Bangkok?'

'As I explained, Sir ...'

'Who gave him permission to leave the border area? Who? ... Who?'

'I don't know, Sir.'

'Do you remember that Bangkok is forbidden without my permission?'

'Yes, Sir.'

'Try remembering who gave this man his orders.'

'I'm sorry ...'

'Get out!' The officer was paralysed by this onslaught. 'Get out! And tell them to leave Blake alone.' Krit waited until he heard the door closing downstairs before walking across to join Pong. 'What are those corrupt pigs up to?'

Pong shrugged. 'General Chu's daughter is in town.'

'I know that. So what?'

'The word in Bangkok is that she's tired of the jade

business. She has been seeing all her father's associates. She has been talking to Shan insurgents. She is feeling out the ground, trying to see whose commitments are flexible. I believe she would like to get back into the family business. The Border Police have always been very helpful to her father, which is hardly surprising, given that, as you know, they could not live on their little salaries without General Chu's generous donations.'

Krit listened without drinking or making a sound. 'Why follow Blake?'

Pong shrugged. 'They might think he is acting for some of the Shans. Would it be the first time?'

This infuriated Krit. He pitched his empty glass across the room at Blake, who didn't move. It flew wide and broke against the wall. Krit's wife wandered into that half of the room to check the damage. Instead she saw Blake's blood on her sofa and screamed,

'He's ruined it. Look at that. Marea should never have gone to live with him.' Her voice changed to idle curiosity. 'Where is she? Didn't she bring this man?'

'She's waiting in her car,' Spenser said.

'Marea likes music. She should come in.'

'Shut up.' Krit had clearly had enough. He stared about in search of how to bring order and calm into his life. 'Get out of here, Blake. You know I'll expel you if your friends become involved. Or you.'

'In what, General?' Blake got painfully to his feet. 'I'm in the rattan business. With a reputable journalist.'

He was helped down the stairs by Spenser, who as he left the room heard Krit instructing Pong, 'Go to see the Chu girl. Find out what she's up to. For once things are running smoothly here. I don't want her raising the ante.'

When Spenser and Blake appeared outside, Marea made no sign of emotion and busied herself in the darkness directing how the injured man should be laid across the back seat of the Land Rover. Spenser asked only one question as they drove away,

'You're a friend of Mrs Krit?'

Marea answered, 'I used to see her. She's an idiot.'

The driver continued around the deserted town until he came to the river, which could be sensed rather than seen in the obscurity. They followed it for fifteen minutes, after which the road cut away from the river bank and they went on to a mud track that slid down to a compound on the water's edge. Two slight men appeared out of the darkness from within the garden, rifles in their hands. Beyond them was the outline of a sprawling one-storey house. They helped Blake inside and to a cushioned wicker sofa in a long room which looked out on to the grass and beyond that no doubt on to the river. There were screens on three sides of the room. Two ceiling fans turned. The floor was cool tiling and the fourth wall was littered with photographs.

Spenser took in little of this. Instead he asked to be taken back to his hotel.

'You will sleep here tonight,' Blake replied. 'It would not be safe there alone.'

Spenser began protesting, but Marea stopped him. 'In any case the boys are too tired to go out again.'

They led him to a bedroom which also looked towards the river. It was furnished only with a wicker-framed bed and a chest of drawers. Nothing else – except a coloured print of Jesus Christ on the wall and a single fan on the ceiling. He lay in bed unable to sleep, a mixture of dissatisfaction and annoyance still hanging over him from the experience he had just been through. The whine of mosquitoes came from the other side of his screen and beyond that sounds of life rose up from the river.

Then he heard Marea's voice in the next room. There had been no hint of footsteps passing in the corridor to warn him that she was near. Blake's voice answered her, which meant that even in his shaken state he moved silently. A light was switched on, throwing pale lines out into the garden, and in its wake came her laugh, a clear, childlike ringing that bore no resemblance to the woman he had seen. There was silence for a time, then he heard confused sounds of movement. At first it was only the creaking of a wooden bed, but gradually Blake's breathing grew until its pattern came through the wall. Above it rose a moaning which seemed scarcely human. He knew immediately that it was her. He could sense her moving and, as the moaning grew, he could feel her presence creeping through into his own room until she was there, present beside him, a tangible force attacking his feelings. The sound expanded into the chorus of the mosquitoes and on into the river noise so that they were all shouting at him and he lay frozen in his bed, unable to move. Then there was momentarily silence. Then the insects began again, without accompaniment.

Spenser was awakened by a voice declaiming in the garden,
   'And Ehud put forth his left hand and took the dagger from his right thigh, and thrust it into his belly.' This was followed by a second, quiet recitation from someone speaking another language. There was a pause and the louder voice dropped to a corrective level, 'No, no. Try this word.'
   Spenser saw that his clothes had been picked up from the floor, ironed and laid out on the chest. Only his shoes were missing, so in socks he followed the corridor to the large screened room. This time he noticed a number of orchid plants and a low coffee-table covered with pocket-books, through which he glanced. Most were old copies of classics. The photographs on the wall were in thin teak frames, each carved with a different decoration, but always invoking a cross, and then varnished dark brown. The images showed one of three men in a multitude of surroundings – usually at the centre of what Spenser took to be a Lahu congregation.

The oldest prints were of a patriarch in white, posed as if living up to his unexpected deification. Most of the others showed a more relaxed man – Blake's father – who had given up white and resembled a prosperous American dirt farmer. Finally there were two of Blake himself, carrying a rifle in the company of a small group of men. In all cases, the Blakes towered over their parishioners by two feet.

His shoes were sitting on the steps outside. Spenser opened the screen door upon a domestic scene – Marea, sitting at a table, repotting an orchid in the shade of a tree; the driver of the night before across from her, behind piles of paper. Blake stood leaning over him. In daylight the driver appeared to be constructed in miniature; perhaps because he was a collation of sinew and muscle which covered him in gradations rationally built one upon the other.

The only reminders of Blake's evening were two scabs on his face and a black eye. He saw Spenser and clapped his hands with pleasure, 'Ah, here you are. Sorry we didn't see you. Would you settle for rice soup?'

Marea looked up in a distracted way from her potting. Her hair was tied loosely on top of her head in a series of coils, so that for the first time he could see her face fully, if only in the shade. The eyes were as large as he had first thought, but perhaps that was only by contrast with the delicacy of the rest. At the back, a few hairs too short to be caught up in the coil lay black on the eggshell skin.

'I don't eat breakfast,' Spenser answered, and tacked on, 'thank you.'

Blake drew up a chair for him. 'Hope our talking did not wake you. We are translating the Bible into Lahu. No one has done it since my grandfather and he did it badly.'

Spenser didn't sit; instead he smiled politely, 'What I'd like is to go into town.'

From the expression on Blake's face, this might have been the most surprising of requests, but he appeared to pull

81

himself together and put himself on the road towards his guest's idea. 'Why, of course. I'll take you.'

'Now. If possible.'

'Yes, yes.' And as an afterthought he indicated the Lahu working on the Bible. 'Did you meet Jalaw?'

'Last night.'

Again Blake showed surprise. 'Ah, of course. Well, come on.'

As he turned to go, Marea looked up from her plant, 'Thank you, Mr Spenser.' The words were calm and motherly.

On the ground floor of the Mitr Niton Hotel across from Santana's house, a solid wall of floor-to-ceiling shutters had been folded back, revealing to the street four rows of wooden tables and chairs, which faded back into the shadows. Beneath each table was a tin spittoon painted with flowers. A single ceiling fan hung stationary in the centre of the room, waiting for a customer, and on the street the hotel owner had already set up his cage of noodles and was busy lighting a fire beneath the vat of water. Next door, the Thai Military Bank was not yet open. Across from it, the Jine Senn Jade House was shuttered behind its protective wall. Farmers and people from the hills passed on their way to the market.

Blake cut his engine outside Santana's shop. 'An unhappy man.' He indicated the house. 'Look at that basket of fruit hanging from the porch. That is for the spirits. How strong can his Buddhism be when his own example cannot influence his wife. He is not much of an example anyhow. I will be at your hotel in an hour to see how you made out with him.'

The missionary tone was something Spenser had heard enough of in the art world to be able to bear, but this assumed right of interference was too much. 'Listen. We've been spending a lot of time together by your choice or need. Fine.

I'm happy to have been your alibi. But I don't remember asking for your help.'

He said it so quietly that Blake didn't register the meaning at first. When he did, a look of wounded innocence came over him, which left Spenser feeling guilty at his rudeness. Blake raised his right hand, large, square and clean, to rest on the other's shoulder for a brief second, then drew back in shyness. 'But you need my help,' he said with simple assurance and added as an afterthought, 'unfortunately.'

The reply was so unexpected that Spenser could do little more than stare at him in silence, then open his door and climb down. Before walking away, he shot out at Blake, 'What did you mean by promising Krit a statue from me?'

'If you do not give it, he will take two ... or more.'

Spenser turned away. Five mules were tied up near the monkey cage beside Santana's house. Most traffickers unloaded their mules thirty miles outside town, where the track became a road, and brought their goods the rest of the way in pick-up trucks. But that meant bribing the army patrols who hung about on the outskirts of Mae Hong Son, so Santana's brother-in-law led his mules right into town on footpaths.

Spenser followed Lik, the Spaniard's son, who was carrying a large mule basket in through the front door. The room was littered with unwrapped blankets, baskets, statues of the Buddha, fragments of statues, lacquer boxes, carvings and leaves that had been used as extra padding. In the air was a smell of rice gruel, which no doubt had been for breakfast. A small man leaned glumly in the corner. He wore cheap city shoes, polyester trousers with a broken fly pinned together and a stained white T-shirt and he resembled Santana's wife, except that an aura of endemic dysentery clung to him; a drained look left over after the physical had encircled the spirit and destroyed it. Santana was bent down, picking his

83

way through the mess in disgust, his finger clutching from time to time by what seemed a fourth articulation, and raising an object briefly, only to say something to his brother-in-law in an insulting tone.

From this position he saw Spenser hovering at the doorway and went on searching through the packages without saying a word, except to shout for his wife, who came in and turned on the light and began spraying under the tables with her insecticide.

'Go on, spray,' he shouted at her. 'Your family brings the mosquitoes.' He straightened up and turned his back on the mess. 'You come here for nothing,' he said to Spenser. 'There is nothing here for you.' He repeated it in Hua, so that his wife might share her brother's failure.

'I don't care,' Spenser reassured him. 'I want to talk to you.'

Santana was always nervous in the mornings, probably more so this particular morning from fear of missing the monk's death. 'Talk?' he echoed in confusion. The word appeared to have no meaning for him. There was no talk in his life. Silence. Silence had significance. He leaned back to catch his breath against a cupboard filled with large betel boxes and waited.

'Is there somewhere we could sit?'

There was no reply, so Spenser came forward into the centre of the room and himself leaned awkwardly on a cabinet before explaining his proposition. When he had got far enough to make his meaning clear, Santana showed interest and interrupted him to translate the essentials for his brother-in-law. After that there were several interruptions for translations and a heated conversation between the Spaniard and the Hua, who was clearly on the defensive. This came to an end without any resolution, so Spenser asked, 'Doesn't interest you?'

'It is a good idea,' Santana replied. 'Who will finance the trip?' He hadn't spoken so much in a very long time.

'I'll arrange that.'

Santana translated and another heated conversation began. This time Santana's wife joined in shouting at her brother. Again it ended without apparent resolution.

'How would you pay me?'

'I could give you a lump sum, or you could get more by taking less in advance and a percentage of the sales over time.'

Santana nodded in long, slow nods as he listened, his lips pulled over his teeth. 'I can send these statues anywhere you like once they get to Mae Hong Son. That is a big risk for me, but I can do it.'

'What about the hard part?'

This started the family row again. As Spenser understood nothing, he began looking through the shipment scattered around the room. His eye was drawn to the shadow of what resembled a large standing buddha. He looked up and saw it was Blake hovering motionless in the doorway, as if he had always been there. The American raised his hands in prayer and bowed to Santana and his family, who fell silent. Without moving any farther, Blake said,

'The problem is that they cannot do what you want, Mr Spenser. Santana and his family are traders, not operators. They buy, transport and sell. They do not produce or take. Secondly, they are small operators. They don't deal in controversial material because they are unprotected travellers on disputed trails. Disputed by rival armed groups. Thirdly, they only go up the trail as far as Taunggyi. That gets you through the Shan jungle to the edge of the Burmese plain, but it doesn't get you across the plain to Pagan, where someone still has to take the statues.'

'And if I pay them to go that far?'

'That is what Santana had been telling his brother-in-law. But he will not go. It is not his kind of risk. He is a hill-man. He deals in the Shan jungle, not down among the Burmese. If he does what you want, he might incite a Burmese reprisal.

His friends would not forgive him for that. They would kill him. And his family lives within the Shan States in a village on the Mae Hong Son trail.'

Spenser felt a strong grasp on his arm and found that Santana had come silently forward. A smell of wax rose off him. He spoke carefully, moving his tongue with difficulty in the cavern of his mouth,

'You need an outsider to do this. Blake is the man. He can get the statues. He knows the private armies, so no one will touch him on the trail. And I take over when you reach Thailand.' This got no reply from Spenser, so he added, 'Blake hates the Burmese. He does not care. He has nothing to lose. We make good partners.'

Still Spenser was frozen in silence by the feeling that he was being trapped into what he didn't want to do.

'Let him think about it,' Blake said and evaporated from the room.

Spenser had no reason to stay, so he followed and found Blake staring up at the five monkeys, who had turned their backs in conscious disinterest. On his face was the wistful air of a preacher before his parishioners. He turned as he heard Spenser come forward.

'Why don't you want my help?'

Spenser felt a mixture of sympathy and irritation. It was so rare that someone spoke as Blake did, with clarity, asking the question directly, the way a child would. 'Field told me to keep away from you. He said I'd end up paying you to fight your own battles. From the little I've seen, his advice was correct. Your battles are too rich for me.'

An audible sigh of despair came out of Blake and he turned back to the monkeys. 'Don't you think Field has his own little games?' he asked over his shoulder. 'Not for money. Field doesn't care about that. He likes to interfere in other people's lives. His own is such a mess. As for my battles, they are over. Why do you think I went into the furniture business with him? To make a few bucks. I'm the only one who can take what you want ...'

'That part is easy,' Spenser interrupted. 'Pagan is abandoned. Ruins.'

'You said there was a museum.'

'Hardly. I believe it's more of a shack.'

Blake shrugged. 'That doesn't change your problem. And I have the most to gain by succeeding. The money, Spenser, is not just money to me. It's my freedom. The freedom to pack up and take Marea out of here before they throw me out. When they do, I won't get a penny for my house. That will be confiscated. There is not one thing I can earn a living at in this world, except exactly what you are after. I need your job and you need me.' He appealed with simple earnestness. 'I can get those statues for you.'

Spenser avoided his eyes and said, 'Perhaps.' All he wanted to do was end the conversation. 'I'll think about it.'

It was something Blake could grasp on to. 'Good,' he said. 'I will come to see you tomorrow.' He walked rapidly away towards the road and his Land Rover. As he climbed in, Spenser called out from behind,

'Listen.' He walked forward quickly to catch up. 'If I agree, what will you do?'

'No. Think about it. I will come to see you tomorrow morning,' Blake repeated. 'We can decide then.'

Spenser thought of going back into Santana's house. Instead he walked across the road to the hotel to collect the photographs of Pagan. His body was covered in sweat, so he went downstairs into the shadows of the noodle restaurant where there were a few other clients. Spenser's arrival tipped the balance for the owner. He switched on the lights and the ceiling fan and turned up his radio, sending forth a sound that had digested the worst of the electrical guitar and of middle America only to blend them with Thai folk music. From the owner's daughter, Spenser ordered noodles and a beer. The

87

bottle-top was flicked off to reveal a growth of rust which she cleaned away inside and out with a dirty finger. He spread the photos on the table to see whether daylight would give them any extra life, but his attention wandered with anxious frustration. Why was he sitting waiting for them?

He had come to this place wanting something badly and needing, even expecting to find people who could help him by providing services for a fee. Instead they had been lying in wait and leapt on him the moment he appeared. He could feel webs shooting out to entangle him. Already he wanted to cut himself free, the way he had in London, but for the moment he felt bound by his own ignorance. He had no choice but to play their games. He would have to control them by keeping on his own course. Whatever they did, he must keep that clear in his mind.

Half an hour later Santana went by in the direction of the monastery. Then, across the road, the gate of the Jine Senn Jade House swung open. Khun Minh's nephew drove out in a green T-shirt in his Mercedes sports car and turned towards the airport. Two men, wearing holsters, closed the gate behind him.

Spenser paid his bill and, hugging the little shade which remained along the edge of the road, went off in the direction of the monastery. Nothing had changed from the day before. This time he climbed on to the porch of the temple and sat on the floor under the protection of the wood awning. The old monk lay twenty yards away, Santana and the others seated around him. Spenser was immobilized by the heat, waiting for small gusts of air. After a time he heard a thin voice calling out in Victorian English. He looked up to see the old monk pointing in his direction.

'Who is there?' The voice was frail, but with a piercing quality. 'Who is there on the temple steps? Are you death come to take me? Come death, I am ready.'

The other monks waved the Englishman away, but he was

transfixed by the transparent finger and did not know in which direction to move through the aura of heat. Santana remained with his back turned.

'Death, do not fear. I shall embrace you.'

Eventually Spenser withdrew inside the temple, out of sight, and after a time the old man stopped calling. It was natural, Spenser thought, that he should have spoken in English. Death is a stranger and white men speak English.

# 6

Beneath his naked body Spenser's feet were balanced on the tiny foot rests sticking out at either side of the porcelain bowl, like defective wings twelve inches above the ground. The enclosed corner which served as his bathroom was also equipped with a bucket of water waiting to flush the bowl or shower the body. It was a balance he could keep while standing, but scarcely while crouched, the balls of his feet overflowing on both sides. This manoeuvre was interrupted by the sound of the room door opening – he thought he had locked it the night before – and a moment later by the appearance of Santana in the bathroom entrance.

Without any suggestion of having intruded, he carefully pronounced, 'Good morning. You have agreed with Blake?'

Spenser stayed where he was, letting his head fall back down to a natural position. 'Pretty well. How much do you want for sending the pieces abroad?'

The reply began with a sound of sucking, and when his mouth was clear of saliva, Santana said, 'The customs man must be paid $20 a kilo. That is calculated on the weight of the total package. This is very reasonable because there are no drugs. Maybe we can save a bit by rolling a large piece in a rug or packing it in a crate of fruit. But I get a discount for bulk. All that we work out after. For me you have to pay $10,000.'

Spenser didn't look up. His mind was only half on the conversation. 'I can't afford that. Not with Blake to pay as well. Take a percentage.'

Again there was a sound of sucking. 'What good is a percentage? I do not deal in that kind of money. Look at me.' He said it not as an entreaty, but as a statement of fact. Spenser twisted his head up and saw that nothing had changed. 'If I do this, it is for immediate profit.'

A sense of relief came over Spenser. 'I'll give you $5,000 to show faith before I go into Burma. I'll give you another five on the sale of the first piece. And another five on the second.'

'You shit well, Mr Spenser. My insides stopped working long ago.' His eyes searched the bathroom. A look of concern came over his face and he disappeared, only to reappear holding a copy of *The Bangkok Post* which Spenser had brought with him two days before. He ripped the front page into four equal parts.

'Thank you,' Spenser said and took them, almost losing his balance in the process.

'You need to store the statues until you want me to send them. I have a place.'

'Good,' Spenser replied. 'Do we have a deal?'

'A deal.' Santana smiled, but the effect was to reveal the black hollow of his mouth. He waited for the Englishman to nod in reply before leaving the room.

It was another half-hour before Spenser came downstairs to the restaurant. A girl slipped in from the street and pushed a piece of paper into his hand. She was gone before he registered her face. It was a message, written in a solid, clear style, instructing him to walk out of town on the main road in the direction of the border. 'Thank you, Matthew Blake,' was at the bottom. Spenser stuffed the paper into his pocket and set out past the bank, the jade house and the twenty or so wooden houses which separated him from the scrub-covered hills.

The road was empty, except for an occasional motor bike. Here and there a hut had been built of split bamboo with tin on the roof – a sign of urban opulence which ensured that their peasant owners would bake inside. Apart from a few banana trees, nothing had grown more than a foot high. There was little sound, except occasionally on his right that of the river flowing down to the town, and no smell, except that of the burning on the distant hills. Ahead there were steeper slopes covered by a tangle of jungle.

He put himself in the centre of the road and strode along, properly alone for the first time since leaving London. The morning sun burnt his confusion away. Blake was the man. Why resist merely because the events were not of his own making? Blake was precisely the man he had been seeking. Field had been wrong. Wrong out of jealousy or wrong because the north made little sense when you were sitting in Bangkok. Spenser could not sneak up one of these trails with a second-rate smuggler as his guide. He needed a man who could weigh the risks and who wanted to succeed. Blake was desperate for money. Well and good. There was no need for him to understand Spenser's drives so long as they were both after the same result; and yet, on reflection, their drives did not seem so terribly different. Both of them sought freedom to pursue what they loved. Spenser found an unexpected pleasure in the idea that his own passions were comparable to those of Blake; that Marea was in some way equal to the beauty of a statue at Pagan. Or of twenty statues. That in both cases the beauty lay in a reservoir of static energy.

It was a mile before he saw Blake's Land Rover pulled up beside the road. The door swung open and Jalaw leaned out from where he was dwarfed behind the wheel.

'Good morning, sir,' he called, then waited until Spenser had climbed in and they were driving down the road before asking, 'What is "dirt" in the human body?' He had a pert way of talking.

'I don't understand.'

'Me too.' Jalaw replied. 'It is Ehud who has thrust his dagger into the King.' He quoted from memory. '"And the half also went in after the blade, and the fat closed upon the blade, so that he could not draw the dagger out of his belly; and the dirt came out."'

'That dirt. What does Blake say?'

'He says God's word is literal.'

'In that case, it means the innards of an evil man. In your case flowers would come out.'

Jalaw gave a great laugh and said nothing more except, 'Must have been fat, eh?'

A mile before the house the growth began and with it the sounds. The compound had been cut from this tangle as if no other civilization existed in the world. The fence around it seemed to hold back everything, with barbed wire along the top to protect against the plant life, not people. Behind this defence, the house itself was encircled by five small buildings.

Blake waited at the gate, where he took Spenser's arm and led him to a one-room building. It was filled with boots, rifles and waterproof gear. Blake closed the door before drawing two chairs to the table in the centre of the room. He made certain that Spenser was seated, then said,

'We do not want people to focus on what you are doing with me. Interest means interference. That always costs money.'

Spenser shrugged, 'I enjoyed the walk.'

Blake stared at him without understanding. 'We have one clear month before the rain starts in July. Maybe six weeks. The trail is difficult in the mud. What do you want to transport?'

'Twenty stone statues. Two hundred pounds each. Three feet tall.'

'Ten mules. $500 each including the handlers. They feed themselves. O.K.?' He waited only for a sign of disagreement.

92

'Plus a horse for your pack and probably for you, with a handler. $900. That's a return trip price.'

'Do I need it?'

Blake pulled a pile of military maps on to the table and arranged them end to end. He placed a wide index finger near the bottom, where Mae Hong Son was marked. 'This paved road runs ten miles towards the border, then turns east and runs parallel to it. The twenty miles between the road and the border is a no man's land. Several tracks lead off the road to separate camps and from there they twist to join the main trail, one after the other. Each camp is controlled by a different private army, each of which claims to be a revolutionary movement against the Burmese and lives by taxing the smuggled goods they allow through. The big earner is drugs. The Karen are the farthest away, here. Then General Chu's Chinese, here.' His finger jumped a little nearer to Mae Hong Son. 'We take the closest' – the finger jumped – 'the Shan State Army. They're the main nationalist group and they control most of the trail.' He moved back again. 'This camp in the middle is our only problem. Khun Minh's outfit. The Shan People's Army. He runs ninety per cent of the opium out of Burma; that converts to sixty per cent of the world's heroin. He used to bring most of it down the old trails east of here. But now he wants to use this one, so he's fighting with my friends, the SSA, the Shan State Army.

'We drive five miles up this track, then walk fifteen miles to the border. There we pick up our SSA protection. Obstacle number one is on the far side of the first mountain range – here – where the track from Khun Minh's camp hits the main trail. Then we cross six more ranges to get to the Salween River. That's the next problem. Khun Minh controls the ferry crossing. After that it's easy. We climb up the north bank on to the Shan plateau and cross that to Taunggyi. 200 miles on foot. There we get a truck to carry us and a few SSA boys down into the Burmese plain, load the statues and whizz back. Maximum three weeks each way.'

'Where are the Burmese in all of this?'

Blake gathered up the maps. 'Forget them. They have garrisons in a few Shan towns, but they're afraid to come out.' He returned to important things. 'The truck at Taunggyi costs a few hundred. A thousand for miscellaneous bribes – on the border, in villages, for small ferries. I think $10,000 for the SSA. Oh, and General Krit's memento. One statue.' He stared over the maps with satisfaction.

Spenser followed the route again with his eyes. 'You say Khun Minh controls the Salween ferry. So how do we get across?'

Blake threw himself back in his chair with an open smile – the first hint that he might have any humour. 'You can't afford Khun Minh. But he might settle for a statue. What are they worth?'

'Theoretically about a million. As stolen goods, a few hundred thousand. It isn't just their value. I mean, they are the finest. The most beautiful.'

Blake nodded. 'He would like that. To have the best. Plus it gives him a chance to demonstrate his power on the trail. He likes to exercise his muscle. That's how he finds weaknesses in his enemies. Better your statues at risk than his opium. All you have to do is convince him.'

'I do?'

Blake thought this very funny. 'Oh yes. Jalaw and I are leaving now to set up the SSA. That will take four days. Remember the weedy guy who came into Honey's? I told you he was Khun Minh's nephew. His name is Charlie Tsoi. Ask for him at the jade house. He will take you up to Khun Minh's camp if you can make him want to. Only don't mention me. We had some trouble when I was working for the Americans. He was small-time drugs then.' Blake pushed his chair back with an air of 'meeting over'. He pointed at the boots along the wall. 'Find a pair that fits you. And some clothing.'

Spenser hadn't moved. 'What about General Chu? Why was he having you followed?'

'Chu? Forget him. In his time he sold more heroin than anyone else. That is finished. He is senile. His men are out of it.'

'What about his daughter then?'

'She's a child.'

It wasn't really an answer and Spenser cut in sharply, 'What about you, Blake? How much for you?'

'Me? $60,000. Half up front in case there is a disaster – for Marea.'

Spenser shook his head. '$10,000 up front.'

Blake's self-assurance disappeared without warning. 'Is that all?' as if money were unreal, even mythical. It was something other people had and appeared to spend easily.

This childlike reaction left Spenser unsure of what to say. He redid the figures in his head. He would have $5,000 over for emergencies and to last him until the first sale. 'I'll give you $30,000 from the first sale and 30,000 from the second.'

Blake nodded mutely, then stuck his hand across the table to take Spenser's. 'Agreed. Stay have lunch with Marea.' He jumped up, stopping at the door with a last thought. 'Tell her nothing about our conversation.'

Spenser tried on various bits of clothing and left a pile on the table. He went out to the front of the house. The air was not as oppressive there as in town, although between the shade of the trees the sun weighed heavily. A slight movement of air wafted from the river to give a hint of relief. A man, who resembled Jalaw, lay on the ground just inside the gate, with a shot-gun at his side. He wore shorts that hid a part of the blue dye covering his thighs down to his knees. Below that, various messages had also been tattooed.

She was seated where she had been the previous morning, this time reading, so Spenser called out from a distance to avoid surprising her. She put the book down on the table and

95

waved him over. He saw it was *The Realms of Gold*. The only other thing on the table was an orchid, whose mottled leaves were dwarfed by a single green stalk, arching up and out more than a foot and on the end of which a large flower sat, its peach-tinted open pod hanging out beneath the baroque crown of three long, flesh-like petals. It was placed before her, as in a Carpaccio painting, the single object in view should she chance to look up from her book.

'Smell it,' she insisted, seeing his eyes fixed.

The musk flowed into the air which, because of the flowers in her garden, already had a rich texture.

'I didn't know you were here,' she added. 'Matthew has gone off on a trip, but you must stay for a while. Your name is James, isn't it? What are you doing here?'

'I was asking your husband's advice before he left.'

'He's not my husband.' She laughed. 'I didn't mean here,' she pointed at his feet, 'I meant, what are you doing in Mae Hong Son?'

Spenser pulled a chair out from the table and put it on the grass not far from her. 'I collect sculpture.'

She wasn't very interested in that and began to ask him questions about London and what people did with their time. At one point she apologized, 'If it weren't for the magazines I get sooner or later, I'd be asking you what they wear and what they read.'

'You know more than me. I'd have guessed you were transplanted from Knightsbridge yesterday.'

'Except for the race.'

He shrugged. 'Knightsbridge plus.'

She laughed. 'Hardly.'

'You do all right.'

This meaningless comment interested her. 'I had planned to go. To London. To America. Everywhere. Before, you know. Then I couldn't.'

There was something in all her words, something in the way she threw them out quickly, then seemed to withdraw to take her distance from them. He couldn't identify what it was, except that it changed the sense of whatever she said without clarifying the meaning.

'Before?' Spenser echoed her, but she ignored the question.

That was in the middle of lunch, which was brought to them outside. The Thai idea of summer cooking involved quantities of small green peppers so hot that Spenser could hardly talk. It also killed the taste of the vegetables and the pork and the chicken. Between mopping the sweat from his face, he had been answering her questions, trying to hold her attention. He couldn't remember when he had last tried so hard to hold a woman's attention. It was a gratuitous effort because she was more than willing to give it, which only made him try harder.

'This is a rare place,' she added. 'Isolation which also offers the comforts of civilization. I mean civilization, not modern life.'

'What I don't understand is how you got here.'

'I found Matthew and that decided it.'

'No,' Spenser said. 'It must be more interesting than that.'

'You know, Matthew's notorious reputation has nothing to do with him having a wild character. He's a very ordinary man. Probably more ordinary than either of us. It's just that his normal rules of action are those of the jungle, so he's a bit out of place in the world we know. Either he acts like a wild man who has strayed by error into polite company or he appears quite disarmed. Childishly gentle. Like a YMCA director. Out of his depth.'

'I still don't understand.'

Abruptly she took on an air of dismissal, as surprising on her face as her openness had been seductive. 'A pleasant conversation doesn't necessarily bring on my life story.'

97

Because her beauty came from her flesh, not from a dominant bone structure, her whole character changed when she changed expression.

'Sun, heat,' he joked, in the way of an apology.

She smiled again, but the openness had gone from the conversation. After lunch he was driven into town in an old jeep by the man who had been lying on the grass. His place was taken by another who appeared from behind the house and began to fiddle with the shot-gun.

Spenser got out just before the first buildings of the main street and walked. He went to the jade house where he pulled a bell at the gate. A woman slid open a small peek hole and told him that Charlie Tsoi wasn't there. During this brief exchange, which passed for a conversation, Spenser saw through the opening that the Mercedes sports car was parked in the courtyard. He went back to his hotel and waited in the noodle restaurant in the heat for something to happen. When nothing did he went up to his room and turned the ceiling fan on to four so that the whole machine rattled and swung in its sockets as the blades whirled.

Shirley Chu stepped out of her father's house on the mountain crest at Mai Plan, her lime green skirt, bought in New York six months before, shining unwrinkled beneath the late afternoon sun. She avoided looking behind at the tiled roofs curving down and out of sight into the jungle. This was her father's town. They were her father's people.

She got into her BMW sedan before any of the officers could appear and drove quickly away past the other stone house on the crest, built for General Krit. It had been a minor offering from her father. One of many minor offerings of various kinds in various places to various people and it sat empty most of the year, symbolizing the gratitude of Chu's Chinese to a representative of Thai authority, General Krit.

The road twisted smooth and paved, first past the town

gardens and then down through the jungle past two separate barriers where soldiers saluted. It was her father they saw, not Shirley. Her plain, sensible face was already a reflection of his. This she knew, but would not admit. Her hair had been cut and set to sweep back. In New York this had given a hope of elegance to her square face. Here it only drew attention to her familiar features.

Somehow, everything was a trap. Her father's declared purpose had always been to give her stability and respectability; independence, in fact, from his own twisted career and the fate of his followers. Yet somehow it had all led full circle.

At the third barrier a young major stepped into the road ahead of his sergeant and saluted, forcing her to stop. She recognized him immediately. Douglas Sung. They had begun school at the same time sixteen years before and more or less grown up together until her disappearance to the States. She pushed the button opening her window – 'Hi, Douglas' – and waited patiently for the expected criticism. It came in mandarin.

'Forgive me, Khun Chu, you should not travel without protection. At least one man. Your father would never have risked this.' His voice had a physical edge when he addressed her, missing the distance of the others. And yet when they were children, he had always hesitated before using her first name. Now he avoided it completely.

She met his gaze in search of its meaning. 'I don't matter, Douglas, not like my dad.' Shirley was conscious enough of her own plainness to suspect any male interest. She looked for signs of ambition on his face. No. It was physical. He blushed under her attention. She remembered suddenly how at school Douglas Sung had always been on her side; an unquestioning supporter. She gave him a warm smile – which only made him blush more – and drove on.

Full circle. The idea stayed while she drove. Everyone at

Mai Plan addressed her in elegant mandarin as if she were a gold-plated child. They asked only that she accept the game rules and therefore lead them, neither of which she wanted to do. Even the elegance of their language annoyed her. It was still another sign of the isolated, artificial world they had created. Reality was New York, even Mae Hong Son, but not their little collection of dolls' houses in the jungle.

She jammed a cassette into place. The soft, reassuring sound of Barry Manilow billowed out around her, shooing away the uncertainty. Yet some remained. She shoved the air-conditioning lever up to maximum. It was stupid to go alone. That was what she kept thinking. Childish. What was there to gain by taking such a risk? She braked abruptly, came to a halt in the middle of the road and began reversing up the two hundred yards of curves to the last barrier. Douglas Sung had rushed out when she came swerving back into sight. Her fingers cut the cassette and the air-conditioning before lowering the window.

In mandarin, she said, 'You come with me, Douglas. And you do what I say.'

He went into his guard-post to radio for permission. Shirley could tell from his end of the conversation that his superiors were delighted. When he came out she stopped him,

'Get in the back, Douglas. In the back.' He climbed in meekly and she skidded away. 'I'm a great chauffeur, huh?' Douglas said nothing and so they drove in silence, except for the sound of his just audible breath. He was a perfect product of General Chu's artificial world.

Understanding and accepting her father's life had never been difficult, she reflected. What could he have done in 1949 other than retreat before the advance of Mao Tse-tung's communists? At least he had withdrawn his Second Army south into the Shan States of Burma – a far more courageous direction than that of the other Chinese armies who had leapt on to boats for Taiwan. Perched on the border of the northern Shan States, he had been well placed to counter-attack. In the meantime, he and his men had to survive. He had the largest armed force in the area, so he got American support in return for becoming their ally on the front line of the cold war; then he took over the opium business to pay for food and guns plus extras.

Gradually the Burmese forced him south, until his army and their wives and children were tucked into the jungle mountains of the Thai border; still on the front lines of the cold war; still living off the drug trade. And all this time, General Chu stuck by his men.

What they needed was stability, so he constructed a world of mirrors around them at Mai Plan, where a fortune was spent creating an air of normalcy. Even Shirley's name was the result of that. General Chu bought two hundred prints of old American movies in 1958. The soldiers built a cinema and ran the projector off their generator. The first film show was *Rebecca of Sunnybrook Farm*. Her mother, the daughter of a Shanghai businessman, had loved it – pastoral America; so unthreatening, so comfortable, so different from the jungle into which fate had thrust her. Shirley Temple became her idol. She was pregnant at the time.

'Hey, Doug Ah Fong,' she called over her shoulder. That was what they had called Douglas Fairbanks in Chinese. Douglas couldn't help laughing. 'Looks like you turned into a swashbuckling hero, just the way they hoped.' He didn't understand swashbuckling. 'A knight errant.' He didn't understand that either. 'Now we're going to play movies, Douglas.'

'Play movies?'

'You get down on the floor with your pistol out. Go on. Don't make a sound. Don't move.'

He slipped down obediently. Her father's world of mirrors was also political – to the north there were the Shan chiefs who became General Chu's front men in the collection of

101

opium; to the south there were Thai generals and politicians who left his army in peace and gave free passage to the heroin he produced from the opium. In return they expected nothing more than generous and varied offerings.

'Hey, Douglas, has Krit been up to stay in his house?'

'Not since last spring. He wanted extra money. We all had to play up to him.' There was disgust in his voice. It was an emotion the other officers would not dare to show. To admit disgust would be to admit that their position was unnatural; dependent on bribes and the goodwill of men like General Krit.

Shirley looked back at Douglas stretched out on the floor. There was self-loathing on his face. 'You can't do anything about that,' she said. 'That's part of our condition.'

Shirley Chu had been brought up to believe that the Shan chiefs were at best of average intelligence and, more often than not, stupid. How many had her father been through, all of them gradually becoming self-important and eventually a hindrance. That fortunes were at stake did nothing to make them wiser men. The Thais were much smarter – expert at manoeuvring, but more often than not just for a quick gain.

'You remember, Douglas, that Thai general my dad was working with who claimed a big reward for a heroin seizure, then turned around and resold the drugs? He ran off to Hong Kong with his stack of money, only he was so excited he had a heart attack on the plane and died.'

They both laughed. Had all the Thais proved so inconsequential, life would have been easy. But there were others. Steadier. Greedier.

Now her father was confined to the house he had built in Mae Hong Son, away from the border and close to the airport that led to the ouside world; senility left him at best capable of stumbling around like a child, and the 30,000 Chinese at Mai Plan, his people, looked to her. Douglas looked to her.

They didn't understand that she was free of them. Why else had General Chu bribed and wheedled until he got Thai citizenship? He and his daughter could not longer be expelled as refugees. Why had he sent her to school and college in the United States and pushed her to succeed at the Harvard Law School? Why had he used every Pentagon and State Department contact to get her a Green Card? – except that she might escape to the States and lead a normal life.

She had done as he intended: gone from Boston to New York the moment she graduated the year before; moved into the apartment he had bought a decade earlier on the East Side; entered the law firm he patronized. She had also delayed visiting her father in Mae Hong Son, though he was close to death.

Most of her college friends had preceded her or followed her to New York and there they went out together, gave parties, had a good time. None of them were Chinese – none, therefore, knew her background. In their company, Shirley quickly lost her virginal obsessions followed shortly by her virginity. She had even found a boyfriend; a bit pink and hairy for her tastes, but he was yet another wall built between her father's Second Army and her new normalcy.

She looked back at Douglas. Unless puritanism had waned at Mai Plan, he would still be pure as fresh-driven snow. Muscular snow, she reflected. Ardent snow. In a hot country.

'You got a girlfriend, Douglas?' She could sense him blushing.

'Why do you ask me that?'

'Forget it.'

Maybe he had a girl in Mae Hong Son or went to Honey's massage parlour. 'Have you been to Honey's, Douglas?'

There was no answer. No. Honey's wasn't his style. He revelled in his purity. He belonged in silent movies. He probably still had wet dreams and was ashamed in the morning.

Shirley's boyfriend had never been to Asia; had never heard of General Chu; knew only that her father was in the jade business and her mother dead. He was concerned about Shirley's future as a lawyer and his own and whether he gave her pleasure in bed, which wasn't the sort of thing you talked about in Mai Plan. No more than Mai Plan was a subject for New York.

She had arrived back in Mae Hong Son six months before with a round trip ticket valid for thirty days. None of her New York friends would understand what was keeping her. A few had written enquiring little notes. She hadn't answered. What was there to say?

'You remember, Douglas, the way they always told us at school how important Mai Plan was for the free world, fighting away on the frontiers of communism?'

'Yes.' He didn't sound as if he took that seriously.

'In New York they've never heard of the Second Army. None of my friends. And I know what they're thinking about me right now, if I even exist once I'm out of their sight – what's she doing over in that hole? That's what they would think. I mean, I've got the best education in the world. I live in New York – the best city. I've got full access to everything American. That means the best. I'm one of them now. That means I'm lucky. So what am I doing here when I could be a corporate lawyer and have brunch on Sunday?' Douglas didn't understand brunch. 'Like *dim sum*,' she added.

He shifted his back on the hump running down the centre of the car, before saying, 'Why go back to Disneyland when you come from the real world?'

She didn't answer. Pirated cassettes of the Disney show were very popular at Mai Plan. In Douglas's mind, America was Disneyland. Mai Plan was the real world. The disorder in her family's affairs had initially held her there. Her father's fortune would soon be Shirley's, so she was obliged to get it on to a sound footing. But General Chu's affairs were inextricably confused with those of Mai Plan – and both were in equal confusion. To make matters worse, no succession had been agreed among the officers of the Second Army, which meant their opium trade was slipping away in the absence of leadership. This, Shirley turned her back on, as she always had. Drugs may have been at the heart of her father's fortune and therefore of her own, but she pretended they did not exist. Instead she applied herself to the family jade commerce in Mae Hong Son and in six months outstripped Charlie Tsoi's efforts. She had always had a flair for the practical side – the jade itself – but now found she could play the margins and make good profits. These, of course, were nothing compared to the cash flow and margins of the opium business. In past years, twenty-five tons of refined heroin had been a small annual turnover. Sometimes, but not often, she thought of this at night, lying on her narrow mattress in her childhood bedroom.

At school in Boston she had been taught about morality and profits in that particularly ambiguous manner proper to the United States. What did any of it mean on the Thai-Burmese border, with endless bands of Shans fighting each other for the trade? Thirty thousand stateless Chinese looked to Shirley and if she were to keep her mind averted from their needs, which included control of the opium trade, she would have to go back to New York.

Instead, once a month, she drove up to Mai Plan on her own, without any protection, to inspect the school where she herself had learnt mandarin, or to donate new equipment to the hospital. Then she would visit wives to listen to their problems and inevitably she would finish the day around a table with the town elders. Some had been her father's junior officers. Others were second generation exiles with whom she had begun school. It was all slipping away, they would repeat; not just the opium and the money, but with these the ability to manipulate the Thais. Though Chu's own family now had

Thai passports, his people were still stateless and if they ceased to be useful in some way to the Thais, they would be driven out. Again, today, she had allowed herself to be dragged into their affairs and in truth, when she looked at them, she knew they were her family.

At the bottom of the long descent she turned right on to the main road in the direction of Mae Hong Son. Before the heat of the valley could seep through into the car, she pushed the air-conditioning lever back up to maximum. Perhaps it had always been a trap. Giving her an American background – what normalcy did that buy? Every drug official in the United States knew who she was. Every passport officer saw immediately into her secrets. Of the partners in her law practice, some had known from the beginning. Sooner or later they all would. What kind of career did that leave her? Did her father really expect her to go to an office every day to earn a respectable income when a fortune and 30,000 people waited on the Thai border?

It had all been a trap; the kind of clever, unspoken trap he had used all his life to control people. Well, she had only to turn her back and walk in the other direction.

She jammed the cassette again into place. The reassuring sound covered the silence between herself and Douglas and shooed away the dry jungle on either side so that she scarcely noticed the track cutting off to Khun Minh's camp. He was the man, her father's officers said, who was stealing most of the business for himself. He and her father had once been linked in a way so obscure that even she could not grasp the relationship; but now Minh had broken free and, more to the point, was developing his own links with the Thais.

It was Douglas who, despite being on the floor, realized where they were. He raised his voice over the music. 'Khun Minh got a caravan out last month. A small one. Twenty-four mules. All opium.'

'You didn't try to stop him?' Shirley asked.

'We could have. Easily. Someone would have had to give the order.'

'Did you discuss it?'

'Hardly,' Douglas grunted. 'If we discussed it, we would have to admit that no one would give the order.' It was a reproach aimed at Shirley.

'So he's doing well?'

'A real Doug Ah Fong. A star.'

Shirley didn't laugh at his joke. Like all the Shan chiefs, Khun Minh's flaw lay in his ego. Already he was too famous; too much the opium war-lord. Her father's success had turned on his discretion. Still, Minh was succeeding.

A few miles on she passed the cut-off to the Shan State Army Camp. They were more to her taste: old-fashioned nationalists. They could always be outmanoeuvred. Their nationalism had no chance in an area numbed by forty years of anarchy. Nobody could weld the Shans together while there was so much money to be made by keeping them apart – and there were more than enough rivals to ensure that happened. She had only to drive along this border road past camp after camp of insignificant private armies to be reminded of the myriad Shan rivalries that had made it so easy for her father to orchestrate his business.

She slowed the car to look for the opening. It would be a rough dirt track no different from a hundred others. A yellow rag lay on the pavement and she turned sharp left before it, braking until the car bumped forward at a crawl with branches scraping along the roof.

'Quiet now, Douglas. I'll call if I need you.'

Still the dust rose up obscuring her vision. Twenty yards in, a Land Rover sat among the trees. A man leaned against it, picking his teeth; a thin, dried figure in green fatigues who fitted the description she had been given of Lao Sa. Shirley stopped the car at a good distance and waited.

Her eyes strayed down to the dashboard and considered it.

She cut the motor but not the ignition, shut the air-conditioning, lowered the cassette and opened her window half-way. Douglas would be able to hear her, while the music would cover any small inadvertent sound he might make. She looked up at the man. He had not moved, but there was a wan smile on his face to indicate greeting. Behind the smile there was nothing. He wore a holster.

Lao Sa was Khun Minh's number two, though in his time he had also worked for the Burmese, attempted to set up his own army and been allied in various ways with General Chu. For the moment he was entirely loyal to Khun Minh. She looked carefully and was glad that she had not come in search of a trustworthy ally. She opened the car door and climbed out, walking slowly over the rough ground.

He put his gold toothpick away in a leather case and came forward, raising his hands in respect beneath his chin before bowing,

'Good day, Khun Chu. How is your father?'

Shirley bowed in return. 'He sends his greetings to you.' It wasn't true. Her father knew nothing of the meeting, nothing of anything, but Lao Sa brightened at the words, so she added, 'You two worked great together.'

Lao Sa nodded, 'Those were good days. We both made good money.'

There were no sounds on the track; no sounds of other soldiers; only Barry Manilow rising into the jungle trees. Shirley gained confidence. He had come alone. Perhaps it was to report her proposition back to Khun Minh, perhaps out of curiosity, but perhaps also because he was hungry. There was a dissatisfied air about him, as if he suffered from congenital hunger. She regretted now having brought Douglas. If he made a sound, everything would turn to violence within seconds. Well, she would go quickly.

'My dad is sorry you're not together anymore. I guess you're happy working where you are. But that doesn't mean we can't renew old ties.'

Lao Sa nodded in agreement. 'We should not forget our ties.' He was obviously asking himself what she wanted and was probably expecting an offer.

'We ought to think, Lao Sa, each of us on our side, and figure out if we can't help each other.'

He continued to nod slowly, examining her all the time. 'So the Second Army has a new Commander?' At least in that his curiosity was satisfied. 'You will take his place? General Chu is lucky to have a clever daughter.'

'What I want are friends, Lao Sa. My dad's friends and their guidance. I want you to think about that.'

He smiled, his eyes fixed on Shirley. She could read the meaning – there was contempt because she was a woman. Worse: a plain woman. The sort he would never sleep with. On the other hand she was smart. She would want men around her. She already had the Chinese, but there was room for a Shan. She would need that.

Shirley broke the revulsion she felt beneath this stare by reaching into the pocket of her skirt. She pulled out a small object. 'I've got an offering here for you from my dad.'

Lao Sa held the piece firmly while he examined the metal. It was an amulet of the Buddha stamped on to a block of gold weighing four ounces. 'You must thank the General. I am sorry I have nothing for him except my good wishes.'

Shirley dismissed his apology. 'We've got to think, both of us, about our friendship. Who knows?'

That was quite enough for the day. Shirley gave him a sign of parting and turned back towards the car. She could feel him waiting behind, but restrained herself from looking until she was seated with the air-conditioning flicked on, the cassette turned up and the car moving in reverse.

Lao Sa had not moved. He watched her go, his face showing as best it could that he was favourably intrigued. Shirley registered this and wondered what her boyfriend in

New York would have thought had he witnessed the scene. Their interpersonal relationship would no doubt have been altered.

When she was back on the main road, she said to Douglas, without turning her head, 'This is between us. You tell no one at Mai Plan. No one.'

'If you say so, Khun Chu. But do not trust this man.'

'Trust! You gone nuts, Douglas? I'll use him for our benefit. I trust Doug Ah Fong.' He was pleased by that. 'We'll have dinner at the house, Douglas. You can say hello to dad. He might remember you. There's lots of spare beds. You can go back up in the morning.'

# 7

Signs of life were slow to come from the jade house the following morning. Seated in the front row of the noodle restaurant, Spenser studied his map of the Pagan ruins and watched. Santana went by on his way to the monastery, paused for an awkward bow at the sound of Spenser's greeting, and moved on without a word. Just after nine-thirty the shutters began to open.

Spenser waited thirty minutes before crossing the road to ring the bell. When no one answered, he rang again, the air growing hot around him. The slot opened revealing the central third of a face – that of the man who had closed the gate the day before. His tongue was moving between his teeth in search of grains of rice.

'I want to see Charlie Tsoi,' Spenser said.

'Not here.' The man shook his head, scraping his skin against the metal edges of the opening.

'His uncle wants to see me. Tell him that.'

'Uncle?' the man repeated. The word was unknown. He closed the slot without waiting for an explanation.

Spenser put his hand on the bell and left it there until he heard the bolts of the gate slide back. The door opened enough for the man to come out. He was a wide rectangle, without a neck.

'You go away.' In order to say the words, the tongue stopped its search for rice. He moved forward.

Spenser stepped back. 'Tell Charlie Tsoi I want to see Khun Minh.'

The man kept coming forward, forcing Spenser into the middle of the street. 'Go away.' He put a hand out on to the Englishman's plexus and pushed. This motion appeared to be nothing, but Spenser found himself winded and on the other side of the street. By the time he had his breath back, the gate was closed.

He retreated to the noodle shop where he scribbled a note. Santana's boy Lik rode by on a small motor bike and waved as he passed. Spenser suggested in the note that Khun Minh would miss something if he didn't agree to a meeting. This paper he pushed through the mail slot of the gate, then went back to his table, where he switched from smoked green tea to beer and studied his Pagan map. At eleven, Marea was driven up in a jeep.

'A bit early for beer,' she called out from her window.

'Drowning my sorrows.'

'Come and drown them at the house.'

This wasn't doing much for the discretion Blake had insisted on; that at least was the reason Spenser gave himself for moving quickly to drop money on the table and climb in behind her. When the jeep was headed out of town, she asked, 'Have you anything to do today?'

'Not until later.'

'Good!' She turned around and put her hand on top of his. 'You can spend it with me, if that doesn't bore you.'

'How could it bore me? Is curbing my tongue part of the invitation?'

111

That made her laugh. 'You found me difficult did you? I thought conversations were supposed to be smooth and uncompelling. You're not meant to penetrate the soul of everyone you meet. You must learn to sail on smooth water if you spend time with me.' When he made no comment, she added, 'Ten years in an English Catholic school in Hong Kong does nothing to increase a taste for soul-swapping stories. Besides, I'm a little slow, living out here with Matthew.'

'Slow perhaps, certainly compelling.'

She took her hand away, but looked back at him with pleasure.

They spent much of the afternoon in the little greenhouse where she worked on her orchids. There were two rows of plants, most of which were waiting to bloom with the rainy season. At the far end was a section of new hybrids she had begun.

'It takes seven years to produce a flower, so I haven't been here long enough. I won't know what I've created until they bloom. Sometimes Matthew finds me unusual plants on his trips into the hills. Look at this.' It was a washed-out flower. There were pale brown spots on a mauve pod and two leaves, with a third leaf lightly striped green. 'This is my project for him. It's a Paphiopedilium Wardii. When Ward discovered it in 1922 these colours were dark and rich, but all the offshoots have degenerated into this, pale and weak. Now if Matthew could find me an original, I'd create a sensation in the orchid world. I could sell each offshoot for $500.' She wasn't satisfied with his appreciation of this fact, so she nudged him with her wrist. 'Then I could buy some new clothes.'

Spenser looked closely at the flower. 'They're unnerving.'

'Because they look like naked people. And because they suggest a difficult ego, which humans don't like in their animals and plants.'

'When you lived in Hong Kong, you probably felt the same way.'

'Ha!' she said with surprising force. 'I hated Hong Kong. Parties and gossip and more gossip. There's nothing to do except make money and spend it, and there's nothing to spend it on except clothes and food. They buy a lot of glitter and noise and call it fun. All my friends were in a constant state of depression, physical or mental. I prefer my orchids.'

'So you picked up and left.'

She looked at him quizzically. 'No. I came here after my husband died.' She watched Spenser's surprise with enjoyment. 'Too young to be a widow? Well he wasn't so young. I was eighteen and I can tell you my mother didn't give me much choice. After three years he died and I didn't do very well with what he left me. So I came to visit a friend in Chiang Mai. That was ten years ago. I found I liked being in a real place instead of cooped up on the floating casino. Then I met Matthew.'

'How long ago?'

'Five years. Happy years, I believe is the phrase, in this case accurate.'

Spenser calculated. 'Which makes you thirty-five. We're the same age.'

'I don't think so. The years aren't of much importance.'

'I see. You weigh the years by how difficult they are. I don't agree. Doing what you want is what counts. Or trying to. That might make me the older.'

Spenser had lost all desire to chase after Charlie Tsoi. It was late afternoon before he forced himself to go back to town and to the front row of the noodle shop, where he waited to be summoned across the road. At least this left him free to think about his day with Marea. He was also in the shade and probably the coolest place in Mae Hong Son, apart from the temple; but he didn't feel like being mistaken a second time for death.

The light fell early and with the sunset the gate of the jade house opened. Spenser jumped to his feet and ran the few yards to block the Mercedes as it pulled out. From behind the wheel, Tsoi stared impassively. Spenser moved around to the driver's window, but as he did the engine roared and the car disappeared behind him. The rectangle-shaped man closed the gate as if nothing had happened.

'Fucking bastard,' Spenser mumbled, then abruptly strode the few yards to Santana's house.

The door was open, although the lights in the shop were off. He went through, calling, until he heard a faint reply from above and climbed the stairs. Santana was stretched out on his bed, his shirt off, so that his rib cage stuck out and his trousers could be seen to swim around the absence of flesh. He lay weighed down by indolence. On a low table beside him was his smoking equipment.

Spenser didn't stop to register any of this. 'I'm taking your motor bike.'

There was a slight movement of a hand which probably indicated indifference, so Spenser went back downstairs and set about trying to make the bike work. As he had never ridden one, it was thirty minutes before he set out past the monastery and around the pond.

By the time he got to Honey's bar, her name was flashing in the dark. A small crowd of cars were gathered in worship; most of them Land Rovers or heavy traction pick-up trucks. The only real automobile was that of Tsoi and it was parked closest to the flashing shrine.

The room was full. Most of the men there had walked from town or from the army base; they were all young, with short hair and loose open shirts. The air reverberated with the smell of beer and of perfume and of sweet cologne. Across from the entrance, girls jostled for a seat near the front of the amphitheatre, where they could demonstrate their qualities. It was a much better selection than the afternoon shift. The band, however, had not changed and its disco music was amplified off-key at a level that drowned out the sound of voices. Spenser walked along the outer tier without any luck.

He moved down to the next circle. On the mirrored floor around the band, a few men danced with girls from the cage.

'*Farang!*' Spenser turned to find Honey bearing down. 'You want a girl?'

Spenser came as near as her arched posture would permit. 'Where's Charlie Tsoi?'

She pulled him closer and stretched her lips upward towards his left ear. Her breasts were encased by the heavy silk dress in such a way that they felt like artillery shells. He smelt lipstick among the other fragrances wafting off her decoration.

'What you want to see Charlie for?'

'He's avoiding me. I have a message for him from Blake.'

'Charlie a creep. He in room twelve.' She pointed to a narrow staircase beside the amphitheatre. 'Don't tell him I said.'

'How do I get in?'

She found that very funny. 'No locks here. Got to protect girls you know. I give you deal after.'

'After,' Spenser said and backed away.

The stairs twisted down to a low basement corridor, carpeted black on the floors, walls and ceiling and running in a circle, with doors off towards the centre. Number twelve was a third of the way around. He paused outside. Little sound came through, so he pushed open the door. The room was in the form of a wedge. To his left was a large sunken bathtub. Straight ahead the sharp end of the wedge was filled to the walls by a bed and Charlie Tsoi was on its pink sheets on his back, his pallid body laid out like a slice of cold lard. He was grasping at the breasts of a girl with a spread nose – between his fingers the nipples peeked as might two purple eyes – while a second girl sat astride his pelvis doing a credible imitation of a merry-go-round horse.

Only for a second did Spenser hesitate before walking up to stand over them. 'I want to talk to you.'

The horse slipped off her piston and slunk to the far end of the bed, where she was joined by the two purple eyes, and there was a pause while Tsoi's erection shrunk away with the sadness of an incompleted act. He dragged the sheet across to cover himself and sat up.

'Did you tell Khun Minh I want to see him?'

'No one told me.' Tsoi had an American accent which came out flat and nasal. 'Who cares?'

'Look, I have another way to get to your uncle and the first thing I'll do is tell him how co-operative you were; how concerned for his financial interests. Then you'll care.'

Tsoi turned his back. 'I got to see him tomorrow anyway. Your name's Spenser, right. What's your problem?'

'I'll tell him.'

Tsoi thought about that. 'He's going to ask me. You can be sure.'

'He'll find out when I see him.'

'If. If. I'll give the message.' To indicate the conversation was over, Tsoi reached out for a breast of the nearest girl, closed his hand around it and drew her forward, as if turning a handle.

'Enjoy yourself.' Spenser left them.

He was stopped upstairs by Honey. 'Don't tell me,' she said. 'I find out from the girls. You come with me. Busy time, but Charlie Tsoi a creep, so on the house.'

She pushed Spenser over to the amphitheatre and made him choose number 42; the one specialized in English tastes. She was skilled enough, but little in their hour and a half together seemed particularly aimed at an English market, except that she knew a few words. One phrase in particular she repeated every few minutes – 'You feel nice, darling?' – and when it was over – 'You feel better now, darling?'

'Marginally,' was the reply he thought but did not give.

The following morning he didn't wait for Marea to appear.

She hadn't said she would come and he feared that meant she would not. Instead he rode out to Blake's house on the motor bike. He reasoned that it prevented him being seen with her by everyone on the main street of Mae Hong Son. She appeared delighted he had come. In fact, she seemed to have been expecting him.

They spent the day together doing nothing in particular. He told her about his own life, even trying to explain his passion for genius and what it created. She wasn't in the least interested. Curiously enough, that didn't seem to matter. At least he was allowed to talk of beauty. He was certain she understood that he was talking of her.

She asked him about the rest of his life – and he described his affair with Anne. Marea made absolutely no comment and yet he volunteered that he would never marry her. Once made, he realized it was a declaration aimed at himself.

Marea retreated back into idle chat and dragged him off to help move some plants. In the curious, heavy atmosphere beneath the glass, with the orchid leaves hanging down from above them, he began to see her moving, not in a specific physical way, but somehow moving around him. It was an illusion, he knew, but so distracting that he could hardly concentrate while she told him what she had been reading and what she thought it meant. He forced himself to describe a part of London for her; Holland Park, which had been mentioned in *The Realms of Gold*. The only thing he retained from their conversation was a phrase of Darwin's on the sex life of orchids – 'Nature hates perpetual self-fertilization.' He also remembered that she talked of General Krit as the perfect Northern Commander: he was on everyone's side and got a percentage of everything. That kept a kind of liberal peace in the area by gathering all forms of corruption within his responsibilities.

Spenser was overwhelmed by a desire to touch her, just to touch her, as a beginning. Each time her hand brushed against him he wanted to hold it there. He didn't think of what she might be like naked or how he would try to make love to her. It was all an indistinct desire which would become clear if he could begin by touching her. But there was no time – he kept thinking – no time. Not that Blake came into his mind. Not at all. It was just that in this meaningless town, where he had come merely to pass through, time was non-existent for him. The buddhas alone were real, and they were elsewhere. Afterwards, when he came back from Pagan, perhaps then.

Besides he couldn't tell what she meant. She was two different people. At times she was simply friendly and beautiful. At others she seemed to be encouraging him, although even that was unclear because his vision was confused between the way she moved and the way he imagined that she moved. All of this in such a few hours; but they were not hours of time, only of waiting – something pure, isolated from the complications of the real world.

# 8

There was a message waiting for Spenser at the hotel. Charlie Tsoi had printed on the jade company's transparent paper that he would be leaving for Khun Minh's camp at nine the next morning, if Spenser wanted to come along. It was a child's hand. Across the road, the Jine Senn Jade House was in darkness, as was the rest of the street.

Spenser took a bottle of beer to his room, turned the ceiling fan up to four and switched off the light. Brightness tended to create excitement among the mosquitoes crowded at the screen. His mind switched back and forth between Marea and the temple at Pagan, turning both into questions and confusing the possible answers until knocking jarred him back to the world, where he heard Marea's voice. He wrapped the sheet around himself and opened the door.

She had dressed for her call. Or rather, groomed herself. There was something protectively sleeked-down about her appearance, the grey cotton dress playing more the role of defender than of demonstrator. As she said nothing, he stepped aside and looked around his own room,

'There isn't a chair. You're my first guest.'

Her smile indicated sympathy – an emotion out of place – as she sat at the end of the bed, from where she watched Spenser climb on the other end. The smile faded.

'You're going to see Khun Minh tomorrow,' she said resentfully. 'You didn't tell me.'

'I thought it was best done without advertising.'

'I suppose,' she admitted.

Abruptly, he asked, 'How do you know?' He meant 'why?' not 'how?'.

'Oh, there are lots of people to tell me. I came tonight because of what he might say about me.'

'Why would he say anything?'

'Because he'll know you've been with me. He has the house watched. You wanted to know why I came to live here. You insisted, so I gave some of the reasons. Now I have to tell you the rest or you will think I lied. It's always better to know nothing.'

Spenser wondered what he wanted from her. Isolated in this seedy bedroom, the contact was cut. She was scarcely recognizable. What did he know? Nothing?

'Well, I'll tell you.' She looked at him, then looked away. 'My father was a businessman involved with half the companies in Hong Kong. My mother was his second concubine, his last amusement. She had escaped from Shanghai with nothing and started out in Hong Kong as a sing-song girl in a big restaurant. My father found her there. I was her first and only child, his last. He had nine children. We were all recognized and treated wonderfully.' She caught his

119

eye for the first time. 'People forget now what a common situation that was. I would have been well looked after when he died, but my mother was obsessed by money – you can see why. She negotiated my marrige to my father's partner. They were old friends, the same age. He had never been married and I suppose he thought I might produce a child. Well I didn't.' She said it with satisfaction. 'Then he and my father died in the same month – the real marriage was between them. All my husband's money came to me. It was quite a bit and there I was, suddenly free and rich. So I had a good time. A Hong Kong kind of good time. The only thing my mother hadn't taught me was how to manage money.' With bitterness she added, 'They never teach you that.' She paused as before a hurdle.

'I didn't know what to do. I talked to people. One of my friends was a commodity dealer from Singapore. He had a big office, a Rolls Royce, a wonderful apartment. Lots of people used him. He was the kind of person you could talk to, so I put all my affairs into his hands. I suppose it was about six months later he just disappeared, with everything. Not just my money. It turned out he hadn't been registered. I didn't know he should have been. That left me with nothing. I didn't even own my apartment.' She laughed at herself. 'Stupid, don't you think?'

Spenser thought of how he had been cheated by the dealer in London. 'Not by my standards.'

She ignored this. 'I had met Khun Minh at parties. He used to come to Hong Kong to throw money around. People knew what he did, but they didn't care. A lot of them had started in the same business. Some were still in it. The point was I couldn't tell anyone – all my credit would have been cut off. What I needed was a husband, quickly, but first I needed enough money to bridge the gap, so I could at least choose someone bearable.

'Minh was in town and was playing up to me. One evening I

told him I had a cash-flow problem – by then I knew what that meant – and asked if he could lend me some money. He was leaving the next day for Chiang Mai, but invited me to come with him for a visit. He said he'd be able to work something out. I knew what all that meant. Now, I thought, I'll just have to play my way through.' She said the phrase stiffly.

'He put me up at his house in Chiang Mai and I held him off for two weeks. He was so kind, gentle really, that I stupidly told him the truth about my money – my lack of money. Eventually I said I'd have to go home. He gave in nicely and offered to give me $20,000 if I carried a package of jewels back to Hong Kong. A lot of people did that sort of thing to make easy money. I thought he was just being graceful about having to offer something. You see, if he didn't give me a present, other people would realize I hadn't gone to bed with him. If I took money, it would be his word against mine and people always believe a man.'

She slapped her knee with disgust. 'The plane connected through Bangkok where I was picked up for drug trafficking. I suppose I should have opened the parcel. Dealers usually get life. After two weeks in a terrible prison – a filthy place – Minh turned up. He said he could get me out – bribe the police – but the scandal sheets in Hong Kong had got hold of the story – even the part about my losing my money. I suppose he told them. I suppose it was set up from end to end. He offered to take me back up north, to live with him, obviously. What could I do?' She seemed still to be asking herself and Spenser imagined she had asked herself again and again. 'I couldn't return to Hong Kong. So I lived with him for five years and hated him. Not that he was unfair or even unkind. He was good to me. He's a very straightforward man. If anyone causes trouble, he kills them. To me he was more considerate than a loving husband. Most of the time I was up in his camp or here or occasionally in Chiang Mai. He keeps his wife in Bangkok. No other man would come near me because they were afraid of Minh. Then he was arrested by the Thais and sentenced to life. I'd already met Matthew ...'

'How could you meet him?'

She smiled at Spenser, as if he understood nothing. 'Through Krit. During the Vietnam war Krit worked with the Americans. He also protected Minh. They were a happy little trio. Anyway, I was free and Matthew took me in.' She stopped and corrected herself. 'I went to him and asked him to take me. He's an unusual man. You don't understand about that. I knew he would make me happy. Three years ago Minh bribed his way out of jail.' She looked questioningly at Spenser. 'Now he haunts us. I suppose he wants me back, but I won't go. This is the first time my life has meant anything. And Matthew is happy.'

Spenser wanted to reach out to her, still sitting stiffly at the end of the bed. Instead he mumbled, 'Thank you for telling me.'

Her expression changed from darkness to open pleasure and she got to her feet to come around the bed and put a hand against his cheek. 'What a nice thing to say.'

He took her hand and made her sit down beside him. 'What does your life mean?'

'What? Oh.' She laughed. 'Is that what I said? I don't know. For the first time I'm not sold or selling.'

'And Blake, what about him?'

'I don't think I could explain about Matthew. If you mean, is he just my strong arm? – No.'

Now that he had it, Spenser wouldn't let go of her hand. 'Whatever he is, why stay here? From what you say, your problems come from where you are. I suppose you can't go back to Hong Kong, but you can go anywhere else. You could come to England.'

'Is that an invitation?' She looked at him with curiosity. When he hesitated she began to giggle, slipping out of her defensive role into that of someone else. It was the same schizophrenia he had sensed earlier; as if she were an essence disguised behind a series of screens.

'I suppose it is.' He started to smile himself and let go of her hand.

'There's one good reason for me to stay here. Not too many suitable men come along with offers. And when they do, they're like you – not serious.'

Spenser fumbled for the right words. 'You mean you would go?' It wasn't what he'd meant to say. She was looking at him again with curiosity. 'Leave Blake?' He tacked on, 'Would you leave him?'

She got up and turned away. 'Of course not. Why else would I stay?'

He followed her and turned her around. Then took his hands off her. 'It doesn't matter what I mean. But if you wanted to leave, I could help.'

'You're probably talking about freedom and choice. The magazines and novels I read are full of that. You don't understand about me. I'm not interested in freedom and choice.'

Spenser couldn't tell if she were teasing him. 'Nor am I,' he said.

'No. You're interested in objects.'

'Not objects. Wonderful creations that capture not just beauty but ...'

'Beautiful objects,' she teased. 'I'm not one.'

'They're more than objects.'

'In any case, they're not human.'

Spenser couldn't understand why she was going on about this. 'In a way they are, because there is genius trapped inside them.'

'I don't want to capture or be captured.'

'Neither do I,' Spenser said. 'Neither do I. But I would like you.'

She stepped back as if surprised and tapped the fingers of one hand against the wall, once. It made a curious clicking sound. 'You would?'

'Yes, now.'

'And do you want me short-term or long-term?' She was teasing him again.

Why was she teasing him? He couldn't understand. He could scarcely see her. Only sense her dissolving around him. She was still a yard away. He put out his hand to touch her throat. It was firm and warm. He slid his palm against it gently, then around it, pushing her back up against the wall. He moved the hand over her flesh with his fingers spread, to hold her where she was, and slipped it down across the cotton dress between her breasts towards her chest where he could feel the heart. He could not understand why she was allowing him. He came forward and closed his arms around her. She weighed nothing. She was a ghost. His eyes blurred as he came close to her face, then he felt her lips seal his with softness and more warmth, a precursor of her body.

Behind his sun-glasses and the wheel of his car, Charlie Tsoi didn't talk; perhaps it was the early hour or weariness from the night before. Perhaps he didn't like the company. Certainly all the life blood he had available at that time of day was invested in driving his Mercedes as fast as it would go and as close to the edge on the corners as the laws of survival allow. There were few straight stretches, but when they came he lost interest and released his left hand from the wheel to pull at the solitary long hair on his lower cheek.

They passed Blake's house. Spenser saw the jeep sitting where Marea had no doubt left it upon returning the night before. It was out of sight before he could reconsider what had happened. A hundred yards beyond they swerved to climb up through a tortuous valley road clinging to the side of the river. There was still in the air a hint of coolness that was seeping away as the sun began to cut through the dry trees. After twenty minutes of climbing, Tsoi abruptly put his foot to the floor and the Mercedes exploded into half-controlled screeching. A khaki motorcycle pitched out after them from an invisible lane behind. The man on it must have been caught off guard because he wore only khaki boxer shorts.

When the motor cycle appeared in Tsoi's mirror, he whispered, 'Slow. Too slow,' and then, 'Aaah,' like a child on a roller-coaster while they skidded around a curve. The cycle reappeared twenty yards behind them. On the next curve he again let out a long, 'aaah,' then snorted when he saw the man was gaining. This went on for twenty-three corners, or more than a mile, by which time the cyclist was so close to their bumper that he put out his right hand and thumped the car's trunk.

It was like a hypnotist's signal of release – Tsoi lost interest. He reached into his pocket for a small pile of hundred-*baht* notes, which he held out of the window, the gold chain blowing and twisting around his wrist. His foot eased off the accelerator until the cyclist had drawn up beside, right hand out. He snatched at the bills, but Tsoi jerked his arm and let them go with a triumphant laugh. They scattered in the air over the road and the ditch. The cyclist screeched to a stop and turned back to gather them up.

Tsoi gave another laugh of contempt and for the first time looked across at Spenser. 'He was good this morning.'

'What was that all about?'

'That,' Tsoi jerked a thumb in the direction of the still floating notes, 'was the Border Patrol collecting a little cash to let us by.'

'This isn't the border.'

'So what? They don't like it up there. Oh no. No basic comforts. No roads for their cycles. No pretty girls. They like the big town. What difference does it make? There's only one road.'

'And what was the money for?'

'For letting stuff up the trail to the Burmese black market.'

'We're not carrying anything.'

Tsoi's tone changed to indignation. 'You think I'd let those pigs search me? You got to treat them like waiters – the pay's so bad they live off the tips.' He went back to concentrating on the road for a minute before speeding up, then tried to be friendly. 'Hey, you're English, eh. What school you go to?'

'What do you mean?'

'Khun Minh's got a kid at Eton. He says it's a good place. Where'd you go?'

'Not there.'

'Too bad. He'd have liked that. He likes good schools. His number one son's at Yale.' The places took on a curious resonance in his mouth – something exotic. 'Number two's in Japan. The girl's in Paris. Good education. Good contacts. He sent me,' Tsoi tapped his chest lightly with two fingers, 'to Pennsylvania. That's a good college.' Nothing more was said for a few curves. 'You know that Shirley Chu? That fat one?'

'I've heard about her,' Spenser said carefully, his attention suddenly revived.

'Never met her, huh? She doesn't go out much.' There was a dissatisfied edge to his voice.

'Then you don't know her yourself?' Spenser provoked him.

'I used to.' Tsoi regretted the words immediately. 'Plain Jane now, huh? Plain Jane.' He laughed at the phrase, but there was still a dissatisfied look on his face.

According to Blake's description, the road should have veered sharply twenty miles from the border and run along parallel to it. With the constant weaving it was impossible to know when it actually turned rather than merely twisted. Spenser watched on the left for the tracks going up to the first base camp. Nothing they passed appeared to lead anywhere. He was about to ask Tsoi when they swerved across the road into a dry mud clearing where a Land Rover was parked by a small bamboo lean-to. Tsoi screeched his car up beneath a tree and jumped out. The three men in the lean-to gave him a half-hearted greeting as he climbed into the Land Rover. Spenser followed. The men were sitting on a poncho spread out over the dried mud, with three rifles and a portable two-way radio beside them.

One of them got to his feet and climbed behind the wheel. They began grinding their way up a zigzag course on what gradually tilted into a sharp mountainside of pot-holes laced together by sharp rocks. Beneath the skidding of their wheels, the road surface rose fine and clay-like into the air, only to settle down upon them, the eye of their own dust storm. Spenser followed Tsoi in tying a handkerchief around his head to cover his nose and mouth, though the dust still managed to clog his pores making him suffer doubly from the heat.

He was drawn from this purgatory by a yank at his sleeve. Tsoi had inched down his own handkerchief and leaned up close. The dissatisfied look was still there. Seen from so close it was childlike.

'That Chu girl. You know. She went to Harvard. That's a good school too.' He seemed to be hoping for a denial.

'Sure.'

'I mean, you think it's better than Penn?'

'Penn?'

'Pennsylvania.'

'I wouldn't know.'

Tsoi seemed relieved that there could be any doubt, even based on ignorance. 'I hear things about her. You know. I hear.' This declaration gave him satisfaction and dispelled the doubt. He shouted into Spenser's ear, 'What'd she come back for? Huh! That was a dumb thing to do. General Chu's all over. He's history. It's too late for her now. She wasting her time.'

Spenser pushed him away to get relief from the shouting. 'I don't know what you're talking about. Do you understand?'

Tsoi didn't seem to care now that he had had his say. His eyes shifted around to indicate the dust which enveloped them. 'Once the rains start it's worse. You've got to ride up.' It was an hour before the Land Rover came over a sharp rise to a ridge occupied by a village. Behind it to the right and left the climb continued in the form of sugar-loaf humps, on one of which there was a temple. Ahead they could see range after range of hills obscured in a mixture of heat haze and smoke.

Machine gun posts dotted the crest of the ridge. The village itself was laid out geometrically with what looked like a crude swimming-pool in the centre. Nearby was a generator and an open square designed to double as a parade-ground or a basketball-court. Low plywood huts ran in rows off the square. They were painted white and were very neat; it was an attempt to recreate the look of a California retirement village for blue-collar workers, but the huts were like cheap false fronts of the real thing and were set on packed dirt. On a little rise off to the left was a larger house, surrounded by the only garden – a small one – and trees. Its size alone distinguished it from the others, and the fact that it had brown varnished shutters cut with a decorative edge. The Land Rover drove slowly across the village – where the dust did not rise because the ground had been dampened down – to the edge of the garden. Not far away there was a sound of children chanting in a school. The few people moving about outside were in green fatigues or were women coming from a laundry hut. The place smelt of what it was; an isolated military camp.

Tsoi led the way through a picket gate and up some stone steps to the porch of the house. The garden had been laid out in rows of Chinese pots holding flowering trees. The inside of the house shone from its white painted walls to its varnished wood floors, with the inevitable minimum of rattan furniture to cast shadows. The only signs of the modern world were air-conditioning units and, in one corner, a video machine; beside it, an open shelved cabinet was filled with cassettes.

An elderly woman padded through the room in bare feet to bring them glasses of water, then padded out again. Spenser chose one of a group of chairs that faced the windows over the village and there waited in the silence of the house. Beside the water on the table before him was a glass vase jammed with carnations whose scent crept up to fill the air. The room was remarkably similar to that in Blake's house – perhaps it was just a standard look – empty to dispel the impression of heat. It was even emptier than Blake's; as if no one lived there. He looked about, trying to imagine it as Marea's room, and stopped when he realized the same exercise in Blake's house would have been equally unsuccessful. She didn't mark her physical surroundings. Probably she didn't try. She passed through them, indifferent. In any case, he had no desire to imagine her there.

The door behind opened without his hearing and Khun Minh came through on the flat of his bare feet. He wore no jewellery, not even a watch; nothing except a white cotton shirt open at the neck and a grey cotton *longyi* wrapped around a stomach curved out in an opulence that did not suggest fat. His haunches, however, stretched against the cloth and caused him to walk with a feminine sway. This weight had appeared upon him recently, so that he carried it with some embarrassment, as if expecting it to melt away just as fast. He had come across the room and sat at an angle to Spenser before the guest could turn or rise. Minh's head was large and square; young for a man in his fifties, with only a slight red puffiness encircling his eyes to detract from what was a kind, fatherly expression. He slouched into the chair in a relaxed way that confirmed this impression.

'And what does my friend Blake want?' The voice was filled

with the assurance of a man in charge; the kind of commander who wants to know the details of each private's life.

Everything about the arrival had been surprising, so Spenser took the time to recover, looking gradually up at his questioner, who should have known nothing about Blake's involvement. The old woman came back into the room with a crude package of thin Burmese cheroots and an ashtray. Khun Minh lit one immediately in a smooth series of movements and grasped its very tip with his lips in something resembling a relaxed pucker. 'My opium.' He smiled and pushed thick hair back over his head.

'Blake doesn't want anything,' Spenser said politely. 'I do.'

'No matter.'

Silence followed. Spenser took it that he should state his case and did so clearly, even quickly, leaving out only the question of what Khun Minh would be paid. He had the impression that every word was listened to intently. Somewhere in the background Charlie Tsoi was standing; but his presence had evaporated now that the person, of whom he was a shadow, was in place. Spenser had hardly finished before Khun Minh broke in,

'So Blake has a new profession.'

'Blake has nothing to do with it. He's simply giving me some advice.'

'Oh, I doubt it. And really it doesn't matter one way or the other.' He didn't remove the cheroot while he talked. 'Poor sap. He's done so many things unsuccessfully. It will be amusing to do business with him again.'

Spenser was now careful to show a little surprise. 'You've already worked together?'

'But, of course. I'm surprised he didn't tell you. That one time he was actually successful. In the days when he was leading his hill-men against the communists, why do you think they were so loyal? Because he sold their opium for them. Flew it out on his army planes. And I bought it for a very high price because I supported the free world against the communists.' He apparently detected a hint of disbelief on Spenser's face, which even Spenser hadn't realized was there. 'Oh, I did business with a series of Americans. First there was an officer called Gerten. They got rid of him. Then Blake. He went the same road. Then … well they all did business with me. They had no choice if they wanted to fight the reds. It doesn't matter now.' He laughed in a self-deprecating way. 'Blake's a good man. Naïve. Not as Lahu-come-Shan as he would like. Nor as American. And now he has that woman on his hands.' He paused to inhale his cheroot. 'How is Marea?' He looked kindly at Spenser while he asked.

'I don't think I know her well enough to say.'

He smiled again. 'You surprise me. No doubt she's fine.' He called over his shoulder, 'Charlie. Find Lao Sa.' When Tsoi was gone from the room he asked, 'What do you propose offering to entice me into helping you?'

Spenser remembered Blake's phrase. 'I don't think I can afford you. But then I'm not asking much. Safe passage, that's all.'

'Our long friendship has not been long enough to justify free passage. That would be bad business. Besides I am not a very rich man. My 2,000 men are expensive to maintain. Their families live better than any other villagers in the Shan States. And there are all the putrid politicians and soldiers I must constantly make payments to. Burma begins at the bottom of the slope beyond this village. The privilege of being a Thai guest is costly – especially when there's a large reward for my capture. And then I have to sell my goods for so little. The Chiu Chau Chinese in Bangkok make the money; and your dealers in the States and Europe. All I can do is try to protect our peasants so that they continue to earn their pittance from the opium. In Chinese – because I am half-Chinese, only half-Shan – the characters for objective things

131

have greater weight than those for abstract ideas. So what is your objective offer?'

'One statue.'

'We may be talking among Christians, but I don't like stealing from temples.'

'You should think of Pagan as a museum.' Spenser's curiosity got the better of him. 'Do you mean you're a Baptist?'

'God no! Not one of Blake's fundamentalist songsters,' he shouted good-naturedly. 'I belong to the real church. St Peter's rock, my friend.'

The door was shoved open and a small boy ran in, then hesitated for a moment when he saw Spenser. Khun Minh's face lit up,

'Come here.' The boy ran over and threw himself against the man's side, where he was caught in an embrace. 'Speak of the saint. This is Peter. Mr Spenser.' The boy put his hands together under his chin and gave a quick bow. 'Peter, now you can ask how your mother is. Mr Spenser is one of her friends.'

Spenser was overcome with confusion. 'I'm afraid I don't ...'

'Marea,' Khun Minh cut in.

Peter shouted impatiently, 'When is she coming? When is she coming?'

'I ... I'm afraid I don't know.'

'Did she send a message for me?' he insisted.

Spenser stared and felt blood rushing to his face. The boy's fineness made him resemble Marea. He must have been eight or nine.

It was Khun Minh who answered. 'No, she didn't.' Then more to himself than to his son, 'Why would she?' He turned to Spenser. 'You see what a good-looking boy I have. Do you find Marea in him? ... No, you won't answer that, will you? I think not. I see myself. Eh, Peter?' He pulled the child closer.

132

'A strong, handsome boy.' Peter flexed his arms with a big smile. 'You see. And my soldiers are all the same. All healthy. Why then do the youth in your world destroy themselves with heroin? They die. But they choose to do so. Each one of them. And if there is a nuclear war, who will have chosen? No one. No one at all. And my soldiers do not destroy themselves with drugs, though the material is so easy to come by. So you see, I am only an instrument of choice for your degenerate society.' He gave the child a kiss. 'Now leave us to work.' Before the boy could ask anything else, he was gently pushed away. Khun Minh waited until the door was closed. 'You see what good English we teach up here. I have a very fine school.' The cheroot had gone out between his lips without his realizing. He crushed it down in sudden impatience and lit another. 'She didn't tell you?' It was obvious from Spenser's reactions that she hadn't, but that he had heard something. Khun Minh saw this and threw down his fresh cheroot. 'I can imagine what she did tell you. About her forced marriage to the old man? Was that the story? You should have seen how she made him suffer with her affairs. The humiliation was what killed him. And her widowhood?' He pushed the ashtray an inch to the right, then back to the left, then picked up the cheroots. 'Hong Kong talked about nothing else. She had a couple of queers who took turns taking her to parties so she'd be free to pick up whatever she wanted for the night. Then she lost her money to the last lover she could afford. And how I tricked her? Eh? She knew what was in the package. She said she couldn't stand being poor. She would have done anything to get back to the gay life in Hong Kong. Even then I had to save her. And the thanks I got was that she ran off the day after I was arrested. She's a disgusting woman. If you can help Blake make enough money to take her away, I'll feel the air clear around me.'

They looked up to see that Charlie Tsoi and Lao Sa, wearing green fatigues, were waiting across the room. In the midst of Khun Minh's excitement they had opened the door unnoticed.

'You wanted me?' Lao Sa asked.

'Don't interrupt!' Khun Minh turned away from the two men, now frozen in place, and attempted to calm himself. He focused on Spenser with a distant neutral stare. 'One statue? That's not quite enough. Tell me about Shirley Chu.'

Spenser sighed, 'I've never even seen her. There's nothing I can tell you.'

'Don't be silly, Mr Spenser. Perhaps your trip to collect statues is just a trip to collect statues. But what about this girl and Blake?'

'I wish I could help you. Really. I know of nothing.'

'Don't waste my time. You were with Blake in Bangkok when he killed that Border Patrol agent. Yes. Of course you were. And that agent, as I'm sure you know, was working for the Chus. So what's going on?'

'I don't know.' Spenser tried to think of something that would satisfy him. He went back over the conversation at General Krit's house, attempting to make sense of it. 'All I've heard is that she's bored with jade. That she'd like to get back into the family business.'

Minh's voice retreated into the distance. 'You heard that from whom?'

'A friend of General Krit ... I can't remember his name ... A man with buck teeth.'

'Pong. The night Blake was arrested.'

Spenser could only nod. The man seemed to know everything. 'That was all he said. And Blake has never mentioned her.'

'All right. Now listen. When you see the Chu girl ...'

Spenser interrupted, 'Why would I see her?'

'Be quiet.' Minh said it kindly. 'When you see the Chu girl, you tell her that if she so much as moves, moves you understand,' he raised his hand as if to squash a fly, 'splat!' He laughed good-naturedly. 'Is that graphic enough?' Minh waved the same hand over his shoulder without looking around. 'Come here, Sa.' He smiled as if to himself, 'Splat!... Here. Mr Spenser, this is my number two. Mr Spenser wants safe passage to Taunggyi and back. He has it.'

Lao Sa nodded, without expression. His dried features showed complete acquiescence. 'I'll send a messenger.'

Spenser tried to concentrate on what was happening, but his mind was still on the small child.

'Put in the message,' Khun Minh added, 'that he will come back with a load of goods. He is to leave one statue on the trail at the cut-off to this camp. One large statue. Have someone there to take delivery.' He rolled to his feet to lead Spenser out, his arm around the Englishman's shoulder. 'Leave a little something for my boys on the ferry at the Salween. Cash. They like that. They can dream about spending it one day.' His humour had come back by the time they got to the door. As Spenser bent over to put on his shoes, Khun Minh added, 'Tell Blake it's for old times' sake.' And when Spenser was half-way down the steps, 'Hey, my friend, don't forget.' Spenser looked back to see a large smile. 'Splat!'

They were in the Land Rover about to leave when Spenser was overcome with a feeling of revulsion at his own indolence before Minh's words.

'Wait a moment.'

He jumped out and ran back up the stairs, but Minh had disappeared. Spenser hesitated, his revulsion turning to fury, then abruptly sloughed off his shoes and went in. At first he saw no one; the room was perfectly still. Minh was standing with his back turned in the far corner before a large cupboard which he had opened. Spenser crossed without being noticed. Minh was lost in contemplation before a shelf covered by a piece of dark blue silk. In the middle sat a silver cross. Spenser thought it was a small private chapel until he noticed a framed photograph of Marea beside the cross. It was very much a society photograph, showing off a necklace of stones and hair in place. Propped up in the corner of the cupboard was a cheap automatic black umbrella and on the floor an expensive looking pair of hiking boots.

Spenser came to a halt scarcely a yard behind Minh, who turned slowly at the sound. The expression on his face was a confusion of self-pity and anger. The two men stared at each other for a moment, till Minh looked back over his own shoulder at the photograph and said sheepishly, 'Funny eh?' Then he laid the frame face down on the shelf and pulled himself together. 'You see those boots. I had them built by a Mayfair boot maker.'

'You've been to London?'

'He comes to Hong Kong once a year. My dentist too. I have terrible feet. He looked down at them, bare on the wood floor. The joints of the big toes were deformed outwards at the ball into nodules that resembled nascent toes facing each other. 'Bunions. My feet are half-numb most of the time. The man from Mayfair, he made me walk. A real saviour, eh?' He laughed.

'About your message for the Chu girl. I won't deliver that. It has nothing to do with me. If you want more statues or money, say so. But I'm not in the drug business. You've got lots of messenger boys, I'm sure. Tsoi, for one, is dying to look her up.'

'Sure,' Minh said. 'I'll tell Charlie.' He seemed to lose interest. 'You make sure I get the best statue.' He turned away to close the cupboard and walked out of the room.

Charlie Tsoi said nothing on the way down in the Land Rover through the last light of the day, but when they were in the Mercedes he burst out, unable to hold back his malevolence, 'How do you think the Thais caught him? You don't just arrest Khun Minh. You got to trap him. She was the one who set him up. You won't hear him say that. He can't bring himself. But we know. He came down to Chiang Mai for a meeting with some new dealers. They turned out to be journalists with cameras, and two creeps from the drug office – straight guys. With that kind of press he couldn't buy his way out. Even Krit had to go along with it – in fact, he took credit for the capture since there was some good publicity going around. She's not just disgusting. She's worse than a girl at Honey's. At least they tell you how much it's going to cost.'

Spenser made no comment, not even to himself; he couldn't so long as Tsoi was near, polluting his mind.

They were a good way down between the hills and swerving through the darkness before Tsoi opened his mouth again. 'You want to know something. I'll tell you. OK. Since she left him he hasn't touched a woman. He could have as many as he wanted. He doesn't want any. And you know, it's not because he can't forget her. It's because he feels stained; dirty, you know, after what she did. He can't look at a woman. She poisoned his feeling for them. I mean, he's a real saint now. A celibate. All his men know that. They admire him for it.'

Just before they passed Blake's house, Spenser said curtly, 'Let me out here.'

Tsoi pulled up a hundred yards before the compound, where the jungle still hung thick over the road. He emitted a restrained mocking sound as he waited for Spenser to climb down.


# 9


The guard let Spenser through the gate without any sign of surprise at the hour or at the direction from which he arrived. He cut across the grass towards the living-room, where her silhouette was distorted by the light cast through the screens. She was sitting alone, her eyes fixed on what she read. On the table before her was the orchid with the arching flower which

137

had been in the garden the previous day. He stared without knowing what he would say or why he had come.

'Is that you, James?' She looked up towards the door. 'Don't stand out there. Come in.' As he came through, she smiled. 'Even in the dark you don't look like a Lahu.'

He waited at the end of the room.

'Is something wrong? ... What did Minh say?'

'He introduced me to your son.' Without intending to, Spenser said it harshly.

She flushed – at first he thought it was embarrassment, but she spoke with anger. 'They told me Peter had been sent away to school. God!' She began tapping her nails on the book. 'His other children are sent off to every wonderful place on earth. He keeps mine as a hostage.'

'I would have thought he was too young to be sent off.'

She looked up, suddenly aware that Spenser was criticizing her. 'Do you think he should be brought up there? By that man?'

'I suppose you lost your say by leaving. How old was Peter then?'

Marea grabbed up the orchid plant in a wild gesture and threw it at him. The pot smashed just short of Spenser and the plant itself rolled forward to his feet. She looked at the mess and struggled to her feet. Her voice was bleached out, 'Is that what he told you?'

'And that you arranged his arrest.'

She was crimson now, but turned towards him coldly. 'Do you think I wanted his child? Do you think I had a choice? I brought Peter here with me. Did he tell you that? Did he tell you how he came here the night he bribed his way out of prison? He came looking for me. I was in town with Matthew. He and his men killed a guard and two women and he kept shouting my name while they searched the house. Sai was never interested in the child – he only wanted it as a trap to hold me. I see you are a righteous judge of others. – What

138

would you have counselled me then? "Too long a sacrifice can make a stone of the heart." Is that romantic enough? Too practical for your tastes? And I had nothing to do with his arrest. I wish I had. What could I plot, cooped up in that camp?' She paused as if to speak to herself before throwing out, 'Why should I care whether you believe me?'

'Why should you care?' Spenser repeated listlessly. 'Because I care.'

'You have no property rights.'

Spenser was astounded. 'That wasn't what I meant.'

'You meant something? What would you expect me to do?'

'Expect? It's not me for, Marea. You have a choice. You can refuse things. That old man you married. Minh. Blake.'

'You. Don't forget yourself ... Wonderful. What do you suppose men have bodies for? To use women. So I get used.'

'That's ridiculous.'

'As well. Wonderful. How do I refuse? What do I ... Who do I hide behind? All I have is my body and how it gets used. So ... sometimes I hate it. And sometimes the man has needs like mine. You'd call that love, wouldn't you? But don't tell me that because he creates a child I'm his prisoner. Oh no!' She shouted at him and then seemed to forget he was there. 'Not such a stupid trap. You want to lock me in place. To tie me up with your stupid sex. Oh no! None of you can come near me.' She was trembling.

Spenser had started towards her when he heard talking outside and turned to see the light of two cars coming through the gates.

A group of men had returned with Blake. They milled around in the shadows of the garden with rifles over their shoulders waiting for orders. He found Marea and Spenser standing at opposite ends of the room.

'You are here late,' was Blake's only comment. It was a friendly inquiry. He saw the orchid on the floor and moved immediately to gather it up.

139

Spenser bent to help him, 'I'm afraid I dropped it.'

'Only the flower is crushed,' Blake said. He propped the plant in a corner on the largest shard.

All this time Marea was trembling on the edge of tears. She half shouted, 'He's just come from Minh!'

'Has he?' Blake replied. He looked more carefully at them.

'One of the old women found out. I suppose you instructed Mr Spenser to tell me nothing.'

Blake ignored the comment and turned to Spenser,

'Was it successful?'

'Yes.'

He nodded slowly. 'In that case we will go tomorrow. Jalaw will drive you to town now. You collect your things and come back out with him for the night. Since everyone knows we are doing something, at least we can keep a touch of suspense about when we do it.'

'What are you doing?' Marea shouted at him. 'I have a right to know ...'

Blake folded her in his arms before leading her away towards their bedroom. Spenser was overcome by self-loathing as he watched this. He stood alone waiting for something to happen. Nothing would happen without his provocation. He knew that.

Jalaw drove him into town, where he packed up his belongings and counted out the $5,000 for Santana. All that time Spenser could see Marea flowing over with anger at the world. He banged at Santana' door without getting an answer and went back to the hotel to write a note which he sealed in an envelope holding the money. This he was about to push through the door of the house when he thought of the monastery. Jalaw waited while he walked down to the compound. There was a light on in one of the huts, with the monks inside seated around the old man, who even in this long departure had kept the proper position on his right side with his head propped up by his right hand. Outlined by the

140

light of the oil-lamp behind he appeared already dead, transparent like a rabbit stretched and dried. Spenser gestured to Santana from the doorway. He came outside.

'I'm leaving tonight.' He stuffed the envelope into the Spaniard's trouser pocket. 'Here is the money.'

Santana was lost in the effects of his smoking, from which he had been called to the monk's side. 'Tonight,' he said. 'I think tonight.'

When Shirley Chu heard a car approach the house, followed by the noise of someone being questioned, she stopped reading the *Asian Wall Street Journal*. It was late for a visit. She looked around at the heavy furniture and up at the gloomy heights of the ceiling and reflected upon the railway station atmosphere of the room. Her father had given into his worse desires for grandeur without comfort when he built this house in the hills on the edge of Mae Hong Son. Its five white cement pillars rising up three storeys along the blue façade were like drainpipes. Since return home she had noticed a nostalgia for the suburban cosiness of her American friends' houses materializing from somewhere within.

A middle-aged man was led through and allowed to kneel on the floor beside her chair. She had known him for a long time. He was a butcher. He supplied meat to Khun Minh's camp as well as to her father's house; more to the point, he had always been loyal to her father. It was a loyalty she had reactivated by asking him to organize her meeting with Lao Sa.

He had gone to Minh's camp again that afternoon and Lao Sa had given him an oral message which he had now come to deliver – a curious message that made no sense. Not a message really. Just information. Shirley listened without understanding. The Shan State Army was sending men up the trail to collect statues for an Englishman. They were asking for Khun Minh's safe passage. Why would they do either? It made no sense. And Blake? She knew all about Blake, which left her even more confused. Somehow the Englishman was the key. What interests could he represent that would draw these people together? Not statues of the Buddha. They might be using him? Or was Lao Sa using her? Perhaps he had told Khun Minh of their meeting. She questioned the man closely, but he repeated everything just as he had explained it the first time.

She gave him some money and went up to her father's room. He had developed a phobia about air-conditioning over the last few months. In his lucid moments he insisted that the cold air congealed his brain, and the evidence supported him. He had insisted on moving to a small, plain room where they installed screen windows and fans. The only furniture he allowed was a wicker table, a chair for visitors and his metal folding army field bed, on which he had slept during his last campaign against Mao Tse-tung and throughout the long retreat across Burma. The walls of the room were bare.

Shirley shooed the nurse away and took her place by the bed. He was asleep, with saliva running in a small trickle from one side of his mouth. She wiped it off.

For a month now she had been casting lines in every direction. Suddenly the fish were jumping. Earlier in the week Pong Hsi Kun, General Krit's Bangkok financial backer, had paid a visit. That was a good sign. Pong's friendly questions had in fact been statements of flexibility: if she were planning to get into her father's business, General Krit wanted no public upheavals. Whatever she could get hold of quietly she was welcome to, provided the General's kindness was recognized in a concrete way. There was no rush. They could negotiate a price later.

In the meantime, Pong had offered to organize an evening on her next visit to Bangkok. He said he knew lots of suitable young men. Shirley thanked him without mentioning that

142

she'd already met the suitable young men on her last few trips down to Bangkok. The advantages they offered were: indifference to her background, as theirs were much the same, and fortunes equal to or greater than her own. The disadvantages were harder to pin down. They were elegant boys – weightless seeds floating on the breeze of their family money. If it came down to Chinese men, she preferred Douglas Sung. At least the young major was resolutely physical. He had the earthy, solid weight that could hold her – in his arms yes, but also in a storm. He could protect her. She had the intelligence and drive; all she needed was a Lancelot. Even so, Douglas Sung's warm stare left her indifferent. She seemed to have lost her taste for Chinese men.

A week before, a letter had arrived from her boy-friend in New York. She knew at once it was from him by the plain white envelope. He was a straightforward man without soft edges even in the details. On the reverse he had printed 'A Robinson' in clear, neat letters. It was the first envelope in two months, but in it he offered to come to Mae Hong Son for his holiday. There was an enthusiastic, ingenious quality to his assertions of affection and of loneliness, even in the way he scrawled 'Andy' at the end. To himself, he was Andy – never Andrew. His worldly innocence somehow didn't match with his sexual assurance. No wonder the Tarzan myth had been so popular in the States. She wondered if she could get through a month without him finding out about her family and all that surrounded her. It might be worth a try.

What a pity she couldn't present it to him as a game. He, the budding corporate lawyer, would like that: gamesmanship at its most monopolyesque. The problem with the young men in Bangkok, apart from their boy scout view of women, was their unearned cynicism. The secret to her father's success had been his denial of cynicism. He had enjoyed manipulating the Shans and the Thais. It had all been a game.

What would he have done now? She wiped a line of dribble

away and he stirred, half opening his eyes.

'Watch for Chu-Tse,' he mumbled. 'Too fast for us.' He slipped back asleep. Her father's mind was entirely consumed by refighting the campaign against Mao.

Shirley knew already that the options had been reduced by time. She could not play, as he had, with four trails leading from the opium fields to Thailand. The three to the north were now partially in the hands of communist guerrillas. Rumour had it that they needed the opium income because the Chinese had cut off their subsidies ... True or not, that left only the trail leading to Mae Hong Son. The rivalries for its control appeared endless, but the only real player was Khun Minh; and she knew far more about him than he did about her. If only she could work out the meaning of these statues.


All of the lights were on when Spenser arrived back at Blake's house, though no one except the guard was in sight. The moment he came into the living-room he heard indistinct shouting from the other end of the corridor. He carried his bags along to his own room, where the sound came through the wall in a grinding noise. The words were garbled but their cadence was unpleasant – there were silences of a few minutes or even of a half an hour and then it would start up again. Eventually Spenser took a sheet out to the living-room, where he tried to sleep. He had no idea how much time had passed when Blake stumbled in and switched on the light. He had a half-empty bottle of Mekong in one hand and his face was grey.

He saw Spenser, but took the time to bring him into focus, then waved him away, 'Get out of here.' It was a slurred, unfriendly order. He waved again. 'Go away.'

Spenser went back to his room where he lay on the bed, incapable of a specific feeling or thought. The electricity running through the house consumed any individual emotion. From time to time he heard crying in the next room. He began to wonder how he had ever let his attention slip away from the essential – the statues at Pagan. When light began to appear outside he crept down the hall to find Blake unconscious on the sofa. Beside him on the floor was a neat pile of vomit and the empty bottle of Mekong. Spenser went back to his room where he stayed like a prisoner until after nine. By then Blake was gone and a basket of flowers sat on the table. There was no sign of life in the house.

An old woman in the cooking shed gave him rice gruel as if he were responsible for all the world's evil. He felt she was probably right and retreated to the garden to examine the Pagan photographs yet again, though without much success. He wanted to go in and force Blake to pull himself together, but knew it would be stupid to try. Once he heard Blake shouting at Marea in a tirade that ended with a bottle breaking.

This was followed by a quiet void until after midday when the sounds of an argument drifted over from the gate. Spenser got up warily and walked around the outside of the house to find one of the men Blake and Jalaw had brought back talking through the wire grille to a young Chinese woman dressed in tennis clothes. She could hardly have been twenty. A large BMW sat on the roadside behind her.

Spenser turned away to avoid becoming involved, but the girl had seen him and called out,

'Excuse me! Please, excuse me. Could you help?' She had an American accent of the eastern seaboard variety.

'I can try.' Spenser good-naturedly came up to the gate.

The girl calmed down and did her best to act older than her age. What made this endearing was her inability to hide a certain juvenile enthusiasm. She was what the English would call 'very American'.

'I came over to see Matthew Blake, only he' – she pointed at the guard – 'won't take a message in.'

'Was Blake expecting you?'

'No, not specifically. I mean I've been away for years, but I'm sure he'd like to see me.'

'He's sick. He's asleep.'

The girl seemed amazed by this, but she recovered. 'I know. I mean, is Marea here?' It was as if they had lunched together the day before in New York just off Madison. 'I feel kind of stupid talking to you through a fence. Who's in prison? Me or you?'

Spenser couldn't help laughing. Perhaps the girl was a friend who had come to give moral support. He made a sign for the guard to open the gate and sent him off to find Marea. The Lahu seemed to know who the girl was; still it appeared safest to take her to the living-room which was the farthest place from Blake's bedroom.

Her first words once through the gate were, 'You must be James Spenser.'

He betrayed surprise.

'This is such a small town. You're from London?' She sat on the sofa facing the Blake photographs. 'Quite a family.' She pointed at them in tribute. 'I hear you're in the antique business.'

'That's right.' Spenser stopped at that when he saw she expected more. 'What about you?'

'Oh,' she dismissed herself. 'I'm a lawyer. I'm home on holiday. My name's Shirley Chu. You wouldn't think there'd be any antiques left around here.'

'I'm not fussy.' It took Spenser a moment to place the name, then he wished he hadn't let her in.

His silence apparently didn't bother Shirley, who chatted on, and he found himself watching, mesmerized. So this was the girl they were all worried about. She was certainly plain. Plain Jane. Charlie Tsoi had been right. But more solid than fat. There was nothing remarkable about her, except her obsessive self-interest. Even in this idle chatter her focus was so all-consuming that no one else existed.

'I hear you're taking off for Burma with Matthew. I guess the pickings are better there.'

Suddenly Spenser realized she had come to interfere. He remembered Khun Minh's message – 'splat!' – and was tempted to deliver it. Instead he walked over to her. 'You know, I don't think Marea is going to come. She's been up all night.' He took her by the arm. 'I'll open the gate for you.'

Shirley showed genuine disappointment. 'Jesus. You don't think so? I really wanted Matthew's advice. I got this message. Well, more a threat I guess, from Khun Minh. I thought maybe Matthew ... well, could you tell him?'

'Of course.'

Shirley hadn't budged. He was about to make another attempt at moving her when Marea rushed into the room, hesitated a second on seeing the other two and ran across in wild strides. Her face was swollen from crying. She grabbed Shirley by the shirt and dragged her up while she screamed at Spenser,

'Why did you let her in? This isn't your house!' With her other hand she swung at Shirley, aiming for the face but it caught the back of the head. 'You're filthy people! Filthy!' She dragged the strangely submissive girl across the room.

'Hey, I'm sorry Marea. OK, I'm sorry.'

'Never come here! Do you hear me? Never!' She tried to strike out again, but this time Shirley defended herself. Although the heavier of the two, she was dwarfed by Marea's fury. 'Get out. Go on. Get out.'

She pushed the girl through the screen door into the garden where Shirley stood dazed for a moment, then started walking doggedly towards the fence. Marea waited blocking the door until she saw the gate close and the BMW drive away.

Tears were streaming down her face by the time she came back into the room. Spenser had only to look at her for a second to feel all his emotions slipping free and drowning the doubts he had felt about letting her divert his attention from the statues. He tried to take her in his arms but she brushed him away.

'No. Leave me alone. I made a mistake.'

He moved to block her way.

'No. Stay away. Please stay away.' With surprising force she pushed past him and disappeared down the corridor. He could hardly chase her in her own house. He could hardly shout down corridors what he felt.

He sat for a time in the living-room, where the old woman brought him supper just before the light fell. The food went untouched. It was an unfriendly room in which to be alone; the Blakes staring down with the full power of deities still held to be divine. Eventually he went to bed. There he could hear Blake's voice through the wall – the words were still unclear. They had the cadence of someone out of control.

Spenser half dozed without any consciousness of time in the atmosphere that billowed around him. He woke up in the night to hear Marea crying. It was a sustained, mournful sound, which was interrupted by Blake's voice. Then a door opened and she went past down the hallway. He lay still. There was a noiselessness that drowned out the river sounds. He listened for what seemed the passage of a full night without hearing Marea come back down the hall.

When he could stand it no longer he got up, put on his dressing-gown and went out. As he came closer to the living-room, he could hear her. She was attempting to catch her breath, without being able to do so. Each rasp broke off in a moan.

Through the darkness her body was only half visible, twisted up on the sofa across the room. He went over and sat down beside her without there being any sign that she had noticed.

'Marea, listen.'

'There's nothing here.' It came out of her in the unsettling rhythm of gasps. 'You don't understand … I'm nothing … I offer nothing … I am a very ordinary person … That's why I am so lucky that Matthew wants me.'

'Then why did we make love?'

'Because I'm a very ordinary person … I'm sorry.'

The sound of her gasping invaded him, breaking down the walls of his separate existence until the distance between them became unbearable and he reached out to lift her into his arms and hold her against him where he could soothe her and rock her. She was wrapped in a cotton dressing-gown through which he could feel the convulsions rise up as if to break her body. He held her tighter to squeeze them out, but the gasps went on, each one like a fit of suffocation, in the labour of which she sweated great waves of her own heat, soaking the cloth between them.

They stayed like that while he unconsciously began breathing with her and sweating and he could no longer bear even that separation. He reached up to pull her gown aside, at first slowly, without thinking, but then with growing urgency.

She put out a hand to stop him – he could no longer tell whether it was in protest or a caress. He heard her say, 'Don't.' The word meant nothing and was lost beneath her heaving sounds. In any case there was no power in her arm next to the strength with which he moved. He pulled his own covering back and felt the warm sweat of their bodies slip together as he pressed her body hard to his, her breasts melting against him. His hand searched frantically over her body and he heard her say again, 'No, no,' but he covered her mouth with his to drink her in. And when he penetrated her, her body cleaved to his, but he held himself still until he felt her juices coming and the walls moving about him and he knew that it was all right. She went on crying as he moved in her and now the gasps came with their movements and her moans were like the breaking of despair.

149

The rest he had no memory of, except that he held her in his arms long after it was over and they were still. Only when she pulled herself away did he realize that she was still crying. It was a sound which lingered after she had left the room, wrapping her gown about herself, so that he didn't know whether what he had done had been right. He lay as at the bottom of a pool of still, clear water; freedom motionless about him. A freedom he could keep if he sacrificed himself to her. As Blake did. Then he wondered about what had happened and was horrified. The night noise rose up from the river to engulf the silence around him and Spenser went back to his room, thinking he would be unable to sleep.

He was shaken hard into waking, how much later he couldn't say.

'Get up, you bastard.'

The ceiling light was on and he was being forcibly turned over. Outside it was still dark. John Field bent close to his face, the smell of accumulated sweat coming off him. 'Wake up. Come on.'

'What are you doing here?'

'What am I doing? I drove ten fucking hours over the hills from Chiang Mai in the hands of some pseudo go-cart champion just to get here. You come with me.' He dragged Spenser to his feet and out along the corridor. 'Now where do they keep the booze in this holy place?'

'He'll have drunk it all by now.'

Field stopped his search around the living-room to consider Spenser. 'Smart fucking guy. If you were so smart I wouldn't be here, eh. You took my advice. Right? I shouldn't have said a word.' He went back to searching until a litre of Mekong turned up in a cupboard, then sat in a chair and drank from the bottle.

Spenser complained, 'Everything was fine before he went on this bender.'

'Nothing was fine. Listen, you tell me one thing. What

happened to Marea? I'm used to his disasters, but the message she sent was pure panic.'

'You've seen her?'

'Sure. If that's what you call it. Blake's out cold on the floor in their room and she's asleep in the bed. Sure, I had a peek. She looks terrible.' Field was considering Spenser, noticing his unease. 'And you, tell me how you brought this about, eh. Samson of the jungle.'

Spenser listened with growing impatience. He hadn't left London to be lectured at by an alcoholic. 'I'm not accountable to you.'

Field thought about that while he took another drink. 'All right. Who are you accountable to?'

'I remember you telling me this was the home of anarchy.'

'Don't talk crap to me. You know the difference between situations and people. Listen, I could get you expelled from Thailand in two minutes flat. Nothing could be easier.'

Panic engulfed Spenser. 'I told you, everything was all right before he went on this bender. And I did take your advice. He forced himself on me. You know him. I'm sorry I gave in. Now I've got to make the best of it.'

'You don't get it, do you? You can't deal with Blake like a reasonable human being. Look at those pictures. He was brought up on all that fundamentalist stuff. Retribution. Black and white. Fire and brimstone. In Wisconsin that doesn't mean much. You leave your fridge on Sunday morning just long enough for a cathartic experience. By lunch-time your microwave tells you it was all just words. Blake didn't learn it that way. Up north with the Lahus life really is black and white. Not that extraordinary things are happening, but uncomplicated ethics work. Retribution works. Being a minor deity with people acting upon your actual words; that works. So the words aren't words. Life can actually be lived on the level of a parable.

'When Blake was thrown into the Vietnam business, he saw

it as just another parable – better even. It was the proving ground for his beliefs. All those boys who came from Wisconsin or wherever got caught up in a moral crisis by trying to weigh the obscure ethical values life in the States had given them. None of it made sense over here so they ended up betraying themselves or not doing their jobs. The other people who did Blake's job went completely nuts.

'But our friend didn't hesitate for one second. He waded right in with his childhood lessons and they all proved true. You could say he was still a child. So he made these things happen. These terrible things. He did some of them himself. He followed his own logic into the cataclysm – the burning bush is not consumed because it contains the holy ghost. So he put himself to the torch and he wasn't consumed. Still, the weight of what he did built up; the weight of being true to himself. But you know, he just refused to consider anything in the light of adult contradictions. And when it was over, he protected himself by remaining a child. He still is.

'Only he doesn't work quite right. He's a flawed child. Unlike a normal person he has no street sense. No links to the real world. He doesn't automatically know how to act. Oh, he tries. But the word is "act" and it's a bad performance.'

'Then what does Marea want with him?'

'Marea's got nothing to do with it.'

'That isn't what I mean.' Spenser grasped for another way to ask, 'One minute she ...'

Field cut him off. 'So she did her number on you. That's just an extrapolation of what she reads. That has nothing to do with life. Marea is a survivor. She and Blake are both actors. She's the serious one.' Field had lost his distance the moment he said her name. 'Blake is Marea's "good work". She's earning merit. Making up for her past life.' He seemed annoyed with himself for having said this. 'My private interpretation.'

'You're probably right about Blake. But listen. He doesn't have to "act" on my behalf in the real world. I'm paying him to take me through his private country. What could be better, for him and for me?'

Field paid no attention. His head slipped to one side and he fell into a stupor of exhaustion and drink.

A young boy, who had joined the monastery only a few weeks before, came to fetch Santana at three a.m. The Spaniard followed him down to the temple for the second night in a row. This time they knew he was going to die – he had come out of the hazy fits that had obscured his mind over the last few days, and begun reciting the Buddha's words with ethereal clarity. To all intents and purposes he was already dead. By the time Santana arrived, the old monk was naming the parts of his body in the way of a check-list, which once completed would free him from his physical cage. When it was finished, he lay silent for a time, willing his life to come to an end. Santana could feel the waves of that will filling the dark room, calling on the body to give its release. Then the light began fading from the monk's eyes and when it was gone and his lids had closed by his own will, his lips moved with a power no longer arising from the physical, 'All compound things must decay,' after which it was finished.

They sat staring at the body. Santana saw that two of the monks were weeping. He felt pity for them, no, contempt, lost in their own weakness when they should have been overcome with joy. He clambered to his feet in disgust with a force he had forgotten. The old man had proved by dying so well and with the ease of a perfectly elementary lesson that he, Santana, could do the same. But that was in a distant future. For the moment his life was a series of contradictions that seemed to block the way. There was no longer any need for guidance, only for strength; the strength to strip off the contradictions. Suddenly the idea of returning to his bed and waking up in Mae Hong Son, with his wife sleeping at his feet, was unbearable.

Santana went back to his house, where he searched

through cupboards for his army boots and pack. Into the latter he stuffed a few pieces of clothing, his pistol and his smoking equipment, along with a good piece of opium. His wife had awoken and watched all of this with misgiving, but without comment. He shouted at his son Lik to get ready immediately, as they were leaving to visit his family's village. Santana was a strange enough figure at any time, so no one asked why this had to be done at four a.m. Just before going, he gave the envelope holding $5,000 to his wife, with a brief squeeze of her hand in a sign of affection and instructions to look after it until he got back. He sat down on the porch of his house to pull on the jungle boots he had worn twenty years before and was surprised to find the feeling agreeable.

The two men rode out to Blake's house on the small motor bike; Santana balancing behind with exhilaration. When they arrived at the compound, he was relieved to discover from the man on the gate that there had been some delay, so he would not have to bounce on up the road to catch them. As the guard would not let them in, he and his son unrolled their blankets to lie on the ground before the gate.

In the morning Blake came out, pale but sober, and saw them. He had the gate opened and went to give Santana a shake,

'What are you doing here?'

To the Spaniard it was obvious. He sat up. 'I come with you and give help.'

'You will only slow us up,' Blake said as kindly as he could.

'We'll see.' He saw that Blake wasn't convinced. 'When I slow you up, you leave me behind.'

'This is hardly a trip for an old man.'

'I am not old yet. Why should I not come? I know the hills as well as you. At worst I could die.' He dismissed this as nothing by waving his arms from his position seated on the ground. 'You must accept the passage of time. In any case it will pass.'

# 10

Voices filtered across the garden through the screen doors and drove Spenser from his refuge of sleep. He went out into the early morning air to find the Lahus milling about the Land Rover without their rifles; Jalaw crouched above them, loading packs and gossiping. Unarmed they might have been mistaken for a Sunday school group about to leave on a picnic.

Blake appeared from behind the house carrying a hunting rifle and an army pack, both of which absorbed his attention until he had handed them over to be stacked. Only then did he notice Spenser.

'So you are awake.' It was a matter-of-fact observation. He went off in search of something else, but called over his shoulder, 'Your gear is loaded. If you want any personal stuff, get it now. You have fifteen minutes.' Blake paused to make his point clear. 'You need nothing. It will only weigh you down.'

The cloud has lifted, Spenser thought as he walked back to his room, the cloud has lifted. The words alone cleared his mind. Once they were on their way, Blake's weaknesses would be his strengths. Even Field had agreed with that. He threw two shirts and some socks on a towel. Into the socks he stuffed an envelope of dollars and another of Thai *baht* for minor expenses and bribes. His papers lay on the floor like a dead past. He shuffled through them, eliminating everything except a map of Pagan and the photographs of the Ananda Pagoda statues. The rest was irrelevant. He bundled up the towel.

All this time no sound had come from Marea's room. He went out to see if she were in the living-room, but found only

Field, slumped and snoring in the chair where he had collapsed the night before. He walked back down the corridor and stood for some time outside her door, then knocked. Nothing happened. He knocked again and tried the handle. It was locked. He called her name.

'Why don't you just go away.' Spenser turned to find Field leaning against the wall at the entrance to the living-room. His shirt was half unbuttoned and he took the time to stretch like a fallen and shop-worn angel before adding, 'You know, just take your circus and move on.'

Spenser looked back at the door and knocked again. In the silence that followed, an unexpected sense of relief came over him and stayed like an aura as he walked down the corridor past Field to join the others. Yes, he would take his circus, he thought, and he would get his statues. That was what he had come for. Nothing else. If he could keep his mind clear, nothing else was relevant.

Blake was in the Land Rover; his feet, encased in old running shoes without socks, were up on the dashboard. He pushed the door open, revealing the faces of Santana and his son in the back seat. The Spaniard smiled one of his black smiles, broken by the grey bars of his seven teeth, and inclined his head.

Blake volunteered, 'At least they know the jungle. Get in behind.'

Jalaw threw Spenser's bundle of clothing into the back before climbing up to the wheel. A second Lahu hopped up beside Blake.

'Now we go,' Jalaw announced and threw the Land Rover into gear.

Only when they were through the gate did Spenser realize the others weren't coming. 'What about our escort?'

Blake laughed. 'Not them. Their job is to protect the house.' He twisted about to find a perplexed look on Spenser's face. 'People know I'm away. I suppose Field will

156

hang around as moral support. He's always ready for another try.' Blake caught Spenser's reaction. 'Relax. I do not take risks like that. Field is not up to much with girls he doesn't pay.' He grabbed Spenser's knee and squeezed it. 'Relax. Now the fun begins. Hey, Santana, tell our friend to relax.'

Santana smiled obligingly with his head nodding in long strokes.

It came as a surprise to Spenser that he appeared unrelaxed. In fact he felt at ease for the first time since his arrival – now that he was on his way. He pulled a roll of hundred-*baht* notes from his pocket and counted off five. 'Give this to the Border Patrol.'

Blake hesitated, 'I can talk us by.'

'I'd rather pay,' Spenser cut in, 'and get on with it. We're already a day late.'

There was no sign that this registered. Blake took the money dutifully and held it with care between fingertips. Suddenly Spenser felt foolish. He leaned forward and put a hand on Blake's shoulder.

'Shirley Chu came to the house yesterday.'

'Did she?' He appeared intrigued.

'Marea threw her out.'

'Did she?' It was said with delight. 'What did she want?'

'She knew about the trip.'

Blake said nothing. He just nodded, waiting.

'She wanted your advice on Khun Minh. He threatened her. I forgot to tell you: when I saw Minh, he also gave me a message to deliver to her.'

'A message?'

'A threat. That if she so much as moved, he'd …'

'I am sure he would,' Blake cut in. 'So she wanted my advice on your message?'

'I didn't deliver it.'

'Good.' After a few minutes of silence he repeated, 'Good.' The Border Patrol motor-cyclist appeared ahead and Blake handed him the five hundred *bahts*.

An hour later they turned north on to the dust track Spenser had passed without seeing on his trip to Khun Minh's camp. It wasn't surprising. Branches on either side brushed in through the windows and a ridge of weeds stood a yard high down the middle. For twenty minutes they lurched through a cloud of dust. Then Jalaw dragged the Land Rover around a corner and the track abruptly ceased before a small village called Narplachat. The huts had bamboo frames filled in with a matting of woven leaves. The roofs were tin sheeting.

Blake leapt out. 'End of the road.'

He pulled his rifle and his pack from the Land Rover and started off up a dirt trail between the houses towards the far side of the village, where the path degenerated into a muddy stream. The second Lahu turned the Land Rover around and disappeared back towards Mae Hong Son. By then a few peasants had come out to watch them pick their way up the edge of the stream, Blake leading, with Spenser behind, then Santana and Lik, who carried one small pack for his father, and finally Jalaw, in shorts and running shoes. On either side rice paddies were terraced into the slight incline, with hills beyond rising to block the horizon.

A young man watched them disappear before he rolled a motor bike out through the bamboo stockade surrounding his house and drove down towards the main road, where he turned left in the direction of Khun Minh's camp. A Land Rover was waiting to carry him up the hill.

Blake followed the path back and forth across the stream, into stretches of eucalyptus and bamboo, then out again into rice paddies. After an hour Santana picked his way past Spenser. The Spaniard's dissected walk was very precise. Again and again during his life he had covered hundreds of miles in the worst conditions and his experience slipped into play automatically. He soon caught up to Blake, but walked one pace back and to the side, as if about to pass. Blake looked over his shoulder,

'In a hurry?'

Santana mumbled, 'I like a clear view when I walk.'

At midday they came into a dusty clearing empty except for a thatched hut. A young Thai in army issue underwear came running out with a machine gun in each hand. He saw they were white and shouted,

'Hey you! What you doing?'

Blake stopped to lean leisurely back on one leg. He called, 'Where is Captain Sai Harn?'

The man didn't understand and shouted back again, 'Hey you! What you doing?' Then fired a burst over their heads.

Spenser ducked to the ground only to discover no one else had moved. Already the sound seemed unreal, almost comic.

'Idiot,' Blake whispered more to himself than to the others and shouted back in Thai before turning to Spenser, 'Give me five hundred *baht*.' He walked forward, waving the bills in the air. The conversation that followed ended in back-slapping and the party moved on.

'What was that?' Spenser asked.

'More crummy Border Patrol.'

'That was the border?'

'Oh no!' Blake laughed. 'Not yet. The border is too dangerous for those idiots.'

They climbed sharply over a low rise into a second valley, where a row of huts stretched out for a good 200 yards on either side of the trail. In place of the tin roofs were swatches of large circular leaves dried to a dark brown. Behind the huts on the right were rice paddies, behind those on the left rose a hill covered in jungle. A viaduct of split bamboo poles came off the hill and ran above their heads down the central path, with smaller poles carrying water to each house. The grid was low and the three white men had to duck as they walked.

The entire population came out to watch the group file by. They were a heavy-set people with fair skin – both the men

159

and the women wearing loose trousers wrapped twice around their waist and tied. They discussed the peculiarities of the travellers the way two old women might comment in loud voices on an unusual breed of dog seen in the street, with Santana's son-gathering the most interest because he had the features of his mother's tribe, but was thin and almost as tall as his father.

Kharhan was a Shan village – refugees from the other side of the border had found there a no man's land into which neither the Burmese nor the Thai army ventured; with the added advantages of good rice paddies and a constant stream of smugglers going both ways.

Half-way through the village, Blake stopped outside the house of the local Chinese merchant, who bought all the Shan produce, the rice and the opium carried down from the hills. He then sold it to the bigger Chinese merchants who passed through with caravans. He also ran the local store and stable. His house was larger than the others, its walls of bamboo slats rather than woven leaves. Blake began an involved conversation with the owner after being invited to sit down outside to drink tea.

The five men crouched on the porch – two planks balanced on stumps a few inches off the ground – and stared back at the villagers who had gathered around them. Spenser was exhilarated by a freedom seeping again into his consciousness. Freedom from what? He had imagined it would be hidden inside his communion with beauty. That was what his statues promised, half-locked within their stone; not a key to their secret, but a way to break down the physical. An inversion of alchemy. And yet he had felt it with Marea. Dead weight being scraped away. Passages appearing in walls. An exhilaration. Then he noticed that his boots were soaked from crossing and recrossing the stream. In the heat the spongy feeling of his socks was a relief. It was curious. He concentrated on that soft coolness and realized it was the most important thing in his life at that moment.

He didn't have a physical imagination. His passion for genius throbbed only when he saw and held something beautiful. Until he had the statues of Pagan beneath his touch, he would have to drive himself on with only an abstract idea of what the emotion would be. Were Marea to appear among this crowd of Shans, in a second she would melt any promise of other emotions. But she was not there. And so she also became an abstract memory.

A small, tough-looking horse arrived, saddled with a heavy rope brace around its lower neck to support the weight of the load on steep slopes. Its handler wore sandals and a *longyi*, while his head was protected by a flat straw hat. He pulled the horse forward to be inspected, then stared curiously up at the white man from his one good eye. The other was laced over with a filmy growth. The man had a gentle, doe-like expression which suggested a simple mind, but might, in fairness, have reflected a man at peace with himself.

Blake gave the animal a quick examination. 'He looks fine. You do not want one any bigger – already a mule would have been steadier. Pay $300 now. Another 200 when we return it and its handler. Do you want to ride?'

'No. No.' Spenser said quickly. 'Can he see?'

Blake missed his meaning at first. 'Oh, the handler. They all have glaucoma here. The half-blind are more careful. We will tie your pack on, and maybe the ammunition.'

At the far end of the village a clearing of flat ground opened like a breath of calm air. It was fifty yards across and on the other side a wall of hills rose up with the suddenness of a cliff. Beyond, other hills loomed still higher. The wall before them was hidden behind a tangle of vine and bamboo and trees, all faded to a brownish-green by the dry season. From within that morass sounds as if from a power station radiated towards them – vibrations were mixed with disordered cracklings and bird cries which sounded unbird-like in the

161

midst of the writhing noise.

The moment they entered the jungle the village disappeared from view. The trail went straight up in the bed of the stream – a maze of roots enfolding the rocks on which they had to find their foothold while ducking beneath the brush that had collapsed above to form a tunnel. Little sunlight penetrated. No water flowed. Spenser began second in the file, but was soon last; with only the handler remaining behind in deference, and the horse, which picked its way over the easiest ground without hesitation.

One hundred yards up they were ejected on to an open ridge. There was a momentary clear view of the village lying like a haven of peace – the outer edge of the defined world; for those who came down the trail the other way, from the north, Kharhan would have been the first harbinger of civilization and, like most civilizations, it was fickle. The Shans had gone into their houses, having already lost interest. The parade was over.

Blake looked back over his shoulder with open pleasure, as if to say, 'Your world ends here. Ahead there is no modern, no medieval, no industrial revolution. Only a world devoted to those with the will to survive'. Or, more simply, a place where he was still relevant.

The jungle engulfed the small party and they began to pick their way up a series of hills, broken only by one river across which they waded in bare feet.

For two hours the sweat poured off them like layers of flesh, until they came to the bottom of what looked like an enclosed watershoot for a turbine. It rose almost vertically, each side curving around some eight feet of dry clay to the top, covered over by a web of collapsed debris. The bottom was strewn with boulders among which a little water flowed. They heaved their way upwards in semi-darkness for another half-hour when a voice called from somewhere above and Blake answered.

Minutes later they struggled out on to a flat ridge twenty yards wide, on the other side of which the trail plunged downwards with the same urgency that it had risen. A machine-gun post commanded each side, while off to the right the ridge widened and continued to climb. Above, in a grove of tall, elegant elms, were a collection of huts built on cleared ground. The only decoration on this black surface was the bamboo railing that led with the delicacy of a child's model from one hut to the other for guidance in the night.

The group stood catching their breath while Blake questioned the guards. They pointed towards the huts.

'Come on.' Blake looked back at the others, still recovering. 'Come on, Spenser. You wanted an escort. Well here we are. Gwe Houk. SSA base camp. Four thousand eight hundred feet up. Be glad you're here in the dry season.'

Spenser had cooled enough for a chilling breeze to coagulate the sweat that swam on his skin and soaked his clothes. He pushed himself forward, looking about with disappointment. Men in peasant clothes mixed with bits of uniform straggled out of the huts to stare impassively as they approached.

'Captain Sai Harn?' Blake shouted ahead.

They pointed to a hut on the higher ground. Spenser took Blake's arm to stop him,

'Listen. You said the Shan State Army was bigger than Khun Minh's. This is a dump compared to his camp.'

Blake gazed at Spenser's fingers grasping his sleeve. 'That is because Khun Minh is in the opium business. That camp is his headquarters. This is just a taxation point for the SSA. Less than a hundred men. We are not even over the border yet, so this camp is here only as long as the Thais put up with it. What we are interested in is our escort. Minh conscripts his men for life and pays them $18 a year plus threats. The SSA soldiers get 100 a year and sign on for a fixed period. The main army is up north where the fighting happens. And my friend Sai Harn is one of us.' He moved his arm until it was free from Spenser's grasp. 'I told you, relax,' and turned away to greet a slight figure wrapped in a *longyi* who appeared out of the hut above them. 'Eddie.' Blake folded the small man into his arms and unfolded him like a yo-yo. 'Captain Sai Harn, commander of this place. James Spenser, your guest.'

Sai Harn shook the hand without tightening his grip. Only his left eye focused on the Englishman, which produced a sinister expression. But when he looked away, his face was gentle, verging on delicate, with smooth, long cheeks from which any sign of age was absent. Blake drew him on ahead,

'Did you get the message?'

'Sure,' Eddie answered. 'Twenty-five men ought to do it. They need a diversion. It's been like a summer resort up here. Tomorrow early enough?'

Blake looked back at Spenser. 'I don't think he can do any more today.'

Eddie shrugged with indifference. 'No rush. Ah, I'm looking forward to this. We'll make the Burmans look like fools. It's a good trick. Who's the old man?'

'Carlos Santana. He trained the Hua for my father.'

'Before my time.'

'He left in '63. Took a Hua wife.'

Eddie stared sharply at Santana making his way towards them. 'The opium smoker?' He put his arm around Blake to drag him forward. 'You sure pick them.'

The hut had a dried mud floor with a smoking bonfire in the centre and a raised wooden platform along one side. Eddie slipped his sandals off before jumping up on to it and sinking down among a jumble of blankets and papers. When Spenser had followed suit, the Shan turned to him with great interest,

'Now you must tell me about Lady Di.' He saw bewilderment on Spenser's face and thought he had mispronounced her name. He put his left hand out in

164

encouragement. On his third finger a cabochon ruby stretched in narrow elegance from the knuckle to the joint. 'The future queen!'

'Whatever for, Sai Harn? Spenser laughed.

'No. Eddie. I'm Eddie. His father,' he pointed at Blake, 'converted my father. So I'm baptized Eddie. A royal name. We are among Christian gentlemen.' He made signs of self-mockery. 'Some of us, gentleman-gods. Oh, yes. But you are the first white in this place except for Blake. He doesn't count.'

'I was here,' Santana grumbled, 'when there was no camp.'

Eddie ignored him. 'The only news we get is from the magazines the traders bring up for us. We get *Time* quite often. *Time* and Coca-Cola. Sometimes *Newsweek*. *Paris Match* is best for pictures, but rare. Once we got *Queen*. That was very interesting. You see, I've been in the hills for sixteen years now, ever since school. So tell me what she is like, Lady Di.' Before an answer could begin, he added, 'And do you know about Margaret Trudeau? She is of great interest to us. Do you suppose that her unusual behaviour is a sign of intelligence?'

Spenser answered a stream of questions about every young woman who had managed to get her photograph into a weekly magazine, in general by marrying someone. Eddie knew more about them than he did; but the occasional morsel of new fact which Spenser contributed made a great impact. This went on through tea and a dinner of fried eggs swimming in oil and covered in pepper. With the darkness a soldier knocked out the struts holding up the shutters and they slammed shut, trapping more smoke inside. Tea reappeared and Santana began to unpack his pipes.

Eddie stopped him. 'You cannot smoke in here.' His childlike voice was suddenly filled with authority and contempt. 'If you wish to, you must go to another hut.' He shouted and a soldier led Santana away with his son. Eddie's off-centre stare followed the Spaniard out of the hut. In the firelight they became yellow-brown shadows. 'I cannot bear an opium smoker. They are a burden. They cannot even make a child.' He paused to put the incident out of his mind, oblivious to a cockroach that climbed up his bare leg. When it reached the thigh he unconsciously flicked it off. 'And Jane Fonda? Here we feel she has too many muscles. She is not attractive. What do you think?'

# 11

Spenser made a down payment over breakfast of $5,000, before following Eddie to the narrow ridge where his men were milling about. On a boulder a few yards from the group, Santana sat staring out towards the Shan States.

A number of Eddie's soldiers had faces deformed by scars, friends having sewn them together after clashes in the jungle. The twenty-five men were dressed in a variety of green combat clothes, buttoned high in the cold morning air. Some wore running shoes; others, canvas combat boots. The headwear ranged from baseball caps to wide-brimmed hats, with one side sewn up. The hair beneath had been left to personal taste. Disorder reigned even in the weapons; there were more M16s than Klashnikovs, a good number of short machine-guns and grenades hanging here and there.

Eddie said to Blake, 'I'll send ten on ahead and ten behind. Five with us in the middle.' This was offered as information, not for comment.

'Do you mind if Jalaw goes with the advance group?' Blake's voice was matter-of-fact.

'No confidence?'

'As a messenger, in case your radios fail.'

Blake's bible translator ignored the conversation and leapt down among the boulders, leaving Eddie to watch him disappear while he considered the complications.

Eventually, Eddie betrayed the doubt in his mind, 'You do have Khun Minh's agreement?'

'Yes. Which does not mean I am a trusting man.'

The Shan was indifferent to the explanation. He sent ten men over the ridge. Twenty minutes later he started out himself, the whites and five soldiers behind him. The last ten watched them pick their way down the boulders of the shoot towards the border.

It took three hours to reach the synthesis of heat haze and smoke that hung in an unbroken wave filling the lower valleys and making it difficult to breathe deeply. There they set off on a gradual climb, winding their way along the side of a hill where no light penetrated and electric vibrations again filled the forest. They could see further up into the trees than they could ahead or behind. Out of the mass above, thick vines hung down 100 feet, bare and brown with knots as if waiting to be swung upon, or twisted like a corkscrew. They added a festive note. The ground evened out, then the forest broke and they were in a muddy clearing some hundred yards square, littered with collapsed bamboo huts. The only fruit of the mud was a blanket of mosquitoes that hung around their ankles. A single hut still stood, the walls edged black with decay, and in its entrance there was a pregnant woman holding a child. The soldiers called out to her and she called back in an oddly pitched voice, before screaming with pleasure.

'A woman who does noble service,' Eddie joked. 'Even in the dry season this place stinks with water. We used to have a camp here, but the malaria was awful.'

A macabre atmosphere hung over the clearing and pushed them on faster.

'Where are we?' Spenser asked.

'Narmonlong. The border,' Eddie laughed. 'Can't you tell?' He looked back at the woman waving after them with wide sweeps of her free arm and great energy. 'It's on the map.'

They slipped into the shade of the forest and climbed slowly up along the edge of a valley. Eddie walked just in front of Spenser to keep up a conversation.

'It is my belief that Mrs Kennedy should now marry Mr Trudeau. What do you feel?'

'She's too tall,' Spenser replied, his voice lost in the vibration of the jungle.

'Too tall?' Eddie re-evaluated in silence. 'Do you think he would mind?'

'What about her?'

'Her? Can you think of anyone taller?'

'Well, Edward Kennedy for a start.'

'That would be incest.' Eddie expressed shock.

'Surely not. There's no blood involved.'

'"Thy brother's wife." Ask Blake.'

'I can't think of anyone else offhand,' Spenser had to admit.

'Then she must forget about height.'

At midday they came to a clearing that stretched for a mile along their side of the valley. The trees had been cut and the undergrowth burnt in preparation for crops. The impression was of a battlefield gone cold. The trail led across it down into the belly of the land where a village of twenty woven huts had been squeezed together behind a bamboo wall.

On the edge of the village, one house stood alone with its own palisade. Over the doorway there was a wooden cross. Before they could pass, a Lahu ran out and threw himself on his knees before Blake, holding the American's hand to his cheek. Without letting go, he dragged him in under the porch. The others followed, except Santana and his son, who walked on towards the main palisade. This was his wife's village.

Eddie resentfully radioed ahead to stop the advance guard, then dropped on to a stool and turned with a smile to Spenser, who was taking his boots off. 'An hour for lunch?

All right?' Spenser nodded. 'Good.'

The owner of the house produced a Bible in Lahu, with a photograph of Blake's grandfather opposite the title page. He went away to fetch a postcard of Christ on the cross, followed by a dozen other devotional cards brought out one by one, then crosses, then Christian sundries, until the stock was exhausted. Only then did tea appear, smoked and heavily salted, along with pieces of grilled pork and corn cobs cooked on cinders.

In the afternoon they started over a mountain range where comfortable steps had been worn into the earth by smugglers moving up and down the trail. One of these caravans appeared ahead later in the day – six mules laden with transistor radios and nylon clothing for the black market in Rangoon – and was squeezed by.

Much of the dirt path was less than a yard wide, with the hill rising up sharp on their left and dropping away at an eighty degree angle on their right. They could not see farther than ten yards ahead in those precarious moments; instead there was a spectacular vision hundreds of feet down over the jungle's disorder. Out of that tangled mess dried stumps of broken bamboo suck up like stakes waiting to impale a cavalry charge.

Blake pointed at these. 'You see why we prefer the dry season.'

'Why?'

'Because you are walking on clay. In the rain it becomes like ice.'

Spenser looked back and caught sight of his horse handler, who had so far addressed not a single word to anyone; in fact, his walk was so discreet that for hours at a time Spenser forgot the man was only two paces behind. The trail levelled off at about 4,000 feet on to a long plateau, where the trees were high and the undergrowth sparse. There Blake broke away from the group to search the rock face on either side.

'What's the matter?' Eddie asked.

'Looking for a flower.'

Spenser joined him. 'What flower?'

Blake pulled a photograph from his pocket. It was of a purple-brown orchid and the image drew Spenser's eye like a relic that converted itself into Marea.

'The flowers will not come out until the rain starts,' Blake examined the picture again, 'but I said I would look.'

'May I help?'

Blake's arm materialized to block the way. With the same movement the rifle slipped from his shoulder into the other hand and was raised towards a branch hanging low a foot before them. Softly he ordered, 'Now move backwards slowly.'

Spenser did as he was told. Blake followed suit, then picked up a stone and pitched it. The leaves exploded and the branch whipped into the air. Something green crashed to the ground in a tangled mess that frantically unravelled itself into a narrow snake a yard long. It hesitated a moment before evaporating into the brush.

Blake went back to searching. 'Not very venomous. We would have had time to get you to the hospital in Chiang Mai. Thank you. I will look on my own.'

After that Spenser followed in Santana's footsteps, with Marea still in his mind. Desire for her came rushing out unexpectedly and filled him to such a degree that he could scarcely see where he walked. When he pushed her away, she returned. He pushed again, but as with his visions of beautiful objects, will-power played no role. Then, like water settling, she became less defined and the jungle began to reassert itself. He found he was concentrating on the steps Santana took. They were precise, chosen moves, each of them. The old man never brushed against a branch or a bush. He side-stepped the clumps of grass which broke out on the track. What he was avoiding was impossible to see, but Spenser began to feel there were things to be kept at a distance; that the sound which engulfed them had a meaning. By then Marea had slipped away so completely that the thought of trying to summon her up again did not occur.

The far side of the mountain was traced by a river twenty yards wide that rushed over a bed of rocks. A caravan was resting on the near bank; the mules loaded with rubber sandals and with birth-control pills which were illegal in Burma. Eddie waded through the clear water and started to climb again.

The afternoon was fading when they picked up a radio call from their advance group, who had reached the intersection with the track from Khun Minh's camp. There they had found seven men waiting under the command of Lao Sa, Khun Minh's number two.

Blake's placid face abruptly tensed and he turned on Spenser, 'What is this about? What did he tell you?'

The Sunday outing atmosphere evaporated. Spenser was unnerved as much by Blake's attack as by the news. 'Only that he would send a messenger to clear the way.'

Blake and Eddie stared at each other, but neither could guess what it meant. The Shan broke off impatiently,

'Let's get there before the light dies.'

They doubled their pace down into the valley and in fifteen minutes reached the advance group, crouched on the trail by a fire, drinking tea. Twenty yards on, Khun Minh's track slipped innocuously in from the right. A tent had been pitched in the narrow opening and a fire lit before it. Lao Sa and his seven men, six of them in matching khaki uniforms with long trousers tucked into jungle boots, sat before their tent, also drinking tea. The two parties faced each other, with their rifles at their sides.

When Spenser's group appeared, Lao Sa jumped to his feet and shouted out, 'Welcome!' Beneath the enthusiasm, his voice was without life.

Eddie strode across the no man's land. 'What are you doing here?'

'Khun Minh's idea.' Lao Sa shrugged. 'If I travel with you, there will be no problem at our posts.' This produced no reaction. 'It's a friendly gesture.'

Eddie met his smile with one of equal width, his left eye fixed on the man. 'Your men will travel in a separate group behind us.'

'Why not?' Lao Sa agreed quickly. 'Do you mind if I walk with you? And my runner?' He indicated the only member of his group not in uniform.

'As you wish.'

Lao Sa cheered up at that. With genuine warmth he added, 'Let me give you dinner. Oh, I tell you, the last thing I needed was another trip to the Salween. The thought of doing it alone.' He nodded in the direction of his own soldiers. 'Alone with them. Worse than alone. At least now I'll have some company.' He put his arm around Eddie, drawing him towards the fire.

His runner was also his cook and, like the soldiers with Spenser, he had been gathering leaves and flowers along the trail. These were now fried or steamed, with a little smoked pork added for taste. Apart from being a cook, he stood out because his entire trunk, his upper arms and his thighs were tattooed solid blue. He wore only a T-shirt with narrow straps over the shoulders and shorts, as if to show off his decoration. There was also a message tattooed across his forehead. All of the Shans had tattoos on their arms and legs, even Eddie, but this was quite different. Lao Sa volunteered his story.

Tattoos were worn as armour and this man's father had proved that it worked. During the war he had fought for the Japanese and had been hit on the chest by a British bullet. The bullet had struck a tattoo and had bounced off. There

172

had been witnesses. The skin had been bruised, but nothing more. With this miracle he had become a local celebrity and, by necessity, a prophet of the tattoo. He had forced his children to go beyond the norm by covering every important part of their body. Lao Sa's runner had interpreted his protection as a vocation and on his twelfth birthday had enlisted to fight. He was Khun Minh's only volunteer; a fact not mentioned in the story. It was a proof of loyalty that made him valuable.

Dinner was half-finished when Santana withdrew from the circle and walked back down the trail to where his son had laid their ponchos and blankets. Lao Sa watched him go, then produced a small leather pouch from his breast pocket. From the pouch he pulled his gold toothpick and began to run it methodically down between each tooth, his lips pulled back to expose the roots. He stopped to tease Eddie,

'So you travel with opium smokers? At least we only sell it.' He went back to his teeth without missing a space. 'I mean, can you imagine being weak enough to touch the stuff. Unless you were a tribesman, of course, living in filth.'

Eddie flushed. He put aside his dish and wiped his hands, as if to dismiss the conversation; but this calm lasted scarcely a few seconds. Suddenly he put his right hand up to his right eye and popped it out on to his palm, only to lick the glass ball up into his mouth and suck it loudly. Lao Sa stopped talking. The eyelid sank over the empty cavity. Eddie spat out the eyeball and examined it in the firelight before drying it off carefully with his handkerchief. He looked straight at Lao Sa with his good eye, propped open the empty lid with his fingers and slipped the eyeball back into place. For the first time, Spenser noticed that there was a scar running from the side of the eye up into his temple, where it was lost in the hair.

Eddie got to his feet and walked off to his men. Later in the night, Spenser overheard him talking with Blake. Blake's voice was soft and reassuring,

'We will watch him, that's all. They are only eight. What can they do?'

'He's a pig!' Eddie interrupted. 'He always was, even at school.'

'Forget it.'

'In Taunggyi he was three years ahead of me at the Chief's school. Since then he's fought on every side. You know that. When the Burmese burnt my village, he was working for them. The Burmese like pigs – drug runners they can encourage so the nationalists don't have a chance.'

'We are rid of him at the Salween. Just control yourself.'


They moved on the next morning in four straggling groups. The trail was wider and followed the straight line of the valley, with a stream on their left. They met a caravan going south; its dozen mules, loaded down with boulders of jade, had been pulled to the edge of the trail to let the soldiers by. Lao Sa made a point of walking at the front to reminisce with Eddie about school. Spenser got Blake's attention and drew him to the rear of the group.

'What happened last night?'

'Eddie? He joined the SSA when he was eighteen – the year the Burmese arrested a lot of students. He was just married. His wife was pregnant. He sent his wife back to their village up north so that he could go off into the hills with the guerrillas. A year later, he and two others from the village made a lightning visit home – their group had been operating in the area. Somehow the Burmese found out. In those days, Khun Minh's army was acting as a local militia for the Burmese – a sideline to running opium. They staged a quick raid to catch the guerrillas. The village was flattened and everyone was killed. Eddie saw his wife and child burnt up, then he got shot in the eye. One of his friends dragged him out. In those days, Lao Sa was the local militia chief.'

They could hear him ahead telling stories about a teacher that Eddie had also endured; one of the last Englishmen to teach in the school. Behind them, Lao Sa's tattooed runner was chatting to Spenser's horse handler in what passed for a monologue, with the handler making every effort to avoid the attention paid him.

The stream grew into a small river with grass-covered banks that spread back into what might have been a European meadow. Profusions of butterflies swooped across their path. The horizon was blocked by a single banyan tree rising a hundred feet from a tangled series of central trunks that altogether measured fifteen feet across. In its shade there was a worn, wooden buddha and a small platform, which had once been the floor of a hut.

Blake was surprised. 'What happened to Mong Mai?'

'The Burmese raided this far three years ago.' Eddie pointed towards a low hill. 'They burnt everything. A few peasants hung on. They've built a new village on high ground.'

'What about the SSA toll-gate? It was under the tree.'

'Khun Minh cut a side path around through the hills. We weren't making any money, so we moved the barrier further up the trail.'

Lao Sa interrupted good-naturedly, 'You can hardly blame us. Besides, this isn't a safe place. The trail from General Chu's camp comes in near here. You were always afraid he would catch you off-guard.'

Mentioning a third party in their rivalry, particularly a Chinese, drew the two Shans together, if only for a few minutes while they watched for Chu's trail. It was Eddie who pointed out the narrow overgrown path.

Lao Sa mocked, 'Old men don't cut their grass.' He thought this very clever; so much so that the tone of his voice re-awoke the enmity between him and the others.

A wedge of rice paddies appeared on their left, then

expanded until it covered the bottom of the valley. The paddies were dotted with women deep in the mud and water, the legs of their loose trousers tied up around their waists. The trail skirted along the edge before crossing over on a dirt causeway to the other side where a village was hidden in the trees. There Lao Sa left them. He said he would catch up.

Three miles on they came to a second village, called Homong. The jungle again pressed in on both sides, hanging above them from impossible cliffs. This was the new Shan State Army taxation point. The first village, Muglang, where they had left Lao Sa, was a Khun Minh outpost. He had settled a handful of soldiers there with their familes. While the women worked in the paddies, the men were attempting to cut a side trail around Homong and its taxes. So the two villages lived in a state of undeclared war, the women working within a few feet of one another and both groups of men waiting for a chance to kill the other.

Eddie called a halt for the rest of the day. They spread out on the wood floor of the largest hut, ten feet above the ground, with the warm smell of water buffalo coming up between the boards. Children appeared in small delegations to stare at their first white men, though what they saw was limited by the film growing over more than half the eyes. Spenser had wanted to push on. He had intended to say something. He said nothing. There was an atmosphere in the air that deformed any personal desires. The trail was a black thread being drawn by an invisible hand through thickening green paint. There was no apparent progression, no apparent goal, only an ill-defined sense of continuity. Spenser found this suspension of the individual will surprisingly agreeable, and not because he knew it was temporary. The suspension was so complete that it included not thinking rationally enough to divide the permanent from the ephemeral.

When he went out to use the jungle, Eddie told him with pride that Homong had a latrine – it was therefore a better

place than Khun Minh's village down the trail. A child led
Spenser to a small bamboo hut built over a hole eight feet
square and ten feet deep. They were followed by the entire
population of children. A bamboo platform had been built
across the hole, with a square opening in the centre. The smell
proved it had been in use for months.

Spenser stooped but the area was so cramped he had to
drop his trousers at the entrance and work his way backwards
across the platform. The children watched all of this in
silence. When his feet were almost at the hole, he felt his toes
trying to slide out from under him. He leaned to right himself,
but they continued to slide and in a panic he fell backwards.
Then he understood. His weight was double that of the Shans
and the bamboo was giving way. The bottom of the pit
rushed towards him with horrifying richness. He threw
himself forward and landed half-way out of the door, his
hands grasping at the grass for support. The children laughed
with delight. Spenser worked his legs out, got to his feet and
pulled his trousers up to the cheers of his audience. He gave
them a shaky bow and went off in search of some cleared
jungle.

The next day they crossed two mountain ranges without
seeing more than ten yards ahead or getting a clear view of the
sky. Then a village broke the monotony for the few seconds it
took to pass by. The land rose a last time and on the reverse
slope the forest sounds began to swell. At first the volume was
simply higher, then it divided itself into two parts; with a new
sound growing ever louder, like warm, aeolian music which
drew them on until it drowned out the electricity of the
cicadas and became a roar.

They climbed down and down from clay to rock that had
been carved or worn into narrow footsteps. The light was
blocked by the hill, so that they worked in obscurity. The roar
echoed back and forth across the invisible valley. They could
not speak above the noise. Abruptly the trees opened into a

tunnel and at the end they saw the Salween flowing. The closer they drew, the greater the expanse of water became, until at last they were on the river's edge. The other bank was at four hundred yards and it rose up, a wall of jungle, as steeply as theirs had fallen. The water flowed beneath a smooth surface, but with speed and with the colour of great depth.

Their advance group was waiting beside the opening, where the bank had been dug away to create a small breakwater. Across, on the other side, was a group of huts.

Lao Sa drew his pistol. 'Will you fire or will I?' he asked Eddie.

'Go ahead.'

There were four explosions in the air. They echoed off the facing mountain and back and on down the canyon. A few minutes later, two long, narrow speedboats, like the fast water-taxis in Bangkok, set out from the other bank.

# 12

The Salween ferry consisted of the two boats fixed side by side five yards apart, with planks laid between them and lashed into place. Twenty men went over on the first trip, standing clasped together, the whole mass swaying as the boats moved in tandem and the boards shifted beneath their feet. Spenser had hung back to avoid crossing with Lao Sa. The man repelled him for no concrete reason. It was a question of vibrations.

Darkness had begun to fall when the ferry set out on its second trip, Spenser facing upstream at the edge of the boards. He could feel agitation and jostling behind him as the soldiers shifted at each lurch of the boats, their fingers grasping to hold the next man's shirt, the horse moving uneasily in the centre. The excited chatter was drowned out by the roar of the river and of the two engines whose drive shafts stretched yards behind, their propellors filling the air with water.

Spenser forced all of this from his mind. His eyes were fixed on the mass of the Salween rushing towards him down a thousand miles from Tibet with another seven hundred to flow before reaching the sea. The water was dark, the sun having fallen behind the cliffs. The river called out to him in an unending chorus – divide, divide. Behind him, on the shore just abandoned, lay the mediocrity of his former life, of London and of all the binding cords. On the other side he sensed he would be without dead weight, at least until time forced him to travel back across; but by then he would carry with him the secret to eternal freedom. He would be married to the children of genius. The cords would have been cut finally away.

They landed at a small dock, behind which a beach rose up steeply twenty feet to a dozen solid wooden barracks. Blake proposed they stay in two huts offered by Lao Sa, who had gone off with his local officer. Some fifty of Minh's soldiers stood here and there idly watching.

Eddie interrupted, 'We're not sleeping in this camp.'

The tone surprised Blake. 'It's almost dark.'

'I don't care. We can get a little way.'

Spenser looked around at Khun Minh's $18 a year slaves. 'Eddie's right. Let's get out of here.'

As they left, Lao Sa reappeared, anxious to keep their company. Blake said only that they were pressed and would pick him up in a week or so on their way back.

The trail rose as sharp and twisting as that on the south side of the river. They climbed for half an hour before finding a sliver of flat rock scarcely large enough for them all to lie down. Blake baptized it 'Eddie's Folly'.

Without waiting to be exiled, Santana placed himself on the edge of the group, where the ground was least comfortable. He sat snipping at his nails while he waited for the first pipe. It was a curious mania. He worked on his fingers daily, cutting off minute amounts in order to maintain a narrow quarter-moon of black. Each time a clipping flew into the air, the boy looked up from his work to see where it fell. When he handed over the pipe to his father, he set about finding the slices in the dark – counting carefully until there were ten in his palm. By that time the others had finished chewing at their cobs of corn and Santana had slipped into his own world. His son disappeared to bury the clippings.

They slept badly and so started at the first sign of light climbing for three hours until the trail ejected them on to a summit. Ahead, a plateau undulated into the horizon, its sweep broken only by occasional eucalyptus trees and sudden outcroppings of rock. This was the Shan highland that stretched all the way to Taunggyi. The soldiers set a fast pace, perhaps because they were glad to be back on their own ground, perhaps because the air on the plateau was cool and invigorating. With the sky open to them, the claustrophobia of the jungle evaporated; and everywhere, as if by a miracle in the dry earth, primroses, clematis and wild roses lined the trail.

On that first morning, Spenser used the wider path to walk beside Santana. The man was treated as a social leper, for which Spenser could see no good reason. Besides, they shared a common interest. But Santana seemed not to hear the conversation at his right side and didn't bother to reply. After several attempts without success, Spenser was about to drop back into line, when the Spaniard suddenly hooked his arm around the younger man's and leaned on him as they walked.

'I am a weak man. They are right to treat me that way. But why should I care what they say to me? I try not to exist.' Santana fell silent. 'I think I will be happy only when I am no longer here. Anywhere.' He laughed, opening his dark mouth wide. 'These Christians, they are so quick to judge. In Shan, the word for "convert" means to eat a religion; if you conquer a town and live off it, they also say you eat the town.' He pulled Spenser close by pushing his own arm through further. 'Blake – Does he believe? I have asked myself that question.' Santana closed himself in reflection. 'Does he believe that he believes? Those two, they have traded drugs while I only smoke. I do not judge them. It is their problem.'

'Eddie traded?'

'The SSA sold opium for years.' He waved that subject away with the long fingers of his left hand. 'Do you know that the old monk died?'

Spenser shook his head.

'They will preserve him in honey for a year; then cover him in perfume and paper flowers and put him on a pyre, three tiers high. He will never know the rot of the body. He will escape the worms. When they burn him, it will be a big celebration in Mae Hong Son. They do it for the wrong reasons, but he was a good man.' Santana was both leaning on Spenser and drawing him forward. 'The statues of the buddha mean nothing. A European contamination. There were none until Alexander the Great came east with his idols. I do wrong to sell them. But it does not matter when they no longer give hope to people. There is no hope in a museum or in a statue dug out of the ground.' He thought about that before bursting into laughter. 'You see. Any man will construct a morality to meet his own needs. I am no different. But neither are they.' He was looking at Blake and Eddie and pulled his arm free. 'I am happy to see this place again.' Like the Shans, he was walking faster, encouraged by the light.

For three days they moved across an unchanging landscape. The occasional caravan was met and passed by; a few others were overtaken, loaded down with everything from dismantled motor cycles to plastic buckets. It was the last flurry of smuggling before the rains made the way impassable.

Near Mawkmai the main trail went off to the north, while Spenser's group edged over to the west on a smaller track that avoided all roads and towns. This cut across the flow of the rock so that river after river blocked their way. At each crossing there was a village and a peasant who owned a raft. He charged them a tiny sum and passed them over quickly, before the Burmese heard that a rebel band was in the area and destroyed the raft. These ferry masters also sold chickens and fresh pork to the travellers.

On their fourth day north of the Salween they climbed to a higher plateau that rolled into more valleys, each of which was a few hundred feet deep and divided by a river. The hills were covered by pine forests and the valleys with a profusion of flowers. At the first ferry crossing of the day, they bought wild strawberries and ate them as they balanced on the raft.

After another four days the trees began to take on fantastic forms – first the poinsettias, entirely red, like multiheaded buzzards. Then the swedows, like great oaks, but covered in creamy, flesh-like flowers. The soldiers picked whatever blossoms they could reach and steamed them for dinner.

The following afternoon Eddie ordered silence and an hour later they came to a dirt road which led into a clearing at the base of a cliff. The rock face was pierced by caves, each lined with buddhas.

Jalaw left with a message while they set up camp in the caves. It was Santana who slipped farthest in among the statues and stretched out in their shadows to await his first pipe. By the time it was ready, Jalaw had reappeared in a 1940s pick-up truck driven by a Shan. The truck stopped long enough for Blake and Spenser to climb up beneath the tarpaulin hood, then swerved around and headed back to Taunggyi.

After five miles they came on to a badly paved road and climbed over a last hill. The truck stopped. They heard the driver being questioned by a soldier at what must have been an army check-point, then he accelerated. Taunggyi was divided into two parts by the road. On the mountainside to their right were summer villas built by the British, who had come there to escape the summer heat of the plains. On the lower ground were wooden palaces with store-fronts. These had belonged to the Indian trading class until they were expelled by the Burmese, who now occupied both sides of the road.

Spenser saw all of this through the slit in the back. 'Are we safe, camped so close?'

Blake was seated on the floor, strangely uninterested. 'The caves are off limits because there are terrorists in the hills around town. We are the terrorists.'

They turned up to the right, by a large, stone house in the Scottish baronial style. It had been the governor's residence. The windows were shuttered; the garden, though overgrown, was filled with mauve jacaranda trees. After passing three smaller villas, they pulled into a courtyard. The gate was instantly shut behind them.

Blake hopped out. 'Quick! Inside!'

It was a white house, two floors high, whose stucco had not been repaired since the British left in 1947. They dashed across the courtyard into the grand hallway, where Blake paused to gaze around. The slats of the wood floor had separated so that dirt filled the spaces in between. On the walls, the wood frames had pulled away from the stucco infill. A cheap sliding iron gate had been fixed across the doorway, as if it led into a warehouse elevator.

Blake sighed and led the way up the wide staircase to a landing on to which a conservatory and bedrooms opened. All the entrances and exits to it were fitted with iron grilles, as were the windows, and all of them were slid across and locked. Only the gate through which they came at the top of the stairs was open. In the centre of the landing was a circle of heavy teak armchairs with rattan seats. In one of them was an old man who shouted as they came into sight.

'So, Matthew, you come back! And everyone dead except me.'

Blake took his hand before sitting beside him. 'You are still young, U Thaw.'

He had a brown army toque on his head and wore a fawn Shan jacket. A wool blanket was pulled over his knees. At his feet were a white spittoon and a bone cane. He put a stained handkerchief to his mouth to wipe away the saliva. The chair had a slanted back for lounging, so that each time he talked he had to pull himself forward with a hand grasping the teak frame between his thighs. 'You see, I have kept the house for you. You see in what good shape.' He waved at the room with the same hand so that his body fell backwards. The air smelt of dust and fish oil. On a table before them were plates of fried garlic and tea pâté. 'Eat this. Go on. I have kept the house and the trade, so much of the trade. I am rich now.'

'I see that,' Blake agreed.

'So it was good that the British left.'

'Very good.'

'You see.'

'Yes, I see, U Thaw.'

'No you don't. You wanted to stay.'

'I loved it here. We were different. We would have stayed if they had let us.'

The old man pulled himself forward. 'You cannot love what is not your home,' and let go. His body fell back.

'I was born here.'

'So you were. I am glad to see you, Matthew.'

'I'm glad to see you.'

'You see how rich I am.'

'I see.'

'No thank you to the Burmans! Poor Shans.' He pulled himself forward to repeat, 'Poor Shans.'

The conversation went on until it was exhausted and Blake said, 'I need a truck for forty-eight hours. A big truck.'

'I have all the good trucks,' U Thaw insisted with great pleasure, so he laughed. 'What do you want?'

'To carry ten men plus 4,000 pounds of cargo, plus it's got to have a covered back.'

'A very big truck.' He pulled himself forward to spit into the spittoon.

None of this made much sense to Spenser, who thought a small truck would do.

'And in good shape, U Thaw. No bad engines. No bad axles. I am taking it down to the plain. In it I need tools: crowbars, mallets, five two-men slings and twenty cloth sacks.'

U Thaw nodded, 'I have a Chevrolet truck. In very good order. 1948. Only you must pay a great deal for my petrol. I shall tell you the price. In Rangoon, three and a half *kyats*. In Taunggyi, thirty-five. Poor Shans. Poor you who must pay.'

'All right. Plus I need ten mules with handlers waiting for me here to make the trip back to Mae Hong Son. Each has to carry two packages, 200 pounds each; so baskets won't do. They need rope bags.'

U Thaw appeared confused by the mention of Mae Hong Son. 'How did you get here Matthew?'

'Across the Salween.'

'Khun Minh would not let you across!' He grimaced with astonishment.

'Have you got the mules?'

'How can I give you these things. I do not want to make an enemy of Khun Minh.'

'You are not giving, U Thaw. We are paying.'

'No matter, Matthew! No matter!'

'But you would make an enemy of me?'

The old man stopped to consider this. 'I cannot make an

185

enemy of the past, Matthew.' He avoided Blake's eyes. 'I love you. You know me. But I am too old to make an enemy of Khun Minh.'

'You won't, U Thaw. He knows I am here. My friend, Mr Spenser, negotiated with him.'

U Thaw looked at Spenser for the first time to see whether he could be believed, but Spenser sat in silence, shocked by this turn in the conversation.

Blake broke in, 'You remember my father, U Thaw. You worked in this house. We are not a family to lie.'

The old man nodded but said nothing.

Spenser broke in impatiently. 'Of course Khun Minh knows. How do you think we crossed the Salween? There's only his ferry. You don't think Blake was disguised as an enchanted princess, do you?'

U Thaw laughed. 'So he knows. You see he is loyal to nothing. His father would be unhappy to hear this.'

'What about the mules?' Blake insisted.

'Oh, mules. Lots of mules. But these are expensive at the end of the season. I will not get them back until the rains end. So he let you across?'

'Yes, U Thaw.'

They paid $500 per animal, just as Blake had promised. The truck was another $300. Returning to the cave they sat side by side on the floor of the pick-up. Spenser had been silent since his single intervention. Now he asked,

'What did the old man mean about Khun Minh's father?'

'My father was military governor here for two months after Taunggyi was liberated from the Japanese; just until the English sent someone. The province was in chaos. Guerrilla bands, black markets, assassinations. Khun Minh's father was one of the worst. My father had him hanged. After that things worked pretty smoothly in the area.'

Spenser managed only a weak, 'You didn't tell me.'

'It wasn't relevant.'

186

'Not relevant!' Spenser grabbed him by the shoulder, 'Are you crazy?'

'Stop shouting.' Blake unpeeled the hand with ease. 'I've had dealings of all sorts with Minh for twenty years. Why should his father suddenly become relevant?'

'What else are you hiding?' There was no reply. 'I suppose Marea knew.' More to himself he added, 'Why wouldn't she?' Then to Blake. 'I know you're all playing with me. I'm your bauble this month. I know that. It doesn't matter. You get me my statues, Blake. I don't care what game you play so long as I get my statues.'

Blake listened to all of this with a display of embarrassed patience – his embarrassment was for Spenser. When the tirade finished, he said firmly, 'I came to get your buddhas. That is our arrangement. You will get them.'

They were woken in the morning by the Chevrolet truck. The driver neither cut the motor nor climbed down. He was probably afraid to get out or afraid the motor would not start again. Eddie had chosen his ten strongest men, who ran across and jumped up into the back; he himself was in civilian clothing so that he could ride in the front to deal with any crisis. Blake, Spenser and Jalaw completed the group; then at the last moment Santana appeared, without his son.

'You stay here,' Blake said. 'You're not strong enough to be of use.'

Santana didn't bother to reply. He climbed up on his own.

The truck coasted down the twisting road from Taunggyi to the lower plain of He Ho and from there on down to Kalaw, the tea-planting station on the edge of the Shan hills. In Kalaw it was stopped at an army check-point. They wanted to know where the truck was going and what it was carrying. The Shans in the back waited, their rifles ready, as Eddie replied to each question with painful slowness so that the Burmans had to stand longer in the sun. He said they were

187

carrying blankets and offered 300 *kyats*, which was a generous bribe without being extravagant enough to raise suspicions. They were allowed to drive on.

The road plunged from Kalaw down to the plain, restricting the driver to first gear, exhaust fumes rising into the enclosed back until the men began to cough and crowded up to the rear flap. Near the bottom they were attacked by an arid heat which slipped above 100°.

The rest of the morning was spent pounding over the dry countryside of the plain. The roads, paved or not, were a series of pot-holes and dry river beds without bridges. When the sun was at its highest, they opened the rear canvas to let in air and began to skirt south around the rail centre of Thazi on a dirt track. The fields were empty. The land was flat and grey. After a time it became flat and red. In the middle of the afternoon the monotony was disturbed by a dead volcano, Mount Popa, a lone deformation of the plain. Then the flatness rolled up into small hills covered with grape-vines, which were succeeded by sugar-palms. Beyond them the horizon was broken in an irrational manner that could only have been man-made.

Small pagodas and temples began rising like young corn in the fields on either side. This crop grew thicker and the ruins larger until the truck was rolling through a forest of ruins, each of which sat calmly, throwing long evening shadows across the ploughed land. There was no hint of the people they had once served. All the houses, even the palaces, had been built of wood and had disappeared a few years after Pagan was abandoned. The truck stopped because neither the driver nor Eddie knew which way to go. Spenser was sent forward to squeeze into the cabin. He had no need of his map; the plan of the site was fixed in his mind. The dirt track he directed them on to wound through the ruins aimlessly – he did not say he had chosen it in order to pass by what he would not get another chance to see. They should have noticed it in his eyes or by his silence, because he said not a single word; only raising a finger periodically to point the way, his mind lost among the beauty of the ruins. Eventually he brought them to a halt beneath a large square temple, the Sulamani, which stood like a two-tiered wedding-cake a mile from the core of the site.

A heavy kick broke the rusted chain holding the temple door closed and they all filed into the first corridor. The Shans left their shoes at the entrance, went in to kneel before a large ruined brick buddha, then settled down there in the dust, while Spenser climbed up a narrow flight of stairs to the first terrace, fifty feet above the ground.

The sun was setting beyond the Irrawaddy, which flowed two miles wide and brown at an unhurried pace. On its near bank a cluster of a thousand temples were silhouetted. To either side and behind were thousands more – square and circular players set for an unknown game.

'Where is the museum?'

Spenser did not hear him the first time. He heard nothing extraneous. Blake touched him on the shoulder and repeated the question. Spenser turned to find him examining the buildings through his field-glasses, and Santana, ashen from the effort of the stairs.

'You see the largest building between us and the river?' Spenser pointed. It was a white square of six receding storeys, on top of which sat a golden pagoda that tapered to a pinnacle. 'The museum is 100 yards beyond it and to the right.'

Blake was still examining the white and gold pagoda. Apparently he had not expected anything so extraordinary.

It was Santana who noticed and said, 'That is the Ananda. The most wonderful.'

Spenser broke in without thinking, 'Two hundred and ten feet high, built as a cross, two hundred and ninety feet long each way.' He was chanting an incantation to beauty; to the immortality of perfect form. 'The central cube is an eighty-two foot square, begun by King Kyanzittha in 1091 with the finest workmen of Asia. Inside, there are one thousand five hundred statues sitting untouched in the niches for which he had them sculpted. In the world there is no building more symmetrical or complete. Or abandoned.'

He hardly noticed the discomfort caused by this impassioned recital and turned away from the two men to sit on the stones of the terrace until the day was gone and the moon had risen and the golden pinnacles had ceased to reflect light. Now that the jungle was behind and he had the Ananda in sight, within reach, its spires and domes entered into communion with him; they danced for him, dragging in their train all of the temples and the pagodas; the thousands of ruins coming alive with the only living thing that remained in them – the genius of man. No. Not of man. Transmitted through man and free of his temporal human touch the moment the creation was complete. Spenser ceded to the dance for as long as there was light and when all was still on the obscured horizon he rose to his feet to find the other two men no longer there.

# 13

At one a.m. Blake and Jalaw went out on foot to cut the electric and telephone wires. They came back at three, able to confirm that the peasants and the few guardians were asleep in their huts. Twenty minutes later the Chevrolet rolled into the clear night as quietly as could be managed.

The museum was divided into two parts. First, a small, recent, one-storey building. Second, what resembled a covered market, enclosed only by a low wall, around the inside of which large stone sculptures had been mounted.

The Shans waited in the truck while the three whites and

Eddie climbed over this wall. They walked the full circuit, shining their lights on the statues. These were in stone and close to five feet high. They were also coarse of creation, though Spenser alone noticed this. When he had come full circle, Eddie said in a strained voice,

'I was told two hundred pounds. This stuff must weigh four or five hundred. We could get them loose from their mounts. We might even be able to get them on to the truck. But the mules can't carry that much.'

The four men stood awkwardly, their lights still playing over the statues, who stared up at them with the quizzical expression of the Buddha. In the darkness, Spenser could feel their eyes focusing on to him. He turned away.

'Let's have a look at the other building. There must be smaller pieces.'

They climbed back out and walked the few yards to the closed museum. It had no windows and the roof was fixed tightly on to the concrete walls. Their lights shone over the door. It was a steel sliding panel.

'Well,' Blake said eventually, 'we could open this with a grenade or a few shots. That would also wake up the world. There must be some military in the area, so the question is, can we load statues while we fight off an unknown number of Burmese?'

'No,' was all Eddie said.

'Come on! We can't just walk away.' Blake became impatient. 'What about all those temples? If they're locked the way the first one was, we have no problem.'

'The Ananda,' Spenser broke in. 'The best is in there. I can guarantee each piece would have a market. And ... it's 100 yards from here.'

Santana pushed forward with sudden violence, his light shining into Spenser's face. 'You knew! You tricked us. You knew we would agree after coming this far.'

'I knew nothing,' Spenser protested.

Santana grabbed at him in the darkness and came up with his collar. 'You knew! Listen to your voice!' He seized hold of a shoulder with his other hand and tried to shake Spenser. 'Listen! Listen!'

'Shut up.' Blake ordered.

But he didn't interfere. Both he and Eddie seemed to be digesting the situation and left Spenser to struggle on his own. The old man's grasp was strong. He was in a kind of frenzy and kept repeating, 'Listen. Listen.' – though he whispered it now, holding Spenser close, the breath of each word enveloping him with the smell of rotting apples. Spenser ripped himself free and stood at a distance, panting.

'What's the difference, Santana?' he managed at last. 'These aren't temples. No one worships here. They've been empty for 600 years. The whole place is a museum. You said so yourself. No one comes here with hope, so it doesn't matter.'

'I came!' Santana whispered. 'I came!'

Spenser stared at him amazed. 'Don't be ridiculous.'

'I'll kill you if you take from the temple.'

'Shut up!' Blake grabbed Santana and shook him. 'Shut up. You will do what you are told. You are here by your own choice, not ours. So shut up. Eddie, drive the truck over there.' Blake pushed Santana hard against the museum wall and set out to walk the distance by himself. No one else moved.

'Matthew,' Eddie called after him, 'the men won't do this.'

'Order them.'

'I can't. Because I'm a Christian. I can't do that. They would think it was because I am a Christian.'

'All right. Just get the truck over there.' Blake walked on.

Spenser could hear the Spaniard breathing deeply somewhere in the darkness, almost gasping. He was about to apologize, but realized it would do no good. Instead, he went

192

after Blake. Moonlight threw the shadows of the Ananda across the ground, exaggerating the size of its twenty spires and lighting it enough for the planes of white walls to appear ivory.

The soldiers hung back from the west door while Blake twisted the chain with a crowbar. When the metal was taut, Spenser jammed a second crowbar into the padlock itself. They wrenched in opposite directions and the lock fell apart.

The doors opened on to a hallway thirty-five feet high that stretched 100 feet before them – at the end was a colossal carved figure protected by gold leaf. Its head was lit by moonlight through a single window and the expression on the face was benign. The buddha's palm was held out towards them in a gentle admonition to stop. Their flashlights played over the walls and picked out sixteen niches, in the shadows of which were statues. No one moved forward.

'This way,' Spenser whispered.

He broke through the knot of soldiers to stride down the hall past an open pair of teak doors that rose to the ceiling. At the base of the golden buddha he stopped, flashed his light up its full height and turned right into the outer circular corridor. Both walls were a honeycomb of niches that rose seven levels towards the ceiling. Those near the top appeared dark and empty, except for reflecting eyes. His light played over the bottom two tiers of the outer wall and black lacquered faces leaned out, only to disappear as he went on. These were what he had come for. Eighty figures set in niches around the four sides of the temple explaining the Buddha's life in chronological order – this they did with an elegance and realism devoid of flowery degeneracy. Emotion began to overcome Spenser as he saw the outlines, but he suppressed it and came forward to examine one of the figures closely, rejected it and moved on to the next. He gave the buddhas no chance to move or to talk to him.

The upper row was too high to be got at quickly. That left the forty statues around the bottom, from which he had to choose twenty.

The soldiers had by then caught up with him. 'This one,' he ordered. It was of the Buddha as a child, having not yet seized his destiny. The lips were tender. Such innocent lips. Unviolated. No. Brilliant. He caressed the lips with his fingers. They felt warm. 'They're only mortared into place. A little leverage will get them out. Don't worry about the lacquer chipping. It has to come off anyway.' He looked back towards the Shans who stared at him without moving. They were in bare feet. Their running shoes must have been left at the door. They had clustered together in a group and now stared around the hall and at Spenser. There was awe on their faces, but it was more than that. More an expression of shock. Standing in bare feet in their bizarre uniforms they appeared tiny. The hall soared above them, while the jungle had been fitted close to their measure. He realized that Eddie was not with them. 'This one,' he repeated.

Blake materialized from the shadows with a crowbar and jammed it beneath. The sound echoed around the corridor and on into the central maze. He levered with the full weight of his body. The statue moved sideways. He looked straight at a soldier. 'Get the slings.' It might have been a commandment of the Lord, but no one moved. He released his weight and the statue settled back into its place.

'Temple,' one of the men called out. The silence of the others was in agreement.

The appearance of Jalaw carrying the slings into the hall caused a momentary interruption. Blake walked over and slipped his way into the midst of the soldiers. They were obliged to move aside and to spread out around him. He was a good foot taller than any of them.

'This was a temple,' Blake said in Shan. Spenser made Jalaw translate. 'Now it is finished. No one comes to pray. We are here to make fools of the Burmans. This was their temple. They keep it as a memory of their power. We will show they have none. We will take their buddhas. We will not destroy them.' He put his hands on the shoulders of two and led them towards the statues. 'This is a Burman place.' The others followed. 'Take the slings.'

He levered the statue again and within a minute everyone was working. The first sling was stretched out before the statue, where two soldiers knelt to the floor with their hands in prayer, then stood to manhandle the stone forward. Spenser walked on to choose the others from around the square of the temple. How little there had been in the vague, flat photographs – from which he had tried to work – compared to this reality. He had taken a mallet and a chisel with him. Now he scratched an X beside each statue he wanted.

But to make that choice, he had to relent and open his heart to their magic. Before long he could feel them beside him, moving and talking. They communicated with the tier above and those with the next level and so on up to the niches where Spenser's eyes could see only darkness until all seven tiers were filled with life. Sometimes the sounds seemed close, harsh, unholy. These were rats, he thought, or perhaps snakes. The temples were famous for their cobras – at home because Pagan was abandoned. He reached the north side, then the north hallway where there was a second colossal figure. An idea came to him. He walked farther down the hallway into an inner corridor, turned right and shone his light on to the facing wall. There was a row of bas-reliefs. He examined them one after the other and, as expected, found a damaged scene – the remains of the fragment he had bought in Bangkok for Percival Gordon. With his tools he hammered carefully at the stone; it showed the Buddha seated with three fingers of his left hand touching the earth. On the edge he felt the legs of the disciple, which had been missing from the piece in Bangkok. The stone came out intact. It was three inches by two and only an inch thick. The edge running down the centre of the scene was sharp and curved. He slipped it into his pocket, then turned to find his way back to the central hall. A yard behind him, Santana was waiting in the darkness. He blocked the corridor. Spenser had not heard him come, nor could he see the expression on the man's face. Spenser looked to see if there was a way clear behind him. It was a dead end. He forced himself to speak,

'What are you doing here?'

Santana came forward out of the shadows until he was very close. Even clearly seen, it was impossible to read his expression. 'I said I would kill you.' He raised the pistol in his right hand.

Spenser started lifting his light to blind the man, but stopped himself. Santana would probably fire blind. He was impervious to surprise. Spenser knew he had to break the silence. 'Then Blake would kill you and he would still take the statues. Don't you see? You're not stealing them. I am. And you're not selling them. I am. It's my responsibility. What's your rush to judge me? I have more love for these buddhas than this empty place could ever give them. Even the people I sell them to will want the buddhas for their beauty. Here they are dying. You said on the trail that you left Blake and Eddie to themselves; that they should leave you. How am I worse? All I asked you to do was ship the statues. If you don't want to I'll find someone else. You should worry about yourself, Santana. Judge yourself. That was what you told me.' He waited for the Spaniard to say or do something. The pistol was pointed and steady, but nothing happened. There was silence. 'What do you expect of me?' Spenser threw at him. 'How am I supposed to guess your standards?' Still Santana said nothing. Spenser put his hand out and pushed the gun aside. There was no resistance. 'I don't understand you. Why come with us? Here they are nothing but stone sculpture.

There was more hope in your old monk. I want to bring them back to life.' He brushed by towards the outer corridor. 'I'm sorry, but I don't understand why you came.'

There were no sounds of footsteps following, though that meant nothing as Santana moved silently. He walked on the darkest side with his light off, forcing himself not to run. When he found the others, he stayed close to them and set about leading the Shans to the marked statues.

The last of the buddhas was loaded just before six a.m., with its face, like those of the other nineteen, turned forward and a sack pulled over for protection. Blake dragged the temple doors closed and replaced the chain as best he could; then climbed up on to the back of the truck, where the men had squeezed into the little remaining space. Santana appeared silently from the fields at the last moment and climbed into a corner. The nervousness, which had run through the soldiers while they were in the dark corridors in the act of stealing, evaporated as the Ananda receded. They talked quietly to each other until the last of the 5,000 ruins of Pagan was behind and the truck was on the open road. The thud of the pot-holes in the tarmac came as a sign of release with the truck speeding up, creating a rhythm from the broken pattern of the road. Suddenly the men became boisterous, shouting and joking. Only Santana and Eddie sat in silence, each of them closed upon himself.

Spenser joined in the laughter without understanding what was being said; but behind his pleasure there was an empty feeling and he fell into depression. Blake nudged him with his foot from across the truck,

'As promised.' Spenser gave only a slight nod in response. Blake nudged him again and offered a sympathetic smile. 'It always looks easy when it goes well.' There was a pulpit edge to his voice.

Six hours later they were labouring back up the wall of the Shan plateau with the extra weight of the statues forcing them to stop every few miles to cool the motor. At 2,000 feet – half-way – they drove under a layer of cloud and rain began to fall.

Blake pulled aside the tarpaulin to stare out at the downpour. After a time he said, 'A freak storm.' That answered no questions, so he added, 'We are ahead of schedule.' It was an assertion, not an apologetic remark.

By the time they reached the caves, where their remaining soldiers had waited, it was dark. They spent the night in dryness and were woken by the arrival of the ten mules and ten handlers at the first sign of dawn; all, that is, except Santana, who had smoked himself into oblivion the night before.

The rest of the party set about loading the mules in the rain. The statues were thick at the base, with a fairly straight back and a tapered front, which meant tying them on upside down, their backs against the mules and their fronts facing out. They were carefully wrapped inside the burlap sacks before being lifted into the rope baskets. Still their form came through clearly. Blake had them all unloaded and sent Jalaw off to get more sacks. With a double wrapping the form of the Buddha was lost.

The rain stopped at noon, just as their long unwieldy caravan of animals and men was ready to set off. They took this as a good omen; so good that Eddie came out of the depression that had held him since Pagan, unless it was his relief at getting back to what he knew.

He changed their marching orders. Only five men were sent twenty minutes ahead, followed by the mules and the whites. The rearguard was half an hour behind with twenty men, watching for signs of a Burmese search party.

The good omen lasted until mid-afternoon, when clouds appeared, wet earth turning to light mud as they advanced. With rain falling steadily they were wrapped into semi-isolation by their ponchos, unable to talk to each other without shouting, and sweating under their rubber protection in the warm air. The sweat drew mosquitoes that began to hang thick over the trail and managed to find their way beneath the layers of clothing. It was an isolation that suited no one except Santana, who had closed himself into a heavy, unbreakable silence and walked at the end of the central group, with only his son Lik behind him.

Night fell before they reached the first river, but Blake insisted they move on. He wanted to be well into the hills before the Burmese pulled themselves together enough to do some reconnaissance, which would soon pick out the caravan. A garrison sent out from Mawkmai could intercept them easily. Spenser stood waiting in the mud on the river bank for the ferry to come over and found himself working through a calculation that he guessed Blake had already made. The rain was slowing them. The mules were slowing them. The strain of keeping eleven animals and forty-two men on the move at a steady pace left them with the impression that they were making good time, but it had taken a full day to reach the river. On their way up the trail they had covered that distance in two hours. And now they were faced by the first of a long series of ferries. With the rain, the river was already moving faster and, if the rain continued, each river would move faster still. More important – each ferry had taken the original group across in two trips. But animals were another matter. This raft could only take one mule at a time. Others might manage two.

All three whites went over with the first crossing to the village on the other side. The ferryman's hut had a wooden porch with an overhang – beneath this the party squatted on the boards to wait. In a few minutes they were surrounded by villagers, huddled under cloth caps and straw hats, their faces lost in the rain and the darkness. They squeezed up to the edge of the porch, until the ferryman's wife rushed out to shout and push them back.

She brought a paraffin lamp and tea and offered to sell them food. When she produced a leaf basket of wild strawberries, Spenser bought it and gave a handful to Blake before forcing some on Santana, who crouched in his dripping poncho staring, not at the villagers, but through them into the night. He allowed a few berries to be tipped into his hand. These he ate without interest, then pulled out a knife to work at his nails. His son had stayed down by the river to watch the animals crossing. He was not there to gather up the clippings.

They waited an hour. Still three animals were on the other side. Frightened by the rain and the raft and the shouting in the dark, each of them balked before being loaded. In the midst of the mules already across, a villager ran from one to the other feeling the sacks and smelling them. The handlers chased her away, but she crept back in the shadows. They chased her away again. She ran over to the ferry master's house and pushed her way through the other peasants to get up to the edge of the porch. There she leaned forward to stare at the white men. They couldn't help but notice the harelip and the crazy look. Her tongue ran repeatedly up into the deformity to clear away saliva. Her head was uncovered, the rain running down her face, her hair a tangled mess. The other peasants fell silent to watch her. She fixed on Santana and leaned up to within a few inches of his face to ask a question. It was a curious, unexpected voice – soft and graceful. But Santana spoke no Shan. He waved her away. When she didn't move, Blake volunteered an answer. She repeated it and disappeared through the crowd, towards the mules.

'What was that?' Spenser asked.

'Wanted to know what we were carrying. I told her jade.'

There was a shout from behind the crowd and the woman shoved her way back through. She took a quick look at the whites before turning to the peasants and shouting at them.

200

Her voice was completely different – wild and shrill. There was no reaction. She threw herself into the air and began waving her arms, first at the villagers, then at the men on the porch. Two peasants tried to hold her still, but she went on screaming in what became an uncontrolled chant.

Spenser felt the sound penetrating him. It was unbearable. 'What's going on?' Blake was listening to the mad woman carefully and paid no attention to the question. 'What's going on, Blake? Stop her.'

Blake smiled. 'She says we should not be allowed to pass. She says we are evil. But you see the villagers don't agree. They want us on our way before the Burmese turn up.'

'That's not all. What's she saying?'

'Forget it.' Blake turned away to call the ferryman's wife. He questioned her and relaxed. 'She's the local *aulan hsaya*. The witch.' He turned back to say that if she were not removed, they would not stay on the porch. In the interests of commerce, the witch was dragged off. She stopped screaming the moment they took hold of her, but kept her eyes on Santana so long as he was in sight.

'Local colour,' was Blake's only comment.

The rain paused, then started again as they left the village. Spenser waited on the porch until all the animals were past before setting off himself. He was in no hurry to go out into the night. As he walked away, a noise behind made him turn. He saw the witch run out from behind a house and throw herself on her knees near the porch. She scooped her hands into the mud and lifted them up before her eyes, with the black liquid running through her fingers. Spenser searched in his pockets. He had lost nothing. Perhaps one of the others had. He ran back to scare her off and when she saw him coming through the mud, she screamed and leapt away. Had she found it? He followed her to behind the first few houses, where the darkness of the village closed in. Blake and the caravan were probably out of hearing. He hesitated. From somewhere in the obscurity she mocked him. Crazy. The woman was just crazy he told himself, turning away. He went back and looked around in the mud and on the porch, but found nothing except two black clippings of Santana's nails. With his boot he swept these from the wood planks in disgust.

They walked through the rest of the night and crossed two more rivers. In the early morning Spenser and Santana were struck by violent pains and diarrhoea, which they put down to the wild strawberries. The caravan stopped until Spenser felt better, but Santana walked on with his stomach torn by cramps.

These stayed with him all day and on into the next, although he kept his silence so that the only visible signs were the slowness with which he walked and the strain on his face. That night he smoked three extra pipes of opium to calm the pain. It was there again in the morning and he was unable to eat even the few mouthfuls of rice which had been his diet. He walked on at the tail of the central group, still without a word of complaint, merely greyer – a greyness which became pallid as the days passed and the pain increased, as did the quantity of pipes. The others noticed little, buried as they were in their ponchos, their eyes fixed on the mud in search of hidden rocks that might turn an ankle, their attention held by the mosquitoes invariably lost within their clothing. Violets and honeysuckle lined the way.

On the afternoon of the fourth day, the caravan was stopped by a scream. Blake and Spenser ran back past the mules to find Santana sitting in the mud tearing at the laces of his boots and shouting,

'I feel them! I feel them!' He wrenched off the first boot and flung it aside. His sock was soaked with blood. He ripped it away and turned to the other boot. 'God! The rot! The rot!'

Blake drew his knife as he kneeled beside him. He took the foot in his hand, examined it, and flicked at the skin with his blade. 'Give me the other one.' He repeated the process before

202

standing up. 'Leeches already. Stay away from the bushes,' he said to Spenser. 'These are land leeches. They jump on to you from the leaves. You won't see them until they are full of blood.' He turned back to Santana. 'Be more careful. You know better.'

That night they stopped in a village. Spenser pulled off his boots to find his socks a dirty red and three swollen leeches inside. They had fallen off when they were satisfied, but the wounds kept bleeding. He had felt nothing. Another leech was edging through an air hole in his right boot. It was more like a maggot – pale white and an eighth of an inch long. It stood on end, dancing gracefully, smelling for skin, then leapt forward a fraction. Spenser crushed it between his fingers. He washed his wounds, with a feeling of disgust for his own skin which surprised him, and bandaged them. In the morning Blake made him soak his socks in salted water before putting them on. That may have reduced the attacks. Spenser couldn't judge. With the continuing rain the leeches multiplied and multiplied, until even he began to pick them out where they waited on the edges of the trail. And each night he had new bleeding sores, while the old wounds festered quietly.

The Shans dealt with the epidemic by rolling their trousers up as high as possible and walking in bare feet with a long knife in their hand. They had smooth, hairless legs and their eyes could pick out a leech the second it landed. The knife flicked and it was gone. They also chain-smoked loosely rolled green cigars, lighting the next one with the last one. The smoke was meant to keep off leeches and Spenser imitated them, though the raw taste of the cigars was too strong to put up with for more than thirty minutes at a time.

On the sixth day Santana walked so slowly that Blake forced him up on the horse. It was unclear whether this slowness came from stomach pains and weakness or from such quantities of opium that he was in a permanently drugged state. Lik walked beside the horse handler with the same devotion that he gave to preparing his father's pipes and cleaning his wounds. This sickness produced a curious change in the caravan. Eddie's men, the Shans, began to rally around Santana. They brought him leaves meant to calm his stomach. They took turns walking behind him to make encouraging remarks. At first this change from indifference to devotion made no sense to Spenser. But then he remembered that Santana had been the only one to hold on to his Buddhist devotion at the Pagan temples. Eddie confirmed that this was the reason. Santana's sickness brought out the soldiers' sense of shame and by ministering to him as they might to a monk they hoped to wash away their own betrayal.

That same morning Spenser's rice and hard-boiled egg had slid through him in a violent immediate motion. He had been obliged to wash out his trousers and wear them even wetter than before. There was no continuing pain, but he would gladly have ridden on the horse, had it been free. The next day his stomach was no better and he thought of Khun Minh's man, Lao Sa, waiting for them in comfort in his dry hut somewhere ahead on the shore of the Salween. It was a depressing image.

They were another five days walking and sleeping in the mud or in village huts before they reached the cliff above the Salween late on the twelfth afternoon. The trail, which had seemed steep on their way north, was now also slippery. Santana was obliged to climb off the horse. As they slid and struggled their way down the rocks and roots, the roar of the invisible river rose up with a force far greater than that they had left behind. The smooth warmth was gone from the sound. Instead it shouted at them in the voice of an avenging god.

They found Khun Minh's camp at the bottom, clinging to the edge of the water that had swollen to bury the beach and now rushed by, grey and brown, laden with debris and eager to rip whatever it could from the banks. Lao Sa came out beneath a poncho,

'So you have them! You have done it! They can't catch you now. Come in out of this filthy stuff. We must celebrate. I have whisky. Not Mekong. Real whisky!'

# 14

Lao Sa threw open the door. 'We must dry you out. Come in. Come in. We must warm you up.'

He rushed across to add wood to his fire. The cabin was built on the highest ground with a large window overlooking the river. Inside was a bed, a table and two chairs – all luxuries in such a place. The rest was bare board. They threw off their ponchos and dropped to the floor to unlace their boots. Spenser counted eighteen sores on his legs before looking up to find Lao Sa bent over him expressing concern.

The tongue clicked. 'Oh, I see they've started. I hate these leeches! I hate them. And now I shall have to walk out of here in the time of their prosperity.' He dashed back across the room to grab his bottle of whisky from a shelf and filled a cup, which he emptied. 'At least we must celebrate before we go.' He held out the same cup. There was no other. 'Here. Who'd like some? Blake, you used to be a drinker.'

Blake shook his head and joined Eddie at the window. There was neither screen nor glass – just a shutter held up by poles.

'It's rising fast.' Eddie was watching the water toss a mangled log about in its arms.

'At least we don't have to cross in a week's time.'

'Leave that!' Lao Sa shouted. He had given the mug to Spenser, who drained it in the hope whisky would kill his stomach pains. 'Tomorrow we cross. Tonight we give thanks.

Hey, you Christians, aren't those the words? Eddie, come drink to the Shans. Hey, you've buggered the Burmans! Drink to that.' He held out the bottle.

Eddie took a long drink from it and Lao Sa matched him. There was good reason to celebrate. Now they were back in the jungle, the Burmese could not hope to find them. The game was won. This sense of victory spread to the soldiers in the other huts. Drink began appearing here and there and the division between the two armies melted. Among them was Lao Sa's heavily tattooed runner, who had rediscovered Spenser's horse handler and was again devoting himself to someone the others considered insignificant. This time the drink helped their conversation.

When darkness had fallen and his guests were at ease, Lao Sa withdrew into a corner where he wrote a letter. Spenser watched him wrap this sheet around a small gold amulet and wrap the whole package in heavy paper. When Lao Sa went outside, Spenser crossed to the window. From there he saw the letter being given to a man in peasant's clothing, who then began across the river on the ferry. Spenser took Blake aside to explain what he had seen.

'Relax,' Blake replied immediately. 'Minh would want to be kept informed. We use messengers here the way you would probably use the telephone.'

When Lao Sa reappeared in the cabin, he brought a second bottle of whisky. Early in the morning he and Eddie began singing English songs they had been taught as boys at school; the sort of songs Spenser hated, but he was drunk enough to join in. The three men fell asleep arm in arm on the floor. Blake had not touched the whisky, but he had listened with amusement and was the last to close his eyes.

He and Spenser were woken by shouting. Through the window there was a damp, grey light. Around them the others still slept. They went outside to find Lao Sa's tattooed runner fighting with Spenser's horse handler, or rather, the handler trying to get away from him. It resembled the sort of stupidity that follows a night of drinking. Blake told them to stop, but was ignored.

'What's going on?' Lao Sa had appeared in the doorway.

The runner could not control his excitement. He held an arm around the man's neck and shouted that he was a deserter from Khun Minh's army. He had run away seven months before. His name was Ba Thein. By now everyone was standing outside listening. The handler had lost his calm, gentle look. He was flushed and tried to interrupt, denying that his name was Ba Thein, but Lao Sa came down from the porch into the rain to stare at him and declared that he did, in fact, remember the face. He ordered the man to be tied up. At that the handler tore himself free and plunged through the soldiers, appealing for help to Eddie's men, who were sympathetic but had not been told what to do. While they vacillated uneasily, the others caught hold of him. He struggled on, shouting for someone to help.

Spenser watched all of this still in a haze of alcohol. He said to Blake, 'That's my handler.'

Blake nodded but said nothing. It was like a play; the handler was almost comic in his excitement.

'What's he done?' Spenser insisted.

'He is a deserter.' The moral edge had disappeared from Blake's voice. It was cold and distant.

'What do you mean a deserter? I hired that man. He's my responsibility.'

'It is none of our business.'

Spenser took hold of Blake's arm to turn him around. 'He's my responsibility! Yours!'

'We are twenty-five to fifty-five.' At first Spenser didn't grasp his meaning. Blake concentrated on him with a measure of contempt. 'Do you want to get killed? For that matter, do you want your statues?'

The handler had dragged himself and his captors towards

the two whites. He screamed directly at Blake, repeating the American's name again and again in his appeal. He was belching with fear. While Lao Sa watched with a wry smile, Blake stared impassively at the man. They forced a gag into his mouth, at which Blake said quietly to Spenser,

'He belongs to Khun Minh. I do not like Minh. I hate him. But the rules are clear. You cannot have safe passage if you don't accept the rules.' His eyes were wide and enfolding.

In the confusion Spenser saw Lao Sa put a thin colourless hand on the blue arm of his runner and take the man aside to talk urgently with him. Seconds later the runner disappeared. Spenser thought at first that this was an attempt to drop the matter peacefully by removing the instigator from the scene. But the handler was not released and went on forcing out indecipherable sounds while he was dragged through the camp along the river bank towards a copse of trees. When they were gone from sight only an uneasy feeling remained, the soldiers of both armies waiting with a sheepish air. Spenser broke away from Blake to run after them. He had no idea what was happening, let alone what he could do, but he could not stand like a zombie, waiting.

Near the trees he thought he heard them talking, though the words had no form. It was more like a drum without resonance. This rhythm led him into a clearing where he came upon the five men. The soldiers had found wooden poles and they now stood spaced around their prisoner clubbing him in a rotating order. The air of the clearing was filled with the echo of wood on flesh. The handler was on his knees. One of the blows had knocked the gag from his mouth, but he was not screaming or crying out. Only when a club hit his torso was there a hollow rushing sound of air. On the ends of the clubs there were delicate frescoes of red that held Spenser's eyes mesmerized while the fence poles danced and the frescoes became like torches and the clearing was speckled with the same colour.

As the body no longer moved, the soldiers dropped their weapons on to the ground and walked out of the clearing past Spenser. They were flushed from their work. He stood alone for a time which he did not measure, then vomited into the grass. These convulsions went on and on. When he came back into the village, no one asked him what he had seen.

Only Santana said kindly, 'None of them works for him out of love.' They were his first normal words since Pagan. Spenser went into the cabin in search of the whisky. There was none left. The others were quietly packing their kits, except Eddie, who stood by the window. He motioned Blake over and pointed at a boat lurching away through the current towards the other bank of the river. It was one half of the ferry. The second boat was already on the far side, drawn up behind its reduced breakwater.

'Give me your field-glasses,' Eddie said.

Blake handed them over before instructing Lao Sa in a business-like way, 'You had better get your boats back on this side. We're crossing immediately.'

'Time enough. Don't rush me.' Lao Sa pointed at Spenser. 'Look at yourselves. You need a good breakfast.' He laughed. 'At least, I do.'

'Get the boats back.' It was Blake's church elder voice. 'We are loading in an hour.'

Lao Sa threw his hands up in mock submission and pulled on his poncho. 'I'll see what I can organize.' He banged out through the door.

The moment the door shut, Eddie came to the table. 'The tattooed man. Lao Sa's runner.'

'Well?' Blake asked.

'He was crossing on that boat. He's gone up the trail.'

Blake didn't appear surprised. He turned away, lost in contemplation.

'What are we going to do?' Eddie called after him.

At first there was no reply. Blake stared out of the window

at the rain and the rushing water of the Salween. 'Warn your men. We will see what happens.' There was no sign of concern in his voice.

Spenser managed his first words since the handler's death. 'What about the messenger last night?'

'What messenger?' Eddie half-shouted.

'I told Blake.'

'Blake!' Eddie went over to his friend. 'What's happening?'

'Don't panic,' was all he replied, before sitting quietly in a corner.

'Don't panic!' Eddie repeated. 'Don't panic! I asked you a question.' But no answer came and he was lost in indecision, staring across at Blake.

It was half an hour before Lao Sa reappeared. 'All is organized.' He threw off his poncho with relief. 'In the meantime, food.'

'Skip it,' Eddie cut in.

'Oh, no. Do as you like, but I'm hungry. You forget, I have to come with you.' The door opened. 'Anyway, here it is.'

The two soldiers pushed in carrying trays, which they set down on the table. Lao Sa pulled off the cloths protecting the food from the rain.

'River fish! How can you resist?'

Spenser glanced at the two large fish and attempted to reassemble a memory of hunger without success. Then he noticed Santana get up from the floor in the corner with his son's help and stumble to the window, where he stared across the river. From behind he appeared so fragile that even to look at him might have caused pain. Without comment he made his way back to the corner to fiddle in his pack.

Lao Sa had thrown himself down on a chair and attacked the food with his fingers. He glanced up long enough to catch Eddie's attention. 'Look at this.' He raised a small white vegetable between his fingers. 'We are all Shans. What meaning has politics – capitalism or communism – in a country where they still take the time to pick the heads off the bean sprouts.' He laughed and went back to eating alone.

After a few minutes, Blake joined him, then Eddie, both picking at the food with their fingers, but not sitting down. Spenser alone saw Santana come across the room to stand close behind Lao Sa. The Spaniard paused like a bird of prey, then his right hand flew to grab Lao Sa's hair and wrenched it hard to one side. The man crashed on to the floor. He tried to scream but his mouth was full of food that choked out on to the boards. By the time he looked up, Santana's revolver was pointed at him.

'It's a trap,' the Spaniard rasped. 'Go look. The boats don't move.' Lao Sa tried to scramble to his feet, but Santana kicked him in the face. 'His runner goes to Khun Minh. They will cut us off. Stand up.' he ordered.

The man pulled himself off the floor into a chair, where Santana again held him by his hair from behind. Through all of this the others had not moved. Blake still seemed lost in contemplation, but Eddie looked through the window.

'Santana's right.' He went outside under the guise of talking to one of his men, then came back into the hut. 'All his soldiers are standing around out there with their rifles.'

'Finished chat?' Santana said. His face was flushed from exertion, making him appear surprisingly alive. He bowed down over Lao Sa as he pulled the hair to one side. 'How you call the boats back?'

'By radio.'

'Where?'

'At the dock.'

Santana let go of his hair long enough to grab the man's right ear. He pulled it out and up, stretching it flat. 'Now you call the boats back.'

He put the barrel of his gun against the stretched transparent skin and pulled the trigger. The appendage split into shreds like a cabbage, out of which blood began to spurt.

Lao Sa was thrown across the table by the shock. Two of his soldiers burst through the door, but stopped when they saw the pistol at their officer's head.

Santana snatched up the cloth that had covered the food and shook off the debris of fish before handing it to Lao Sa. He waited for the man to be capable of understanding, then ordered into his other ear, 'Tell them they call the boats back.'

Lao Sa gave the instruction in an uneven voice. Once the door had closed behind the soldiers, Santana's face drained to its normal grey and he began to tremble. Blake took the gun from his hand.

'Help him to sit down,' he ordered Spenser, who in moving found his hand to be clutched around the buddha fragment in his pocket. 'Next,' Blake said to Lao Sa, 'we are going to call in one of your soldiers. You will order them all back into their huts. They are to leave their weapons on the ground.' He had put himself back in command with no hint that he had ever let it go.

Lao Sa was by then moaning with pain and slipping into shock, but he gave the order to a man who was followed outside by Eddie, to ensure the instructions were obeyed. When the mud was littered with weapons, the SSA soldiers collected them up and threw them into the river. Without any protest, Lao Sa's men allowed themselves to be herded into one of the barracks.

The boats arrived and had to be strapped together with their planks, after which a pair of mules and ten soldiers were loaded. The soldiers were to make certain the other bank was safe before climbing up to hold the top of the cliff. Eddie added his fastest man to the load, with instructions to overtake Lao Sa's runner and kill him. If he failed, he was to keep on to the base camp at Gwe Houk and send back help. At the last moment, Blake sent Jalaw, his Bible translator-cum-chauffeur-cum-bodyguard, along with him.

The mule handlers did their job badly because they were

nervous. They weren't the kind of men who went on risky caravans; even in the opium collection season they didn't carry drugs. They were simple servants of the black market – transporters of radios and shoes – and suddenly they were caught in the middle of something incomprehensible. They pestered Eddie for explanations, to which he gave reassurance instead of answers and kept them moving.

The crossing made matters worse. They had all done it in the dry season. But now they stood on the bank watching the first load set out, with the precarious catamaran pitching from side to side as the boats tried to keep even with each other and the current. If one were to fall behind, the boards would twist and send everyone into the water. The men clung to each other and to the animals, the whole compact group swaying heavily, their heads bowed beneath the sheet of rain. From then on the remaining handlers held back and had to be forced to cross. After the second load Eddie saw through his glasses that those on the other side were not starting up the trail, either from fear or from reluctance to climb the cliff-like slope. He crossed over himself with a few soldiers to get them under way.

Six hours later all but a pair of the mules had made the crossing. Blake came out of the hut holding Lao Sa, a pistol at his head to avoid any misunderstanding by the soldiers who watched from their barrack. Spenser, Santana and his son Lik followed him down to the dock, where they climbed aboard with the few remaining Shan soldiers. Not a word was exchanged. As the ferry drew away, Lao Sa's men came out and lined the shore. Their hands held weapons they had found inside.

The mules were in the centre for balance, with the men standing around the edge – Blake on the upstream side, Santana opposite him and Spenser at the bow with his back to the water holding on to the men farther from the edge for balance. The heads of the mules were just before him. It was the first time he had consciously noticed them since the caravan began. Their heads were gentle, bent low side by side, listening to the water strike beneath the boards. The soft fawn of their bodies faded into a softer white near the eyes.

The two handlers began chattering to each other the moment they saw Blake get on board with his pistol and Lao Sa with his shattered, bloody ear scarcely bandaged. Blake lowered the weapon out of sight and told them to tend to their animals. They stopped talking, but the mules sensed the nervousness and moved on the slippery boards. Blake berated their handlers. This only frightened them. The ferry was by then into the current and began to pitch so that everyone's eyes were fixed on to the rushing water. They could feel the two engines struggling to maintain the course. The mule on the downstream side of the boards shied backwards and brayed, then balked towards the edge. His handler fought to keep control of the harness, whispering and chiding the animal until it calmed, but then a log rose out of the waves and glanced off the bow. The men shouted at the impact and the mule kicked out, moving hard to the edge. Santana's son ducked beneath the belly. But Santana was frozen between it and the water. Spenser grabbed hold of his poncho and yanked him forward.

Suddenly the mule saw the water looming up. It pushed in panic back towards the centre, causing the ferry to keel heavily to Blake's side. Everyone shifted in desperation. The ferry heaved the other way. The mule misjudged the roll and struck out with hooves. They flayed into the air till the animal lost all balance and pitched into the water carrying Santana's son caught up in its legs. The two bodies were sucked away from the boat by the churning current, the boy howling with fear and struggling to get free of his poncho. The others heard this without seeing, lost as they were in trying to find their own balance and to steady the other mule. Only Santana called out to Lik in a plaintive cry. The pilot on that side threw a rope with elegant nonchalance high into the air where it floated above them before dropping on to the boy, already a good twenty yards downstream. Lik clutched at it and sent the line slipping away. The pilot yanked it back into reach. This time Lik caught hold and twisted his body around it, still screaming, which he did the whole time he was dragged in. His cry was taken up in terror by the mule driving its legs to keep afloat with 400 pounds of sculpture still strapped to its back. The stone gradually took its effect and all the animal could do was bray mournfully as the current carried it downstream and beneath the surface.

Santana squeezed his son with an emotion he would have regretted in normal times, a binding emotion; but when the noise of the mule was gone, he looked around and realized that their pack was missing. There had been little inside except the opium.

'You lose it?'

Lik nodded in fear. His father slapped him. There was no way to avoid the blow and the boy waited for a second, but Spenser caught the hand and whispered,

'You'll panic the other mule.'

The ferry fell silent as everyone tried to gain control of himself. Spenser found his eyes had fixed on Lao Sa. And yet his mind was filled by the two statues gone beneath the water. Which had they been? The wrappings made it impossible to know, but he had some idea which pieces had been loaded on which mules and the Buddha as a young boy had almost certainly been one of those lost. He remembered the innocent face, the warm lips he had touched in the temple. They faded and Lao Sa's image was in their place. Innocuous. There was nothing memorable about it, and yet, something radiated from the man. Not emotion. Not fear. Not even hatred. He thought again of the lost statues. Not just lost to him, but completely lost. Waves of life had flowed from them – waves of burning emotion which he accepted at communion on the altar of genius. No human values were involved. Nothing moral. Nothing conscious. Only genius and beauty. Yet the waves coming from Lao Sa contradicted these feelings. Since his first meeting with the man he had sensed vague, repelling vibrations. The death of the handler had focused them. Spenser knew it was evil. Not a directed or lunatic evil. Apathy lay at the heart of it. Indifference to the state of other men and to civilization. This he knew, but now staring at the empty face on the other side of the raft he felt the evil, felt it like a steel blade cutting away the memory of the lost statues and slicing the images to nothing. But if that were so, beauty was not a neutral state as he had always told himself. His own indifference to the ordinary was also evil. What had he been searching for all that time? What kind of false isolation?

The pilot threw a line to Eddie, waiting alone on the river bank. They drove the remaining mule on up the cliff before pushing the two halves of the ferry out into the current with unpinned grenades in the hulls. The boats drifted thirty yards before the grenades blew them in half.

Lao Sa and the two pilots waited crouched on the ground.

'Kill him,' Eddie said.

Blake sent the two pilots a few yards away before turning to Lao Sa in a quiet voice, 'What message did you send with the runner?'

Lao Sa bent his head sharply back to look up into Blake's face. The rain struck his eyes. 'Why don't you trust me? Why follow the paranoia of an addict?' There was no reply. 'What could I tell Minh? That you were safely back. That we were on our way.'

'Listen to the pig!' Eddie shouted. 'How many lies are you made of? Is there any part of you that isn't a lie?'

Lao Sa twisted around to look at him with contempt. 'Don't be hysterical. You talk like a woman. I have no reason to lie.'

Blake lifted his foot and slowly pushed Lao Sa over into the mud. 'If you waste my time I will kill you. What did you say to Khun Minh?'

'I told you! That we are on our way.'

'What will he do with the information?' Blake began to play with the pistol still in his hand. He cocked it, then as if for amusement, kicked mud at Lao Sa.

'I don't know.'

'You are wasting my time.'

'I suppose he'll send out men.'

'Send or lead?'

'What does it matter? Why would he tell me that? You know him. I'm nothing. I hardly exist.' The bitterness in his voice was quite real. 'He tells me nothing.'

Blake nodded in agreement. 'He will come to trap us.'

'Hurry up, Matthew.' Eddie touched Blake's shoulder as if to wake him. 'Kill him. We know what's going on.'

Blake shook him off. 'You have a smaller ferry down river, don't you?'

'Ten miles,' Lao Sa volunteered.

'We might have two days on them.' He waved Santana's pistol towards the other side of the river, where already they could see the activity of organization. But they will soon catch up.' He balanced the revolver reflectively in his hand. 'We will take him with us. The pilots too, at least to the first village.'

Eddie started up the hill rather than admit that he had given in. At first Santana slowed the pace, groaning as he raised himself from step to step, his body buried deep in his poncho. Even so, they soon caught up to the last mule and Blake had to push by to speed the handler. There was little he could do. The animals moved at a certain pace, neither faster nor slower, which was how they managed to carry so much so far without collapsing or slipping. It was dark before they found the entire caravan crowded together at the top awaiting the order to camp. The handlers stumbled about in the mud, trying to raise the courage to say they were turning back, but the darkness, the rain, the pressing jungle caused such confusion that they couldn't organize themselves. The air at that height and that hour was cool, so that any pause left the body shivering in dampness.

Eddie pushed through the mêlée, ordering his soldiers to get everyone on the move. He argued and threatened and eventually took the lead himself, stopping just long enough to shout back to Blake, 'Kill him. I won't march with him.' He disappeared among the shadows of moving animals and of men walking with paraffin lamps to light their way.

When the advance soldiers and the mules were out of sight, Blake pushed Santana up on to the horse and sent him off, leaving only Spenser and the rearguard. Lao Sa had said nothing all this time. He was crouched in the mud, a thin layer of soaked clothes clinging to his skin.

Blake wandered up to him with almost a jaunty gait. 'Eddie is right. I cannot justify keeping you alive.' He cocked the pistol and moved it against Lao Sa's head.

The man was trembling with fear and cold. 'Listen, will you leave me if I tell you one thing?'

'One thing?'

'I'm more on your side than you think. I can save you.'

'We are saved.'

'Come on, Blake.' Lao Sa was whining. 'You know better than that. Listen. Yesterday, after you arrived, I sent a first runner.'

'We know that.'

'To Chu's daughter.'

Even in the dark Blake's astonishment could be sensed. 'Shirley Chu? What for?'

'She wants back in, Blake. She came to me. She wants to get Khun Minh.'

'What was in the note?'

'That Minh would be sent the same information twenty-four hours after her. The man I sent works for me, not for Minh. He'll take the message to a butcher in Mae Hong Son who works for the Chus.' Lao Sa stopped to see if so much detail was having any effect. Blake stood impassively above him, waiting. 'I didn't sign it, just in case. I wrapped it around a buddha Shirley Chu gave me. She'll remember.'

'What does all of that mean?'

'Don't be stupid, Blake.' He was talking up into the rain, water running into his mouth. 'It means I'm giving her twenty-four hours on Minh. She knows what he'll do. She knows he'll come to cut you off. She's smart.'

'And what will she do with this information?'

Lao Sa fell silent. At last he said, 'Truly, I don't know. She asked me for a sign of good faith. I've given it.'

'Good faith!' Blake mocked him. 'The words stink in your mouth.' But he thought about their meaning for a time, then turned to Lao Sa with a sharp kick that knocked him over into the mud. He shone a light along the trees lining the trail until he found a strong one and cut off the lower branches with a knife, 'Bring him here.'

The soldiers carried the almost limp figure forward.

'Tie him upright to the trunk.' Blake stood back idly turning over his knife in one hand and holding his light up in the other so they could see. 'With his arms out.'

'Hardly the type to merit a crucifixion,' Spenser said from over his shoulder.

Blake ignored the remark. When the soldiers had finished, he examined the knots, then ordered the men to move on. While they filed out of sight, he gazed in a dreamy manner on to Lao Sa, who had paid no attention to what was being done to him and now hung, like a common thief, with his eyes closed. At last only Spenser remained as a furtive witness. Blake was by then so close to the victim that, in the shadows thrown by their lights, he appeared to be caressing him with his lips. He drew back abruptly and spat into Lao Sa's face.

The Shan's head didn't move. Blake walked away from him, hesitated, and walked back. With a clumsy gesture he wiped the spit from the man's skin. 'Let's go.' He took Spenser by the neck and pushed him forward.

Spenser shoved the hand away. He stopped to look back at Lao Sa and felt waves of evil floating off the slight figure half hidden by the brush. No. Blake was wrong. He understood nothing about the nature of man. Spenser took hold of Blake's poncho, 'You must kill him. You can't leave him here. You can't make a deal with that kind of filth. Eddie was right. If you won't kill him, I will.'

In the half light of their lamps, Blake leered at him. 'Anything to get your statues. Already happy to kill?'

Spenser struck out at him and missed. Blake seemed to have dodged. They stood immobile on the track, not looking at each other. It wasn't for the buddhas, Spenser said to himself. That much he knew. In the darkness Lao Sa had taken on a grotesque form. To Spenser's eyes it was the deformation of evil. A physical emanation that would destroy all he loved. 'Don't judge me, Blake. I'm not a parishioner. Just kill him.'

'You don't understand.' Blake's voice was solicitous. Out of place. 'Better to leave him here with the leeches. He is not very competent. In a few days, when his friends get to him, he will be even less competent. They will have a new leader by then so it will take time for them to sort that out.'

Spenser knew the argument was false, but the will slipped out of him and he allowed himself to be led forward. What was Blake's game? Why had he feigned indecision on the other bank of the river? Spenser was certain he had feigned. Something was escaping him, but he had no idea where to look. There was no support for him in this mud and tangle, neither physical nor moral; not even from his statues, hidden as they were beneath their wrapping.

He walked for a time in silence before Blake took the lead,

then slowed and asked over his shoulder, 'Did you know that we would have to steal from the temple?'

'Of course,' Spenser replied quickly.

'Why didn't you tell me in the beginning?'

'You wouldn't have taken me.'

Blake had no answer to such bluntness. He moved his head in understanding and walked on.

They pushed themselves through the night, overtaking first the rear guard, then the caravan picking its way down the mountain-side. Santana was at its tail, swaying dangerously on the horse. His confrontation with Lao Sa followed by the climb up the bank of the Salween had so drained him that he no longer tried to avoid the branches laden with thorns and leeches. Eddie's soldiers persisted in taking turns walking behind to encourage him.

This undergrowth had ripped at the sacking around the statues and in the grey morning light, faces peered through, upside-down and close to the ground. Orchids burst out from the overhanging rock or in clusters from trees, but it was the gaze of the buddhas that held Spenser. Their reappearance was like a friend coming unexpectedly to offer reassurance and he hung back near the mules where this could be felt.

The caravans preceding them had also been caught by the early rain and had turned the dirt steps into a morass. Hooves had slipped one after the other into the same grooves, digging troughs increasingly deep. These were filled with water and too narrow for a foot. Between them were ridges a few inches thick, crowned by a hard and slippery surface resembling oiled glass. They ran across the track like rungs of a ladder laid on the ground.

The men balanced from ridge to ridge or skirted along the edge, pushing back the undergrowth. Either way they slipped through the mud up to their calves in constant risk of breaking an ankle. All except Spenser were now barefoot with their trousers rolled up.

They took all day to reach the first village, yet Blake would have pushed on for a second night had Santana's state, and Spenser's and even that of the handlers not made it impossible. Ten men were posted to hold the trail.

Santana was carried reverently up into the headman's house by Eddie's soldiers and laid near the cooking fire. This constant celebration of the Spaniard's right action at Pagan was something Blake appeared to find unbearable. There was nothing wrong with moral right in others if it didn't imply moral wrong in himself. To be put in the wrong by a marginal and an addict only made it worse. Eddie took it little better. He had been forced into a Christian position before his men. What's more, it was thanks to Santana that they had got across the Salween. Even Spenser was affected by guilt, though he reacted by taking Santana's side.

The cooking fire gave little heat; less than what seeped up from the water buffaloes beneath. The hut's walls were of matted leaves, as was the ceiling under which they stooped. A wooden chest against a wall constituted the furniture. Santana's son stripped him of his sodden clothing. Leech wounds were scattered over the body; five alone on his neck. Had the pallid skin not shivered, it might have been taken for that of a dead man. They wrapped him in blankets.

'Opium,' was Santana's only word.

Blake asked the headman, who denied he had any. It was impossible to know if this were the truth.

Spenser turned to Eddie, 'Someone in the village must use it.'

Eddie went out into the rain with disgust. He came back later to say there was none, then disappeared to check his men.

Spenser said under his breath to Blake, 'He's lying. What difference can it make to him?' There was no reaction. 'If the man needs it to kill the pain, why not?'

'I am not going to start searching the village.' Blake looked across at Santana. 'His problem is not pain.'

'Predestined to be a loser?' Spenser was surprised at his own bitterness. He could not have explained where it came from. 'Is that it?'

Blake began stripping off wet clothes and hanging them from rafters near the fire. 'You would do better to look after yourself.'

'I don't understand,' Spenser persisted. 'Eddie used to trade opium.'

'That was his choice.'

'And Santana? Whose choice is he?'

Blake walked over to crouch by Spenser. 'Eddie's father was an official in Lashio State. He had a weakness for opium which ruined his career. He's dead now. Eddie's younger brother prepared the pipes, like Santana's boy. Eventually he started smoking. He's still up in Lashio. His mother looks after him.'

They hadn't heard the footsteps on the stairs. Eddie crossed to the fire, his outline shaded by the smoke that spread through the room rather than rise into the rain. He sat down at the edge of the coals and popped out his glass eye, which he began cleaning. After some time, he twisted about to look at Spenser, without putting it back in.

Spenser said doggedly, 'Perhaps we'll meet some caravan handlers who use opium.'

'A caravan,' Blake laughed. 'Once the rain starts, everyone turns back. We won't meet a soul.'

Spenser pulled his socks off. An odour crept into the air. He examined the sores and realized it was they that smelt.

Santana's thighs had to be tied to the horse in the morning. As the men climbed, they were squeezed in by an explosion of growth until their vision was limited to a crack through the indigestible green. Near the mountain top the cloud and the jungle thinned to reveal a profusion of hanging orchids. It was like a breathing space. The caravan slowed and stretched apart without anyone exerting the will power to keep it bunched up. Spenser walked staring down at a buddha's face that melted into the final, liberating wisdom. Even Blake wandered off looking for the orchid he had promised Marea. It seemed a crazy thing to do, but Blake's strength made everything he did appear normal.

He was at the head of the caravan, where the trees were spread out and the ground reasonably clear. Here the orchids prospered in a climate so unhealthy that the leaves in the trees had a yellow tinge. He stopped and laid his rifle against an outcropping of rock from which orchids grew.

'Spenser, come here!' His thick fingers attempted to unfold the wet photograph. 'Look at this!'

The flowers had a mauve pod and three petals; two mauve and one rising above striped green. Spenser crouched to compare. A distant image of Marea clouded his mind. The real mauve had a texture of flesh; the pod suggested a relic of the human body discarded by evolution.

'Perhaps.'

'No!' Blake insisted, 'This is it. I'm sure it is.'

He bent close to cut away the plant with its flowers and rolled them in a cloth which he laid inside his pack, so mesmerized by his task that he ignored the shouting behind. The shots awoke him.

'Go on.' He gave Spenser a violent yet careful push. 'Get the animals moving faster. Quick. They can get around us on this open ground.'

He ran back through the brush while Spenser caught up with three mules preceded by Santana, tied on to his horse. The handlers had stopped with the first shot. Six animals were somewhere out of sight behind.

'Move! Move!' Spenser broke off a branch and struck the front mule. He ran back to the third animal.

The shots had a clean, cold, invisible sound, no more than

mildly hypnotic, but the handlers kept glancing over their shoulders and slowing the pace. Spenser suppressed this fear within himself by driving his legs faster from man to man, encouraging them and striking the mules. An almost imperceptible moan from the statues swept after him in anguish. He heard shots to the side, much closer. The animals shied off the trail, turning in disorder. He knew how near the soldier must be, but stopped himself from looking and beat the mules back on to the path. There was another shot and the handler next to him fell. There was no cry. Spenser shouted for help and snatched up the loose reins. Shots thudded close behind him. He turned to see blood spurt from the animal's neck. Colourful fountains. The mule reared and broke away through the brush towards its assassin, before falling to its knees and on to its side, wheezing with death. A buddha lay prone in its harness, rising and falling with each breath. Though Spenser could not see the face, he knew the figure's exact expression – a poignant pessimism so unexpected in a saint teaching. The statue reached out to him for help.

Panic cut its way through him. The other two animals had been abandoned. He threw himself behind a ledge and shouted again for help. There was a flurry of shots, then silence. Blake's voice floated coolly from a distance,

'Get off the ground! Keep them going!'

The fighting was again far away. Spenser found the two handlers and dragged them to their mules, but neither man moved forward. The animals needed to be led and both men were paralysed with fear. The third handler lay dead on the trail. A few yards ahead, Santana's horse turned in a circle around Lik, who held the reins, but sat on the ground crying. The Spaniard's hood was thrown off and his head rotated wildly in its socket, his teeth shaking with such violence that the sound came through the air in a clear rhythm.

Spenser had lost all sense of time. He noticed only that the firing eventually stopped. Blake reappeared and went straight to the first handler. He put a rifle to the man's head, moved the barrel to one side and fired. The man was electrified by the explosion and whipped his animal forward.

'We can discuss it with them later,' was all Blake said.

He had left Eddie behind to hold Lao Sa for one hour at a narrow piece of trail. By then it would be dark. Blake himself went on to find a defendable camp where he would have the advance guard dug before the caravan arrived. He put an arm around Spenser and squeezed him,

'Once we get down into the jungle, there is no way around us.' It was meant as encouragement. 'They shot one of Eddie's men.' Blake took him by the arm, 'Get them going will you.' He said it kindly. Spenser had never seen him so calm.

Close behind in the brush were two of the buddhas. He stared back at them. One was crushed by the dead mule. The other still reached out for help to be carried on. It was no longer a force of communion. The exquisite pessimism of the face betrayed resentment, as if asking why it had been brought so far to be adandoned, and Spenser thought of Lao Sa, who would soon walk down the trail with his innocuous air and find them lying there unprotected. And what would he think? What would he do? Spenser could feel anger and tears welling up. He forced the eight animals tight together and drove them on faster.


# 15


From that moment, Spenser was left to himself. Five men went ahead; the rest fought behind, falling back twenty, sometimes ten yards at a time from one narrow place to the next where Lao Sa's soldiers could pass only in full sight. Neither side was unfamiliar with the game.

That left Spenser in the middle, charged with the mules and the handlers and Santana and the whole reason for him being

226

there – the sixteen statues – hanging bare in their harnesses, staring upside-down at the world. They were his only company; their robes flowing, their hands dismissing worldly detail. He kept the mules bunched up and moving. Blake had given him Santana's pistol, though he did no more than wave it in the air when the handlers ignored his pacing and began to straggle.

Every few hours Blake ran forward, paused to give encouragement and ran on to check the advance group. He moved back and forth from one end of the caravan to the other with the jealousy of a female cat protecting her brood. Spenser forced his way through the mud and watched Blake's legs drive ahead and on out of sight for the third time. What fuelled the man, he wondered. The impetus went far beyond any desire for money. It was animal. Not brute force. Something from which reason was absent. Spenser sensed and understood that. Perhaps it was a desperate wish to beat an old enemy. Field had said that whatever Spenser paid Blake, they would end up fighting Blake's wars. But what were Blake's wars? A grudge match, one against one. Surely not. Khun Minh hardly merited such an effort. Perhaps it was the money after all, the freedom it would buy to take his Marea and leave. To have her to himself. But no, there was more than that. Something more basic. Something in Blake's soul. It was as if he wished to bring the interminable disorder of the jungle into line, as if he could master it, make it stop where it was, if only for a moment.

Was it fear then that drove him? Uncontrollable fear at his own isolation, devoid of the supports other men enjoyed. Spenser wondered what had made him put his own hopes into such hands. But no. It was good that Blake's drives, whatever their origins, enslaved the man, because those drives would carry the buddhas to safety. Yet where was the guarantee that these incomprehensible reasons would not rush the man off in some disastrous direction?

Spenser had calmed down, now that he was alone with his sculptures, lost with them in a sea of permanent communion where fear could scarcely breathe. Even his stomach spasms and his festering sores were gradually expelled from his consciousness. Even the mosquitoes became a distant background noise. Most of the time he was perfectly content. Once, he found himself thinking of Marea and what he would do about her when they got back to the other world, the world in which Blake would shrink down to human size, and wondered whether that would make any difference? He tried to remember how she had felt in the dark of the house in Mae Hong Son and the sound of her breath, that gasping, desperate sound, as if her soul had a physical consistency; but the air around him was filled with the living buddhas so that the little impression she made succeeded only in breaking their cocoon and revived his own pain with all its violence. And when Percival Gordon dreamt of breaking out into reality while he sipped his champagne and lounged in his Peking chair, was this what he imagined? After all, it was only a fantasy. Of one thing Spenser was sure; this pain, this nightmare of a Sunday stroll was true to his own dream. Not because it was a nightmare – that was of no importance – but because his statues were there with him, coming with him, dissolved into his own destiny, into his very being. And when he turned again to his conversations with them, the stabbing pain melted away.

The mud on the descent was so thick that it took two days to cover the distance. They could no longer move at night – their lights would have provided targets – they wrapped themselves in their ponchos and stretched out along the edge of the troughs, having long since forgotten the line between dry and wet. It was not surprising that Santana's fever worsened under these conditions until Spenser felt obliged to stuff a handkerchief into the man's mouth. According to Blake, this was a malarial attack – the recurrence of something caught long before. It was a tidy diagnosis.

On the second day there was an outbreak of shots well behind. Blake passed forward in late morning with the news that another soldier had been killed. Spenser recognized from the description which man it was, more a boy as he remembered. But there was no emotion in an unseen death. The visual shock had been missed. And the true weight of death – the absence for the living of someone cared for – was not his to carry. The news had no meaning. He had his own men, his mules to push forward and his buddhas to placate. From unseen roots high in the trees, the vines twisted down thick and bare, like a field of hangmen's ropes.

They descended into the valley which led from the Shan State Army's village, Homong, to Muglang, three miles farther on and controlled by Khun Minh's supporters. Layers of cloud, cumulated above, dropped a solid sheet of rain. The streams feeding the rice paddies had flooded the entire valley, creating a lake more than five miles long and a few feet deep. At the sight of it, Santana threw off his poncho and fought his son's attempts to put it back on.

'Maggots!' he shouted. 'A sea of maggots! Stay away! Go back!'

The leeches had been transformed in his mind. He saw maggots everywhere. He felt them swarming under his shirt and tried to rip it off. In desperation Spenser reached up and hit him hard.

Santana froze, tensed like an animal before a strange sound. He twisted backwards to fix on the nearest buddha. Its eyes filled him with terror and he spurred the horse forward, his own face covered by a hand. After that, the boy struggled constantly to hold the horse in place. Santana was led out into the lake with water streaming off his bare head and his eyes squeezed shut. Sounds came from his mouth. At first they were garbled and drowned out by the splashing feet, but with time they grew louder and clearer, accompanying

229

the caravan with an endless dhammic chorus.

'There is no fire like lust. There is no grip like hate. There is no net like delusion. There is no river like craving.'

The handlers could not understand the English words, but saw his fear of the buddhas and began to say among themselves that he was possessed.

It was not safe to rest at Homong, its stilts rising out of the lake, with Khun Minh's village so close and the risks of a trap awaiting them. Blake strengthened the advance group by ten men and bunched them up just before the animals. Behind this phalanx, he waded out in Spenser's company, their feet sinking through layers of liquid and mud.

'Six more days,' he announced.

'We did it in two.'

Blake shrugged, 'Then it was dry.'

'Are we doing so badly?'

'Badly?' Blake was amazed. 'We are doing very well. We are almost home. Lao Sa is a fool. He can drag along behind us taking pot-shots if that makes him happy. It won't slow us down. Jalaw should be at Gwe Houk by now. When Khun Minh hears fresh men are coming to meet us, he will fade away. He never likes a big fight. No. Things couldn't be better.'

'And Santana?'

Blake looked back at the bare figure on horseback. 'I got engaged to a girl at college. After we graduated she came to stay with my parents in the house at Mae Hong Son, to see if the life suited her. She liked it out here all right. Six weeks after she arrived, they sent me into northern Laos during the rains, just like this. We got slowed down. The army guessed we were cut off. They radioed out to all their insurgent contacts for information. One of them confused us with another group and replied that we had got killed. That was what the army told my parents, who told my fiancée. Two weeks later I showed up. She was happy enough to see me alive, but she went back to the States.'

Spenser watched Blake speak. At a distance the man fascinated him, but up close he was insupportable. To every unsatisfactory situation he had a perfectly satisfying answer – satisfying to himself. His ego was so complete that he automatically became philosophical about other people's misfortunes. Spenser stumbled on the edge of a paddy and looked down in search of a pattern beneath the water. 'I'm certain that will be a great consolation to Santana's wife.'

Blake stared at him with a curious eye. 'What does that mean?'

'I don't understand why you let Santana come.'

'He wanted to come.'

'I forgot,' Spenser said coldly. 'Of course, you might have discouraged him.'

Blake's voice filled with indulgence. 'You tell me I judge you. I think it is the other way around. You seem to expect something from me. I promised you your statues. Nothing more. Tell me. What else do I owe you?'

'Nothing,' Spenser mumbled. 'Nothing. In a few days I'll have my statues and you can go back to translating the Bible and killing people in alleys.'

Blake nodded. 'You want moral standards in the thieves you hire – lots of brother's keepers and good deeds. You confuse sentiment with scripture, Spenser. There isn't a word in the gospel about good deeds leading to salvation. And salvation is what counts. Christ calls us to follow him. There are no preconditions. We don't have to change first. In following, you hope to be changed. So I follow and I do the best I can. Maybe that is not enough for you, but there is no 'good Christian' clause in our agreement. Santana wanted to come. I made no judgement. I let him follow.'

The confidence in the voice irritated Spenser's nerve-ends. Why couldn't he simply ignore the man? 'And if Marea had wanted to come, you'd have done the same.'

Blake stopped. The mules behind stopped in imitation. Fury drowned his eyes. 'I know you, Spenser. You think because you sleep with a woman once, part of her belongs to you, even if you never touch her again. You chisel your little initials on to your bit of the territory.'

Spenser forced himself to keep walking. The voice followed from behind, uneven with passion. Had Marea told him? Was he guessing or was it some underside of his missionary paternalism?

'Sure you get something when you sleep with her.' Blake strode without lifting his feet from the water till he had caught up. 'But nothing you can keep, Spenser. You can't keep Marea just by sleeping with her. Sex is a small part of the bargain. The rest is what counts. Look at Field, he could never give the rest. Never.' Blake grasped hold of Spenser's shoulder. 'Maybe he is better than you. He knows what he would have to give and realizes he can't. You don't understand that do you? I know what kind of man you are. Your statues. Why do they obsess you? I see the way you stare at them. You are a pagan. You need a hewn idol to get it up.'

Spenser pulled away from his grip. 'You know nothing about me.' His mind was buried in swirling clouds.

'What is there to know?' Blake shouted after him. 'That passion is the rent veil! The veil, Spenser! how many veils close you out? Is it fear or ignorance that has got you this far? It certainly isn't devotion. I have seen all three. There is no devotion in you. Only an obsession. Obsessions come from fear and ignorance. They have nothing to do with love.'

Blake broke away to join the soldiers and left him alone between them and the caravan. A great fatigue came over Spenser, a fatigue beyond pain. He stared back at the buddhas to see only cold stone, their heads riding beneath the water as if they were standing on their hands. He watched Blake instructing the Shans. The fatigue weighed so heavily upon him. He wished only to stop, to stop and to lie upon the opaque surface.

Through the rain the trees surrounding Khun Minh's village took form. Blake hesitated and everyone with him, like a flock of awkward sea-birds. He made a sign and his fifteen men began running behind him, their knees lifted high to clear their feet from the lake. It was a comic scene – the boyish men, with outsized rifles held high, leaping out of the water again and again until their forms merged into the seascape and only the sound of splashing remained. Then even the water noise died away.

Spenser looked around for reassurance and found Santana staring at him with his mouth hanging open, the rain pounding on to his head.

'Empty,' he intoned. 'Empty, empty, empty.'

Spenser wanted to take him in his arms and hold him like a child. They waited. Then the sound of a single man running swelled towards them. He materialized into a Shan soldier. They had found the houses closed up. The villagers were probably inside, praying that locked shutters would be accepted as a promise of safe passage. Spenser began to laugh wildly, his body shaking. Then he heard Santana laughing in imitation and stopped, suddenly frightened by his own state.

Shirley Chu lay in bed, her boyfriend linking his arms around her from behind. She could feel his chest hair, still warm and sweaty, matted against her spine. He had fallen back asleep, but she felt quite awake and stared around with a smile of satisfaction. Outside, the morning shower seemed far away.

He had arrived three days before. At the last moment she had moved into her parents' room, with its enormous carved and gilded bed and its thick Tientsin carpet. She had also asked for silk sheets. Her mother had always kept the air-conditioning so high that even in the June heat she had been able to sleep between silk. Somehow in the rainy season it seemed more justified.

Not that Shirley was in need of justifications. When she had brought Andy into the room he had burst into laughter and wandered around inspecting each extravagant decoration. She watched him, so out of place in his solid shoes and heavy cotton shirt. When he felt the sheets they had laughed together and he had pulled her down on to the bed. It was all like a game.

In those three days she had shown him how the jade business worked, had taken him off on little expeditions into the country, had made him eat food filled with the hottest chillies and start the morning with noodle soup. He seemed to enjoy everything, smiled all day and dragged her off to bed as often as possible. He asked only once about her father and she replied that he was too frail to be seen. She was perfectly happy.

A girl slipped through the door, listened for activity with her eyes averted and when certain of silence came forward to kneel by the bed. The servants understood nothing about knocking or privacy. The girl whispered in mandarin – the butcher was downstairs with an urgent message. She unlocked Andy's hands and threw back the sheets.

'Don't get up yet, Shirley.' He opened his eyes to discover the kneeling girl and pulled the sheet to cover himself.

'I'll be right back.' She caressed his arm, the reddish hair flattening under her fingers.

The girl held a heavy silk dressing-gown ready. Shirley slipped on to the carpet pile and wrapped the gown around herself. It had been her mother's. Worn without high heels, it trailed on the floor. She hitched it up on her solid waist and went out barefoot.

Her moving into the large bedroom had not made a great impact on the servants, but when she asked for the silk sheets it was another matter. No one had used them since her mother's death eight years before. If Shirley had the right to sleep between these, she had the right to everything. They interpreted her demand as an assumption of full power and began presenting her with a multitude of relics, even her mother's clothes, as if each object were an additional seal of office. They were discreet enough to recognize that Shirley had inherited her father's shape and refrained from presenting clothes that called for curves or natural elegance.

The butcher handed her a note, with apologies for its tattered state. It had been brought in an hour before from across the border by a runner. She unwrapped it from around a small amulet which she recognized as the gold buddha given to Lao Sa a month before. Her fingers straightened out the creased and stained paper, then flattened it on a table where she read it slowly; then again a second time and turned the buddha over in her hand.

What did Lao Sa mean? Why tell her that Blake had returned to the Salween with twenty statues? 'Messenger to Khun Minh tomorrow. Will attempt to slow Blake.' She didn't want their statues.

'When are you expected to deliver meat to Khun Minh's camp?'

'When you wish.'

'How about this morning?'

The butcher nodded without a word. He seemed more intimidated than usual. Perhaps it was the peacock, embroidered in richer colour around the full sweep of the dressing gown than a living bird could have managed. She handed the unfolded note to the man.

'See if you can find out anything that makes sense of this.'

That same day, Lao Sa's official runner arrived back in Khun Minh's base camp, having been protected on the trail from everything except mud by his solid blue shield of tattoos. He splashed through the thick brown sea that had flooded the camp right up to the doors of the cheap plywood barracks. At the main house he was allowed in, despite his filthy condition, and led to the living-room where Khun Minh was dozing. Minh found it difficult to stay alert once the rainy season had started. The air was too heavy. There was too little to do.

The runner delivered the message from Lao Sa and answered the questions that were asked him. Khun Minh accepted the runner's words at face value, as he knew the man to be perfectly loyal; probably the only one of his soldiers to be truly loyal. But there was little to the message, except that Blake's party had reached the north shore of the Salween with the statues.

Khun Minh scribbled a few words to General Krit. The air was so damp that his pen scarcely wrote. He sealed the message in an envelope and gave it to the tattooed runner, still covered with mud, who was sent on down to Mae Hong Son in a Land Rover.

From his window, Khun Minh watched the machine churn across the mud to the edge of the camp, then disappear. He looked up through the rain at the dark sky before calling an orderly, 'In thirty minutes. 100 men to go up the trail. Two weeks' provisions.'

He felt a surge of energy and strode across the room, his haunches swaying slightly with the extra weight, which he felt altering his step. The sensation was dismissed as of marginal importance. Now he must go fast; fast, he thought, like Mao or Ho. They were men to be admired, men he had always admired, but now he felt himself stronger than either – stronger because he had a tougher heart. That was Krit's problem. He had no steel. He was westernized, destroyed by guilt, a western problem. He was divided from himself. Khun Minh felt in perfect harmony with himself. He shouted again for the orderly.

'I want three extra mules in the party. Strong ones. You make sure. Don't load them.'

In the corner he swung open the large cupboard on to his relics. Next to his silver cross, the photograph of Marea lay face down as he had left it after Spenser's visit. He wasn't surprised. None of the servants would have rushed to raise her image. He took the frame in his hands. Minh hardly recognized her. She had been dressed up and made-up Hong Kong-style for the photographer. Her real flesh was disguised. No. It was once-removed from flesh that could be held. And time had cut away any remaining links. Now she was twice-removed by make-up and time. He stared again at the photo. No. He felt nothing. It was so long since he had touched her or any other woman. More than the memory was gone. He had lost the habit. He had no physical needs.

Minh put the frame back in place, with her face staring out but away from the cross, then pulled on his Mayfair hand-made boots and laced them. They felt very reassuring. When he stood, the orderly was waiting with a short raincoat. He also delivered the daily report on Shirley Chu's movements. There was nothing in it. Just detail. But Minh already knew enough to be certain she was on the verge of something. Well, he had warned her. Now was the time, if he were going into the jungle, to immobilize her. He knew exactly what the Chus thought of him: only part Chinese and the rest Shan. Out of the hills. That was what they thought. Well, he had warned her. And she hadn't listened.

'I want something done in Mae Hong Son.' The orderly leaned forward expectantly. Minh said the words slowly. 'The Chu house. Kill the old man.'

In the corner was the black umbrella with its aluminium shaft. He drew off the sheath, held up the shaft and pushed the spring button. The umbrella opened with a whoosh. He was always relieved to find that the works had not rusted.

Shirley's butcher arrived in the camp to find that the supply officer, with whom he normally dealt, had gone away. The young man standing in for him apologised that he had no power to take meat orders. He also explained that Khun Minh had ridden out a short time before without notice, taking a party of men that included the supply officer. The butcher thanked him and wandered over to visit a friend in the kitchen itself. Before long he learned that the party had been 100-strong, followed by ten mules loaded with provisions and equipment and behind those, three extra mules carrying nothing. He was back in Mae Hong Son by mid-afternoon.

The caravan waded on towards Mong Mai. Only the last mile leading up to the river was above water. Beyond it, the great banyan tree towered over the SSA's former taxation point. The river they had waded through a few days before was now chest high and churning so fast that Blake alone dared struggle across to fix a rope along which the soldiers, the eight mules and the horses were led.

There, they were stopped by Eddie, running towards them from behind. He had not left the rearguard since Lao Sa's reappearance and his face was lined with fatigue. He had cut the legs off his trousers rather than support their wet bulk rolled up. His skin was badly scratched, his poncho had been abandoned.

He had seen Lao Sa lead his soldiers into their village, probably for the night. He suggested the rearguard hold the river bank so that the main party could camp for once on firm ground before pushing over the last two mountains. Blake offered to go back to take his place for the night.

The banyan tree was vast, its foliage thick and the ground beneath it rose in a gradual hump that came as close to being dry as anything they had seen since the rains began. A jumble of wood fallen from the tree and from the old taxation hut lay about in a condition fit for burning. The Shans lifted Santana on to the platform at the base of the trunk, while Eddie set about organizing the camp. He was interrupted by the handlers and some of the soldiers, who came forward in a delegation led by a man they had chosen as spokesman. He began an earnest speech in Shan, but was soon interrupted by the comments of the others, until they were all talking at once.

Eddie listened with impatience. Eventually he gave a sign of agreement and dropped down with a guffaw on to the platform beside Spenser and Santana.

'What is it?' Spenser summoned just enough curiosity to ask. Since the lake at Hmong, his will power had been draining away.

'Oh, nothing. Is there anything to eat?'

'Cold rice.'

Eddie looked around at the debris. 'For once there's some wood that will burn. Let's have hot rice. You're shivering.'

'It's just my stomach.'

'Some warmth will help.'

He gave orders for a fire. 'Ah, what would Ronald Reagan do if he were here? He is a great star. But what would he do in all this mud, without Nancy and with no photographers to cheer him on?' Eddie peeled off his clothes and wrapped a blanket around himself. 'Fame is a curious thing, I would like to be, just once, in one of those magazines for famous people. Just to see how it would feel. You know, with Elizabeth Taylor on the back of my page as a soft padding. She would be holding on to a new husband. She is a very matrimonial woman. I think she likes ceremony. And on the facing page, Brooke Shields. Oh, I realize she may be a virgin and hard to deal with, but that's who I'd have.' He stopped when he saw Spenser was not listening.

With darkness came a group of soldiers and handlers pushing a man before them. His rough white robe stood out among the filthy uniforms. He was an old man, as thin, if not thinner than Santana, and without teeth. They forced him up on to the platform, where he stared at Santana, then at

239

Spenser, then back at Santana. The sight of two white men seemed to unnerve him, but the soldiers shouted encouragement and he came alive, taking a roll of white cloth from beneath his arm and smoothing it out with a specific orientation over the wood planks. Under his direction the soldiers moved Santana on to its centre.

'What does he want?' Spenser asked.

'The men say your friend is possessed. They say he's a talisman for their own failure and will bring us all bad luck. They won't go on tomorrow unless he's dealt with. This old boy is the village expert.' In case Spenser should protest, he added, 'Just stay out of it.'

At the foot of the cloth the man in white lit a row of fourteen rough candle stubs, beneath which he laid a drawing of the Buddha, then knelt in a silent prayer. It gradually became audible and grew into a shouted incantation for Santana's spirit to be freed – that was Eddie's interpretation. This lasted half an hour without Santana moving. He appeared to be asleep. The light the candles threw on to the side of his face showed him to be breathing heavily. Around the platform, the soldiers and handlers squeezed up to the edge where they commented on each event in a babble of low voices.

The exorcist leaned forward slowly and with a sudden movement grasped Santana's hand. He examinied it and raised his head with a shout that caused a sensation in his audience.

'What did he say?' Spenser insisted.

'Eddie began a running translation. 'That he can see the spirits.'

The old man spat on Santana's palm and rubbed in the spittle. The hand began to shake. The exorcist let it go with a curious smile. He took a metal statue of an ox – a rough, approximate form – from his pocket and shaved off some filings with a knife. These were dropped into a cup of water. When they had settled, he ran the drawing of the Buddha slowly over the candles, the paper flaming into the night. Then he lifted Santana's head to make him drink the water mixed with metal shavings and ashes.

His chanting began again in a deep, strong voice; he called on the devas of the heavens, on the hosts and the evil creatures, on the ogres of the earth, the witches, the dark nats and the ouktazouns. 'I command you to leave. I command you by the glory of the Buddha, the Dhamma and the Sangha.'

Santana awoke with moaning and attempted to sit up, but failed and fell back sobbing. Tears ran off his face and saliva from the side of his mouth.

'Why have you come to this man?' the exorcist coaxed as a father to a child. 'Leave his body. There can be nothing between you. Must I force you to leave?' He took Santana's hand and spat on it again. 'Separate! Separate!'

Santana wrenched his hand free and leaped violently backwards with a force exploding out of nowhere. Two of the soldiers at the edge of the platform grabbed hold to force him down on to the sheet. Throughout the struggle his lips were pressed hard together so that he made no sound.

'What do you want?' the exorcist shouted at him. 'Are you listening to me? You cannot disobey. Will you leave this body.' He dropped into a soft voice, 'I am trying to be gentle with you.'

Santana's mouth twisted into a licentious smile and he spoke in a woman's voice – the grotesque expression was meant to be seductive. There was excited talk among the soldiers.

Spenser leaned forward to Eddie, 'What is it?'

'He's speaking Shan.'

Santana spoke no Shan; Spenser knew that, but he was too

241

exhausted to doubt what was happening. His eyes drifted over towards the mules and the statues. In the darkness he saw nothing.

'I love him,' Santana moaned in falsetto. 'I want to take him away.'

The exorcist flushed with anger. 'You cannot disobey me.'

'I love him! I love him! I love him!'

'If you disobey, I will kill you!'

'I will take him with me!'

The crowd could not help but notice that Santana's trousers had bulged up with an erection. In the shadowy light it seemed inordinately large and the penis moved spasmodically so that even the exorcist stopped for a moment to watch, sweat glistening on his forehead. He appeared calm and made few movements, but emanated a tension that could be felt throughout the group. 'You can want nothing from this man. Nothing.'

Santana broke into the hideous laughter of a stage prostitute and rolled from side to side on his back while his penis danced against his trousers.

'Do you hear me?'

There was no reply except lascivious giggling. The old man went on cajoling and ordering. At one point he gave up and turned to appeal for release from Eddie, who encouraged him to continue.

But Santana heard this and shouted at them – 'Why should I leave? What can you do? You are a weak old man' – and screamed with amusement until the falsetto was an unbearable affront to their ears. Suddenly he wrenched free – 'I must take him with me!' – and leaped up a second time, ejaculating in the same spasm and stretching open his mouth to let out a moaning cry which was somehow that of both a man and a woman. Four soldiers reached up to pull him down. There were stains spreading across the front of his trousers, but what they all stared at was the colour. It was streaked with blood.

'You cannot take him. This is forbidden by the Buddha.'

Santana shook his head violently, 'There is no Buddha! I want his soul!'

Sweat streamed off the exorcist, who trembled with emotion. He slapped Santana hard across the face. As the hand slipped from his skin, Santana fell asleep. The exorcist slapped him a second time and he began to sob in his woman's voice. Mucus ran from his nose. The old man lowered himself over Santana and spat in his face, then slapped him a third time.

'I will call you with the full power of the Buddha and you will come out. I will call you a last time or you will be killed.' He chanted in an uneven intonation worn by fatigue. Eddie reached out with a cloth to wipe the sweat from his face.

While the chanting rose and fell in successive crescendos, the soldiers stopped commenting and Santana lay perfectly still. The only other sound was that of the fire. He lay flatter and flatter against the ground, as if each of his cells were individually relaxing. The tension flowed out of his face, then out of his form, leaving what appeared to be the amorphous shell of a dead man. Then his lips slackened apart and saliva poured out and his bowels opened to stain the white sheet black.

The exorcist's head dropped and he wept with such exhaustion that he did not see Santana's eyes focus to stare about himself with a gaze which was clear and rational. His skin had turned from grey to white. In the firelight he was transparent.

Marea had been laughing all through dinner. To Field it seemed that she had been laughing for weeks, ever since his arrival. He took an inexhaustible pleasure in entertaining

243

her, so that the dinners, which he was certain with Blake were short and quiet, stretched out over the rainy evenings, their laughter becoming like a warm cocoon.

The cook's daughter came creeping in and stood for some time before Marea noticed her.

'Jalaw here,' the girl whispered.

The cocoon evaporated. Field watched Marea force out, 'Where?' He knew that what she wanted to ask was – 'Only Jalaw?' – but she had held that question in.

The girl nodded towards the living-room. Marea got to her feet very slowly. Her eyes passed over Field across the table without focusing. He followed in her steps through to the main building where Jalaw, Blake's Lahu runner, was crouched on the tile floor. He was stained with mud and wore only a T-shirt and shorts. She sat on the edge of a wicker armchair with a reserve that suggested indifference, but Field sensed she could control herself no other way. He threw himself unnoticed on to the sofa.

Jalaw recounted the little he knew, in chronological order. 'I did not stay with the SSA runner. He was too slow. I ran ahead. I did not catch Lao Sa's man. He may have hidden from me. I could not slow down to watch.'

Field looked over at Marea. He could see only that one thing interested her. Was Blake alive? Instead of asking, she listened in silence, with her lips held tight together. Field felt a burp coming on and stretched out his arms to crack his knuckles as a way of preventing it. The snapping cartilage echoed through the room.

'Yesterday I came to Gwe Houk for the reinforcements, but the SSA are no longer there. The camp is abandoned. I kept running. Down at Kharhan the Shan villagers told me the Thai army had come to take the soldiers away.'

Field jumped up. 'Take how? Do you mean force?'

Jalaw looked nervously at Marea, but the tension had gone from her face. Life appeared to be surging back into her.

244

Nothing definitive had happened. Blake was alive. She gave the Lahu a smile of encouragement.

'The Thais climbed up to visit. But they disarmed the Shan soldiers and brought them down and drove them away in a truck not long after we left there to go into the jungle. So I ran home.'

'Krit,' Field said in disgust.

Marea ignored him and looked at Jalaw with warmth. Field felt the complicity of love for Blake that bound the two. He was closed out.

'You must go back,' she said. 'Take the ten men I have here.' She went out to organize the food before opening the storeroom and distributing weapons.

Field followed her around repeating variations of, 'Ten men are worse than none. We must go to Krit. We can pressure him.'

At last Marea turned on him in anger. 'Krit is nothing in this. Nothing. He's a pawn. Leave me alone, John. I can't think. Go back to the house.'

It was ten p.m. before she had them loading the Land Rover. Neither Field nor she noticed Shirley Chu drive by on her way home from a rushed trip to Mai Plan. Nor did the Lahus.

Shirley, on the other hand, noticed them and concluded that a third messenger had got through. If Lao Sa had gone to the trouble of sending one to herself and another to Khun Minh, it wasn't surprising that Blake should be asking for help. She was beginning to understand just how much was at stake.

Her butcher had returned from Khun Minh's camp halfway through that afternoon with his tale of Minh disappearing up the trail at the head of 100 men and it had immediately made sense to her. It was so typical of the Shans. They were obsessed by outmanoeuvring each other and so always forgot to look over their shoulders. They knew they should be suspicious, but were not clever enough to know of what. Well, they had made a mistake. Each of them. Even Khun Minh. Even Blake, which surprised her.

She told Andy to look after himself for a few hours and drove alone up to Mai Plan, where she gathered the officers together in the conference room of her father's house. The fifteen men fell into place around the table in order of precedence without hesitation. Douglas Sung filed in with the junior officers and took his place near the far end of the table. His eyes were on her like those of a loyal dog starved for affection. The company of his fellow officers only heightened his confusion of embarrassment and devotion, so she smiled at him. He looked away nervously, but seconds later his eyes came back to her. She saw a physical hunger in them which he would have denied was there. Apart from Major Sung's devotion, it was a calm, structured society that General Chu had created. Far too calm, Shirley thought.

She explained that, according to her information, Khun Minh was in the process of isolating himself on the trail, along with his number two, Lao Sa, and that with them they had no more than 200 men. Probably as few as 150. She suggested they seize the opportunity to cut them off. With luck they could be destroyed. She paused.

Silence hung over the table – neither a silence of refusal, nor one of enthusiasm. They were officers, who therefore responded to orders, but they had not been given any for a long time. Not real orders. Only instructions regarding daily details. Shirley suddenly realized the weight of this lethargy. She had expected her words to sweep it aside, but no one moved. No one rose to the challenge. Her confidence began ebbing away as the silence persisted and the fifteen officers stared at her. She forced her eyes to stare back, shifting them from man to man around the table, examining each face. Most had passed the age of fifty. She knew where the problem lay – they had lost the habit of action. They talked about wanting it, but the habit was gone; at least among the elders. She stared at her father's number two, in his mid-seventies. Beneath the girl's harsh look he reached to pick up the cup before him. His skin had the same frozen quality as the porcelain.

Her eyes came to the junior officers at the end of the table. They, of course, dared not speak. She fixed on Douglas Sung, who betrayed the pain he was feeling for her. Why not, she thought.

'What would Major Sung recommend?' Her voice began weakly, but grew by the third word into an aggressive challenge.

No one said a word, but a feeling akin to the shattering of glass spread around the table. Douglas Sung looked down in embarrassment. When he looked up, Shirley was still staring expectantly at him, as if to say she was throwing herself into his arms.

'Forgive me,' he managed. 'I am ignorant in these matters ...' No one agreed or disagreed. 'Perhaps 500 men would be enough. If we send them along the track towards the main trail ... when they reach the trail, they would assure themselves that the caravan and Lao Sa had both passed before blocking the way with ... say, 200 of our men, just in case there are more behind. The remaining 300 would chase Lao Sa. Then they would have to look for an opportunity to destroy Khun Minh.'

'Great!' Shirley enthused. 'Does anyone think this can't work?'

The silence persisted. Now that a proposition was on the table, the silence was in her favour. She looked at her father's number two. He began tapping his fingers on the teak. It was a habit he had picked up from General Chu. She chose a tone of respect before speaking to him. 'Who will command?'

The old man reached again for his cup and sipped the tea. She wanted to smash the porcelain. Her father had done his

247

trick of mirrors too well. They believed Mai Plan was a real place, not a refugee camp at war. There was too much porcelain, too many gardens. After peering around the table he fell upon a middle-aged man in fairly good shape. 'Colonel Lin might consider this honour.'

Lin looked neither pleased nor displeased; no doubt he was imagining the conditions on the trail. Shirley knew him well enough to be certain he would take no risks. That was good.

'Thank you, Colonel Lin,' she said, carefully implying that he had volunteered. 'We must also decide on an officer to lead the pursuit group of 300. Given the season, I suggest a junior officer.' She pretended to examine all of the younger men, until her gaze came back to Douglas Sung. His shyness was gone. Now that he had spoken for her and no one had disagreed, he was ready to do anything. 'What about Major Sung?' Shirley asked.

The young man looked hard at General Chu's number two, but this was unnecessary. The old man passively indicated agreement. So that was that. No one had questioned her authority. No one had doubted her judgement. Was it only the power of inheritance or did they recognize some quality in her? She no longer cared.

'Thank you.' Shirley stood up. 'It's late, but you've got to leave today. I'll let you get on with the details.' She was careful not to look at Douglas again.

The moment Shirley left the camp, it began to evaporate from her memory; but not so quickly nor so completely as before. She would think of them again when it was time for the next step. Meanwhile she let Andy back into her imagination and he chased the table of officers away. He would be reading or in bed by the time she got home.

The house was in darkness. She padded up the stairs and along the familiar corridors without switching on lights; hesitated outside her own room and went on towards her father's at the back. There was light beneath the closed door.

This hardly surprised her as he was now often frightened by the darkness. She slipped open the door.

His nurse was lying in a curious position on the floor at the end of the bed. Shirley's eyes swivelled towards her father. He lay peacefully. But a man stood beside the bed, a knife in his hand. He was naked except for a pair of shorts. His eyes met Shirley's and they stared at each other momentarily. Then Shirley began screaming,

'Don't touch him! Don't touch him! Help! Help me!'

She screamed in English, which the man was unlikely to understand, but nothing was clear in her mind. She screamed louder and louder. The man took a few steps across the room, the knife raised to silence her. Shirley was paralysed. She couldn't move. She just kept on shouting. There was doubt growing in the man's eyes. He looked back at General Chu, who was now awake and trying to sit up, his face opening at the sight of his daughter's panic. The old man began to echo her with a sound like sobbing, as if he were dead and she had come to mourn him. There was no meaning to the sounds, only a great refrain of moaning.

Seconds later, there were shouts in the corridor, and the echo of servants running towards the room. The man with the knife stepped back to strike out at General Chu, but was distracted by the crescendo of noise. Indecision ceded to fear. He ran towards the window screen he had cut, and slipped through. The servants arrived as he disappeared.

Shirley ran forward to take her father in her arms. There was froth around his mouth. She put his head against her chest and held him, unable to say a word. Then she felt someone take her from behind. She looked around to find Andy saying calm words,

'He's OK now, Shirley. Come on. You're upsetting him. They got the guy downstairs. Come on. See, the nurse is OK too. He just knocked her out.'

She allowed herself to be drawn away.

'Poor Shirley,' he said as he led her along the corridor back to their room. He had his arm around her waist. 'To think he was once *the* General Chu.'

Shirley stopped and looked up at him, her heart pounding again. 'What do you mean?'

'Well, it must be tough to see him get old that way. And terrible for him.'

'No, Andy. I mean about *the* General Chu.'

'Well, he doesn't look like the greatest dope dealer of all time, does he?' Andy laughed. 'I guess he had it good for a while. Looks like he's still got his enemies.'

What did he mean? Shirley could make no sense of what was happening. She said nothing until they were in the ornate bedroom, where Andy stripped off his clothes and threw himself on the bed.

'If you knew about him,' she forced herself to ask from across the room, 'why didn't you say anything before?'

'God, Shirley, I thought maybe you'd tell me sometime. I thought I should leave it to you. I guessed maybe you were sensitive about it. Who'd want to kill an old guy like that, eh?'

'How long have you been waiting?'

'Oh!' Andy sat up in surprise. She wanted him to take hold of her, instead she listened for him to answer. 'Oh, I see what you mean. Not long. I mean, once I wrote you to say I'd come over here, I thought I'd better do some boning up. You know me. Always on top of the subject. I couldn't arrive like a tourist on a package tour. I'd have been rude to you. So I looked through some books. I kept coming across this General Chu. After a while I figured out he was your dad.'

She sat down on the edge of the bed, trembling. 'What do you think?'

'About what?' Andy reached out to embrace her, but she kept her back to him.

'About me? Me and all of that.' She felt tears welling up.

'There's nothing to think. You're you. Someone else has

the drug business now. I'll tell you what interests me. Those 30,000 Chinese on the border without citizenship. There's an interesting legal question. Do you ever go up there?'

'Sure,' Shirley said, unable to hide the break in her voice. 'They're my people.'

'You've got to take me up there. I'd love to see that.'

'Sure, Andy.'

He pulled her around and discovered tears streaming down her face. 'Hey. Hey. Come on. They didn't hurt him. Hey. Come on.' He pulled her on to the bed and hugged her. 'Come on. It's OK.'

# 16

Santana's son was piling wood on the platform when Eddie came past him through the early morning drizzle and dropped a parcel wrapped in bamboo leaf on to the Spaniard's chest.

'I've brought you a present.'

Spenser drew his legs into a foetal position to break his stomach spasms before he could summon up enough curiosity to look over. The will to move had left him. A cockroach running across his thigh distracted his gaze enough for him to shift his right hand to knock it off. The gesture was one of habit. He watched Santana reach down to unwrap the leaf, inside which was a spongy block of green-black opium.

'I have the equipment,' Eddie reassured him. 'A man in the village sold it to me.'

Santana pushed the opium away politely. 'I do not need.'

Eddie laughed. 'You won't get on the horse without it.'

'Why get on the horse? I need nothing. My needs have burnt out.' Santana's eyes slipped shut, apparently in comfort.

251

Eddie stared about in confusion. He fixed on the boy piling wood along one side of the platform. 'What's he doing?'

The eyes edged open. 'Maggots,' Santana whispered. 'If you leave me behind, the maggots will eat the flesh.'

'We're not leaving you behind.'

'I would die before you crossed the hills. You would leave me rotting on the trail.'

Eddie turned away to watch the boy stack the wood. 'What is he doing?' His voice trembled uncertainly.

'My life is completed. I am free of all needs. Now I will end it.'

'You're a fool!'

Santana seemed scarcely to listen. In a gentle tone he reproved, 'Christians always want life when the time comes for death,' and pushed the opium towards Spenser. 'If you chew a bit, it will calm the pain.' His eyes slipped shut again.

Spenser's mind moved from the gelatinous block to the stack of wood and for the first time asked himself why it was there. The boy piled in alternate rows, first one way, then the other.

'Come on, old man.' Eddie crouched down beside Santana and pulled him into his arms as if cradling a baby. 'It's not so far. I'll put you on the horse myself. I'll pad the ropes well before I tie them. You won't feel a thing. Listen. When we get back I'll heat you a pipe myself. You'll see, I do it well.' Neither man moved, apart from the gentle motion of Eddie rocking them and from time to time coaxing, 'Come on, old man. It's not so far.'

Santana's eyes stayed shut in a trance. At last the Shan laid him back on the platform and jumped down to help collect the wood. Within minutes the news had spread through the caravan and the handlers gathered to join in the work. Then Spenser understood. He took his clothes from beneath his blanket, where he had tried to dry them overnight, lowered himself to the ground and began picking up branches in a

252

sudden frenzy that died away to nothing when the pyre was finished. It stood close to five feet high. They stuffed kindling under it before lifting Santana on to the top.

'You must light it as you leave. Not before,' he instructed his son and with that lost interest in the proceedings.

He began to recite verses of the Buddha. Santana was so calm, so detached, that all emotion was cut out of the air while those around him, who planned to continue on, were slowly filled with doubt as to whether theirs was the real world.

Spenser collected his belongings from the platform. He hesitated until the others, including Eddie, had bowed in Santana's direction and set off. When the last mule disappeared down the trail, leaving only Santana's son and himself, he snatched up the block of opium and stuffed it into his trouser pocket. The boy watched him. There was no judgement in his eyes, not even interest. He had lit a torch, but fear and confusion made him look towards Spenser in search of help. What could Spenser offer? He withdrew to the edge of the clearing, from where he watched the boy wait for some sign from his father – an indication of farewell or instruction – but none came and the torch burnt slowly down towards his hand.

Spenser knew what Santana believed – that he had been punished for stealing the buddhas. Yet in his punishment he had found some sort of freedom. It was only punishment, Spenser reflected, because Santana believed himself to have done wrong. None of that was true for himself. He was bringing the sculptures back to the world, where they would be seen and loved. He was freeing them. Any penalty there might be for him to pay would come due if he failed to get them out.

The words flowed through his mind in an empty formula. How well he knew his own arguments. His own sensations. Since childhood he had been rising to the pleasure of them.

And now he felt nothing. Nothing for the statues. He had not even glanced at them upon waking. He knew that if he looked he would find nothing but sixteen lumps of inert stone. In truth he felt only an empty vortex swelling within him – the emptiness Blake had seen, that no doubt anyone could see. The pain of his body flew around him like an endless dressing that swathed his depression beneath layer after layer of physical reality.

The boy turned away from him in despair and crept forward until the movement of his feet, rather than a specific gesture of his hands, brought the torch up against the pyre. The kindling exploded with unexpected speed. This gave the boy enough confidence to light the wood at the other end, beneath the head, before taking three steps backwards. He bowed stiffly. There his courage failed him and he remained hypnotized by the flames shooting up around Santana, who continued to recite in an even voice the parts of the body, as if once he had named an organ, he was free of it.

'... hairs of the head, hairs of the body, nails, teeth, skin, muscles, sinews, bones, marrow, heart, spleen ...'

Spenser was obliged to go back to the pyre, where he took the boy's hand and led him away. By then the fire had licked up around the edges of the wood and shot into the air, layering it with a smoke tinged first by the smell of hair, then of skin. They could hear Santana's voice for sometime after they left the clearing,

'... intestines, stomach, excrement, brain, bile, pus, blood, grease, fat, tears, sweat ...'

The recitation floated through the rain and the jungle. Twenty minutes later, Blake and his rearguard arrived to discover the platform being consumed in a bonfire. A smell of pork filled their nostrils as they hurried by towards the mountain-side and the junction with the track from Khun Minh's camp. Before long they had caught up to Spenser and the caravan.

Blake drove them on faster, then fell back again to assure the rear. His enthusiasm produced a short-lived effort in Spenser, who soon lagged again. He no longer found the strength within himself to sustain the drive. The trail continued to degenerate, making each step harder than the last. The hoof troughs were now so deep that each mule's belly rubbed against the ridges. Spenser tried looking down at the buddhas for encouragement, only to find what he expected – meaningless figures whose heads were coated thick with the mud through which they were dragging. Had their eyes been clear, he knew he would still have felt nothing.

Instead, pain pounded within him. The original leech sores were now a quarter of an inch deep and seeping with pus. The lymph glands on either side of his groin had swollen to fight the infection, making the movement of each thigh difficult. As for the cramps, they ran through his body on a roller-coaster that brought him close to fainting.

Master of inanimate beauty – the words sang in his mind in a mocking refrain. Blake saw him as Spenser had seen his own father. Was that the prize he sought? Freedom from the fear of uncontrollable life; from animate beauty that could not be frozen into lifelessness? He pulled the buddha fragment from his pocket and ran his thumb over the undulating surface. It seemed no more than crude stone. From the other pocket he drew the bamboo-leaf package and unwrapped one side. It smelt of compost. He held it against his stomach as he stumbled along, then broke off a small crumb. It had an oily, yet acrid taste and within an hour his stomach had ceased to be the sole focus of his existence. He broke off a second piece. It brought him a deadening calm that further slowed the pace of the caravan.

Behind – behind Lao Sa – Shirley Chu's 500 men came on to the trail, where they found spent cartridges and other signs of fighting. Before nightfall they had dug in with machine gun posts facing both ways. By then Douglas Sung had moved on with 300 of them and passed through the clearing where Santana's charred remains lay half-buried in a bed of ashes. He did as he had promised Shirley he would; he pushed his men hard until they were close behind Lao Sa, but without revealing themselves. Then he began looking for an opportunity.

The next morning, the soles of Spenser's feet felt scalded when he tried to walk. He discovered small holes scattered across the surface, as did the handlers on their own feet. They were still arguing about this when Eddie dropped back in search of company and explained that it was a fungus which multiplied during the rains.

'You won't be crippled before five days.' Spenser's dulled reaction to this joke made his condition clear. 'We'll have you to a doctor by then.' Eddie got him on the move and walked along at his side, clearly anxious to help but unable to find the words. When Spenser pulled out the opium to break off a piece, the Shan exclaimed, 'You see. That's how our peasants use it. The opium cure-all. The rest they sell for your people's pleasure.' He looked over at Spenser, who hardly heard the words. 'One family of peasants makes $50 a year with their poppies. That's why the heroin is for you.' His attempt at provocation was ignored. 'How lucky you are to have Lady Di. Such a pure example for everyone to imitate. Think what a wonderful romance she could write about her life. What a pity. I fear they would not let her publish it. Think how much *Paris Match* would pay for the serial rights. More than the price of all your buddhas, Spenser. We are in the wrong business. Why don't you go home and marry a princess? Do you think your buddhas might make you so famous that everyone would want to know you? Spenser of Pagan. Then you could marry a princess and make a fortune. Not one of those Monte Carlo girls! I forbid you. They are nothing. The shadow of nothing. They will take any man who dances well or has money. No. You need a real princess.' He considered what was available. 'Luxemburg might do. But nothing less.'

Spenser forced a small smile. He was stumbling on with Eddie chatting away when a soldier ran back from the advance group. They had seen movement on the trail ahead. Eddie sent a handler to stop Blake, told Spenser to keep the mules where they were and loped forward up the hill.

He found his men on a flat piece of ground where the track ran straight and the jungle was woven so tightly together that it had no particular characteristics. His soldiers lay squeezed to the sides in the mud. The front man had seen something move and heard what he thought was talking. Since then there had been silence. Eddie tried to creep ahead, but whatever he did left him exposed. He crouched to turn over the options. Was it better to go on waiting or to find out who blocked the trail? If the way was actually closed it was better to know. There was nothing to be lost. He called out. After a moment's silence a voice answered. Someone moved no more than ten yards away. Nothing was clear through the narrow opening. Eddie looked for the target, but just in time saw it was his own runner – the man sent with Jalaw for reinforcements when the caravan had crossed the Salween. The runner hesitated uncertainly on the trail, looked behind himself, then walked forward.

'It's all right,' Eddie shouted and got to his feet.

Rifle fire exploded from the jungle. The impact carried Eddie through the air on to the brush at the side of the track. In the mud, a few yards before him, the runner also lay dead. There was no other sound.

Firing broke out on both sides, echoing down the hillside to the mule train, on past it to the rearguard and beyond to Lao Sa, waiting in the swamps for an opportunity to present itself. Blake ordered his men to hold their position, then ran forward alone along the empty trail, past Spenser and his animals who had come to a halt in a small clearing and on towards the firing. From a distance he saw the men crouched against the edge of the trail firing blindly ahead and, just beyond them, Eddie's body spread-eagled backwards on to the tangled jungle. He crept as far forward as he could, without being able to reach the body. There was no way through. They were blocked at both ends.

Sporadic firing went on into the afternoon without anyone being hit; then there was silence from the invisible rifles ahead, followed by a voice shouting for a truce. Blake ordered one of his men to reply that if they wished a truce they should show themselves. A few minutes went by before a soldier appeared on the track with his arms raised. The hands trembled. Even at a distance the fear could be seen on his face. He shouted out that Khun Minh wanted to talk with whomever was in charge. Blake told his man to agree, provided Minh showed himself first. Blake's name was not mentioned.

Nothing happened for thirty minutes, then the silence into which both sides had lapsed was broken by the noise of an animal coming up the path. The horse's head appeared first, followed by that of Khun Minh on its back. There was a pleasant expression upon his face. One hand controlled the reins, the other held his black umbrella, open and upright. Its nylon skin brushed against the leaves on either side to make a curiously urban sound. Blake told his men to train their rifles on the exposed figure, then got up himself and walked forward.

They met where Eddie's body lay arched on its bed of vines and thorns. His gaze was turned towards them with the lids open, but the glass eye had reversed in its socket so that only the white showed. There was blood on his mouth and an ochre colour here and there on his body, where dirt had mixed with the blood. A distant observer might have mistaken him for an angel suspended over the conversation of the two men, as in a baroque painting; except that Blake was distracted by his presence, while Khun Minh seemed not to have noticed it.

'So, this is your party.' Minh paused for Blake to answer. When none came, he leaned slightly forward in his saddle to get a clearer view down over the horse's head. 'And I suppose you would like to get by.' He raised his umbrella with dismay, as if to let in more light. 'You and your men may continue. But not the statues. You, no doubt, are unaware that the Burmese are quite upset. As a Burmese citizen, I must use my advantage to see that they are returned.'

'You have no advantage.' Blake's eyes ran over the horse and its clean and tidy rider until he fixed on the well-made boots hanging loosely at the end of each leg.

Khun Minh raised his umbrella again, this time with indulgence. 'Let us say, my superior position in this stalemate.' He waited for a reply, which meant more than a minute of silence.

Blake finally said, 'I will ask the owner of the statues.'

'The Englishman!' Khun Minh seemed to find great pleasure in that word. 'Yes, ask him, and give him my apologies for this change in plans. If only we had realized what he intended to do.' He made a point of noticing Eddie's body for the first time. 'And do have this poor young man removed.'

While Khun Minh's horse stepped backward with elegance through the mud, Blake lifted his friend from the vines. He did not stop as he came past the soldiers, but ordered them to hold the trail and walked on, with Eddie's body in his arms, back to the caravan.

Spenser took some time to realize what was being carried. Then horror overwhelmed him. He could neither move nor speak. Death raged before him, clawing off his protective layer of pain to invade the emptiness within until he felt he would explode. Blake laid the body on the ground and ordered the handlers to dig a grave by the trail. He allowed no comment on what had happened. His own emotions seemed to have been absorbed into whatever it was that drove him; invisible behind a wall constructed across his eyes and voice so that no one might guess what he felt.

The handlers dug with two small trench shovels. Each lump of mud came away with a sound of reluctant sucking. Spenser tried to concentrate upon this noise, but his eye was drawn back to Eddie's body, lying formless as if already part of the land. Beyond were the eight mules with their buddhas, which he took care to avoid. The noise stopped. He looked back to find that Blake had leapt down into the shallow hole to force the handlers out and had wrenched away one of their shovels.

He drove it into the ground, flinging the muck aside, then hurtled the blade down again. The handlers retreated to where Spenser and the other men waited. Blake dug with violent speed until, at four feet, water seeped into the hole. He wrapped his own poncho carefully around the body, pausing only to straighten the glass eye before closing the lids and lying him on the bed of rising water. In a loud voice he began reciting a burial service. He recited from memory and alone, holding the others at a distance by the power emanating from his back, then filled in the grave with convulsive motions that hesitated for a second once the hole was full; only to swing about and attack the ground around, piling up a mound of weeping mud that rose as high as the grave had been deep into the earth. He stopped in indecision, the small shovel held high in the air while the tension drained out of his back to leave him with the stance of little more than a lost dog. Even then the grave held him. He began reciting in a monotone indecipherable at a distance.

Spenser forced himself over to the grave. When he was very close, Blake's monotone separated itself into words,

'... thus sayest the Lord God of Israel. Put every man his sword by his side, and go in and out from gate to gate throughout the camp, and slay every man his brother, and every man his companion and every man his neighbour ...' Blake broke off when he saw someone beside him.

'Who was it?' Spenser whispered.

'Who? Who? Minh.'

The sound of Minh's name, followed by abrupt silence, released all the panic that had been building up in the handlers. They began to argue with each other, their voices rising to a pitch that frightened them into silence again. They looked over at Blake and Spenser by the grave, then began to argue again. Within this disordered sound one of them gradually took the lead and silenced the others. He walked tentatively across to Blake and explained that a narrow side path began 200 yards behind them and ran for a mile before rejoining the main trail. This was known by only a few dealers, who wanted to avoid the junction with Khun Minh's trail where taxes were often collected. It would get them around the blockage. Blake grabbed the man by the arm before he could finish and pushed him ahead down the track to find the opening.

'Where are you going?' Spenser stumbled after them to block the way.

At first Blake seemed not to recognize him, then elation rushed into his face. 'It's going to be all right. I told you. I will get your statues out.'

'I don't care.'

Blake didn't hear. 'A side trail.'

'And if they find us, Blake? I don't care. What do they want?'

'Want?' Blake looked at Spenser for the first time. 'Minh says he will let us by if we leave the statues.'

'Perhaps we should. Would he keep his word?'

'Of course not.'

'We could try.' Spenser felt himself slipping out of control. He reached into his pocket for the opium.

'Try what? Try to give up?' He saw the crumb going into Spenser's mouth and grabbed hold of him with both hands and shook hard. 'You're giving up, Spenser! Do you

261

understand? If you start to think that this' – he grabbed Spenser's hair tight to the skull and forced him to look around at the jungle pressing down upon them – 'Look at it! Can you see? Look! Can you? If you start to think that this is out to get you, it will get you. If you expect it to kill you, it will kill you. But Spenser,' he shook him hard like the strokes of a clock pendulum until Spenser himself realized how far he had withdrawn, 'it doesn't care about you. It is indifferent. You can take advantage of it as much as Khun Minh or you can let it destroy you. Your mind will decide whether you survive.' He waited to see if Spenser was focusing on him and, when he was satisfied, pushed him aside and disappeared along the trail with the handler.

Spenser dropped down to crouch in the mud. The weight of depression had dissipated, leaving nothing in its place. He could see himself for the first time in days, yet saw nothing. He looked up at the buddhas. Dead. Through his wet pocket lining he could feel the cold stone of the buddha fragment against his thigh. He reached down for another crumb of the opium. The monument of mud over Eddie denied already its origins. Nothing. He felt nothing. He did not feel.

Two hours later Blake strode back into sight. No one had used the side path since before the rains began, meaning its surface was smooth enough to be followed at night without lights. He had the eight mules gagged and turned around and led the 200 yards back to the path's opening. There they waited for darkness.

At ten p.m. their rearguard fired blindly down towards Lao Sa's men. This, plus the answering shots, produced enough noise to cover the animals while they moved on to the path, with Spenser placed behind the fourth mule for his own protection. Nothing was expected of him except that he follow. Only then did Blake's advance guard open fire and rush forward; as if trying to break through. At the explosion of reply they halted, then withdrew slowly down the hill.

When Khun Minh's soldiers heard the shots shrink away, they assumed that the attackers had been driven back and so pressed their advantage. Blake's group had to retreat half a mile through the mud on their knees to reach the entrance of the side path, where the rearguard was still exchanging shots with Lao Sa. They disappeared one after the other down the narrow detour, leaving Blake to pull the vines again into place across the opening before himself slipping away. That left the two factions of Khun Minh's army firing at each other. With a little luck it would be hours before they discovered what had happened.

Without caravans passing to clear the ground, the undergrowth had burst forth to block the path. Barriers of thorn, invisible in the dark, clutched at their bodies as they slid their feet carefully in search of the way. Spenser took hold of the mule tail before him and followed in the steps of the animal. Behind, the rifle fire belonged quickly to another world. This narrow dark tunnel warmed him with the security of a womb. Perhaps it was just the mules before and behind, the heat of their labour enfolding him so that it made no difference whether his eyes were open or closed and so he closed them. He could neither see the mules, nor the statues, but with the warmth he began to sense them there, at first only as part of the comforting darkness, but later as a pulsation that rose above the breathing of the animals and grew to drown them out.

Gradually he realized that his eyes were again open and being drawn to something that separated itself from the darkness. He concentrated on it without understanding. The night had somehow taken on two qualities, one of which married itself to the pulsation in his ears. Was it music? Was it another stage in his body's collapse? He concentrated, seeking a clue to his own weakness. Then light gushed forth to irradiate his face. He accepted this extraordinary sensation as if it were expected, though his mind tried unsuccessfully to

263

register the idea – extraordinary. It lit nothing around him. Not the jungle. Not the animals. Not the handlers. The light grew in intensity, outlining another head before him, a face also irradiating light until it became like a sun. He walked on. The face withdrew at the same pace. Spenser stared at it, not with curiosity or questioning, but with calm acceptance.

It came to him slowly that this was his own face and the light was his own spirit, somehow released so that it glowed from his whole body. No explosion came with this realization, no wave of change. Yet he felt he had come truly alive for the first time, as were his statues all around him.

They were more than alive. His own life force gave them new strength so that suddenly the created and the creators were freed from their prisons to mingle. Spenser could not see the sculptors, but he saw their essence, an amorphous power, and saw the buddhas, their creations, float like witnesses testifying across eternity and take their transitory creators into their arms and Spenser, a mere worshipper, with them and press the power to them until the men became immortal.

There was no desire, no shadow, no double, only the line to be broken between temporary flesh and the love of real flesh, real blood – that which flowed through the soul of beauty – not just the apparent, concrete eternity of some statue or painting, but a chorus of beauty so perfectly conceived that even were the object itself to disappear in a fire or in the seas or in some other vulgar disaster, the resonance of its music would vibrate on through the unconsciousness of time until another creator managed to summon up the spirit.

What was the love of flesh next to this? Not something to which he was insensible. Not something he would refuse or avoid chasing. Yet neither would he sacrifice his other love in its name, no matter what he lost. He could not imagine the pain of this loss lasting so very long; at worst only so long as he himself was alive. What was that, next to his love of these sculptures and the divine service they rendered to beauty?

They were part of the greatest of the heavenly choruses. They were the witnesses of heaven.

The light shone on for a time. He had no sense of how long that might have been. That had no relevance. Then abruptly the veil fell and Spenser saw reality again – the total reality of himself passing towards death. 'But if I am in the presence of eternity all my life,' he said to himself, 'can I not seize this force myself?'

And so he decided, clearly and consciously, that he would do anything to get the statues out. Anything. Eddie's death, that of the others, had weighed upon him. Now they seemed only part of time. They had been cleansing rites that helped him on his way, helped him to understand. And his father's death, which had flooded his vision with a sea of nausea at the least sign of mortality in the world, was itself swept away. Only fear had made him see death as violent. Now he saw no difference between the sudden and the gradual; little change between mortal life and mortal death – merely stages in osmosis. No, he would do anything to get the statues out. And whatever tried to stop him would sharpen his determination.

He pushed by the mule and on until he was past the first animal; whose handler he took by the arm to speed his pace. It was almost dawn before the main trail loomed ahead. Spenser stood on the threshold of the deep mud ridges and encouraged each handler as he went by. Quite apart from the men, the mules had slowed. Weeks of forced march in the mud with a full load could only mean they were exhausted, though their calm white faces showed no sign of it. It was in their speed that the fatigue could be sensed. Mixed in with them was the horse, loaded with ammunition and small packs, but led by Santana's son as if his father still rode on its back. Periodic distant shots echoed from behind.

Spenser drove them fast all morning, maintaining his own strides by force of will and just enough opium to keep

265

physical pain in the background. Late in the afternoon sustained firing broke out at some distance. Blake ran forward in its wake, signalling the caravan to stop. He was bubbling over with delight.

'We have him beaten now!' he called out and put his arm around Spenser's neck.

'Did they try to break through?'

Blake didn't understand the question. 'Oh, you mean the fighting. The rearguard has stopped. They are holding Minh where he is. You can take a rest.' There was a strange excitement about him.

'We don't need a rest. The daylight is for moving.'

'But we have got him, Spenser! Listen. Minh chased down the main trail to cut us off. He was way too late, but he left his own track unprotected. Listen. We got a call on the radio. General Chu's troops are right on his tail. He's blocked both ways.'

'Both ways?'

'Chu and us. He can't go back and we control his way forward. Chu's men want us to block Minh's escape while they pound him.'

'You can't.' Spenser said bluntly. 'Blake, you can't do that.'

'It's all right. Listen,' Blake's excitement carried him on, 'I can hold the trail for weeks. We will get him.'

'I don't want to get him. Blake, while Chu pounds him, he'll pound us. What if you can't hold him? What if he finds a way around? We did. What if Chu's men want the statues? We don't know what they're really after. You see. We can't risk it. Blake, I didn't come here to get even.' Spenser turned away to wave the handlers on, then back to find that his words had had no effect. Anger impelled him. 'Only the buddhas count. We came for them. That and nothing else. We came to get them out. I'm going on. I expect you to be behind me providing protection. If you're not, you forfeit your fee.' Blake seemed not to hear. Spenser took hold of his shirt to keep the man's attention. 'I won't let you. Blake, do you understand what those buddhas mean? They are beauty and light. They are a form of love. We can't risk them. You're big on preaching. Minh is evil. The forces of darkness, Blake. Even I know what the scriptures say – you can't destroy darkness. All you can do is nourish light. So I'm going on.' He walked away after the mules. He dared not look back. He dared not think what would happen if Blake didn't follow. They were so close, Spenser thought, one or two days at most from Gwe Houk. He would push the animals fast and if Blake stayed back to fight, the mules would be over the border before there was time for something to go wrong.

They slipped and pulled and splashed up through level after level of cloud that floated in to cover them, only to float away just as abruptly. The trail was cut into the mountain edge, though they could never see how far the ground fell away because the valleys were filled with mist. But Spenser remembered the plunging chasms seen on their way in, a few weeks before, and the clustered pikes of dead bamboo that reached up to impale anyone who fell. The mud was at its iciest and the hoof troughs at their deepest, running into the hill on one side and into the precipice on the other, so that the men were forced to balance their way from one ridge to the next, holding on to the mules for equilibrium. At the summit of the first mountain, they caught a glimpse between clouds of Blake and his men not far behind. So they had followed. Spenser leapt forward among the animals, slapping the handlers on the back with encouragement. 'Not far! Not far!' It was the buddhas he sang to. When he heard shots behind, they came from such a distance that he suspected they were flying between Chu's men and Khun Minh.

By noon of the next day they were well up the last mountain. The fungus had now peeled successive layers of skin off the soles of their feet, leaving the surface almost too tender to be walked on. Spenser suffered most and was forced

to chew more opium to dull the pain. This also slowed his
pace so that he brought up the rear. The mist thickened,
leaving visible only the first few feet of the precipice on their
left. After a time a breeze moved the cloud away to reveal a
chasm plunging hundreds of feet. The caravan stopped in this
rare clarity to stare down at the trail they had just climbed,
winding up in a zigzag so tortuous that half a mile of track
was laid out within a few hundred feet as the crow flies. Two
turns below was Blake's rearguard. And three below them,
little more than forty yards away, were the first of Khun
Minh's men. The three levels focused on each other and stood
frozen.

'Move!' Spenser shouted. 'Move!' He whacked the last
mule, immobile before him, but the handler was hypnotized
by what he saw. Spenser grabbed hold of the thorns above to
swing himself around the animal and take hold of the man.
'Move! Come on!'

The man allowed himself to be dragged forward a few
paces, but was blocked by the seven mules and the horse
before him. Spenser grasped at the thorns again, trying to
swing forward, but the track was too narrow. A first shot
rang out from below. He pulled Santana's pistol from his
waist, shouting ahead as loudly as he could. The lead handler
stared back at him, frozen with fear. Spenser held his eye at
twenty yards distance and aimed the pistol straight at the
man. 'Move!' he waved the barrel and fired. The ball struck
above him. 'Move!'

Immediate fear overcame the distant threat and the man
rushed forward, dragging his mule, the whole caravan
following in his train. This animation jarred the soldiers
below into a fusillade. The second mule from the lead reared
up with blood streaming down its throat, causing the animal
behind to panic, rising on to its hind legs in an attempt to turn
around. They crashed into each other and reared again. The
handlers let go at the sight of the hoofs flaying and pulled

themselves up into the jungle.

'Hold on!' Spenser shouted and tried to push forward to calm them.

But the twisting bodies spread from mule to mule, pushing forward, backing, rearing on to each other, twisting to turn in search of a way out. They struggled in silence, the sound of their hooves muffled by the mud. The horse alone neighed in panic at being caught in the midst of the disorder. Taller than the others and not weighed down by 400 pounds of stone, it leapt forward, up and over them towards the safety it could see ahead, only to land straddled across the back of a mule.

The sight was so fantastic that the soldiers of both armies stopped firing to watch the mass of bodies rise and hesitate, pause for a second of tangled calm, rise again and tremble on the edge, then topple together over the precipice. The stone buddhas came free as the animals were tumbled on to their backs a first time and then a second and across the next level of the trail, almost carrying two of the soldiers with them. The buddhas rolled ahead down the hill, carried by their dead weight on and on out of sight, while behind, the awkward, flailing mules were impaled one after the other on bamboo stakes until six of them had been pegged in grotesque positions at different levels. The wheezing of death was the only sound. Spenser looked up. The lead mule was still on the trail, as was the animal he himself held. Even the horse had gone over. The handlers and Santana's son hung like decorations from the tangled green above, paralysed by the anticipation of death. Then a cloud rolled into the valley, hiding all that was further away than ten feet. The firing began again, now blind and between the soldiers. Spenser was awakened from his dream by Blake, whose arms enfolded and forced him on.

'Quick! Get going!' Blake dragged the two strongest handlers to the mules. 'Leave the other men here, Minh won't touch them.' He ran back to the rearguard.

Spenser closed his mind and whipped the animals forward. He stumbled on within an artificial peace, not daring to examine his pathetic party. He looked once at his hands to find they had been ripped open by the thorns and were oozing blood from scores of small wounds. The pain left him indifferent. With the horse, he had lost his pack and his remaining money; but the idea of paper value was so abstract that it had no meaning. Four statues, he told himself, still had the power of a sheet of light. There was no greater truth in repetition. No weight of goodness in multiplicity. There was still enough beauty with him to be nourished. This was reason enough to make Spenser push hard. Four, he thought after a time, would have greater value than twenty. One would have to go to General Krit, but the other three might sell for two, three, four hundred thousand a piece. Perhaps more. He would keep one. It was still a great deal of money.

The idea meant nothing to him. It was the thought of the twelve statues lying somewhere below that filled him with sadness. Lost except to Minh. Lost to darkness. They reached the summit and began down for the last time, the magnetic pull of the border dragging him on with the inverted faces of the buddhas crying encouragement. A few yards behind, Santana's son followed aimlessly.

Blake came forward that night to find the four men chewing in silence at ears of roasted corn, now soggy and mildewed. He sat with an aggressive enthusiasm that failed to raise morale.

'You should be happy to have four,' he said after a time. 'If they are worth what you say, you are a rich man. A very rich man.' In bewilderment he added, 'Far richer than I have ever been with all that I have done.'

'What a great place!' had been Andy's first words when he woke that morning at Mai Plan and went out on to the balcony.

It was one of those rare mornings in the rainy season when the sky was clear and the sun brought lightness and warmth to the wilderness of green beyond the town. Immediately below and around him was the grid of paved streets shaded by trees and the solid houses wrapped in flower beds. Shirley had driven them up the night before, having sent a message ahead. It was the first time she had spent a night at Mai Plan since her return from the United States and the town elders treated it as a major occasion. They had filled the house with orchids and organized a banquet with all the officers and their wives.

Only Andy caused some hesitation. Outsiders were not allowed into Mai Plan; certainly not *gwei-lo*, or *farang* as the Thais called them. Two beds had been made up in the house in rooms on separate floors. Shirley laughed when she saw this and ordered the maid to bring Andy's bag to her room.

This question mark over his status caused the banquet to begin in silence, but Andy seemed not to notice. He chatted to everyone, asking friendly intelligent questions that showed respect for the elders. Within half an hour he was being told stories of the campaign in the forties against Mao Tse-tung, then of their crossing the wilderness to the wild mountain that was gradually built into Mai Plan. He had been accepted. Not a word was said of the drug trade.

'The amazing thing,' Andy exclaimed, 'is that none of this exists.' He gestured at the long table of porcelain and around at the room.

General Chu's number two thought he had missed something. 'What do you mean, does not exist?'

'Well, Mai Plan, this whole wonderful place. I mean here you are – 30,000 prosperous, happy citizens of a Chinese Republic that went kaput in 1949 – living on the Thai/Burmese border without being citizens of either country.' He didn't notice the silence falling around the table. 'I mean you don't even have immigrant status. You're not illegal either, because no one has asked you to leave. You're invisible, non-existent.' Andy paused, suddenly aware that thirty people were watching him. Shirley had blushed with embarrassment and stolidly went on eating. 'Legally, I mean.' He laughed. 'I mean, for a lawyer, it's a fascinating case.'

'For you, no doubt,' General Chu's assistant whispered. His English had scarcely been used since 1949. 'You must understand that our unfortunate condition has been permitted to continue because of our continued services in fighting against communism. We are surrounded by corrupt, effeminate regimes that are happy to rely upon our strength.'

He explained at great length the threat of communism in Asia as a phenomenon held back principally by the Second Army at Mai Plan. Again there was no mention of the drug trade. After that Andy was more careful in what he said, but the evening never quite recovered. When he was alone with Shirley he apologized.

'It's my fault,' she reassured him. 'How could you know it was the one thing they never talk about. You're right. This place doesn't really exist. They are great actors and they all know their lines perfectly, so it goes on as if it does exist. My dad didn't help matters by getting citizenship for his own family.' Above all she was glad Douglas Sung hadn't been there to see Andy make a fool of himself and, more to the point, embarrass her.

The subject was forgotten by the next morning when she took Andy on a tour of the whole town. Everywhere he asked questions and seemed to enjoy himself. She left him only once – for half an hour in the afternoon when a runner came in from Douglas Sung. It was good news and bad news. They were making a fool of Khun Minh by cutting him off from support and forcing him to flee down the trail. But they hadn't caught him. And Blake was refusing to hold him up. She talked with the officers in the hope of finding some way to exploit the situation. There seemed to be none.

272

On her way back into Mae Hong Son that evening she took advantage of a straight stretch of road to look at Andy. He was still enthusing over what he had seen. She put a hand out to caress his cheek and in the same moment found herself explaining that part of her army had caught Khun Minh on the trail and were chasing him towards the border.

'The opium king?'

'You read about him too?'

Andy thought this very funny. 'I did my research well. What are they chasing him for?'

Shirley shrugged. 'He's been causing us a lot of trouble. I think he'd like to use Mai Plan as an exit for his opium. Now that we're out of the game, he wants to get rid of us. I'll bet he paid that man to kill my dad.'

'So what do you get by chasing him?'

'That's just it. The officers asked me for ideas today. I don't know. Officially there's a price on his head. He beats that by bribing the men who should arrest him. If we could catch him, that would be something. But just chasing him ...'

'Simple. You write a letter to the paper.'

'Don't joke, Andy. This isn't a democracy.'

'I'm not joking. You write a public letter. Short and sweet. You embarrass the people who should be arresting him so much they have to do it. And who becomes the hero? – the Chinese at Mai Plan.' He switched on the reading light and scribbled on some paper. 'Listen: "Dear X. The Second Kuomintang Army at Mai Plan has for sometime been scandalized by the activities of the opium dealer, Khun Minh, who although sought by the police, continues to benefit from a mysterious immunity that allows him to remain the largest manufacturer of heroin in Asia. Our soldiers have trapped Khun Minh on the trail leading into Thailand near ..." Where is it?'

'K-H-A-R-H-A-N.'

'"... near Kharhan. We intend to force him over the border

where Thai officials may arrest him. We call upon the government of Thailand and the world community to ensure that this criminal does not escape again." And you sign. Little Shirley Chu. Original to the Thai government. One copy for the US Ambassador, to make sure the States puts on the pressure. And one for each foreign correspondent to make sure the papers put pressure on the States. We show the full distribution on each copy. Within an hour of reading this, they'll all be doing their bit.'

'Andy, we haven't got any time. Minh is almost on the border.'

'So? You have friends in Bangkok. We phone the letter down tonight. Your friends type it up and deliver it by hand at sunrise. Zap! Great huh?'

Shirley thought about it as she swerved around corner after corner. It was great.

'You'll be a hero,' Andy threw in. 'A *Time* magazine hero. Good guy gets bad guy. Young girl versus Opium War Lord – young, American educated girl. Being General Chu's daughter makes it even better. They'll love that. Devoted daughter saves father's soul. People are big on repentance at home. They might even force the Thais to give all your people citizenship.'

Shirley kept nodding. He was right. It was a great idea. They drove along for some time in silent darkness. Then Andy chuckled,

'Of course', he teased, 'once you've knocked Khun Minh out of the opium business, the field is wide open. I mean, you could take it over again.'

Shirley hardly dared look across at him. She concentrated on the corners until certain that her expression was under control, then glanced sideways. Even in the darkness, she could see that he wasn't exactly joking. There was something else in his eyes, as if he had known all along. What did he mean?

274

Andy prattled on. 'Now that would be even smarter. Once you're an anti-drug hero, well then you're squeaky clean. You can do anything you want. No one would guess. All you'd need is a front man to take Khun Minh's place. That must be pretty easy to find.'

'Very,' Shirley laughed.

Andy laughed with her.

Jalaw reappeared at Blake's house with his ten Lahus. They had got as far as the mud road leading towards the trail when he found their way blocked by Thai soldiers. He had withdrawn until night fell and tried various detours on foot, but the Thais had stretched themselves along several miles to block every access. He could think of nothing else to do except come back.

Marea reacted as if she had been expecting something like this. She sat thinking in her living-room on a wicker chair while Field stood around impatiently. He knew the options as well as she. No doubt it was the Border Police acting without Krit's knowledge. 'Appeal to Krit,' he said.

She shook her head. Field thought of Krit with his house of interlocking triangles and his clothes and his wife and her jewellery and his bank accounts and his hundred interlocking combinations. Which one was he playing? There wasn't time for a mistake.

'He owes me nothing,' she said. 'I have nothing to offer.' She got up. 'I'll go up to the border.'

She disappeared to get dressed. This left Field with little choice but to do the same. She didn't thank him. It was clearly expected.

They were almost ready to set off when the guard came in from the gate to say that Shirley Chu was at the gate with news of Blake. Field started outside but Marea ran past him, slowing herself to a walk only when the gate was in sight. She did not have the lock removed, so Shirley was forced to talk through the grille. First she shoved across a copy of her letter.

'I just sent this. The copies are marked at the bottom. My people tell me Matthew is ahead of Minh; that means he's alive.' Shirley said this in an encouraging tone. The brim of the baseball cap protecting her from the rain was beginning to sag. 'I'm pretty sure it's going to be OK.'

Field noticed a young man waiting behind the wheel of the BMW. He was staring at Marea with bold, unpleasant eyes from a puffy, shapeless face. She thanked Shirley, though it was unclear whether the girl had come to reassure or to upset her, and went back into the house before reading the letter. She showed it to Field and stuffed it into her trouser-pocket.

They set out an hour later – Marea, Field and the eleven Lahus jammed into the Land Rover and the Jeep. Field tried to distract Marea during the drive, though he wondered if he were not talking really to distract himself.

'God knows what we're doing here. There are so many people who follow the rules and earn their dinner. Sometimes they look pretty good. But they don't matter. It's our weaknesses that rule us. Nothing interesting is going to happen until a man has pretentions. Look at Spenser, eh. Unless of course he also has the conviction of his emotions, like Blake, in which case nothing else matters. But what about you, Marea? What about me? We don't earn our dinner. Not really. We don't have pretentions. We don't have convictions. Just untidy emotions. Why do interesting things keep happening to us? We don't get anything out of it. Nothing.'

The track cutting off to Kharhan from the main road was blocked by soldiers, just as Jalaw had said. Marea jumped down and asked for an officer. She was passed from a lieutenant to a major who came out of his tent into the rain to examine the small party, before asking Marea and Field to follow him through the road block. The Thais were spread up the mud lane in a double row of tents. Fifty yards along there was a larger canvas construction – a miniature marquee. The officer disappeared inside and moments later the flap was thrown open by General Krit. He was half-awake, wrapped in silk pyjamas and his paisley silk dressing-gown. His slippered feet perched on the edge of the dry canvas floor. He focused on Marea, probably trying to make out her features in the darkness, then reached through into the rain to take hold of her poncho and pull her inside. It was an impatient gesture. He hadn't yet noticed Field and asked,

'What are you doing here?'

Marea shook off his hand with anger. 'I don't know why you are blocking the road, but it is our right to go on if we wish.'

Field pushed through the closed flap as Krit walked away towards a table on which there was a glass of brandy left from the previous night. The General emptied it.

'Rights, rights. I understand you are travelling with eleven non-citizens of Thailand, all of whom are armed. Where are you going?'

'You know very well.'

'Ah,' he stopped short. 'To greet returning loved ones. Well.' He turned away to refill his glass, then looked back at her with a wan smile. 'As it happens, I'm on my way up there myself. You can come along. But no weapons. And not your friends. They stay here. The border is off-limits to military groups.' He focused on Field for the first time. 'And to journalists.'

'Don't give me that crap!' Field barged up so that Krit had to lean back against the table. 'I'm coming.'

The General slipped off to the side and took his distance. His good humour reappeared. 'Answer me a question, Mr Field. Why are so many peasants bitten by cobras? You see, you don't know. Because the cobras leave the rice paddies at dawn when the peasants enter them. At dusk, the cobras return just as the peasants leave. Chance timing. Two schedules conflicting for unrelated reasons. A question of absence of discretion. You're a *farang*, Field, but you act like a peasant.'

Field followed Krit into the corner of the tent. 'If you don't let me come, I'll see a number is done on you in every paper that can spell Thailand.'

'Who is paying you for this one?' Marea shouted from across the tent. 'Who and how much? Can we outbid them?'

Krit's eyes darted back and forth between the two while his mouth slipped unconsciously into a sour expression. He forced a laugh. 'All right. To please you.' He called an orderly into the tent. 'Hold the Lahus under guard. This lady and Mr Field are coming with us. Search them and their bags. Confiscate any weapons or cameras.' He apologized, 'It is, after all, a restricted area.'

'Encircled by an imaginary barbed-wire fence,' Field threw out, 'with moncy hanging from every barb.'

When the formalities were over, Krit poured them a brandy and called for breakfast.

# 17

At his mother's village, Santana's son slipped away. He had no reason to go farther. The others pressed on. They were overtaken by the local Christian, who had entertained them on their way up the track. He ran out clutching a bundle of hot corn cobs that he shoved one by one into their hands, as a good Samaritan might press food upon the poor. Certainly they resembled little more than beggars.

From there the trail was clear and the slopes gradual. Spenser reached the run-down hut in the clearing at Narmonlong late that morning. He reminded himself that he was crossing the border. It brought neither relief nor protection.

The prostitute, who had waved them off with such joy,

greeted the three men and two animals in the same state of excitement. She beckoned them towards her hut from the centre of a black lagoon dominated by the hum of mosquitoes. Spenser tried to continue on, but something she said made the handlers abandon their mules. He chased after them.

Inside, the floor was a foot deep in water. Dry on a wooden platform above, the advance guard sat inexplicably drinking tea and arguing with another soldier – someone Spenser had not seen before. None of them spoke English. When Spenser made signs for everyone to move on, they ignored him and he was left to fend off the mosquitoes.

Twenty minutes later Blake arrived with his men, having placed a small group to hold the trail 200 yards before the clearing. The Shans rushed out to crowd around him, all talking at once. The unknown soldier had been at Gwe Houk when the Thais arrested everyone, but he had managed to slip away and had been waiting ever since at Narmonlong for Eddie to return. If the Shans climbed the hill to Gwe Houk, they would have to fight on down the other side to Kharhan, where the Thai army would be waiting to round them up. To march knowingly towards arrest would be the equivalent of desertion. Blake dismissed their worries, but they kept on protesting. He was not their officer, not even a Shan. The risk of arrest wasn't his. He used every argument to persuade them and failed. He could not even call upon his own divinity when dealing with Buddhists. The handlers shouted that neither would they go on without protection. No one could expect them to. The soldiers were sympathetic to this. At last they offered to hold the trail for another hour before withdrawing into the hut. If the shutters were closed, Khun Minh would not touch them. Blake went on arguing.

'Forget them,'Spenser insisted. 'We don't need them now. I can lead the mules.' He felt no qualms. They were within hours of safety.

Black came away trying to shake off his mood. He tied the mules one behind the other so that Spenser could control them, while he himself held the rear. The trail up to Gwe Houk and down the other side would be so narrow and steep that he would be able to block any number of men. By the time they left, his depression had turned to enthusiasm.

'We are better off like this,' he shouted to Spenser. 'Now there is no one to slow us down.'

It was curious – Spenser felt the same elation growing within him. Everything had been cleared away. Only the buddhas remained, and their protectors. Blake stayed with him for an hour and a half; in theory long enough for Khun Minh to catch up.

Not only were the troughs deep, but the trail was so narrow that the statues continually blocked on one side or the other between boulders and trees. Each time, Spenser leapt back to work the mule and the sculptures through, coaxing in a soft voice that Blake no doubt thought was aimed at the animals.

On a bluff overlooking twenty yards of trail, Blake crouched and promised to hold Khun Minh until dark. Spenser was to wait for him on the top at Gwe Houk. No further words were said and seconds later Spenser had climbed around a sharp corner to find himself alone. It was for the first time since the trip had begun. Alone and with no one to follow. The weight of the growth and the rain and the mud closed in upon him. The forgotten electrical vibration surged back to burst against his ears. Without the handlers to focus his will upon, the weakness of his own body asserted itself; calling out for but one favour – to lie down and not move again.

Then a sensation of encouragement came from behind and he turned to catch the gaze of a buddha whose fingers were entwined over his chest and bent delicately out towards the world. Seen upside down, the statue appeared poised to dive into the earth. His face was a pleasant one and Spenser began to talk with him so actively that he almost missed the trail dividing before them.

The mules stopped and waited for direction. Spenser tried to judge which was the main path and which a cul-de-sac. He chose the right and walked on, but ripped from his sleeve a piece of cloth which he tied to a branch as a sign for Blake.

At first the way seemed familiar, but then he wondered. What precisely did he remember? Nothing. The rains had changed the face of the land. The climb was sharp enough to give him some confidence, which evaporated the moment the path dipped down. Seconds later he was trembling with indecision. He had become used to the noise of insects and birds filling the air. Now they made it impossible to think. He broke off a piece of opium and stopped to chew it. His mind calmed without clearing, but enough will-power returned to push his legs forward. Minutes later the trail began up again.

He climbed in fits and starts for the rest of the afternoon, overcome most of the time by a fear which surged from somewhere within him. Only the difficulty of keeping the animals on the move prevented him from turning back to look for Blake.

The light was fading when he came to the foot of the almost vertical chute directly below Gwe Houk. It was as he remembered, with the sides curving up well above his head and the brush collapsed across the top. Only one thing had changed. In place of a trickling stream, a torrent crashed down, breaking over the floor of boulders.

Spenser stood mesmerized. He reminded himself that it was only 200 yards to the plateau. He did this in a loud voice over the drumming noise and pulled the animals forward. They followed into the water up to the top of their thighs; but then Spenser slipped on the rocks and disappeared under the water. They stopped in fear and brayed. He scrambled up found solid footing and pulled them forward. They came on a few steps before he slipped again. The water rushed at his face carrying a mess of small debris with it. He fought his way on to his feet coughing, ignored the scratches on his face and pulled again. For an hour he laboured – choking, fending off debris that flew out of the darkness – and managed to climb some way. The torrent and the sound of crashing water seemed interminable, now below as much as above. He stopped to rest and searched for some sign of the top, but it was impossible to judge how far they had come. The mules allowed themselves to be pulled up around another boulder and there balked.

He shouted and yanked while the lead animal stared at him impassively. He came close to plead into its ears with a song of pity and love, and when that didn't work pulled a stick from the dead tangle above and beat its flanks. The mule lifted a front hoof forward, managed to place it, moved a back leg and slipped, sinking down on to its knees in the water. Spenser coaxed, 'Stand up, baby. Please stand up.' But the animal didn't move and he went back to beating. After a time – in Spenser's world there was no longer any time – the mule lay down in the water. Its head slipped to the side without losing its gentle expression and the mouth fell open to let the water flow in. Spenser climbed over the body to untie the second animal and pulled it forward, but the mule would not move. In a frenzy he began to beat it, 'Move! Move! Move!' The animal sank to its knees. They had both done as they were asked until on the edge of death and now they could do no more.

Spenser sat down on the first carcass, beside the statue that had kept him company all day. The torrent crashed around his waist while he watched the second mule slip on to its side and let its head sink under the water. Then he stared at the face of the buddha, strapped to the body, but now lying flush with the water. The eyes were lowered and the hands were raised in elegant prayer, a flood of water running thin over the face. No. Spenser stared hard. It was not the flood. The water was pouring from the buddha's eyes. He sensed a trembling spread within his own body and grow into convulsions. Tears fell from his eyes as the spasms heaved through his frame again and again and the air seemed to fill with a wailing of which he became part. He was left weeping in gasps, unable to lift the great weight which pressed down upon his chest.

Blake found Spenser sitting there in the falling water and carried him on his back up to the top, where he rubbed him as dry as he could in the mist-ridden air and rolled him in a blanket he found in one of the empty cabins. They lay on the edge of the ridge, with the abandoned camp behind them, listening for sounds of Khun Minh.

Spenser dozed off and on in a trance made up of exhaustion and despair. Twice he woke to hear Blake rambling on without addressing anyone in particular. He registered Marea's name, but little more.

'... Too bad about the statues. Too bad. Doesn't matter. Eddie mattered.' Blake sighed. 'Forgive me. Forgive me. I have tried to follow. Forgive my weakness.' He sighed again and put an arm over Spenser. 'Tomorrow Marea will take us in hand.'

Marea. The name without the image ran through Spenser's mind. 'She knew how to get Minh,' he mumbled. 'Look how she betrayed him.'

Blake sat up to unpack the orchid plant in the top of his kit. He held it close. 'One flower is damaged.' He rolled it up again. 'Marea couldn't touch Minh. She knew nothing about his arrest.' After a while he added, 'There was no other way I could get her.'

These words filtered slowly into Spenser's consciousness and woke him up. 'But they all think she did set it up, even Minh.'

'She doesn't realize I did it.' Blake squeezed his arm. 'You must not tell her.'

Spenser thought about that. 'In case she doesn't want you any more.'

'Field would tell her if he had the guts. He organized the press for me. He would if he thought he could get her. What would he do with her? She terrifies him.' Blake became maudlin. 'I thought this trip would settle it.'

'Settle?'

'It worked. We drew Minh out of his camp.'

Spenser tried to sound bitter. 'You didn't want to get the buddhas out.' Acceptance overwhelmed the bitterness.

'No! You're wrong. We had the statues. It was the rain that stopped us. But I wanted him out here where I could kill him. Then we would have been free.'

'Except for Marea's boy.'

Blake pushed his face up close, swollen with anger. 'What do you know about what is right?' He considered Spenser. 'There is a cobra that grows to thirty feet. In the dry season the female lays her eggs and the male guards them day and night, every day. If you come within his sense of smell he will charge and kill you. He is so fast you cannot escape. Do you know why he guards the eggs with such devotion? Because, as they hatch, he eats his children. Only a few escape. Minh is like that. Once he is dead, his family won't want the child.'

Spenser mumbled to himself. 'What do I know? There's nothing to know. Beyond that. Beyond there's something.'

When there was enough light, Spenser began down the trough on the other side, with the water pounding at his back and his mind empty. He slipped and fought his way to the bottom, then walked through the mud for the rest of the morning, sustained by crumbs of opium. Only once did he hear a shot behind. By mid-afternoon he came to the opening that overlooked the village of Kharhan and the valley beyond.

In the clearing immediately below were a tent and several

hundred soldiers. He considered this array, wondering if he shouldn't wait for Blake to arrive. One of the soldiers saw him standing there and shouted. Within minutes the whole camp was peering up. The tent flap opened and General Krit came out. Behind him were Marea and Field. Spenser stumbled down the last hundred yards of jungle repeating to himself Marea's name. It brought a hint of life to his steps until he was ejected into the clearing in full view of the crowd of soldiers gathered in a ragged line on the far side. As he walked across the empty stretch of mud towards them, the life died away.

No one else moved. When he was half-way across, Field pushed through to take his arm.

'What a mess.' He meant Spenser. 'Where's Blake?'

Spenser indicated behind. His eyes were on the crowd. Marea made her way out from among them. He stared at her without feeling anything, almost without recognizing her.

'What's going on?'

She ignored this. 'Where's Matthew?'

'Coming.' He jerked a hand towards the hill.

Field drew him towards the tent. 'General boy here's got breakfast and booze inside.'

'No. No.' Spenser stopped and turned aimlessly on the edge of the soldiers. He heard Krit's voice in the sea of faces, but could not see him.

'Empty-handed.' It was devoid of emotion.

'Come on.' Field dragged Spenser towards the tent. 'It'll be better this way. You'll see.'

He got him inside and seated before forcing him to drink a glass of brandy.

'So what's happening up there?' When Field got no reply, he shook Spenser lightly. 'What's happening? I can't do anything if I don't know.'

Spenser stared up at him, blank. Outside there was silence. They were all waiting in the drizzle. Spenser poured himself a second glass and listened to the silence. His arrival had changed nothing. For them he was only a bit player. 'Nothing,' he mumbled. His buddhas were nothing. They were waiting not even for Blake, but for something to happen.

'Finished,' he said. Field thought the words were aimed at him. Spenser looked away and repeated to himself, 'Finished. I can leave. This no longer concerns me.'

He stood up and pushed his way out of the tent without Field making any attempt to stop him. Outside, the soldiers looked around briefly, then turned back towards the hills. He walked along the line of men in search of an opening through them down to the village. They were an indifferent forest blocking his way. A soldier behind him shouted. He turned and saw Blake on the ridge above, surveying the group without moving until Marea came forward; then Blake disappeared on the trail towards the bottom.

'Finished,' Spenser said out loud, turning away again with his eyes cast down and pushing through the soldiers in the direction of the valley. They moved out of the way, repelled by his filth. 'Finished.'

Spenser's eyes dwelled for a moment on legs that slid to one side. They were solid blue. He glanced up to find a small man in shorts whose body was a solid tattoo. Spenser stared without moving. Before he could consciously register his thoughts, he mumbled, 'Lao Sa's runner. That's it. That's it.'

He lunged at the tattooed man, catching him with one hand by the hair and the other by the arm and wrenched him off balance. 'That's it!' he shouted and dragged the light body forward, breaking back through the ranks of the soldiers. 'Blake!' he shouted towards the jungle. 'Blake! The runner! Lao Sa's runner!' The small man had recovered from his surprise and begun to struggle, but not before Spenser pushed him with the strength of hatred out into full view in the clearing and went on shouting, 'He's here! Look! He's here with Krit. Don't come down!'

286

Krit shouted from behind and the soldiers took hold of Spenser while the runner melted back into the crowd. They went on struggling until Spenser found Marea staring at him through the heads as if hypnotized.

'Don't you understand?' he shouted at her.

Suddenly she came to life and shoved her hands frantically beneath the poncho into her pockets. She found Shirley Chu's letter and barged over to Krit. 'Here, you bastard.'

'What's this?'

'What it says.'

Krit unfolded the sheet to read. Confusion blunted his eyes. 'Where did you get it?'

'From the lady who wrote it. By now the journalists will be on their way north and Bangkok will have sent you orders.'

Krit walked out of the clearing to get some distance from the crowd. He reread the page slowly and stuffed it into his pocket before looking up. Blake still hadn't appeared at the bottom of the hill. He pulled the letter out again, imposing a calm around himself while he read. A soldier shouted. Above, a group of men had appeared on the bluff and begun down. Behind them came Khun Minh on horseback, with the umbrella held over his head. He paused to examine the crowd below. A few minutes later his men filed in to the clearing, where they spread in a disordered mass across the side closest to the trail. They were separated from Krit and the Thai soldiers by fifty yards. Khun Minh rode out of the jungle and across the open space until he was a few feet from Krit. Behind him came the three extra mules he had brought from his camp. They were now loaded down by two buddhas each. He turned in his saddle to motion the handlers forward. Behind them Lao Sa appeared with an exhausted air. He was on foot, the wounded ear neatly bandaged. His face betrayed a subservient, yet satisfied expression. He waited with the men on the far side of the clearing where he pulled out his gold toothpick and drew back his lips before beginning to

287

clean the crevices. He started at the centre top and worked left.

The six buddhas reached out to Spenser across the mud, shrinking the twenty yards until their strength flowed into him. He felt himself coming back from a purgatory. He could not look away. So Khun Minh had taken the time to recuperate them. The thought of such beauty falling into his hands brought anger swelling into Spenser's body. He stood in a half-collapsed stance, like a monkey, kept up only by the Thai soldiers who held him tight by his arms. Already he could sense the buddhas calling out to him.

Khun Minh climbed down and methodically rolled his umbrella before looking around with delayed focus. He seemed to notice the Thais for the first time. 'My goodness. Quite a party.' He took one end of the umbrella in each hand and wandered over to Krit, with his haunches swaying from side to side in counterbeat to the umbrella. The Mayfair boots made his feet move with an unnatural ease. Krit allowed himself to be embraced. Only then did Minh examine the crowd.

'Where is he?'

'He didn't come down.' Krit's reply darted out.

Minh probably took this nervousness for an admission of embarrassment from the General who had failed to deliver. He waved the umbrella gently towards the statues on the mules. 'You see. I bring more than my agreed share. Three buddhas for you. Three for me.' When Krit seemed unimpressed, Minh allowed a hint of petulance to escape. 'What do you mean Blake didn't come down?' He stared back up at the hill behind them. 'We agreed.'

Krit ignored the question. 'Why have you brought so many men with you? And all those statues? You are beyond your territory here. I have no desire to be embarrassed.'

Minh smiled indulgently. 'A change of plans. Chu's troops are on manoeuvre behind me. I'll have to cut home this way.'

'Manoeuvre?'

'Don't ask me.' Minh shrugged with disinterest.

Krit pulled the crumpled letter out of his pocket, looked down at it in its folded state and put it away.

This obscure gesture was watched carefully by Minh, who began again, 'Well, my friend, even if you haven't delivered Blake, I make you a present of the statues.'

Krit was lost in indecision. He looked up at the ridge and saw no new heads. This apparently gave him courage. 'I have something for you.' He pointed to Marea. 'I'll be glad to have her out of Mae Hong Son.'

Minh considered these last words for what seemed an eternity. A look of weariness came over him. Of reluctance. He brushed the expression away and strode into the crowd of Thai soldiers to take her by the arm. 'We'll go home now,' he said gently.

She pulled her arm free. 'Leave me, Sai.'

His grasp slipped on her poncho, but he seized her again, with greater firmness. 'So elegant in rubber,' and pulled her forward.

Curious to watch this domestic scene, the soldiers let go of Spenser, who himself turned away from the buddhas to listen. The vibrations from the statues made him able to see Marea again.

Field reached out to protect her, but a soldier held him back. 'We're on Thai soil,' he shouted at Krit. 'Minh is a wanted criminal.'

'The border is very indistinct,' Krit replied with a careful politeness more suited to a press conference. 'I can't risk an incident with Burma at this stage. In any case, she isn't Thai.'

By then Marea had been dragged out into the clearing. Spenser suddenly realized he was free and threw himself forward in an attack that verged on parody, because Minh had only to let go of Marea for a second to knock him to the ground, where he lay gasping.

'The eager thief,' Minh jeered. 'So eager to protect the rights of others.' He saw there was a bulge in Spenser's pocket and reached down. 'What's this? Perhaps more stolen goods.' Minh's fingers drew out the remains of the opium block. He smiled broadly. 'My goodness. Look at this. I've caught a drug dealer for you, General. Opium trafficking is worth something in jail, I believe. Or is it life?' He threw the opium to Krit, who caught it with a clumsy cupping of both hands. 'Your evidence,' and pulled Marea close again. Minh's umbrella hung useless in the crook of his left arm.

They were clear of the Thais, out in the middle of the clearing, before Marea realized that no one was going to help. She began to twist desperately on his arm. Her poncho came off, freeing her momentarily, but he took hold of her sweater. She went on turning and pulling away, like an exotic bird chained to its perch.

'Let her go!' The voice came from the jungle above them. 'Minh! Let her go!'

He looked up when he heard his name a second time. It was impossible to tell from where within the green wall the voice came. The soldiers on both sides raised their rifles searching for a movement or a reflection.

Minh took Marea firmly around the waist to hold her before him. 'Let her go, Blake? Why?' He was amused. 'Come down if that's all you want. We'll discuss it.'

A shot echoed across the valley and struck a few inches from Minh's feet.

'Try again,' he shouted up. 'See what a pretty thing she is.'

Krit had melted into the ranks of his soldiers, followed by the handlers, who abandoned the three mules with their statues. Another shot exploded, coming close to Minh's head. It struck one of the soldiers behind him in the leg, causing greater confusion, and panicked the three mules into running off to the edge of the clearing.

'Stand aside!'

Minh stared around trying to make up his mind. In either direction he was twenty yards from cover. He began to carry Marea before him towards his own men, his eyes moving quickly in search of a better chance.

Behind them, Spenser stumbled to his feet and threw himself at Minh with all his remaining strength. In the shock, Marea pulled loose and Spenser threw his arms out to drag her crashing to the ground.

Minh turned in confusion before realizing that he was alone. He raised his eyes towards his own men in mute appeal, but shouted no order. He must have known, as would they, that the distance was too great. In any case, why would they charge out with no more hope than to be shot in his place as mere shields; they who had been forcibly enlisted and forcibly kept in his service. The only man to rush towards him was the tattooed runner, unarmed and scarcely clothed. Minh turned again, trying to bring himself to run, but was crippled by a wave of fear that drained his face to a colour of grey. He seemed not to notice the tiny blue figure sprinting across the mud to his defence. Instead, his feet moved slowly forward in a creeping movement towards his men, while his head was strained up unnaturally with eyes frozen on the wall of hills. He raised his umbrella, pointing it in defence towards the jungle as he crept, his fingers clutching at the button to inflate the black cloth, as if this might protect him. A shot rang out and he fell backwards on to the mud. The tattooed runner arrived in time to throw himself across the body, upon which he lay, attempting to shield it against further shots; but then the pliant stillness of the man beneath became so apparent that he crept away a few yards and crouched on the ground, clasping his knees.

At first no one moved. Then Lao Sa walked forward to stand over the body. He methodically put his toothpick away in its leather case before pushing at Minh's stomach with his foot.

'So he's dead,' Lao Sa murmured, indicating neither despair nor pleasure, and bent down to pick up the umbrella. Just before taking it in his hands, he hesitated, and straightened to stare up into the jungle. 'Blake!' he shouted. 'Minh is dead. You hear me. He's dead.' There was no answer from the wall of green, no sign of movement, and he bent again, this time summoning up enough courage to seize the umbrella. No shot rang out. He turned his back on the body and began to play with the spring button. The umbrella opened with a rush. He looked up, pleased, only to catch sight of Major Sung and his soldiers watching from the ridge above. 'Too late,' Lao Sa said quietly with a laugh. 'Too late.' In a pantomime gesture of abrupt agility, he stepped aside and pointed the inflated umbrella at Minh's body to illustrate his point, then raised the halo of nylon over his head. Beneath this protection he took the few steps necessary to put his arm through General Krit's. 'We must discuss our arrangements.' The General allowed himself to be drawn away, his eyes fixed on the Chinese soldiers above. 'I'll deal with them,' Lao Sa reassured. 'I know the daughter.'

Suddenly the three mules with their six statues had no meaning; no more than Spenser or the other outsiders. Field was the first to realize this. He slipped quietly through the soldiers and across the ground to Spenser and Marea, whom he pulled to their feet. 'Let's get out of here.'

Marea held back, her eyes fixed on Minh's body. She began edging towards it. Spenser thought she was drawn by relief or curiosity to ensure that Minh was truly dead, but when he saw her face it held an expression of tenderness verging on regret.

Field yanked her away and they began across the clearing between the two groups of soldiers who scarcely seemed to notice, their attention being consumed by the men waiting above on the ridge. Spenser glanced around,

'What about Blake?'

ld pushed them on. 'He's at
s way.'

Her face was filled with light,
ike a shield around her and
l a sense of loss; instead, the
n his pocket pressed against
s pace began to lag inexplicably
id's arm leading the way. Desperate
ept from behind, heavier and heavier,
n at made Spenser twist his head back. He
ooking. The six statues were crying out from
for pity and protection. It was not a cry from the
ossessed to the possessor, but from beauty seeking to be one
with him.

Two of the mules still wandered free on the edge of the
clearing. The third had edged back in among the soldiers.
Spenser broke away from Field's fatherly embrace and forced
his legs at a stumbling gait back up the valley towards the
clearing and the animals. He seized their reins and it was as if
the buddhas swallowed him into their purity. He gave no
thought to the soldiers only a few yards away. Both animals
followed without balking and the soldiers paid no attention.
Between Minh's death, the arrival of the Chinese and Lao
Sa's self-crowning, they had other things to worry about. The
only sound behind him came from the pair of buddhas on the
third mule. There was nothing he could do, though their cry
of abandonment followed him down the hill. He had no
choice but to leave them for General Krit. Eventually their
waves of reproach were drowned out by a light which
engulfed the four buddhas and himself.

'Come on,' he whispered. 'Almost there. Come on.' He
pulled the mules faster and caught up to Marea and Field
before the village. She looked at Spenser with astonishment.

'It doesn't matter,' he assured her. 'It doesn't matter.'